IT WAS A SCENE FROM HELL ITSELF.

She lay rigid and wide-eyed as the tornado's hollow tower of fire wavered overhead. It passed over them; and as the sobbing breath came back to her strained lungs, the tornado slammed down beyond them, and with a hammer blow that shook the earth, dug a ditch five feet deep across the Kansas prairie.

Roxanne screamed and clung to Buck; and suddenly a new, ungentle Buck was ripping her clothes from her body.

"No!" she screamed, though he could not hear her in the mighty holocaust around them. But he held her fast, taking her with a desperate urgency.

In Roxanne's trembling body something savage and tumultuous was awakened. Something elemental and fierce, born of the storm and of new wild desires. In pain and terror and in splendor, too, she had become a woman . . .

And in the aftermath of the tornado, she became a wanderer, initiated into the magic of love but searching for its reality.

Warner Books
By Valerie Sherwood

This Loving Torment

These Golden Pleasures

by *Valerie Sherwood*

WARNER BOOKS

A Warner Communications Company

WARNER BOOKS EDITION

ISBN 0-446-82416-X

Cover art by Jim Dietz

Warner Books, Inc., 75 Rockefeller Plaza, New York, N.Y. 10019

A Warner Communications Company

Printed in the United States of America

Not associated with Warner Press, Inc. of Anderson, Indiana

First Printing: November, 1977

10 9 8 7 6 5 4 3 2 1

Contents

To high adventure and wild romance—
long may they endure!

Prologue

San Francisco

Wednesday, April 18, 1906

The great clock on the Ferry Building stood at just after five o'clock, and horse-drawn milk carts clattered about in the early dawn, making their rounds. Soon San Francisco's seven hills would be bathed with light, and the sun would shine on the mixed fleet of steam and sailing vessels that rode the glittering waters of the Bay.

In the fabulous Grand Ballroom of the Golden Palace Hotel, tired musicians played a last waltz while two couples in full evening dress gamely danced the night away. At a table in an alcove beneath the impressive beamed ceiling sat three people—two men and a woman, intent upon what they were saying to each other and oblivious to the scene about them.

The woman was beautiful, sought after, and much talked about. Her name was Roxanne Barrington. Across from her the shoulders of the two men moved restlessly, each man distractingly aware of the inviting sweep of white bosom her artfully low-cut dress displayed under the light from the crystal chandeliers, and the impudent forward thrust of her delicately molded bust beneath her lavish glittering white ball gown.

One of the men was handsome and one was rich—perhaps the richest man on the West Coast—and it was clear that the woman could have either man she chose. The handsome one in the rented suit, the broad-shouldered man who gazed at her so yearningly, had crashed the party—which was being held in Roxanne's honor—without invitation.

Roxanne's fingers toyed with a crystal goblet of champagne as she studied them—these two men who had so shaped her life for good or ill—and a shadow of pain passed over her lovely face, deepening the sapphire of her eyes. She looked down for a moment, perhaps because tears had frosted those thick dark lashes resting now against peachbloom cheeks—which needed no makeup to make them beautiful. Sheer and lovely and celebrated was her fair complexion, her lithe figure so temptingly displayed, her crown of sun-streaked dark-blond hair, piled in Gibson Girl fashion atop her head.

In her brief, wild lifetime Roxanne had been many things. A child of the Deep South, she had faced scandal in Kansas and heartbreak in Baltimore. Alaska had known her as Klondike Roxie; in the South Seas she had appeared an American adventuress. Here in San Francisco she was known as "that Barrington woman," about whom scandal swirled . . . and spiteful glances followed her as, perfumed and bejeweled, she rode round the city in her handsome carriage behind a matched team of thoroughbreds—so thoughtfully furnished by the wealthy gentleman sitting opposite her.

But underneath the silks and the diamonds, underneath the many selves who had lingered in the arms of so many men, was another woman. A woman of raw and flaming emotions, who suffered and shook and knew love's lavish heights and burning depths. And now something of the pain and torment she had known was in her voice as she said, "I . . . heard you," her voice suddenly soft and slurred.

"Then you can give me your answer," said the keen-eyed, aggressive older man across from her. He leaned forward, a distinguished figure in his tuxedo.

The next words spoken at the table might have been heard only by her, for she paled and sat thunderstruck. Then, as if jerked upright, she rose to her feet with a single motion that sent her gilt chair skittering.

"You!" she cried in a choked voice. "You—"

Her cry was lost in a sudden grinding roar. The very earth shook. The musicians, just packing up their instruments, grabbed at the bandstand to keep their footing, and one of them, thrown off balance, fell heavily on the polished floor. Among the departing dancers, a woman in a long pink boa screamed in terror. Both men at Roxanne's table sprang toward her.

At the lower end of Market Street, the clock on the Ferry Building registered fourteen minutes after five.

The great San Francisco earthquake had begun.

As the ceiling collapsed and the great polished beams—now instruments of death—came crashing down about them, both men leaped forward to save her. At that moment, Roxanne's life rushed past her in a mad flash. It seemed to her that everything important began on a day in Baltimore in 1896. But of course disastrous events cast their shadows before them, and so it all really had begun much sooner, on a summer day in Kansas in 1895.

Roxanne had been fifteen years old.

Book I

The Reckless Girl

Part One:

Kansas 1895

Chapter 1

In the hot summer night the tinkle of the banjo swirled around the dancers, who moved like shadows against the light from the lanterns in the Smiths' big barn. On the outskirts of the dance floor a few spectators lounged against the barn's plank wall and clapped their hands and stamped their feet in time to the music. *Swing your partner! Do-si-do!* The girls in their long dresses whirled around; the boys stomped and pranced. They were young, and the night was sultry, laden with the smell of new-mown Kansas hay.

Visible through an upper window of the barn, a yellow slice of moon beamed down and reflected in Roxanne Rossiter's eyes. Face alight, feet skipping lightly, she seemed to be having a better time than anyone else. For tonight Roxanne was unmindful that her stockings were much mended, her shoe soles worn nearly through, her yellow calico dress somewhat out of fashion and faded from many washings. Tonight her laughter tinkled with the banjo. In her tapping feet was the joyous release from a harsh, snowbound winter and a back-breaking spring. What did it matter that she was an extra girl at the dance? That strict Aunt Ada allowed her no beaux, no gentlemen callers? She was young, she was dancing, the night air was soft—and who knew what might yet happen on such a night?

"Let's go outside!" cried someone. "Moon's bright!"

Outside they trooped, a half dozen couples and a handful of watching wallflowers. The music struck up again, the catchy tune "Skip to My Lou," and Roxanne, the prettiest of the girls, found herself swung from one partner to another in the bright moonlight. Around the dancers in the barnyard, past the rail fence as far as the eye could see, stretched the undulating Kansas prairies.

Roxanne's partner slapped at a night-flying insect, and she laughed. It was a light and reckless laugh, as reckless as her challenging sapphire eyes under their sooty lashes.

"Buck," she chided. "You missed a step!"

The young giant grinned and swung her around again, his brown eyes kindling with a hot new light that said he had finally noticed her as a woman.

As she looked up into those eyes. Roxanne's cheeks grew warm with more than the exertion of the dance. Half the girls in the county were crazy for Buck, she knew, and here she was, fifteen-year-old Roxanne Rossiter, dancing with him—*and* holding his attention!

From the sidelines, where she stood leaning against the unpainted barn wall, black-haired Julie Smith watched the laughing pair—Roxanne who, as she stamped and twirled in time to the music, thrust her delicately molded breasts forward temptingly, tautening the yellow calico of her bodice above her slender waist. And Buck—Julia's own Buck, to whom she'd been engaged for more than two years now—swinging Roxanne around, his eyes never leaving her face. He was just being nice to the extra girl, Julia told herself, nice to Roxanne, who had no fellow. Julie's gaze rested lovingly on Buck's giant frame. His coat laid aside in the hot summer night, he looked so handsome. A lock of his ruddy brown hair fell over his brown eyes as he danced. His striped shirt sleeves were turned up to reveal heavily muscled forearms, bronzed by the Kansas sun; his strong farm-boy thighs strained against his dark trousers. For a moment, watching them, Julie's thin hand shook as she smoothed the folds of her new blue linen dress, and a shadow crossed her normally candid gray eyes.

Roxanne didn't notice. It had been so long since she'd danced with anyone—and this time she'd had to sneak away from Aunt Ada, who thought she'd gone to bed early. Instead, she'd put on her one good dress, her best mended stockings, and her only respectable pair of shoes—and had tiptoed from her tiny stuffy room at the back, past the big front bedroom where Aunt Ada and Uncle Josh snored lustily. On downstairs she had crept, careful not to let the stairs creak, and out the unlocked front door—nobody locked their doors in Kansas: Horse-thief law still held good here, and prowlers were apt to get a load of buckshot.

Then Roxanne had run down the rutted dirt lane to the wide plank gate where the young Bonners—Charlie and his sister Jane—were waiting for her in a buckboard.

The Bonners thought it was fun helping Roxanne slip out at night. After all, Roxanne's Aunt Ada was the strictest woman in the county and didn't "hold" with dancing—square or round. Roxanne had arrived in Kansas less than a year ago to live with her Aunt Ada and Uncle Josh, but in that time there'd been few parties, and Aunt Ada had successfully scared off all the young fellows who came around "shining up" to good-looking Roxanne in the churchyard on Sundays. Pretty Roxanne, who had overheard herself variously described in the churchyard as "that high-steppin' Southern gal" and "that pretty little blond from Savannah," walked alone.

She knew boys would have to come courting and make formal calls to please Aunt Ada—but even formal calls were prohibited till Roxanne turned sixteen. Aunt Ada was very definite about that. Roxanne would be sixteen next month, and then she could put her hair up instead of letting it tumble down over her shoulders like a little girl. Next month she could receive gentleman callers in Aunt Ada's stiff front parlor. And maybe even have permission to go to square dances at neighboring farms such as this one at the Smiths'.

That being weeks away, Roxanne, with her vivid face and her restless nature, had decided to pretend she was sixteen now. To dance *now*. So, in whispers, outside the church in Wichita last Sunday, it had been arranged. And here she was—dancing with Buck Wentworth, the most popular boy in the county, to the catchy strains of "Skip to My Lou."

From the sidelines some of those who were stamping their feet and clapping their hands joined in the song. And as he swung his dance partner, Madey MacKenzie, near them, Charlie Bonner—who'd courted Julie Smith before Buck cut him out—leaned over close to Buck's head and with a significant look at Roxanne warbled loudly, "Can't get a bluebird, a yellow bird'll do!"

Buck's face reddened. Roxanne cast an involuntary glance down at her yellow dress and then looked swiftly at Julie's blue one. Compassion flared up in her eyes. Poor Julie! Engaged to Buck, wedding plans made—and then to come down with the dreaded consumption. Dr. Owens had advised Julie against marrying just now, saying she needed rest to recover her health. So pretty Julie had postponed the wedding, but everybody whispered she'd never be well, never be Buck's wife.

The thought chilled Roxanne.

"Let's stop dancing, Buck," she said impulsively. Seizing his hand, she ran over to where the fragile brunette was standing.

"Why did you stop?" Julie, who couldn't dance because it brought on a paroxysm of coughing, asked wistfully. "I wouldn't have, if . . ." Her voice trailed off and she looked down.

Roxanne didn't say, *I brought Buck back to you.*

She said instead, "It's so hot, I stopped to get my breath." And Julie said in her soft voice, "Buck, why don't you get Roxanne a glass of lemonade?"

Buck ambled away toward the white frame house where the punch bowl sat on the porch, and Julie turned to Roxanne. "I don't want you to stop dancing because of me." The words came out in a rush. "I—I don't want Buck to stop dancing because—because I can't."

"Oh, he was already tired of dancing," lied Roxanne, remembering that Julie was the only girl who had been really nice to her since she'd arrived in Kansas almost a year ago.

"Isn't he handsome?" Julie murmured almost to herself as she watched Buck's retreating back. "So strong. So—so manly."

Roxanne studied that sturdy farm-boy figure with its well muscled arms and legs. "Yes," she agreed. "He certainly is." She frowned as she saw Julie's thirteen-year-old sister Nadine skip along and join Buck. Nadine threw back her head coquettishly and laughed at something he said. "You and Buck make a lovely couple, Julie," Roxanne added to distract her friend's attention.

Apparently oblivious to her flirtatious younger sister's behavior, Julie sighed. "I used to think so, Roxanne. But now I'm so thin, my clothes just hang on me."

"Come on now," chided Roxanne. "Don't be so sad. This is *your* party, remember? You'll be dancing yourself at the next one. Why, the first time I met you was at a corn husking, and you were the life of the party then!"

Julie looked away. "I didn't know then that I was so—so sick. I thought I'd be married in a month, living in my own house before the snow blew, and expecting a baby in the summer." She sighed.

Roxanne turned her head and looked out across the moon-silvered prairies and remembered the first time she'd seen them, from the windows of the westbound Pullman car that had brought her to Kansas. As the sound of the train whistle had drifted through that alien corn, homesickness had swept over her. She had scrunched down in her seat and promised herself silently that if she didn't like it in Kansas, she wouldn't stay. She'd run away.

Still, when she'd arrived on her uncle and aunt's quarter section, she'd made a determined effort to like it. All that lonely windswept fall, when the main diversion was going to church on Sunday, she'd tried. She'd tried all that long, lonesome winter with blizzards that made her teeth chatter. Clad in Aunt Ada's worn-out ill-fitting castoffs, she had made valiant efforts to feed the snowbound chickens, fighting winds that cut right through her thin clothing. Then hard-working spring had come and with it the promise of summer and fun—like tonight, and she had almost been reconciled to it all.

But now, caught up in Julie's despondency, something of the loneliness stole over her again.

Roxanne had been born in Augusta, Georgia, where her mother had returned to have her baby after her young husband of only eight months had died up in Pennsylvania. After Roxanne's birth, the young, genteel and impoverished Widow Rossiter had found employment teaching in a select girls' school. But Roxanne could hardly remember those days, since she had been only five when they moved away. Her mother had lost her job, Roxanne wasn't sure exactly why, and they had gone downriver to live with Grandmother Lanier in a tiny house on the outskirts of Savannah.

Roxanne's grandmother was a frail, lovely old lady for whom time seemed to have stopped with the Civil War. She spoke of little else. Mulberry Hall, the plantation where grandmother had spent her girlhood, was one of the many beautiful homes in the path of Sherman's terrible March to the Sea—it had vanished in fire from the Yankee torch. Mulberry . . . her grandmother's voice grew husky as she described it: the avenue of moss-draped live oaks that led up to the gracious fan-lighted front door, the spacious rooms, the whitewashed slave cabins . . . now it was all ashes, its fields charred and left to brambles or wilderness, the land sold long ago for taxes. . . .

Her grandmother told her bitterly of the Yankees who had burned her home to the ground, and how all she had been able to save was a cartload of antiques. Roxanne sometimes wondered where the antiques were, for the tiny house they lived in was so sparsely furnished that her mother sometimes laughingly called it an empty house.

Though they had dwelt in genteel poverty, Roxanne's bearing, as well as her cultivated voice and soft Southern accent, marked her as a lady. Her clothes were cheap and worn and often patched, and she had received no formal schooling, but her mother had carefully taught her all the things young ladies were taught in the fashionable girls' schools of the day—a smattering of French and Latin, a dab of history and philosophy, elementary figuring, good grammar, a graceful copybook script, daintiness with a fork and other social graces. Roxanne spoke well, and she was lovely to contemplate, but of course, since her education had been informal, she couldn't say, "I attended Miss Gilbey's School" or "I graduated from a seminary." In Savannah, where she was known and accepted as her mother's daughter and therefore a lady, that hadn't mattered. Now it did.

Both her mother and grandmother had come down with deep chest colds during a sudden freeze the winter before last, and in a long damp spring in the drafty cottage, they'd worsened and died within weeks of each other.

When her mother—who was never strong—had died, Roxanne had sorrowed—but grandmother was still there. Then in rising panic she had seen the old woman weaken, and at her instruction had telegraphed her grandmother's only other child, Joshua Lanier, who was married and lived in Kansas.

Before Uncle Josh could arrive, grandmother had died, even though Roxanne, weeping a curtain of tears, had sat by her bedside begging her to get well. Her grandmother had patted her hand in an effort to comfort the grief-stricken girl. Dying, she had grown curiously prophetic. She had taken Roxanne's hand and said—"You are too beautiful, Roxanne." She sighed. "And too proud. You may suffer for it. I can leave you nothing of material value—the Yankees saw to that. But you have yourself, Roxanne. Yourself to answer to. Never forget it. And even though much of what you do may not be of your own will, take heart. For to be a woman—a *real* woman—is to strive, to love . . . and to forgive." Her soft voice weakened, and the light in her penetrating old eyes flickered out. Her hand slipped lifelessly from Roxanne's. She lay back on the pillow, not breathing, and Roxanne's hot tears fell on her dead face.

Those words never left her. They were to guide her life.

The next day Uncle Josh arrived in Savannah. As Roxanne turned a tearstained face to greet him, he murmured, "How like your mother you are, Roxanne." Uncle Josh himself had dark-blond hair like her mother's and her own, for that matter, but there the resemblance ended. Uncle Josh was tall and melancholy and romantic-looking, with a weak chin. Her mother had been delicate, lighthearted even at the worst times, and she had had a dazzling smile.

Uncle Josh made a quick assessment of Roxanne's circumstances; she would now be left alone in a rented cottage with no money, for her mother had been destitute and the pittance her grandmother had left was dissipated by the funeral expenses. She was fourteen years old, was without any kind of formal education, and worse, she'd been brought up a lady, which ruled out the only kind of jobs that were open to penniless girls. So, just before he left, Joshua announced that Roxanne was going back to Kansas with him.

But what about Aunt Ada? Roxanne had asked fearfully, noting that Aunt Ada hadn't come east for the funeral.

Her uncle gave her his pleasant melancholy smile. Aunt Ada would love her, he said in his cultivated Southern voice.

That Aunt Ada wouldn't, that she wouldn't even approve of her niece, Roxanne had some inkling. For her mother had always said, "Oh, yes, Ada . . . ," and then her voice would sort of drop away deprecatingly, and she'd change the subject, never telling Roxanne anything about the woman who had married Uncle Joshua.

Yet it was evident to Roxanne that she had no choice but to accept her only relative's well-intentioned offer. So she joined her Uncle Joshua as they boarded the steam locomotive that would take them over the miles into the hard flatlands of Kansas, far away from the gentle lands of the South . . . home.

If I don't like it, she had promised herself, *I won't stay. I'll come back east—I'll get a job*. Even then, she knew that she was whistling in the dark. Jobs weren't all that easy to find. Her lovely mother, with all her charm and credentials, hadn't been able to find a job. How would an untrained fourteen-year-old fare? But she wouldn't always be fourteen, Roxanne had reasoned. Every day, every hour, she was getting older. In July she'd be fifteen—and next year sixteen! Old enough to do anything!

She smiled ruefully. Now that she'd be sixteen next month, Roxanne realized that nothing had really changed. Aunt Ada still disapproved of her, and she was no better prepared to go out into the world than she had been before—except that now she knew how to make butter and feed livestock and milk a cow and scrub floors. All things she had never done in Georgia.

Aunt Ada was strict. She kept her niece working so hard, sometimes Roxanne felt she was a slave. And there was no recreation as she had known recreation back in Georgia. No carefree outings. Aunt Ada didn't hold with those, just as she didn't hold with dancing.

Which was why Roxanne had slipped out tonight.

Nadine came skipping out of the house. "Nance says the food is ready!"

The banjo stopped playing and everyone trooped inside—except for one or two couples who slipped away behind the dark barn and came in tardily, the boys swaggering a little, the girls giggling and smoothing their skirts and patting their rumpled hair.

"You don't have a fellow, do you?" said Nadine in a slightly malicious voice. "You can share a plate with me."

Roxanne followed Nadine into the Smiths' big farm kitchen, which had been "modernized" with an iron hand pump to draw water. Each of the other girls piled a white ironstone plate with sandwiches, which she then shared with a boy. Julie shared hers with Buck, of course, and everybody else paired up. Roxanne gave the giggling stragglers a wistful look. Taking the plate Nadine had heaped high with sandwiches, she headed for the opposite side of the room, away from Julie and Buck. Nadine, discontented with this arrangement, talked absently to Roxanne but kept looking at Buck and pouting.

The conversation faltered. Roxanne, putting flirtatious Nadine from her thoughts, looked around the big kitchen with its plain maple furniture. It was so much cozier than Aunt Ada's barren kitchen. The whole house was much cozier, in fact. She supposed the difference was that Aunt Ada's dour personality spilled over into everything she did. Upstairs here, she knew, Julie's room had pretty flowered chintz curtains and a gay green and yellow crazy quilt, and underfoot a colorful hooked rug. Julie had a little dressing table, too, where she could observe the newfound hollows in her flushed cheeks and study the feverish light in her candid gray eyes.

Roxanne didn't envy Julie; she'd rather have less and be able to dance the night away.

After they'd eaten, Nadine insisted they have just one more dance. Roxanne knew she was going to sidle up to Buck and ask him to dance it with her.

Julie knew it too. As Nadine approached, she jumped up and said with a laugh, "Buck, I can't let you go without even one dance!"

Laughing and chattering, they all went outside again, where the banjo struck up "Camptown Races." Julie Smith, tossing back her black hair, looked pretty standing there slim as a willow wand, but though her smile was gay, her eyes had a desperate light. *She's afraid she's losing Buck*, thought Roxanne with a pang.

Buck hesitated. "Do you think you should? The doctor—"

"Sure, I should!" cried Julie recklessly. "This is my party at my house! Don't I get to dance one dance? Come on, Buck, it won't hurt me!"

Buck grinned. This was the old lighthearted Julie, the girl he'd fallen in love with and asked to marry, to share his life. Everybody applauded as they whirled around to "Goin' to run all night, goin' to run all day!" Charlie Bonner grabbed his girl and joined in, and then the rest followed. But Roxanne, standing this time on the sidelines clapping her hands and tapping her feet, watched Julie anxiously. In his exuberance at dancing with her again, strong Buck was whirling Julie very fast. Her gray eyes were brilliant in the moonlight and she was laughing excitedly.

All of a sudden she missed a step and doubled up, coughing. Buck—indeed all the dancers—came to a halt, and the music died away so that the only sound was that of the wracking cough as Julie's slender shoulders shook uncontrollably. Buck had his arms around her. His face was white.

"I shouldn't have let her. . . ." he groaned. When the coughing had subsided and Julie, white and trembling, looked up at him and tried to smile, he picked her up without a word and carried her back into the house.

Roxanne followed to wait outside Julie's bedroom door. Julie was her special friend, and she wanted to be there in case she could help. Downstairs, Julie's widowed father called querulously from his wheelchair, "Is Julie all right?" And old Nance, who had been the Smiths' hired girl and general confidante since she was fourteen, called down curtly, "Yes," as she shooed a frightened Nadine out of the room and shut the bedroom door in Roxanne's face. After a while Nance came out looking grim, and then Buck left looking stern too, and Roxanne slipped in to say good night.

Julie lay like a collapsed rag doll on the big square bed with its bright green and yellow crazy quilt. Her dark head was propped up by pillows. Tears spilled over her lashes.

"It's no good," she whispered to Roxanne. "No good. . . ."

"Oh, Julie, you just weren't up to it yet," insisted Roxanne anxiously. "Remember the doctor told you to rest—you'll be fine soon."

"No." Julie turned her tearstained face away. "No, I won't."

Because she wanted to cry herself, Roxanne left then, feeling that there was nothing more she could do.

On the way home Charlie Bonner said glumly, "Julie's not gonna make it. Buck's going to bury her—not marry her."

His sister put her hand on his arm and said, "Hush. How do you know?"

Charlie shrugged, but Roxanne felt a chill around her heart for her only real friend on these lonesome prairies.

The next Saturday night there was another barn dance, and Roxanne again slipped out. This time big Albert Dawes got too "likkered up" and tried to kiss her out behind the barn, and she slapped his face. It occurred to her that if it had been Buck who'd tried to kiss her, she might not have slapped him. Which made her angry with herself. Buck belonged to Julie—and as was proper he was calling on Julie tonight instead of attending the barn dance. It wasn't the same without him.

At church on Sunday, seated in the pew between Aunt Ada's poker-stiff back and Uncle Josh's resigned slump, Roxanne watched Buck Wentworth settle himself in the Smiths' empty pew. Julie was still resting in bed, it was said, and Nadine had stayed with her. *That must have irked Nadine,* thought Roxanne, *not getting to go to church alone with Buck.* She stared at Buck's back, remembering how they'd danced, how hotly he'd looked at her. Suddenly he turned and looked straight at her as if he knew she was thinking about him. But she couldn't read the expression in his eyes. Then he faced forward again, and sat stiffly erect all during the hellfire sermon. Roxanne was very conscious of Aunt Ada's disapproval. She cast her eyes down at her hymnal as they began to sing "Rock of Ages."

After church the congregation stood in little groups outside under the cottonwood trees and gossiped. In Roxanne's group all the talk was about that wild Sarah Gregson, who had been caught in the haymow with big Albert Dawes *without a stitch*—no, her ma didn't think anything had happened, but her pa had sure tanned her backside proper. No wonder she wasn't at church—still couldn't sit down, most likely! Roxanne couldn't help smiling. Last week gossip had it that Sarah was clad in her combination undergarment, and the week before she'd been fully clothed. But it sobered Roxanne a little, hearing this new version, realizing how lightly a young girl's reputation was lost.

Beyond the gossiping group, Roxanne saw Buck Wentworth watching her. Their eyes caught, held for a second. There was no mistaking that look. More than interest . . . desire. Then he turned, climbed onto his horse and departed. Roxanne felt quivery inside. Buck was forbidden fruit, but he drew her like a magnet.

Silent and thoughtful on the way home in the buckboard, Roxanne tried to ignore Aunt Ada's pursed lips and deep frown.

When they got home, Roxanne had barely managed to change from her Sunday-best calico to an old dress before Aunt Ada started ordering her about. Barking orders at her was not an unusual occupation for the woman, but this time there was a sharp, bitter note in her aunt's voice. As if she hates me, thought Roxanne uneasily, trying to run everywhere at once under her aunt's strident direction.

"Roxanne"—Uncle Josh caught up with her as she dashed out on her way to clean the henhouse—"Ada knows. Someone told her after church how you've been slipping out nights. Dancing."

Roxanne came to a dead stop. She turned a questioning face to Uncle Josh.

"I know you're young, Roxanne," he said, troubled. "I know you're not doing anything wrong, you just want to be out with the young folks. But—you'll be sixteen soon, and then Ada will let you have callers."

"And go to dances?"

He hesitated. "Ada doesn't hold with dancing. But remember, Roxanne, once you're married you won't have to listen to Ada. You'll have your own house, and you can give parties or go to parties—you'll only have to listen to your husband."

Roxanne gave him a puzzled look. "But I'm a long way from getting married, Uncle Josh."

He closed his mouth as if he had said too much. "We'll see," he said mysteriously.

Prudently, Roxanne skipped the next barn dance. It was well she did, because her aunt showed up in her room in the middle of the night with an oil lamp and shined it in her face. When Roxanne sat up sleepily, blinking in the wavering yellow light, the woman said grimly, "I thought I heard something up here. Go back to sleep."

Bed check, thought Roxanne resentfully. Aunt Ada would probably check her room every night there was a dance. . . .

And then she remembered. Today was her sixteenth birthday. It had passed unnoticed.

She began to feel even lonelier.

Chapter 2

On Monday, Buck showed up at the Laniers' farm on the pretext of borrowing some nails. He found Roxanne, who was making butter in a wooden churn, and went to stand near her. Lounging against the iron outdoor pump, he watched her for a while before he spoke.

"Need some help with that?" he asked, finally.

Roxanne gave him a look through her sooty lashes and shook her head. Her heart was pounding. Buck had come to see *her*. His male presence was almost a palpable thing, as he stood over her, a broad grin on his face.

"Roxanne," called Aunt Ada from the kitchen. "Come carry this bucket of slop out to the hogs."

"I'll carry it," offered Buck, and Roxanne was left working the butter churn while Buck took a big bucket of skimmed milk and potato peelings from the kitchen out to the sleek Hampshire hogs. She could hear the hogs squealing as the delicacy approached.

"The chickens!" called Aunt Ada, peering out the window. "Roxanne, go feed the chickens! And gather the eggs—I'm busy making pies."

Roxanne got some cracked corn from the granary and made her way to the weathered henhouse. There was a mad clucking rush for the grain as she stepped over the feeding chickens carefully and went into the shadowy, deserted henhouse. Standing on tiptoe, she reached up into the top row of wooden boxes filled with straw where the chickens laid their eggs, and began picking up the eggs.

When she had filled her basket, she turned and saw that Buck's tall figure darkened the door. Her heart missed a beat. Without speaking, she brushed by him. Since he gave no ground, her hip and shoulder came into contact with his muscular body, and a kind of electric tingle went through her at the touch. She hurried out, and he followed her at a leisurely pace back to the house. Flustered, she burst into the big kitchen, which was filled with the scent of berry pies baking in the large, black wood-burning range. A moment later she heard the screen door bang and Buck's footstep behind her.

Aunt Ada glared at them both impartially.

Meekly Roxanne set the basket of eggs on the scoured wooden table.

"Here, Roxanne, start shelling these peas," ordered Aunt Ada, shoving a big earthenware bowl toward her and kicking a basket of newly-picked peas in her direction.

Sitting down on a straight wooden chair, Roxanne began shelling the peas.

"Pies smell mighty good," observed Buck, sniffing.

"Julie makes good pies," said Aunt Ada slyly.

"I know, but she hasn't made any lately," Buck replied.

Roxanne kept her eyes cast down. That was the key to all this, she guessed hotly. Julie hadn't done anything for him lately. Julie, for all her dark beauty, was thin, so thin; her very bones seemed to protrude from her shoulders. Her soft voice always sounded tired now. Her fragile health made her incapable of any but the lightest tasks. Roxanne felt angry at Buck. He should be loyal to Julie; she deserved his loyalty and needed it.

And yet . . . and yet Roxanne was achingly aware of those long legs standing beside her, the hard thighs within her range of vision even with her eyes cast down. Buck was a sturdy oak, just as Julie was a weak sapling, and he had a strong physical appeal with his exuberant farm-boy strength and ruddy complexion.

She bit her lip. Aunt Ada had given her a cold reception when she'd arrived in Kansas. Uncle Josh had been kind, but he worked from dawn till dark in the fields. The women she'd met had eyed with alarm this too-beautiful child of the South who'd been dropped unbidden in their midst, and who caused the men's heads to turn—even married men that should have known better. Only Julie Smith had been unreservedly nice to her.

Doggedly Roxanne kept her eyes fixed on the peas she was shelling, dropping the peas into the big earthenware bowl and tossing the pods into the empty slop bucket. Buck talked a while longer, but Roxanne did not look up again until he left.

Roxanne was glad that he was gone. Treacherous feelings swept over her when he came near—her pulse beat faster and her heart rocked. Even when he just looked at her, a kind of surging excitement pounded in her head. She *wanted* Buck Wentworth and she hated herself for it. Because no matter how she felt about him, Buck wasn't fair game. Julie was too vulnerable, too easy to hurt.

Viciously Roxanne snapped the peas in half until Ada said dryly, "You're like to break your fingernails the way you're going at those peas. Why don't you go out and finish churning?"

Grateful to be out of the steaming kitchen and away from her aunt's surveillance, Roxanne set the bowl on the table and opened the screen door.

"And wear your sunbonnet!" snapped Aunt Ada. "You're sixteen now, and you want to keep your complexion fair so some man will want to marry you. Not that there's many good catches in the county, but with that face you ought to get one of them. Time you put up your hair too, and not let it fall down your back like a child."

"It's too hot to wear a sunbonnet," cried Roxanne, sweeping her damp hair back from her forehead. "It's blistering out there!"

Her aunt grunted as the screen door banged and Roxanne feverishly attacked the churn. It surprised her that Aunt Ada had remembered her birthday at all.

At supper Aunt Ada watched her steadily, her eyes hard. When Uncle Josh tried to lighten the atmosphere with a joke, she crushed him by observing that his views were sacrilegious. Uncle Josh subsided, and ate his fried pork chops and peas and potatoes in silence. Roxanne wondered how he stood it. Aunt Ada was fond of reminding him that *her* people had been Kansas pioneers, that they'd come west from Pennsylvania in a prairie schooner when two million acres were made available for settlers in 1854. Come to settle with nothing but a spinning wheel and some corn for planting and what the wagon would carry.

Casting a brooding look at Roxanne, Aunt Ada launched into her favorite subject. *Her* people had put down roots here, she declared grandly. Here in these prairies. Her father had been a "Jayhawker," killed on a raid into Missouri to burn out Southern sympathizers.

At this Roxanne bristled, but managed to keep silent as Aunt Ada went on: But that hadn't stopped her ma. They'd weathered droughts and hordes of grasshoppers and Indian troubles and Quantrill's raiders.

"And Carrie Nation and the Women's Temperance Crusade," Uncle Josh couldn't resist remarking.

"Did she really smash all the bottles in the saloons with an axe?" asked Roxanne, fascinated.

But Aunt Ada was not to be diverted from her tirade. She silenced her husband with a look and told Roxanne how her family had survived the great blizzard of 1886 and the record-breaking corn crop of 1889—which had driven down the price of corn to ten cents a bushel and ruined so many farmers. She added abruptly that she was for free silver and William Jennings Bryan.

Roxanne looked blank. Down south she'd never heard of free silver. As if to punish her for that omission, Aunt Ada suddenly jabbed, "Are you setting your cap for that Buck Wentworth?"

"Of course not," said Roxanne indignantly, putting down her fork. "He's engaged to Julie Smith."

"Just wondered if you remembered that," her aunt said coldly. "Your ma," she added, "up and married another girl's intended. That's why she and your pa went north. The other girl's big brothers were going to horsewhip your pa and—"

"Ada," murmured Uncle Josh reprovingly, "that's enough."

Roxanne looked upset. She'd never heard that about her mother.

"Your mother fell in love and followed her heart," her uncle said kindly. "She was pretty like you, and your father just didn't stand a chance against her. He gave up a big dowry to marry her, Roxanne."

"And so neither of them ever had a thing!" sniffed Aunt Ada. "After all the money your folks spent educating your ma, too! So she ended up teaching in a girls' school."

"It was nice there," said Roxanne defiantly. "I remember it."

"Did they tell you she lost her job because the headmistress's husband took a shine to her?" asked Aunt Ada, furious that her husband had chided her. "Your ma had a face like yours—bound for trouble."

"Ada," groaned Uncle Josh. "That's all water over the dam now. My sister's dead. Let her rest."

"It's because of her we lost all your family antiques," scolded Aunt Ada. And that, Roxanne perceived, was the sore point. "Your grandmother sold them all, Roxanne, when your pa couldn't make it up north and owed so much money. That was what your ma brought him to, with her pretty face and her expensive tastes."

Roxanne fled to her room. She closed the door, fell on the bed, put her head in her pillow and wept. She wished she'd never come to Kansas.

As if in a kind of grim apology for what she'd said about Roxanne's mother, Aunt Ada announced the following morning at breakfast that they were going in to Wichita. All three of them. Roxanne's spirits rose. She seldom got to go in to Wichita; usually Aunt Ada had chores for her to do that kept her home.

Promptly after breakfast they piled into the buckboard and headed for Wichita. Aunt Ada sat stiff and silent, but Uncle Josh pointed out interesting things about the countryside, such as a barn that had been picked up by a tornado three years ago and lifted off its foundations and then set back down *facing the other way*! They called Kansas "Tornado Alley," he added cheerfully.

Roxanne shivered. She had never seen one of those great, whirling, funnel-like twisters that pounced down out of the sky. But Uncle Josh, observing her expression, said she didn't need to worry, they had a sturdy cyclone cellar back at the farm.

Once they reached the outskirts of Wichita, he pointed out where the old Chisholm Trail had gone through. Millions of head of cattle had been driven through there on their way north from Texas to the big Eastern markets—'course, that was before barbed wire had fenced off the prairie and the lowing longhorns had been diverted elsewhere. The sodbusters had won. Corn was king here now, but soon it would be wheat—especially that kind called Turkey Red, brought in by the Mennonites.

Roxanne wasn't listening. Indeed she hardly saw the Arkansas River gliding by. She was staring hungrily at avenues lined with elms and cottonwoods, at the big gingerbread houses. Once this had been a wild cowtown, with signs posted on the outskirts announcing *Anything goes in Wichita* and advising citizens to check their guns. But Roxanne was oblivious to her uncle's account of its past, its wild saloons and roistering trail hands; all she saw was the mansard roofs bristling with wrought iron and the sawtooth gables and the turrets and the gingerbread. Behind those fancy Victorian fronts was a more congenial way of life than days spent churning butter and gathering eggs and slopping hogs and running about at Aunt Ada's beck and call.

Roxanne yearned for that life. She didn't want to be a farmer's wife and live in drought-plagued Kansas fighting grasshoppers and falling corn prices. She didn't want to fall in love with Buck. She didn't want to betray the one friend she had—Julie.

She found herself wondering if her aunt had decided on this jaunt into Wichita to get her away in case Buck came over to borrow some more nails, and so was stunned when Aunt Ada marched her into a woman's apparel shop and bought her a pair of stockings, some high-heeled shoes and a white batiste dress. The dress had a bow at the neck, leg-o'-mutton sleeves and a long bell-shaped skirt with a little train. To this array, a fluffy white parasol and a pair of short white linen gloves were added, though Roxanne was in more immediate need of underwear than gloves, for her own underwear had been mended so frequently that it was near disintegration. Then Roxanne was turned this way and that as the alterations lady pinned and tucked and —on her knees with a mouth full of pins—said everything would be ready by late afternoon.

"Now you look more like a lady and less like a hoyden," approved Aunt Ada, surveying her bewildered charge. "Tomorrow night we're having company," she added. "You'll wear that dress and put your hair up. Makes you look older."

"Who's coming?" asked Roxanne.

"Never you mind," snapped Aunt Ada. "Just you wear your sunbonnet in the daytime to keep your skin nice and white and mind your manners."

The next evening they ate a hurried supper, and Roxanne was told to tidy up the front parlor. So grateful was Roxanne for her new clothes that she would have scrubbed the floor if Aunt Ada hadn't stopped her with a surprising, "Stop that, Roxanne. You'll make your hands rough. And remember to wear your white gloves!"

Roxanne gawked at her. It was true that in fashionable homes back east ladies wore gloves indoors, but this was the first time she'd heard of anybody doing that on the Kansas prairies!

"Hurry and dress," cried Aunt Ada, and Roxanne, galvanized, flew upstairs to put on the new stockings and to slip the new white dress over her threadbare underwear. Carefully combing her hair into an upswept pompadour and anchoring it firmly with combs, she was ready when Aunt Ada bellowed, "Roxanne, someone's here to see you!"

She came downstairs to find their neighbor, portly Ned Witherspoon, peering at her over his bifocals, and bowing so low that the round bald spot on the back of his head gleamed in the lamplight.

"Miss Roxanne," he said formally, in the same sugary tone in which he might have said "Delicious!" of his hostess's cake.

Roxanne paused and looked about, wondering who else was there—someone who conceivably might have come to see her. But Mr. Witherspoon was alone. He stood there wearing a satisfied look, just as he did behind his desk at the bank whenever someone made a really large deposit or paid off a loan.

"Roxanne!" Aunt Ada spoke severely, interrupting her niece's trance. "Take Mr. Witherspoon into the parlor and make him comfortable."

To Roxanne's utter astonishment, she found herself entertaining her unlikely guest in the front parlor. They sat stiffly on the uncomfortable horsehair chairs and talked about the weather and the price of corn and how his married son and daughter were doing up in Missouri. He was a widower, he told her with some emphasis, his wife having passed away a year and a half ago. Roxanne now remembered hearing gossip that Mr. Witherspoon had got most of his money through his wife, a woman with buck teeth and a giant frame, whose people had made their pile in the days when great cattle herds were driven north from Texas. In those days, large herds were sold to Indian agents who were always ready to buy stock to send up the upper Missouri to feed the Indians. These herds often disappeared mysteriously—sometimes by stampede—the very night they were sold; the "lost" herds were then resold the next day to another Indian agent, or perhaps—with connivance—to the same buyer. Roxanne studied Mr. Witherspoon, whose fortune was said to have rested on such shenanigans; he did not look as if he had the courage to face a full grown steer, let alone incite a stampede. No doubt his wife's people had been of a different stripe. She was still pondering this when Aunt Ada served them tea and cookies. Mr. Witherspoon smacked his lips and said they were mighty good—did Miss Roxanne make them herself? Roxanne opened her mouth to say no, but Aunt Ada, who was hovering in the hall, interposed in a loud voice that Roxanne had indeed made them. Roxanne looked startled at this outrageous lie. She was a very indifferent cook, and the delicate butter cookies were a culinary triumph.

Still mystified at the end of the evening, Roxanne bade her gentleman caller good-bye. As he left he promised to take her for a whirl in his buggy on Sunday afternoon; perhaps they'd go into Wichita and see the Chatauqua. Aunt Ada promptly accepted for her.

"Why," demanded Roxanne after he'd gone, "did that old man come to see me? I've never even spoken to him except at church! And he has a granddaughter almost my age!"

Aunt Ada looked at her. "Ned Witherspoon," she said, as if explaining to a not-quite-bright child, "is president of a bank, Roxanne. He is president because he owns most of the stock. He doesn't owe a penny in the world to anyone, and he owns four whole sections of prime corn land. The Widow Carter and the Widow Marley are both out to get him, but you caught his eye. He's a *catch*, child!"

Roxanne was speechless. She staggered off to bed. Was it for *this* that Aunt Ada had bought her the beautiful new clothes, let her put up her hair, baked all those delicious cookies? Was it for Ned Witherspoon that she was to keep her complexion fair by wearing a sunbonnet? She sat down on her bed and began to laugh from pure vexation. And then, surprising herself, she began to cry.

The ridiculous situation went on for a week, as Mr. Witherspoon pursued his courtship relentlessly. On Sunday, as promised, he took Roxanne riding into Wichita in his buggy, which was black and gold and indeed handsome. Her cheeks were flushed with embarrassment, and she had occasion to use her new parasol—she hid behind it whenever they passed young people she knew.

Every time Roxanne opened her mouth to tell her aunt that this May-December courtship was unthinkable, Aunt Ada stopped her by reminding her of Mr. Witherspoon's very visible wealth. Of his big house with its modern conveniences. Of all the things he could do for a woman. As if Roxanne cared! Her dreams of young love certainly didn't include a dried-up old widower whose grandchildren were almost her age!

But he appeared punctually every evening after supper and smacked his lips over the assortment of cookies and cake and pie that Aunt Ada doled out with accompanying assurances that Roxanne had done the baking. Roxanne wanted to scream.

Instead she sat sedately on the little horsehair sofa in the stifling front parlor with her ankles crossed decorously, and tried to laugh politely at Mr. Witherspoon's sly little jokes and to keep from looking pained when he came out with something he thought shockingly modern, such as "Twenty-three skidoo!" or "Oh, you kid!"

Roxanne tried to tell herself this was only a phase Aunt Ada was going through with regard to herself, and that Uncle Josh would understand how she felt. Once Aunt Ada discovered that Roxanne would never be interested in this elderly Lothario, she would soften up and let her niece go out to parties and receive beaux her own age. In the meantime Roxanne must put up with Mr. Witherspoon's persistent calls and Sunday drives until he tired of his unrewarding chase and turned to one or the other of the widows Aunt Ada vowed were after him.

Roxanne had almost convinced herself that this was so when, one Wednesday night, as Mr. Witherspoon got up to leave, Aunt Ada came bustling in and said, "Roxanne, you tell Ned good night now and run along upstairs to your room. Ned and I have some talking to do."

Glad to escape, Roxanne hurried upstairs to light the cheap glass kerosene lamp in her room. There'd be time to read another chapter of a novel Julie had sent to her. But she closed the door so quickly her long dress caught in it, and she heard a little ripping sound. Aunt Ada mustn't see that rip. Roxanne kicked off her shoes and tiptoed back downstairs to get some white thread and a needle out of the sewing basket in the living room.

Pausing on the landing, she could hear Aunt Ada talking to Mr. Witherspoon at the front door. They couldn't see her, and something urgent in their voices made her stop to listen.

"If she gives me trouble," her aunt was saying darkly, "I'll lock her in her room until she's so hungry that she'll do anything I say for a crust of bread!"

Roxanne leaned forward. They were talking about *her*! "I wouldn't want her to act unwillingly at the altar," Mr. Witherspoon sounded upset. "I mean, I've a position to maintain in the community, and if anyone thought I forced—"

"She'll be willing, Ned," said Aunt Ada harshly. "Roxanne likes fine things—like her mother before her." There was a sneer in her voice. (*She's still hating us over those antiques!* thought Roxanne wildly.) "And *you* can give her fine things, Ned—a soft life. That's appetizing to any young girl with no money and no prospects. Right now Roxanne's just a little feisty because she's young and wants to run about free. But once she's married—why, you'll break her to hand real easy. And after the first baby comes along, she'll settle down."

"I hope so," said Mr. Witherspoon nervously. "When we were out riding yesterday, I put my hand on her shoulder—I was just adjusting the cushion at her back," he added quickly, "and she pushed my hand away and turned and glared at me!"

"You don't lay a hand on her until that note is in my possession, you understand?" cried Aunt Ada, her voice fierce. "You promised me you'd cancel Jimsey's note for the four thousand dollars he owes at the bank if I got her for you, and I'm holding you to it, Ned Witherspoon! I'm to get that note back marked 'Paid and Cancelled' in front of the church before you two walk up the aisle!"

"That's right, that's what I agreed," said Mr. Witherspoon, and Roxanne could imagine him standing there wiping his brow with a white linen handkerchief. "But suppose"—he lowered his voice—"suppose Josh objects. I notice Josh is never here when I come calling—"

"He's all tuckered out with work these days, goes to bed right after supper," said Aunt Ada quickly.

"But," persisted Mr. Witherspoon, "suppose Josh objects? She's *his* niece, after all."

"You leave Josh to me," said Aunt Ada in a significant tone. "Josh has never stood against me, and he never will—especially not in this, when you can give Roxanne such a good home. Josh said Roxanne wasn't to get married till she was sixteen, and I respected that. But she's sixteen now. Oh, Josh may buck a little, but he'll come around to it. Same as she will. You'll see, Ned, you'll see.

Roxanne turned and fled silently back up the stairs, her heart beating trip-hammer blows.

Now she understood. Somebody named Jimsey owed a note at the bank, and Mr. Witherspoon, who was president of the bank, had promised to cancel that note if she married him!

Roxanne's legs gave way beneath her and she sank

down on the bed feeling dazed. Was it for this she'd been brought to Kansas? To marry Ned Witherspoon?

She forgot about the torn dress, the white thread. Morning would be soon enough to mend it. She had to think. She sat staring out the window across the rolling moonlit prairies that stretched out lonely and far away.

But no matter how she tried to soften it, it came out just one way: Aunt Ada was *selling* her—just as she might a cow or a horse or a bushel of corn! For four thousand dollars!

Chapter 3

After a nearly sleepless night on her narrow bed, Roxanne had made up her mind. She had to get Uncle Josh on her side. He'd have to stand up to Aunt Ada. Roxanne had no money, nowhere to go, no trade, and jobs were scarce. Uncle Josh was her only hope.

Accordingly, when he announced he was taking the buckboard down to Creightons' to get a wheel fixed, she asked—since the Smith place was on the way—if she couldn't take some cookies to Julie Smith. Everybody knew Julie had had an attack at her own party and had been resting in bed ever since. Aunt Ada said that would be very nice, and Uncle Josh could pick Roxanne up on his way back from Creightons'. Roxanne had a feeling her aunt had assented because the only young people at the Smiths' were Julie and Nadine; even the hired hands were over fifty. And Buck wasn't likely to come calling in the daytime; he had work to do on his father's farm.

All week the weather had been hot, and today was

the worst yet. Roxanne, dressed bravely in her yellow calico, climbed up on the bouncing buckboard. As they drove off, she asked, "Uncle Josh, who is Jimsey?"

He looked uneasy. "I'm your Aunt Ada's second husband, Roxanne. She had a son by her first, name of Jim, who lives way the other side of Wichita. We hardly ever see him. But," he grimaced, "Jimsey has money troubles. He gambles. Ada bought him a farm over there, set him up, but he's about to lose it. Got a note due at the bank."

"For four thousand dollars." Roxanne's voice was bleak.

Uncle Josh looked startled. "How would you—"

"I heard all about it," said Roxanne. "Aunt Ada is trying to sell me to the banker so he'll cancel out that note and Jimsey won't have to pay it."

"Oh, come now, Roxanne," said Uncle Josh, sounding shocked. "Your Aunt Ada thinks this is best for you. Ned Witherspoon is a very solid citizen. You'd live in a fine house—"

"And sleep with him every night," finished Roxanne. "No thank you."

He sighed. "I guess I was wrong to bring you out here to Kansas, Roxanne." He paused, then said hopefully, "May-December marriages often work out. I remember a twenty-year-old girl who married a seventy-year-old man who—"

"Maybe she loved him," interrupted Roxanne. "I don't love Mr. Witherspoon. I cannot learn to love him. He repels me."

Uncle Josh seemed to crumple. "Your Aunt Ada," he began weakly, "is a very forceful woman."

You mean you've never stood up to her, thought Roxanne, her face mirroring the indignation she felt.

His voice was humble. "This place we have—it's her place, inherited from her folks. I never made any money, Roxanne. Not on my own. And we'd have gone under when corn went to ten cents a bushel except for Ada. And when Jimsey got in trouble, she arranged that loan for him at the bank."

Which I am supposed to pay off—with my body!

thought Roxanne angrily. Why, that dress Aunt Ada had bought for her and for which she had been so humbly grateful was just the wrappings on a bed-warmer for old Mr. Witherspoon!

Keeping his eyes on the reins, her uncle spoke again. "Your Aunt Ada only means well for you, Roxanne," he said placatingly, reaching out and patting her hand in a distracted way. "Give it time, child. Maybe you can learn to—"

She snatched her hand away.

"Uncle Josh," she said between clenched teeth, "how could you do this to me?"

On that unhappy note they arrived at the Smiths' road gate, and Roxanne tumbled out of the buckboard while her uncle said a grim giddap to the horses and moved on down the road.

Her mind was a tumble of emotions as she stepped onto the Smiths' front porch. Julie, out of bed and looking lovely and frail, came to the door to meet her. Julie was wearing a checked blue gingham dress that hung on her wasted frame, and her eyes were feverishly bright. She hugged Roxanne warmly and urged her inside.

Immediately Nadine came into the front hall, swinging her hips. "We hear you've got a fella!" she taunted. And burst into laughter.

Roxanne reddened with vexation. But Julie said, "Scat!" to her younger sister and took Roxanne into the comfortable living room.

"Oh, my," Roxanne remembered. "I was bringing you some cookies, Julie. That was my excuse for coming over here, but I forgot them. They're sitting on the seat beside Uncle Josh, and he's a long way down the road by now."

"Never mind," said Julie. "Can you stay to supper tonight?"

Roxanne shook her head. "Uncle Josh dropped me off on his way to get a wagon wheel fixed. He'll be picking me up when it's ready. I'll remember about the cookies then." She gave Julie a keen look. "How've you been, Julie?"

Julie avoided her eyes. "Oh, as well as can be expected, I guess. I got tired of staying in bed in this hot weather, so I got up. But I don't really feel strong, you know." She waved Roxanne to a chair and proffered a cardboard fan, bright with advertisements.

Roxanne took the fan and studied it. It displayed a buxom woman wearing a tightly laced corset.

"Stifling, isn't it?" Julie pushed back a lock of her dark hair that had come loose from its upswept pompadour.

Roxanne nodded, so depressed she could hardly respond.

Julie studied her friend and asked quietly, "What's wrong, Roxanne?"

"Aunt Ada wants me to marry that old Witherspoon man," said Roxanne. "She's going to lock me in my room to starve if I won't."

Julie looked shocked. "And we thought—"

"You thought I'd lost my mind and was trying to marry money," said Roxanne grimly. "I guess everyone thought that."

"No!" cried Julie. "I mean—well, yes, I guess we did, Roxanne. When Nadine said you pretended not to notice anybody, but you were all dressed up riding around town with the president of the bank . . ."

"I felt like a fool, Julie. Oh, Julie, it's awful. Aunt Ada's son Jimsey owes the bank four thousand dollars—and if I marry Mr. Witherspoon, he'll cancel the note! She's *selling* me to him, Julie!"

Julie looked shocked. "That's terrible, Roxanne," she said quietly. "What are you going to do about it?"

"I don't know! I haven't any money. Uncle Josh won't take my part. If only I could get a job—work somewhere."

"There just aren't any jobs around here, Roxanne. You know that."

Roxanne swallowed. She did indeed know that.

From the front porch Nadine suddenly screeched, "It's Buck! He's coming down the road. I wonder what he's doing not working this time of day?"

They ran to the front porch to greet him. He came

into the house, running a hand through his damp brown hair. He had two farmhands off sick, Buck told them, and he'd been checking the neighboring farms to see if anybody could be spared. Julie said eagerly her father could probably spare someone—tomorrow maybe. Her father was taking a nap, but he'd be up in an hour or so. Why didn't Buck just sit down and wait for him?

Buck said he'd do that. It was so hot out there and muggy, it like to roasted a man just coming down the road. He looked speculatively at Roxanne, obviously wondering why she was there.

"Roxanne came over to bring me some cookies," smiled Julie. "Only she forgot them."

For a wild, terrible moment Roxanne envied Julie. Julie who was dying. At least while she lived Julie had love—a man's love, Buck's love . . . and a family who cared for her. Even foolish, temperamental Nadine loved her. Nadine was just young and envious of her older sister's beauty and handsome beau. At that moment Roxanne felt she would have given anything to be loved as Julie was.

Nadine came in and sat down so close to Buck that he grew nervous. She hung on his words until Julie gave her an irritated look. Somehow the conversation came around to the old Hatter place next door. It had been up for sale ever since the bank had foreclosed on it, Julie told them, but nobody wanted an old soddy.

"What's a soddy?" asked Roxanne.

Laughing, they told her that in many parts of Kansas the settlers had found building materials scarce. No stone, just some scrubby cottonwoods and a few willows along the streams. So their first houses were dugouts.

"Dugouts?"

"Sod-covered holes," explained Buck. "And some real sod houses."

"I bet Roxanne's never seen anything like that!" crowed Nadine maliciously. "Bankers live better'n that!"

Julie's mouth tightened. She smoothed her dark hair with thin fingers. Roxanne thought there was something desperate about her friend today, but she put it down to annoyance with Nadine. "Why don't you walk Roxanne over to the old Hatter place, Buck, and show her the soddy?" Julie suggested. "It isn't so far, and I can fix us a snack while you're gone."

Buck shrugged. "The sky looks bad. Might be a storm coming." Plainly, he meant, *I don't like to leave you here.*

Julie's hands clenched, as if with inner struggle. "I've seen lots of soddies," Julie said steadily. "Roxanne hasn't. It's only a little way across the fields. No, Nadine, you may not go! You promised to help Nance with the ironing today and there's a heap of it. It isn't fair for her to have to do it all by herself."

Nadine pouted. And Roxanne, worn out with her worries over being forced to marry Ned Witherspoon, and torn with a desire to be alone with Buck—to be alone with any man who wasn't old enough to be her grandfather—got up and said she'd love to see the soddy at the old Hatter place.

Julie's eyes were hungry as she watched them go. Roxanne saw that look and her heart ached for her friend.

"I hear you've been riding around the countryside with Ned Witherspoon," said Buck as they crossed the yard and went through the gate into the kitchen garden.

"Seems everybody's heard that," said Roxanne.

"Isn't he kind of old for you?"

"Aunt Ada doesn't think so."

"It's what you think that's important, Roxanne."

"Is it?" She turned and faced him. They had gone through another gate and now stood in a cornfield. Ahead of them in the big Kansas sky rose a high bank of clouds moving rapidly from the southwest. As Roxanne turned, she saw from the corner of her eye another cloud mass moving from the northwest, on a collision path with those just ahead.

"You need someone younger," Buck said, his voice growing rich. "More my age."

Her heart was pounding as they moved on through the corn. Buck's meaning was clear. Thinking about that, Roxanne was distracted, as her toe caught in a tangle of morning glories rioting through the corn. As she stumbled Buck reached out to steady her, seizing her slender arm in his big brown hand. His touch seemed to burn her, and she sprang away from the contact, watching her footing carefully, trying to keep a safe distance between them. Cornstalks brushed her and weeds scraped her ankles.

When they came to a barbed wire fence, covered with brambles, Roxanne hesitated.

"Here, I'll help you." Buck reached down and swept her up in his arms. One brawny arm was around her slender waist and the other under the back of her knees, making her legs feel as if they'd turned to butter. He held her that way in the sultry breathless hush, gazing down at her with dark intense eyes, and she could hear the beating of her heart and feel the pressure of her soft hip against his hard stomach muscles and belt buckle. For a wild moment she thought he was going to kiss her; then he swung her up and over the fence, depositing her lightly on the other side.

Back on her feet, she swayed dizzily, then straightened and, with pounding heart, looked away from Buck as he lightly vaulted the fence and strode forward.

I don't want to feel this way, she thought. I won't feel this way! But she was achingly aware of him as they moved on through sticky heat over undulating prairie land, fallow land which hadn't been tilled since the Hatters moved out. Drooping daisies and clover and thistle and clumps of tall grasses rasped against her legs. On distant fence lines she saw tall, straight sunflowers and tumbling masses of morning glories. A rabbit ran past her feet and disappeared into a tangle of weeds nearby. She turned her head from side to side in a fanning effort. She didn't know if it was Buck's nearness or the weather that made her feel so odd. Her legs felt heavy, and her clothes seemed to weigh her down. Even the meadowlarks and wrens were still. A breathless sort of day. The very earth seemed to be waiting for something to happen.

"Roxanne . . ." Buck's voice was caressing. A tremor went through her. She could feel his presence intensely.

When she didn't look up, he said, "There it is, just coming up over the next rise." He pointed to a squat, dingy, boxlike structure. "That's a sodhouse. It's made of heavy slabs of topsoil, held together by roots of buffalo grass. It's a lot better than those boxes covered with tarpaper my granddad lived in when he first came here."

Roxanne came to a shaky halt and drew a deep breath. She had come to a decision. "I didn't come to see the soddy," she announced. "I came out here to talk to you about something, Buck."

Staring at her, he loosened his collar and tossed back his damp hair. Suddenly, he looked up at the ominous sky. "We'd better get on," he mumbled uneasily. "That sky is looking bad."

"Forget about the sky," she said in a level voice, and it took great effort on her part to say it. "Tell me straight out, Buck. Do you love Julie?"

He didn't meet her eyes. "Of course I love her, Roxanne," he mumbled. "I've always loved her. Since I was fourteen."

"You're all she has, Buck—and she's my friend." Roxanne's voice was strong, though her heart hurt to say it. "I came out here to tell you to stop fooling around me, Buck."

She watched him achingly as she delivered this ultimatum. A slight ripple went through his broad shoulders and he frowned, but aside from that his face was impassive.

"That all you got to say?" he demanded, almost roughly.

She opened her mouth to answer with a defiant *yes*, but her voice was drowned in a sudden terrific crash, as if several enormous freight trains had slammed into each other at a crossing.

Roxanne's gaze flashed skyward in the direction of the sound. The two fast-moving cloud masses had met head on, and the thunder had come from that. As she stood rooted in fright, the clouds seemed to break up and roil around in turmoil.

"Come on!" Buck seized her arm. "The Old Hatter Place has a storm cellar!"

They ran forward, Buck almost dragging her. Out of the tumbling clouds snaked a long gray funnel, dangling down from the sky, perhaps a mile long. Leisurely it dipped to the ground and turned immediately black from the debris it scooped up. They could hear its thunderous roar as it sucked up everything in its path and flung its gleanings skyward into the huge roiling cloud that had spawned it.

Onward it came, toward that bleak square building made of the prairie sod.

So abruptly did Buck halt his advance that Roxanne almost catapulted past him, but his grip on her arm held her back.

"Too late," he shouted. "It's coming this way. We'll never make it." He spun about and cut off at right angles to the swaying black tower that leaned toward them cobra-like as if to strike.

Running madly beside Buck over the uneven ground, Roxanne cast a swift, horrified glance at the approaching tornado. It was much wider now, and denser, a looming black funnel of infinite height.

"Hurry," cried Buck desperately.

But Roxanne was already running as fast as she could. Her breath sobbed in her lungs. Suddenly, Buck came to another skidding halt, so fast that she was swung in a half circle around him.

Over the deafening noise of the approaching storm she heard him yell, "It's *turning*!" on an anguished note. And as she followed his gaze she saw that the great black funnel had darted to the side, just as they had. As she watched, that greedy funnel attacked the soddy and the outbuildings of the Old Hatter Place—and in an instant they had disappeared.

In panic now they turned and ran at right angles again, as, relentlessly, the tall black pillar pursued them, bearing down to annihilate them.

"In—the—ditch!" yelled Buck, his voice barely audible above the terrible roar of the advancing monster. He flung Roxanne into a low depression in the ground. In falling, she rolled and landed on her back. Buck threw himself on top of her, shielding her with his body. She could feel his strong chest thudding against her breasts, his heavy-muscled legs pinning down her hips. The breath almost knocked out of her, Roxanne lay still on her back and stared with wide terrified eyes over Buck's shoulder at the menacing whirlwind that approached now from the southwest.

On it came, roaring like a thousand thunders, chewing up the ground as it came. The noise grew so intense that it seemed to merge with her very being and she clutched Buck in terror. When the funnel was almost on them she screamed but could not hear her own voice in the fiendish din. They were going to die she thought and clung to Buck as if she were drowning.

Then just as the sound peaked, it stopped. Abruptly. Some vagary of the landscape had caused the inky funnel to lift a little. As the great vortex—some four hundred feet wide—hung poised over their heads, Roxanne felt the air being sucked from her lungs, and she choked on the strong sulphurous odor. She was looking straight up the inside of the great black funnel.

Above them was a scene from hell itself.

Rotating cloud masses whirled above her, seeming to boil in fury about a great void, their wild gyrations horribly illuminated by a constant vivid electrical display of jagged bolts of blue lightning. Thick, powerful, brutal bolts that made an intricate devil's lacework through that great cavern of air that reached skyward. The rippling lightning was punctuated by hissing, screaming sounds that blasted down at her from the end of the funnel. And at its ragged base the writhing tails of little tornadoes spewed out, hissing, formed and broken away and reformed on the swirling rim of the huge vortex like giant snakes from some unthinkable nightmare.

She lay rigid and wide-eyed as this hollow tower of fire wavered overhead. Then it passed, and as the sobbing breath came back to her straining lungs again, the moving black wind slammed down farther on with a hammer blow that shook the earth and dug a ditch five feet deep across the Kansas prairie. As it touched down, the tremendous shattering noise engulfed them again in a torrent of sound that ripped and tore the senses.

Roxanne was screaming, but she couldn't hear her own voice in the infernal din. She felt Buck's body jerk as the noise came back. Head down, clutching her, he lay on top of her, effectively pinning her down. Had she been on her feet, her panic might have caused her to run madly in any direction to escape the colossal noise. Instead, she lay immobile, stunned by the avalanche of sound that howled over them, through them. In violent reaction she clung to Buck, shaking, clung to those arms she had just forsworn as if her very life depended on it.

Suddenly it was borne in on her consciousness that her legs were being wrenched apart, that her clothes were being pulled from her body, and that Buck—a new ungentle Buck—was straining above her, deaf to her cries—which indeed in the mighty holocaust of sound around them he could not have heard. He was—

"No!" she screamed. She was sure she uttered it even though she could not hear it, as she twisted violently in his grasp.

But he held her fast, with a desperate urgency. His hot breath blew into her ear, his lips closed down on hers—demanding lips that took without asking. His weight shifted on her, so that she felt his body pressed intimately close, her legs against his legs. Unable to move, she felt a sudden savage thrust within her and a sharp pain that seemed to burst inside, making her weak. A terrible lassitude claimed her, a heaviness of the limbs, an unwillingness to move. Suddenly it was all part of the storm—the terror, the pain. And the turmoil within became one with the turmoil without, and her own wild scream mingled with and was lost in the nightmare of sound around her. There was another deeper thrust, and she screamed again, but the sound was torn away. Buck paid no attention to her agonized writhing but held her in a steely grip, working his will upon her, moving rhythmically.

In Roxanne's trembling body something savage and tumultuous awakened. Something elemental and fierce, born of the storm and of new desires that raced unchecked through her being, something wild and free and wonderful. Inhibitions gone, passions suddenly unleashed, she was borne upward and skyward on heightened senses into an utterly new sweet passion that overbore the thrusting pain and the terror of that black doomsday cloud roaring down the prairie. Her feelings roiled until she felt inside her a vortex not unlike the twister, lit by flashing savage responses. Her fingers dug into Buck's back, and she surged upward toward him, feeling a groan quiver through her even though she could not hear it.

In the fury of the elements there on the great wild prairie, they were like mad things, clutching each other, moaning, gasping. A recklessness had engulfed Roxanne. Perhaps it was a reaction to the storm, the horrible rush of sound that had dimmed her brain and rubbed her nerves raw. Perhaps she was only clutching at life. They had been so near destruction, Buck and she. Death's dark, chill wings had brushed them—and now they found themselves snatched from death . . . and they were in each other's arms, young and alive and bursting with emotion. So they lay clasped, straining together in a frenzy of passion as if to make up for time lost, for days that had never been and might never be again.

When their fury was spent, Buck slid away from her and lay silent beside her. Roxanne lay on her back in the deep summer grass and looked up at the sky and marveled. Her whole body knew a new languidness, a warm yielding. In pain and terror and yes, wild desire and splendor too, she had become a woman. And prone beside her in the sweet summer grasses lay her lover.

Her thoughts moved dreamily. This had changed everything, hadn't it? She and Buck . . . she was his now. He had taken her virginity. True, he had done it under the lashing of powerful emotions, but . . . wasn't it always like that? Hadn't the storm just heightened it?

As she lay there dreamily, her mind filled with intoxicating fantasies, she was aware suddenly that Buck had sat up. Her gaze swung toward him, and she saw that his face was averted from her, and his head was in his hands.

"Roxanne, I'm sorry," he choked.

She didn't grasp that at first. Her world was singing and Buck was . . . was sorry?

"Sorry?" she repeated stupidly.

"I never meant to—I don't know what came over me, Roxanne. It was the storm, I guess. I thought we were done for and all of a sudden I couldn't stop myself. I—I just had to have someone, that's all."

Had to have *someone*. Not her . . . just someone. Her singing world crashed down around her with a cruel thud.

"You're saying you love Julie," she said in a dull voice. "That I just—happened."

There was a long silence while, one by one, her illusions fled.

"I'm—sorry," he repeated again, as if the words were torn from his very depths.

Roxanne heard that anguished note in his voice, and deep inside her something quivered and wept. This was the first time any man had held her—really held her—in his arms. And it had to be someone who was sorry! Oh, why, cried her heart, couldn't it have been different? Why couldn't this first time have been someone who truly loved her, not just wanted her out of the need of the moment!

Feeling almost sick with the intensity of her emotion, she leaned forward and put her hot face in her hands. Buck saw that and his tone changed.

"I—I didn't mean—" he stammered. "Roxanne, I'll do anything to make it up to you."

Next, oh God, he was going to say, *I'll even marry you,* she thought wildly.

"You don't have to do anything," she choked. "I guess I could have fought you off if I'd tried hard enough." It wasn't true, but somehow it saved her pride. And she hadn't really fought as hard as she could. Death had seemed so near, a vivid reality, and out of the terrible void of her loneliness she'd wanted—just once—to hold someone in her arms. It just happened to be Buck, that was all. That was what she told herself.

"I'd give anything not to have done it," he said intensely.

She looked away, not able to face him at that moment. He'd give anything not to have done it. What a thing to hear from the man who'd just taken your virginity!

"I never meant—" He was whispering now, and the twister that had spawned this cyclone within them had disappeared, snaked back into the clouds from whence it came.

"I know you didn't," said Roxanne unsteadily. She struggled to sit up.

"I'll carry you back," he cried in an agony of effort to make it up to her.

"No, thanks, I'm not hurt," she said, wincing.

"Oh, God, I've torn your dress!"

"I can hold it together until I get a needle and thread."

Slowly, they made their way back to the Smiths'. They didn't talk, didn't look at each other. A great embarrassment had sprung up between them, composed of shame and guilt and—on her part at least—bewilderment.

When they reached the Smiths' yard gate, Nadine came running to meet them. "We hid in the cyclone cellar while the storm passed over," she informed them importantly. Then she saw Roxanne's torn dress and stared. "Where were you? We thought you'd be hiding in the storm cellar at the Old Hatter Place."

"There isn't any Old Hatter Place any more," said Buck grimly. "Twister tore it all up."

Nadine's eyes widened. "Golly!" she whispered. "Golly!"

Roxanne stumbled onto the porch unaided and Julie opened the front door. Her steady gray eyes took in Buck's worried look and Roxanne's torn, bloodied dress.

"I fell," said Roxanne in a flat voice.

"We tried to make the Old Hatter Place," explained Buck briefly. "But the tornado hit it dead center, and we veered off to the right of its path—and then it turned."

"Golly," thrilled Nadine again in a reverent whisper.

"It came right at us no matter which way we went, but we tumbled into a ditch, and it lifted up and went right over us. I thought sure we were goners." He had a haunted look.

"It was awful." Roxanne shuddered. She looked wan and her legs felt wobbly.

"Come upstairs with me, Roxanne," said Julie quietly. "I'll mend your dress for you."

Roxanne could hardly meet Julie's eyes. She hadn't known it would be so hard. But she followed along, thinking fervently, thank God, Julie doesn't know what happened out there!

Upstairs Julie shut the bedroom door and leaned against it. "I brought you up here so we could have some privacy," she said. "You don't have to tell me what happened—I can guess. It's on both your faces."

"No," said Roxanne, confused. "You don't know. You couldn't—"

Julie's upper lip trembled. "What I'm trying to tell you is that it's all right," she said. Roxanne saw her hands were clenched, the knuckles white. "You see, I—I know I'm not going to make it. I'm engaged to Buck, but I'm not ever going to wear his wedding ring. And I want him to be happy. That's why I sent you two over to the Old Hatter Place. That's why I've been throwing you together so much. Because"—her fingers clenched—"I want Buck to be happy when—when I'm gone."

Roxanne's head spun. She had expected recriminations and was prepared for them. But this! The anguish in Julie's gray eyes, the expression on her thin pale face with its bright spots of color on each cheek, the quiet renunciation in her tone—it wasn't fair that any one person should go through this!

Roxanne's head went up. "Julie," she said in the most convincing tone she could muster, "absolutely nothing happened. Buck was pointing out the sodhouse when the tornado swooped down. He grabbed me and we started running this way and that. I fell once and he dragged me to my feet—that must be how my dress got torn; I was so frightened I don't even remember. And then we tumbled into a ditch and it passed right over us. I've never been so terrified in my life. The noise just stunned us both. And then we got up, scared out of our wits, and staggered back here. But Buck loves *you*, Julie. He's not interested in me. He's just nice to me because I'm your friend."

Wisps of hope sprang up in Julie's eyes. "You aren't just saying that, are you?" she asked, her tone ragged.

"Of course not," said Roxanne sturdily. "Buck doesn't care a thing for me or I for him." Her voice rang with sincerity; she could almost believe it herself.

Julie slumped against the door. Roxanne was afraid she might collapse and slide to the floor.

"I meant to be so brave about it," Julie whispered. "But—but I'm so happy you don't care for each other!" Tears spilled over her lashes. "Oh, Roxanne, it's terrible for Buck having me like this."

"There, there." Roxanne steadied her friend. And any ideas she might have entertained about Buck and the life of a farmer's wife on the prairie went right out the window. It would be like murder. Frail, generous Julie couldn't stand another blow.

Julie twisted her fingers together, and her voice was

anxious, apologetic. "I'm—sorry for what I thought, Roxanne," she said humbly. "It's just that Buck's been so restless lately with me sick. After all, he'd expected us to be married almost a year ago. It's hard for a man to wait."

You knew he was looking around, thought Roxanne, surprised.

"And you're so pretty. And so nice," whispered Julie. "I thought if—if it was going to happen, I wanted the best for him."

Tears welled up in Roxanne's eyes and her throat closed. If she'd ever had any thoughts about taking Buck from Julie, they were gone forever. She would always see Julie's earnest face with its brave sad eyes, and there would be an unbridgeable gulf between herself and Buck.

Julie turned away, hiding her face, her shoulders shaking with dry, wracking sobs.

"I'll go home now, Julie," mumbled Roxanne. "I'll wait for Uncle Josh downstairs."

"No," sniffled Julie. "Your dress—I'll have to mend it first."

Roxanne checked herself in horror.

She couldn't go home! She had a clear conception of what Aunt Ada would think if she turned up with a torn dress and underwear and spots of blood on her skirt. And an ever clearer conception of what Aunt Ada would say. She'd rail at Roxanne, she'd call her damaged goods, but she'd make her marry fat old Mr. Witherspoon anyway! Aunt Ada would lock her in her room and starve her until she was so hungry she'd agree to anything! Hadn't she said so? And if Aunt Ada decided Roxanne might be pregnant, she'd want to get her married even sooner.

"I—can't go home," she choked.

Julie reached out and took her hand. Somehow that frail grasp was infinitely comforting. It said Julie understood. Now Julie's face was determined, and she straightened her shoulders so that she looked taller.

"Roxanne," she said quietly, "I don't know what happened out there and"—she held up her hand to silence the other girl—"I don't want to know. Whatever happened was my fault. I threw you together because I thought that I could bear to give Buck up. But I can't. I know that now. And I've made up my mind. Whatever happens, I'm going to marry him. If I die the next day, I'll have had that anyway. This living in limbo, I can't stand it any more. No more can Buck. I don't blame him if he—if you and he . . ." Her voice trailed off and she gave Roxanne a wild look. "We're going to help you get out of here, Roxanne. We owe you that. When your Uncle Josh comes by, we'll say you fell and hurt your back and that the doctor said it was all right except maybe you shouldn't bounce around in a buckboard for a couple of days. Then we'll put you on a train. Wherever you want to go. Buck has some money saved—enough for a ticket. And you won't have to marry Ned Witherspoon!"

And she wouldn't have to stay and watch with anguish as Buck and Julie got married. She wouldn't have to watch Julie die. . . .

Having made up her mind, Julie went promptly about it. She dried her eyes and matter-of-factly mended Roxanne's dress. Then she poured some water in the big ironstone washbowl on the marble-top washstand, so Roxanne could wash the spots out of it.

"Nance can iron it dry," Julie said, as Roxanne soberly washed the blood out of her worn yellow calico dress. "Besides," she added, "you won't be wearing it. I've got something better for train travel."

She opened the pine hope chest Buck had given her. As Roxanne watched, she pulled out a gray linen suit with wide lapels and a long bell-shaped skirt, a suit carefully folded in tissue paper and smelling of lavender, and laid it gently, lovingly, on the bed.

"I had more figure then, and besides it has deep seams. We can let them out." Julie considered the suit wistfully. "It's part of my trousseau. It was to be my going-away suit."

"But I can't take that," protested Roxanne. "You'll want to have it when you marry Buck."

Julie sighed. "I'm not going away now. I'm going

to marry Buck and stay right here—move right into the little house he fixed up for us on his pa's place. I'll ride there from the church in my white dress and wedding veil." She smiled at Roxanne. "It will be very romantic."

Roxanne smiled back. It *would* be romantic, she thought. More romantic, certainly, than being ravished in a cyclone.

When Uncle Josh came to pick her up, they told him that Roxanne had hurt her back. He believed every word—after all, who had ever known Julie Smith to lie? Especially with Roxanne looking wan in Julie's bed under the green and yellow quilt while they all fussed over her.

That very evening, Roxanne put on Julie's going-away linen suit and a pert gray hat that matched it, a hat that sprouted pink ribbons and gray feathers, and gray kid gloves.

As Julie outfitted her carefully, Roxanne for a stabbing moment thought, You'd think I were the bride. . . .

But then, carrying a little hand satchel packed with her yellow calico dress and a few things Julie had provided, Roxanne climbed into the buckboard and let Buck and Julie drive her to the railway station in Wichita.

On the way there, Roxanne looked at the Arkansas River that flowed down from the Continental Divide in Colorado past Cimarron and Dodge City before it reached Wichita. All the glamor of the storied West was in that river, she thought idly. The land-rushers and the Indians following the buffalo herds and the long-haired gunmen of the plains . . . and their women. She looked at the river flowing by and thought about those women. Had they been like her, dreaming dreams that might never come true? or like Aunt Ada, hard and practical with their eyes on the main chance?

Buck bought her a ticket on the St. Louis and San Francisco Railroad as far as Augusta, Kansas. Julie pressed a little gray purse with money into her hand. "It's best you buy another ticket when you get to

Augusta for wherever you want to go. It's best Buck and I don't know where you're going. Then it can't be surprised out of us." She cut off Roxanne's stammered thanks with, "Hush, now. You'd do the same for me."

I wonder, thought Roxanne. I wonder, in your place, what I would have done. She looked into those brave gray eyes. Hadn't someone said strength was fleeting but love endured?

"Tell Aunt Ada I've gone back to Savannah," she told Julie. "Then she'll look for me in the wrong place."

Julie nodded gravely. "Don't tell me where you're really going," she cautioned. "But . . . write me once in a while. So I'll know you're all right."

"No," said Roxanne quietly. "Letters have postmarks. I'm never coming back to Kansas. Not ever. Good-bye, Julie."

Julie's tear-frosted eyes were grateful. She was being given her chance at happiness.

Roxanne gave Julie a quick, silent hug and turned to Buck. His face was impassive, but his eyes gave him away. They were desperate with wanting her. For a wild moment the storm-wind roared in her ears again, the world crashed around her, and she and Buck were entwined in each other's arms beneath a whirling black holocaust, every nerve raw with feeling, primitive emotions unleashed.

The moment passed.

Roxanne extended her hand. "Good-bye, Buck."

He took that hand, held it briefly. "Good-bye, Roxanne."

Valise and purse clasped in her hands, she got on the train, and amid hissing steam and a great grinding of wheels, it got under way.

Roxanne watched Julie and Buck from the window until their figures grew tiny on the station platform. As the train picked up speed and thundered away, tears glittering on her lashes. This was the last she'd ever see of Kansas . . . the last she'd ever see of her friend and Buck. Whatever part of her heart she had left on these ageless prairies was irretrievably lost.

And yet . . . out of the pain and terror and heartache and wild joy she had become a woman. And it was with a woman's eyes that she looked back across the Kansas prairies and listened to the lonely whistle of the train that was hurtling her through the night.

Then she lifted her head with a new determination and resolutely turned her face to the east where the morning sun would rise to herald a new day.

Chapter 4

At Augusta, Roxanne changed trains, taking one that went south on the Atchison, Topeka and Santa Fe. So, if anyone were to try to trace her, it would look as if she were blundering vaguely toward Savannah. For she had no doubt that if Aunt Ada caught up with her, she would be forced to marry Mr. Witherspoon . . . if her aunt had to break both her arms to make her do it. Riding stiffly, sitting up in a day coach, for she could not afford the comfortable parlor cars or Pullman sleepers, she changed trains several times for short runs, making herself as inconspicuous as possible.

But her pretty face had cost her something. A hard-eyed, rat-faced individual, with a derby hat and an eye for women, noticed the pretty girl alight at Cherryvale, and realized he had seen her the day before going in the opposite direction. He was waiting on the platform to board the train for Kansas City, and when she got on board, he took a seat in the same car and watched her. Crossing his agile legs and smoking a long Cheroot, occasionally looking at a big gold watch with a fake ruby fob, he observed her nervous manner. When they alighted at Kansas City, he saw Roxanne look around furtively and then move to the ticket window. He fell in behind her and watched as she bought a Pullman ticket on the eastbound Union Pacific, then he bought one too. Unaware of this interested surveillance, Roxanne congratulated herself that she had now eluded pursuit. She felt she had made only one grievous error: By mistake she had bought a Pullman ticket, which sadly depleted her funds. Afraid to call attention to herself by changing the ticket—in the innocence of youth she felt Aunt Ada's spies were everywhere—she entered the plush Pullman car and found a seat beside a very stout elderly woman dressed in the drab tailored garb that marked her position as an upper servant.

Unnoticed, the rat-faced man slipped into the seat behind Roxanne.

The elderly woman asked Roxanne her destination. Roxanne said "Philadelphia," and added that she hoped to find employment in some household. Behind her, a derby hat inclined forward as its rat-faced owner strained to listen.

"Ah, there you'll be making a mistake, child," said the older woman. "For since the potato famine in Ireland, so many Irish have come to these shores and raised families that on the East Coast I fear you'll find all the jobs are taken. And with so many other foreigners pouring in at all the ports, too. Regular melting pot we've become!" She clucked her tongue.

Roxanne found this news disquieting. Only this morning she had looked in her purse and found she had barely enough fare to go as far as Philadelphia. Buck and Julie had generously given her what money they had, but they had not dared take either of their families into their confidence. So Roxanne, after her wild perorations about the Kansas railways, now found herself short of ready cash.

She learned that the stout elderly woman next to

her, named Mary Willis, had been in service for many years as housekeeper and companion to a genteel old lady in San Francisco. Her employer, Mrs. Hattie Anderton, was the widow of a captain in the Union Army who had died at Gettysburg. Mary Willis, a garrulous sort, told Roxanne all about the big house high on Russian Hill they had occupied until Miss Hattie's death last month. Miss Hattie, knowing she was going to die, had generously written to her brother in Baltimore, asking him to make a place for Mary Willis in his household. The brother, a Mr. Joab Coulter, had written assenting to her request, but the letter had arrived after Miss Hattie's death. And now Mary was aboard this "steaming devil," as she called the train, headed toward an East she'd never liked and hadn't seen in more than thirty years.

"But why should you go east if you don't want to?" asked Roxanne, bewildered. "Why didn't Mrs. Anderton provide for you in her will?"

Mary Willis shook her head. "Miss Hattie, she didn't have any money of her own, child. All she had was a life interest in that big house on Russian Hill. Her brother, Joab Coulter, had to send her money to keep her going, and now the house will go to him, most likely."

At that moment, the porter came through the car announcing lunchtime. Mary Willis looked astonished when Roxanne refused to accompany her to the dining car for lunch. "Are you sick, child?" she asked.

Roxanne shook her head, unwilling to admit that with her short funds she planned to limit her food to one meal a day. To say so would arouse pity, and Mary Willis might try to buy her lunch. The thought of taking charity from a stranger galled Roxanne. "Just not hungry," she said with a shrug.

The older woman's face cleared. She stood up briskly, remarking that she hoped the Coulters set a good table. She and Miss Hattie had eaten well in San Francisco. Roxanne, observing that Mary could hardly waddle down the aisle to the dining car, could well believe it.

To quiet the pangs of hunger, Roxanne got up after Mary left and restlessly began to explore the train. She was moving between the cars when a man's figure blocked her path. She looked up into a sly, smiling, ratlike face beneath a dark derby hat.

"What's yer hurry, little lady?" he asked.

Roxanne frowned and started to brush past without replying, but he caught her arm familiarly and chucked her under the chin. "You can't seem to make up yer mind where yer heading, can you?" he said slyly.

In the act of drawing back her arm to strike this masher, Roxanne stiffened and stared up into his face.

He laughed. "Didn't know anybody saw you changing trains like that, did you?"

"Go away," said Roxanne in an unsteady voice. "Or I will call the conductor."

"No, you won't," he said confidently. "You won't call nobody. Your face is white and scared. What did you do, run away from home? Bet they're lookin' for a pretty thing like you!"

Roxanne tried to wrench away, but he held her fast in a clawlike grip. "You don't have to tell me now, little lady. But when you get where you're goin', we're going to get off the train together and have a long, long talk about it!" Suddenly he bent down and planted a hard wet kiss on her mouth.

With a sob of revulsion she tore free and plunged back into the car she had just left. The man's nasty laugh followed her.

Heart pounding, she hurried back to her seat. Her train hopping, which she had thought such a clever ruse, had trapped her. It had made this stranger in the derby hat suspicious. If only she could leap off the train at the first station and take another train for somewhere else! She could lose him that way, but her money was almost gone. So flight was out of the question.

And he was right—she dared not call the conductor. She was sure that would bring Aunt Ada upon her in full cry. Biting her lips, she jumped when Mary

Willis came back saying, "You missed a good lunch. The leg of lamb was delicious."

Roxanne gave her a thin smile and listened absently as Mary again regaled her with tales of life in San Francisco. A life which had been far from gay, Roxanne discerned, shut up behind heavy drawn portieres, two old women spending their entire time deciding what they would have for dinner.

She stiffened. The rat-faced man in the derby hat was swaggering up the aisle toward her. As he approached, he gave her a nasty knowing smile and winked. She turned hastily to Mary Willis. "Was Miss Hattie very heavy?" she asked. Let that man believe she wasn't traveling alone, that she was with Mary.

Complacent, Mary Willis did not notice the man's interest.

"No, Miss Hattie was thin. All the Coulters are thin, I gather. Tall elegant people. Real aristocrats. They're a rich shipping family in Baltimore."

Pleased that she had Roxanne's attention, Mary drew from her purse a letter signed "Joab Coulter," which promised to take Mary into his household and demanded somewhat irascibly, "What age is this woman? Is she young or old? You tell me nothing of her."

Mary laughed. "Can you imagine him thinking I might be young? And me a companion to Miss Hattie, who was all of ninety?" She pushed the letter back into her purse along with her ticket to Baltimore and a small roll of bills which Roxanne guessed constituted her life savings. They chatted a little more and Mary's voice began to sound a bit drowsy. Finally her voice drifted off. She was asleep, her head lolling against the seat.

Roxanne looked out the window at the scenery rushing by. She saw no easy way out of her dilemma.

By dinner time Mary had roused herself and was among the first to hurry to the dining car. Famished, Roxanne rose to accompany her. As she did so, she saw the rat-faced man sitting in the seat behind her and paled. It would be hard to escape him if he stayed so close. She could still feel the impress of that disgusting kiss, and she flushed as his insolent glance passed over her trim figure. Lifting her chin haughtily, she followed Mary's determined progress down the aisle.

The dining car was a revelation. Venison, elk, mutton chops, beefsteak and grouse were all on the menu. Roxanne selected the cheapest thing she could find and enjoyed eating in the luxuriously appointed car with its snowy linens and silver finger bowls.

As they finished, her stout companion said, with an almost impish smile, "Do you know, I think I'll just order another meal? I didn't try the grouse, and it looked so good when they had it at the next table." Remaining to keep her company, Roxanne sat by in astonishment as Mary Willis downed another complete dinner.

The rat-faced man was absent when they returned to their seats, and Roxanne breathed a sigh of relief, even though she realized he was probably lurking in the dining car and she had overlooked him there.

It couldn't have been more than an hour later that Mary Willis got up to get a drink of water, started uncertainly down the aisle, suddenly faltered and pitched backward onto the floor. She fell heavily, her purse skittering under Roxanne's feet. A woman screamed, and two or three male passengers leaped up to help Mary to her feet. They bent over her prostrate form and then looked at each other, aghast. A doctor from one of the cars up ahead was hastily summoned. He was too late. When he rose from his swift examination, he pronounced Mary Willis dead. A stroke, he said gravely, and when Roxanne told him how Mary had just consumed two large consecutive meals, he shook his head.

Her people must be notified, he said briskly. They must decide where the body was to be sent. Roxanne interposed that Mary Willis had told her she had no family, but added eagerly that she'd had some money, and bent down to the floor to pick up the purse which had landed almost under her long skirt. As she picked it up, it fell open and everything spilled out: the ticket, the money, the letter, a few trinkets.

Roxanne stared down at them. The ticket and the letter! Her body shielded them from the doctor's view, and her brain was working feverishly. Joab Coulter had never laid eyes on Mary Willis, had indeed written to ask her age! *She* could assume the woman's identity, *she* could take that job in Baltimore until she could find another position!

With only an instant's hesitation, Roxanne kicked the ticket and the letter underneath the hem of her long dress, replaced the money and the trinkets in the purse and, smiling apologetically, handed them to the doctor.

"I don't know where she was going," she said gravely. "But she said she'd lost her ticket and was going to look for it in the dining car when she fell."

The lie had been uttered. She was committed to her course of action.

"Well," said the doctor, counting out the money, "there's enough here to bury her. I'll see the conductor about putting her off the train where I get off. If anyone wants to claim the body, they can do it there."

A search was made of the dining car, but of course no ticket was found, and Mary Willis, victim of her own ravenous appetite, was carried from the train at the doctor's stop.

Before that, however, Roxanne had edged the woman's ticket and letter forward with her foot. Then she awkwardly dropped her own purse and made a great show of stooping down to retrieve the contents which, when she rose, included the ticket and the letter.

Now she knew her destination.

She was going to Baltimore.

But she had reckoned without Ratface.

He caught up with her, in the space between the cars, as she made her way back from watching Mary Willis's body being taken off the train. No one was present; they were protected from view by closed doors. Briskly he stepped in front of her and blocked her way.

"I seen you do it," he crowed. "I seen you pick that dead lady's purse. How much you get?"

In the close quarters between the cars, Roxanne was revolted by his breath, his expression, his whole being. "I took nothing," she said sullenly.

He gripped her wrist. "I seen you grab something and stick it in your purse," he said in a threatening voice. "Now tell me, what was it?"

Roxanne stiffened. In her new desperation she had become wily. Now she glared back at him venomously. "If you don't let me alone," she cried, "I'll say *you* killed her—that you've been following us and you poisoned her."

His jaw dropped open. He was taken aback at the controlled violence of her tone, and his other hand—which had been about to caress her soft white throat—drew back as if the touch might burn him. "The old lady died of a stroke! You heard the doctor!"

Roxanne's eyes narrowed as she played her trump card. "Perhaps. But if I accuse you, the police will certainly hold us both. The worst that will happen to me is I'll go back where I came from. But you—do you want the police checking into *your* background?"

She saw from his expression that she had guessed correctly.

"You she-devil!" he breathed. "I believe you'd do it!"

"You can count on it," said Roxanne in a hard voice. "And if the police looked at me and then at you, whom do you think they'd believe?"

His face contorted at that. "I'll get you for that," he muttered.

"But not today," said Roxanne, her eyes blue ice. "And not for this."

They were both jolted as the train drew to a halt at a little crossroads station. In rage, he drew back his arm to strike her, but passengers coming through on their way from the dining car intervened, moving between them. His eyes, which earlier had been so lascivious, were sick with rage as an agony of emotions played over his venal face.

Suddenly his eyes dilated. "*You* really done it!" he gasped. "For something that was in that purse! You really killed that old lady. You had the chance to slip something into her drink in the dining car—I don't want to be involved in no murder!" With an oath he flung past her, and she saw him disembark onto the empty station platform. Farther down, a driver was turning his horse and buggy in preparation to driving off. The rat-faced man hailed him on the run, hanging onto his derby hat against the wind. As the train began to chug away, Ratface turned and shook his fist, and Roxanne saw that his face was contorted. She smiled grimly, her heart beating a trip-hammer tune.

With a newfound composure, Roxanne sat back in her seat and waited for the train to arrive in Baltimore. Buffeted by events, she had grown up a little and her purpose had hardened. She would be no man's plaything! Especially not such a man as that!

Roxanne Rossiter, with all her young dreams, was gone, she told herself firmly. As Mary Willis she would arrive in Baltimore, and there make a new life for herself.

Part Two:

Baltimore 1895—1896

Chapter 5

Dawn was breaking when Roxanne arrived in Baltimore. The day was warm and cloudy, and a pale sun cast its gray light over the smokestacks, the warehouses and the tall buildings of the big industrial city with its great port. Soon it would be blistering hot.

She alighted at the magnificent new Mt. Royal Station, a monumental building of massive granite set in a hollow of the city, its tall clock tower giving it the austere look of a Norman keep. In the enormous waiting room with its polished marble columns and huge fireplace and oak paneling, she seated herself and read again the letter from Joab Coulter. People came and went. Near her on a comfortable rocking chair a big woman sat stolidly and fanned herself. After a while Roxanne got up and took a deep breath. There was no point in postponing the moment.

She found a carriage for hire and gave the driver the address on the letter. He took her to a tall, frowning brownstone town house on fashionable Mt. Vernon Place.

With her heart beating wildly, Roxanne alighted and paid the driver. Carrying her little valise, she climbed the seven stone steps to the massive front door and banged with the iron boar's head knocker.

To the dignified manservant who opened the door, she said she was Mary Willis of San Francisco and she was expected. Barely able to conceal his surprise as his eyes took in her pert lush figure and fresh-faced youth, he led her into the front hall and told her to wait. Roxanne sank down on a small rosewood chair and looked about the paintings, which she presumed to be family portraits. Their heavy gilt and walnut frames were set against the imported Renaissance-design paper that covered the walls above the dark wainscoting. The backgrounds of these portraits were green and rural, most of them depicting a rolling limestone countryside shaded by enormous oaks and red maples. She liked the faces of the people—open and candid with eyes that regarded her, steadily. The best displayed portrait, lit by a shaft of light from the stairway, was apparently an older painting than the rest; its subject looked to be an English gentleman standing on the terrace of his ancestral holding. He was broad-shouldered, wore a satin coat and knee breeches and had a commanding look about him.

But her favorite portrait was one in the darkest corner, which she could see only by moving closer: It depicted a man of good height and proportions, seated on a spirited horse whose dark mane—like the rider's hair—blew eternally in a painted wind. It was not the man's figure that arrested her, nor his obvious look of command, nor yet his handsome regularity of features. Rather it was the wildness of his green eyes, the humorous twist of the mouth, the firmness of the square jaw. A worldly face, she thought, and wondered who this gentleman was and why he was hidden in the darkest spot behind the stairs.

After a moment the manservant returned and led her into a long dining room where a tall thin man with iron-gray hair and bright, sunken eyes in a cavernous face sat alone at breakfast. He looked startled at sight of her, and his thick dark brows drew together.

"*You* are Mary Willis?" he demanded incredulously.

Unused to deceit, and afraid he would read guilt in her face, Roxanne bobbed a greeting and answered in a stifled voice, "Yes, sir."

He leaned forward. "Surely you cannot be the Mary Willis who was in service to my Cousin Hattie for some thirty years?"

Roxanne hadn't known he knew that. She swallowed and improvised.

"I—I'm her daughter, sir. When she died I took her place in Miss Hattie's household. Miss Hattie trained me, sir. She was fond of me. And it's *because* I'm young that she wrote to you, sir. She didn't want me led into evil paths."

She had not mistaken the fanatical gleam that shone in those eyes. At this last statement the frowning gentleman looked somewhat mollified. He sat back and drummed his bony knuckles on the tablecloth.

"Mrs. Hollister, our housekeeper, informs me we're in need of an upstairs maid. And you can attend Miss Clarissa as well when she returns. You look to be a strong clever girl; you should be able to do double duty as a young lady's maid."

He had accepted her story! Dizzy with relief, Roxanne inclined her head in meek assent.

"Mary." He pondered. "We've two Mary's in this household already."

"My name is Mary Roxanne," supplied Roxanne hastily. "You could call me Roxanne, sir."

"Roxanne." He rolled the name over his tongue. "Yes, that will do." He rang a little bell beside him and the manservant, whom Roxanne now presumed to be the butler, appeared.

"Greaves, tell Mrs. Hollister I wish to see her."

Greaves disappeared and, ignoring Roxanne, the elderly gentleman returned to eating his breakfast.

She took the opportunity to look around the handsome room, which was large and paneled in dark walnut. Occupying a commanding position on one wall, a large mahogany sideboard held a rich assortment of silver bowls and platters from which the butler had obviously just served Joab Coulter his breakfast. Watching him eat made Roxanne hungry, for she had not yet eaten this morning. The table was long, and she decided it must have extra leaves to lengthen it still further, for there were a number of extra chairs set between carved servers and a large mahogany china closet. Overhead a branched crystal chandelier caught the light from the windows and sparkled.

But again the portraits were what interested her most. There were more of them here, crowded into all the available wall space, as if no one must be left out. While the countryside in the background of these paintings was as rich and green as that in the hall portraits, these people were of a different cut altogether. They seemed to represent two distinct types: Most were handsome men and women with carefree faces and the look of pleasure lovers about them, but a few of the faces were cold and austere—and their painted eyes chilled Roxanne. There was a cruel look about the mouths of this latter group; their lips were a trifle too full for beauty, and a kind of knowing malice lingered behind those intelligent painted eyes.

Studying these dining room portraits as she waited patiently beside the long table, Roxanne was puzzled. It seemed impossible that these people could share the same blood as those in the front hall.

Her reverie was interrupted by the arrival of Mrs. Hollister, who gave Roxanne a surprised look, but recovered herself and listened with rapt attention as Roxanne's circumstances were briefly recounted.

Mrs. Hollister, who was plump and stood with her whole body slightly inclined in a birdlike way, listening to her employer's terse words, straightened up and dimpled.

"I'll see to her, sir," she chirped and motioned Roxanne to follow her. In the doorway she turned and gave her employer a sunny smile. "Miss Clarissa will be glad she's so young."

"Time," said Joab Coulter with perhaps unconscious humor, "will correct that."

His tone, though sententious, was slightly scathing, and Roxanne smarted a little under it. She followed dumpy little Mrs. Hollister into the hall, amused to observe that the housekeeper wore an old-fashioned bustle, which made her stout figure appear even stouter.

At a clattering noise from the street, Mrs. Hollister paused and cocked her head alertly. "I believe I hear the ice wagon coming," she said. "He hasn't been delivering enough ice. He'll be stopping at the neighbor's and we're next. I'll just show you to your room, Roxanne, and then I'll come back down and wait for him. You can unpack, and I'll send Reba up to get you started; she'll show you where things are. There'll be little for you to do until Miss Clarissa returns."

"Who is Miss Clarissa?" asked Roxanne.

"She's Mr. Coulter's cousin by his first wife—the one from the Eastern Shore. Mr. Coulter is Miss Clarissa's guardian, and so she makes her home here since her parents died. She's away visiting just now."

"How large is the family?" ventured Roxanne.

"Only three really—except for Miss Clarissa. Mr. Joab Coulter has two sons: Mr. Gavin is the elder son, and Mr. Rhodes is the younger. Neither of them is married." She turned and fixed Roxanne with her bright, birdlike gaze as if to emphasize her next remark. "Both of them are fine young men."

They had almost reached the stairs.

"I don't understand about the portraits," said Roxanne. "They look so different—the ones in the front hall and those in the dining room."

Mrs. Hollister paused and considered her. "The ones in the dining room are of his first wife's family," she explained. "Those in the hall are of his second wife's family."

Roxanne looked down the hall. "Who is the commanding gentleman in the dark spot behind the stairs?"

"He was Mr. Rhodes's grandfather on his mother's

side—a Virginia gentleman. Mr. Rhodes looks just like him."

And his portrait was consigned to the darkest part of the hall. Plainly, Joab Coulter had not cared for his father-in-law. She wondered what Rhodes would be like, a man who looked like that. . . .

On the second floor landing Mrs. Hollister hesitated, a little frown on her face.

"You're very pretty," she murmured. "I think—yes, you should sleep on the third floor instead of on the second floor back with the other maids. It will be more convenient for you, being near Miss Clarissa and you'll be right next door to me." She studied Roxanne thoughtfully. "I sleep soundly, but I don't mind being waked. Just call out if you're frightened."

"Why would I be frightened?" wondered Roxanne.

"Oh, it's a big house," shrugged Mrs. Hollister. "And when Mr. Rhodes is here, he comes in at all hours. Mr. Gavin does too, for that matter. So you might wake up and . . . hear footsteps. There's nothing to be frightened of. Nothing at all."

Roxanne thought uneasily that Mrs. Hollister protested too much.

They continued to the third floor. On the landing, her head inclined as she listened for the iceman, Mrs. Hollister launched into some rules of the house.

Roxanne was instructed that henceforth she would use the servants' entrance, which was below and to the right of the stone steps that led to the massive front door. She would sleep in the servants' wing on the third floor back—which was the top floor of the servants' wing, although the main structure, the front, was four stories tall. She would use the servants' back stairway. Since Miss Clarissa's rooms occupied the entire third floor of the main structure, Roxanne's room would be located close to the main stair landing—where Miss Clarissa could call her conveniently.

Because the rooms in the servants' wing were lower than were the rooms in the main house, Roxanne found herself going down three steps from the third-floor stair landing before reaching the narrow hall where her small room was the first door on the right. A closet used only to store boxes and trunks faced her room and, at the end of the hall, the larger room that occupied the whole back of the servants' wing was Mrs. Hollister's.

There was a clattering noise below. "Ah, that's the iceman now," Mrs. Hollister said and scurried away.

When the door closed on the housekeeper, Roxanne surveyed her new surroundings. Small and square and with only one window, the room was stuffy and airless in the muggy summer heat. Its walls were painted a dull buff. The effect was almost colorless.

Removing her hat, she flung it on the narrow, lumpy iron bed and began to unpack her valise. There was little to unpack, but carefully she hung her worn yellow calico on one of several hooks in the wall. The little toilet articles Julie had given her she arranged in the top drawer of the battered pine washstand, whose cracked marble top supported an ironstone washbowl and pitcher. In a lower compartment was a sturdy white ironstone slop jar. The room was devoid of decoration—there was a roll-up blind but no curtains, a mere scrap of hooked rug was the sole floor covering, and in one corner stood a rickety pine dresser and a straight chair.

Roxanne sighed and taking the pins out of her hair, began to comb it energetically before the cracked mirror that stood atop the washstand. She hadn't expected luxury, she told herself firmly.

While she was combing her hair, Reba came in. Reba was a tall, lanky redhead with dark eyes and a wide mouth that wore a cynical expression.

"Well, old Holly said you were pretty," she observed. "For once she was right!"

Roxanne laughed. "I'm Roxanne—" she started to say "Rossiter" but caught herself and said, "Willis."

"I know. I'm Reba Payne." Reba grinned at her. "Holly told me you were going to be lady's maid to Miss Clarissa." She laughed. "Better you than me!"

"Oh? What's Clarissa like?"

"Miss Clarissa is eighteen years old," said Reba,

"and spoiled rotten. She gives us all a fit what with wanting her dresses pressed right now, and when we're busy always wanting things fetched and carried. She's never satisfied with anything, not Miss Clarissa. So you're to be her maid? Well, well!"

Roxanne began to have forebodings about her new mistress. Life on Mt. Vernon Place might not be as serene as she had hoped. Oh, well, she would endure whatever was necessary, and if she did not like it here, would eventually get herself a recommendation as "Mary Willis" and find herself a new position!

"Mrs. Hollister told me there were two sons in the family. How old are they?"

"Mr. Gavin is in his early thirties. He's the son by Mr. Joab's first wife—she came from the Eastern Shore and was rich. Mr. Rhodes is the son by Mr. Joab's second wife—she came from Virginia and was even richer." Reba plopped herself down on Roxanne's bed. "Mr. Rhodes is in his twenties." Her voice dropped conspiratorially. "The cook we used to have—she'd been here forever and finally dropped dead in the kitchen—*she* said Mr. Rhodes's mother married Joab Coulter on the rebound after she'd had a terrible fight with her lover, else he'd never have got her. They weren't happy together. Mr. Joab Coulter's very religious," she added, "and he likes Mr. Gavin best. But everyone else prefers Mr. Rhodes."

"Mrs. Hollister said you'd show me where things are and get me started."

Reba shrugged and got up and led her to a large step-down linen closet reached by a door from the stair landing. Now Roxanne knew why the box room opposite her was so small: the enormous linen closet reached into the servants' wing and took up most of the space! Stacks of neatly folded bed linens met her eye, piles of blankets and coverlets and towels and heavy quilts—for winters were cold in Baltimore. Although it was dark in the linen closet, all these neat, freshly laundered things gave Roxanne a feeling of luxury and plenty.

She closed the door behind her with a smile and waited for Reba to tell her what to do.

"Look, just make the beds and straighten up and dust," Reba said hastily. She stuck a dust mop in Roxanne's hands. "Sheets don't get changed until tomorrow. Start on the first floor and work your way up. We're working on the ironing, and I've got to get back downstairs or Holly will be screaming for me. When you finish, come on back behind the kitchen. That's where you'll find me—in the laundry."

Reba accompanied her downstairs, chattering companionably. On the first floor she showed Roxanne Joab Coulter's bedroom which Roxanne was surprised to see occupied the large room that normally would have been the drawing room. This was due, Reba told her, to the fact that he had rheumatism, which kept him incapacitated much of the time. Behind his bedroom, at the end of a short hall that branched off to the right of the main hallway, was a small office where business with tradespeople was transacted, and where ledgers were kept. And behind it was a private study that could be entered only from Mr. Coulter's bedroom. Across the entire back of the house, Reba indicated with a wave of her hand, stretched the long dining room; and behind it, in the servants' wing, were the kitchen and laundry and two cubbyhole rooms where Cook and Greaves the butler respectively slept, since Cook needed to be near the kitchen and Greaves was on more or less constant call.

"Enjoy yourself!" said Reba blithely, and hurried away to her ironing. Roxanne watched that swinging stride depart and then, dust mop firmly in hand, went in to make up the big towering four-poster in Joab Coulter's baronial retreat. She found the room vaguely unpleasant with its stiff horsehair furniture and heavy olive drapes and shadowy corners in the dark oak paneling. On the walls were vast paintings of sea battles. Joab Coulter seemed to have a taste for gore. These were not pictures in which the landing of cannon balls was recorded in puffs of smoke—these were close-up scenes of decks slippery with blood as men with angry faces grappled hand to hand, slashing and maiming. Roxanne studied them and shuddered at the mind that would care to regard such scenes before falling asleep at night. Over the mantel was a large lithograph of an angel—but even this angel carried a sword in one upraised hand and had an avenging expression in the eyes that blazed beneath his mop of golden hair. On a handsome commode by the bed lay a large, well-thumbed Bible, open with a velvet bookmark. This mixture of bloody battle pictures and godliness made her wonder about the past of the gaunt man with the fanatical gleam in his eye.

Joab Coulter's private study was a small, darkly paneled room dominated by an ornate desk of rosewood and mahogany with a brass galleried top, ornate front legs and four drawers that opened down the side. Beside it stood a small, glass-fronted bookcase stuffed with letters tied with twine, and numerous other papers. Roxanne, industriously wielding a dust cloth, wondered if her employer spent much time in this gloomy place.

Next, Roxanne went in to dust the office.

The office was better. It had a plain oak rolltop desk, a round oak table and five straight chairs. A calendar with advertising hung on the wall, and the carpet was somewhat worn. A plain, no-nonsense sort of place where business could be conducted, she decided. There were several piles of ledgers and account books and some stacks of business papers weighted down by heavy glass paperweights.

The second floor was devoted entirely to reception rooms, furnished mostly in the ponderous Eastlake style with "Turkish" overstuffed sofas and rich, dark-red tasseled portieres. Roxanne passed it regretfully and went up to the third floor.

Clarissa's rooms were a delight. Her big bedroom stretched across the front, and behind it were a large, private sitting room and a dressing room so big that Roxanne guessed it had once been a bedroom in its own right. All were dazzlingly decorated. Cream satin drapes and billowing curtains of sheer Irish lace adorned the tall windows. The furniture was of walnut and satinwood, robustly Victorian, full of curlicues and carved angels. Roxanne envied Clarissa the elegant cheval glass with its dainty jointed candle brackets. The tall adjustable mirror was a perfect place for a young lady to survey her appearance before going out. And oh, to comb one's hair at that fancy dressing table with its pink marble top and scalloped beveled mirror set between gilt flower baskets! She couldn't resist opening the walnut armoire, which was crammed with stylish clothes, most in shades of peach and pink. She pulled out one creamy lace ball gown trimmed in peach satin and held it up to her own figure. It would have fit her perfectly, she thought yearningly. Turning, she saw that a drawer of the big bureau had been hastily shut. From it protruded a pink corset ribbon. Roxanne pulled open the drawer and was greeted with a jumbled assortment of kid gloves, sachet, lacy handkerchiefs and dainty stockings. She sighed, sniffing the faint perfume that clung to the corset. How wonderful to be rich and carefree and live like this!

She held up the corset and studied its steel-boned construction before she put it away. Then she whirled once before the cheval glass, noting with satisfaction her own slender waist and delicately molded bust. How tightly did Clarissa have to lace that corset to wear those lovely clothes? she wondered. *She* could have worn them without a corset!

Both Joab Coulter's sons occupied front rooms on the fourth floor. She met Gavin Coulter when, believing the room empty, she threw open the door and caught him, standing in shirt and suspenders, in the act of shaving before his mirrored washstand.

He whirled, a tall keen-eyed man, and she was instantly reminded of the dining room portraits. Those portraits of the pleasure lovers—and of the coldly ambitious. Here was a face that strangely combined the two: Gavin had the full sensuous lips of the pleasure seeker but—was there a cruel twist to the mouth? And his eyes, so dark and cold and watchful as he turned.

Suddenly, they seemed to change, brightening at the sight of her. His stance was commanding, and there was about him something that both attracted and repelled her.

Roxanne, red-faced, turned to retreat, but his crisp authoritative voice stopped her. "Who are you?"

"I'm Roxanne, the new maid. I'm sorry to disturb you . . . sir," she added hastily.

"You're not disturbing me," he said. "Someone should have disturbed me sooner. I overslept and no-one called me." His tone was contemptuous. "This house is disorganized. But I'll be finished shaving in a minute, so go on about your duties, Roxanne."

Roxanne advanced on the bed, trying to make herself inconspicuous. She was nervously aware of Gavin's keen eyes watching her in the mirror as he deftly worked up a lather in his shaving mug. Not quite sure what his attitude might be, she scurried about the room as he shaved with swift strokes.

She had been told that Gavin was in his thirties; now she saw that there was a peppering of premature gray in his dark hair. His face, while craggy, was not bad to look upon. Under heavy brows, his dark gaze was very penetrating, and his aggressive stare made Roxanne mindful that her bodice was tight and that she was breathing hard as she energetically plumped the pillows.

"Where were you employed before?" he asked, cleaning the lather from his razor.

"San Francisco," said Roxanne, hoping he would not ask her any questions about the town.

"Ah," he said, "that one." And she realized he knew that Mary Willis had been expected.

"Did you not find it confining—being maid to an old lady of ninety?" he asked curiously as he toweled his face and rinsed out his china shaving mug.

"No," said Roxanne promptly. "That is, I—I've led a sheltered life, sir," she added with an earnest look.

He looked amused. "Indeed, you must have. And yet I've heard San Francisco is a lively city. Had you no desperate young swain to bid you fond farewell at the station and plead with you not to leave?"

Conscious she was being mocked, Roxanne gave the pillow a somewhat harder slap. "No," she said coldly.

His laugh had a tinge of sarcasm. "Miss Clarissa—who'll have you dancing a merry tune to keep up with her wishes when she gets back—has numerous admirers. But she prefers my brother Rhodes to all of them. It's believed they'll marry eventually—when Rhodes settles down enough to propose properly."

"And where is Mr. Rhodes now, sir?"

"God knows. Somewhere on the high seas. We'll know he's here when he comes whistling up to the front door and tells us his ship has docked in the harbor. Rhodes is a wandering boy. He'd never be home at all if he had his way."

Gavin gave his hair a quick brush, shrugged into his coat and—affording her a last narrow glance—went out into the hall.

A little flustered by the encounter. Roxanne looked about the room. The furniture was handsome and, except for the bed, which was a high-headboard Eastlake, almost a duplicate of his father's. But the pictures on the walls were of commerce: of ports, of warehouses, of steamers, of busy docks. There were a few textbooks, a pile of ledgers—no favors from young ladies, no smiling portraits. A serious-minded fellow was Gavin Coulter, she decided, and yet . . . she flushed, remembering the bold way his eyes had raked her figure.

In Rhodes's room, which was somewhat smaller, the bed was already made, so she had only to dust. But she studied it, too, noting that it contained a hodgepodge of furniture, as if everything nobody else wanted had been stuck up here. There was a vast number of books; Rhodes apparently read everything. The walls were hung with pictures of sailing ships; clippers, schooners, tall ships with billowing white sails in romantic settings. Golf clubs, tennis rackets, a fencing foil and mask were stacked in a corner, and on a shipshape desk in a rococo gilt frame was a picture of a woman with smiling eyes and a gentle mouth that Roxanne decided was Rhodes's mother. Although she had not met him, she felt that she would like the carefree Rhodes who had not yet settled down. The breeziness of his room appealed to her. It occurred to her as she dusted that there were two very marriageable young men living in the same house with her.

The thought made her eyes sparkle.

Gavin Coulter had looked at her with more than moderate interest just now. And Gavin Coulter had a brother who was younger and might be even more appealing. Lost in happy daydreams, she finished dusting and went downstairs to find Reba.

She met her in the dining room, just coming through the swinging door that led to the kitchen. Reba's face was flushed and her dress, wet with perspiration, clung to her back. She pushed back a lock of damp red hair that was plastered to her forehead. "Lord, it's hot in the laundry on a day like this!" she gasped. "All finished?"

Roxanne nodded. "I made all the beds, and dusted. Mr. Rhodes's room was very dusty," she added.

"Oh, I forgot to tell you," cried Reba. "There wasn't any need to do his room—he's been gone for months, and no one knows when he'll be back."

So Gavin had said, but Roxanne decided to keep to herself the fact that she had spoken to him. As to Rhodes, perhaps he would return home as capriciously as he had gone. She hoped so. She was looking forward to meeting the man who resembled the interesting portrait in the hall.

"I liked his room," she confessed. "All those sailing pictures."

"And his big square bed," teased Reba. "I'll bet you ached to try that too!"

Roxanne flushed.

"Well, maybe you'll get the chance to try it," said Reba in a voice pregnant with meaning. "Miss Clarissa has, I'll warrant!"

Roxanne turned and frowned. Mrs. Hollister stood in the doorway behind her. It was impossible to tell what the older woman was thinking, but she was considering Reba very steadily. "I've things to do—got to finish ironing," muttered Reba, and brushed past Mrs. Hollister.

"I've finished the bedrooms," said Roxanne.

Mrs. Hollister's face cleared. "I thought you might like to go to market with Greaves," she said graciously. "It will give you a chance to see something of the town, and you can help him carry the baskets back."

Smiling her thanks at Mrs. Hollister—for who would not like to be out on such a beautiful day as this—Roxanne went in search of Greaves. He was the manservant who had first let her into the house, and she found him both courteous and friendly, if a trifle reserved. Roxanne realized that he felt the dignity of his position strongly, and so she tried to maintain a suitable gravity in his presence.

Carrying a market basket on either arm, she accompanied Greaves to the Hollins Market. In the bright sunshine they wandered through some three blocks of outdoor market, walking between rows of stalls where the merchandise was displayed under awnings. Everyone seemed to know Greaves and spoke to him respectfully. Some of the stall owners, Greaves told her, had inherited their businesses from their fathers or even their grandfathers. His sober face looked stern with its big flaring sideburns, as he bent over some tomatoes, testing them for ripeness. Then, moving on decorously, he inspected baskets of snap beans and carrots, and finally selected a large watermelon, which he hefted with ease.

At last, weighed down by a variety of fresh fruits and vegetables, they made their way back to the house. Mt. Vernon Place was very fashionable, Greaves told her proudly. Mr. Joab Coulter had moved here when he'd married his second wife, the Virginia lady who had borne Rhodes. She'd had a great fortune. Not that the first wife, the Eastern Shore lady, hadn't been rich. Joab Coulter had a talent for annexing his own fortune to that of young heiresses, Roxanne guessed. She inquired if he'd made much money himself.

My, yes, she was told. A great deal of it. But—there was a certain hesitancy in the way Greaves said it—Mr. Joab was fanatically attached to sailing ships, and steamers had taken the trade. Much of the Coulter fortune, Roxanne gathered shrewdly, was tied up in this dwindling business.

Why wouldn't the Coulters buy steamers? she wondered aloud.

Mr. Gavin wanted to, Greaves told her. But his father was adamant. Sail, sail was the thing with him. And young Mr. Rhodes, who cared for nothing except the roll of a windswept deck under his feet and a pretty girl in his arms when ashore, took no sides in the matter. Mr. Rhodes always shrugged and let his father handle the business while he was off under sail to the far corners of the world.

Roxanne could easily imagine that commanding pair, Gavin Coulter and his father, quarreling at the long dining table, and Rhodes, whom she envisioned as a ruddy wind-whipped figure with the reckless green eyes of the hall portrait, fidgeting with his wine glass, eager to be gone.

Rhodes who, when ashore, cared for nothing but a pretty girl in his arms. . . . And Reba had baldly stated that Clarissa had tried out Rhodes's big bed. Well, Roxanne told herself, Gavin had said Rhodes would marry Clarissa when he got around to it. It was ridiculous to feel a pang of jealousy for a man she had not even met. Nevertheless, she found herself once again envying the absent Clarissa.

Roxanne ate dinner with the other servants at a long scoured wooden table in the big kitchen. It was bare of tablecloth and the food was served on heavy ironstone plates, but it was good and tasty. Certain delicacies meant only for the main table were jealously denied them by Mrs. Hollister, who explained to Roxanne's surprised look that the household money only went so far. Roxanne supposed that meant if the servants ate pastries they'd have to do without meat—as indeed they did in the mornings. She learned later that breakfast consisted mainly of hot cakes, which were cheap, and blackstrap molasses, the more expensive refined white sugar being reserved for the gentry in the dining room.

At dinner that first night, Roxanne met the staff. The cook, whose name was Mary Scobie, but whom everybody called simply Cook, was a robust bustling woman, weighing almost two hundred pounds. She constantly tasted everything on the stove, and the floor shook when she walked. There were three maids, whose quarters were in the servants' wing on the second floor: Reba, whom she had already met; stocky plodding Lizzie, with her strong hands, who seemed to spend her life scrubbing pots or floors or carrying chamber-pots—all the heavy tasks nobody else wanted to do; and Mary Bridey O'Reilly, whom everyone called Mary Bridey to distinguish her from Cook. Mary Bridey was a dainty Irish girl with gleaming black hair and downcast blue-green eyes. She gave Roxanne a woebegone look, and in the middle of dinner started up with an "Excuse me," and dashed from the room.

"First it was morning sickness—now it's every meal. She's beginning to show," said Reba with a giggle.

Mrs. Hollister frowned at Reba. "Mary Bridey was always such a carefree jolly thing," she sighed to Roxanne, "until . . ."

"Until she made too many trips unstairs and *he* had his way with her," said Reba slyly. "And now she's in the family way and don't know what to do."

He had his way with her. She must mean Gavin, Roxanne thought, recalling how he had looked at her with such a hot narrow glance as she made his bed. Roxanne felt chilled.

"Reba!" Mrs. Hollister's tone was sharp.

"Well, you know it's true," said Reba in a sullen voice.

"I know nothing of the kind," Mrs. Hollister declared. "Mary Bridey's sad because she's leaving us at the end of the month. She's going to live with her sister, I understand."

Reba's jaw dropped. "Mary Bridey ain't got no sister, Miz Hollister!"

Mrs. Hollister frowned. She appeared not to have heard Reba's outburst. "So I suppose instead of helping Reba with the upstairs, Roxanne, it's best you take Mary Bridey's place serving meals. Greaves will instruct you."

Across the table, where he was eating stolidly, Greaves gave a silent nod.

Roxanne bobbed her head to indicate she understood, and before they ate their pudding, Mary Bridey was back. The Irish girl looked very pale as if she'd been sick. Roxanne's heart went out to her. It came to her with sudden force: Was *she* pregnant? A possibility she had not really considered when she left Kansas. That agonizing doubt ruined her evening, although it was assuaged the next day, much to her relief.

As she tossed and turned that first night, it occurred to her to listen for the footsteps Mrs. Hollister had mentioned so obliquely. She soon found herself alert to every sound, but heard no footsteps. Somehow the night passed. Finally, toward morning she fell into a deep sleep, and when she woke the sun was bright.

Realizing that she had overslept, she dressed hurriedly and ran downstairs, cutting through the servants' wing at the second floor. She met Reba storming up the steps—a red-faced, angry Reba who looked as if she'd been crying.

"What's the matter?"

"I've been dismissed, that's what!" Reba cried indignantly. "Old Holly accused me of making off with the linens, she did! But I'll bet it was because yesterday—"

"Reba!" Mrs. Hollister's voice came from below as she flew up the stairs after the girl. She looked flushed and angry, but at sight of Roxanne, she became flustered. "Are your things ready, Reba?" she asked severely, brushing by Roxanne. "I've written you a recommendation so that you can get a new position." Her lips tightened. "Not that you deserve it after—well, anyway, I've said you left us for personal reasons.

You had best come downstairs now and get it before I change my mind."

Her manner was threatening. Reba's mouth closed with a snap. She cast a vengeful look around her and, muttering, following Mrs. Hollister down the stairs.

It was the last Roxanne ever saw of Reba. Later in the day, Roxanne asked Mary Bridey why Mrs. Hollister had dismissed Reba—had she really stolen the linens? And Mary Bridey, whose brows were puckered in thought, answered absently that of course Reba hadn't stolen any linens; Reba had worked here six years and was as honest as the day was long.

Then why had Reba been dismissed? pursued Roxanne. Mary Bridey shrugged helplessly. Mrs. Hollister, who had dismissed maids before on sudden whims, had never liked Reba, always said she talked too much. Mrs. Hollister didn't like people who carried tales.

Roxanne frowned. "Mary Bridey, Mrs. Hollister told me I might hear footsteps at night and that I wasn't to pay any attention. Do you know what she was talking about?"

Mary Bridey gave a guilty start. "I wouldn't know," she cried. "Me, I sleep real sound. You should too," she added earnestly.

Roxanne looked at her in amazement, but before she could pursue that, Mary Bridey said she'd just remembered that she had something to do downstairs, and ran off.

Belatedly it came to Roxanne, that the footsteps might well be Mary Bridey's own, creeping upstairs at night to Gavin's room. No wonder the girl looked so guilty.

Roxanne had the strange, nagging feeling that Reba's abrupt dismissal had something to do with Reba's having spoken "out of turn" to her twice in Mrs. Hollister's presence.

And if that were true, which slip had so angered Mrs. Hollister? What Reba had said about Clarissa and Rhodes? Or about Mary Bridey and Gavin?

The next day a new maid arrived to replace Reba: a subdued immigrant girl who desperately needed the job. Remembering Reba's sudden dismissal, Roxanne forbore to ask the staff any more questions and refrained from answering all she could. But as the days went by, Reba was soon forgotten. The official explanation of her absence was that she had "gone home to her people in Philadelphia."

Chapter 6

The summer heat of Baltimore, which caused irritability among the staff, didn't bother Roxanne. She was used to the sultry stifling heat of southern summers. In Kansas she had been terribly homesick for Savannah, with its lush vegetation, its rows of houses with brick-walled gardens, its gracious tree-lined streets and evergreen-planted squares, its waxy magnolias and moss-hung live oaks. But in Baltimore, to her delight, she met again the pale flowers of the tulip tree, the creamy magnolia blossoms with their heavy scent. Remembering the fan-shaped transoms and arched recessed doorways, the small entrance stoops and fine ironwork of Savannah, Roxanne felt instantly at home with Baltimore's ornate ironwork and white marble stoops and pleasant Georgian houses. It was good to be in a port city again—where the tang of salt was in the air, and tall ships with billowing white sails glided beneath a sky smudged with the smoke of steamers from many lands.

Roxanne came to enjoy her new position as maid in the Coulter household. There was little to do, and Mrs. Hollister—who favored her for reasons Roxanne could not understand—frequently gave her an afternoon off to prowl around the city. She often spent the whole time riding horse trolleys about the town.

Baltimore, she found, was an ironclad city. Great cast-iron fronted buildings such as the Sun Iron Building rose some five stories above the street, and huge warehouses seemed to cover acres. She stood in awe before the massive brick rectangle of the U.S. Appraisers' Stores at Gay and Lombard Streets; four stories high it rose, with arched window tops and heavy cast-iron shutters and brick vaults supporting each floor. From the house on Mt. Vernon Place she strolled the short distance to admire the marble pile of the Peabody Institute, and on very hot days cooled off in the Library wing, looking around at the four handsome tiers of ornamental cast-iron balconies that supported the stacks on all four walls of the reading room.

At the Peabody Library, she browsed through monumental works of history, but at home on Mt. Vernon Place she filched novels such as *East Lynne* and *Lady Audley's Secret* from a cache she had discovered at the back of Clarissa's wardrobe, and read them by the oil lamp in her room. The servants' wing was not fitted with gaslights as was the main structure. Roxanne guessed that Joab Coulter disapproved of such "trashy" novels, and that Clarissa had managed to smuggle them in and hide them from him.

For some reason, Mary Bridey confided in Roxanne. Because she had no one else to talk to about it, Roxanne guessed. Mrs. Hollister refused to admit what had happened; Cook was sullen in the summer heat and went about muttering; Ella, the new maid, kept her eyes cast down and seldom spoke; and Mary Bridey could hardly discuss her problem with Greaves.

In the empty laundry one muggy day before she left, Mary Bridey confided, "Mr. Gavin's found a place for me with a woman who takes in girls like me until they's had their baby." And added proudly, "He's paid her ahead so it's all taken care of, and he said to say I was goin' to live with my sister."

"Why?" asked Roxanne curiously.

Mary Bridey rolled her eyes. "Why, because his father don't hold with a son of his foolin' around with the maids!"

"But what about later? What will happen to you?"

"Mr. Gavin is taking care of that," said Mary Bridey confidently. "He's finding me a new situation and he's goin' to help me with my rent so's I can share with another girl who'll take turns mindin' the baby."

When she asked Mary Bridey bluntly if marriage had never been considered, Mary Bridey looked astonished. "Rich young men don't marry with such as you and me!" she protested, scandalized.

Roxanne bit her lip and told herself fiercely she would never allow herself to be put in Mary Bridey's position. Never! She would not be played with and cast aside as poor Mary Bridey had been.

Her resentment on Mary Bridey's behalf caused her to be almost rude to Gavin. She dared not upbraid him—as she longed to do—because that would have meant instant dismissal. But she managed to turn her head in an insolent way when he was around and to keep her back to him whenever possible.

Now and then she saw a puzzled expression cross his face, and once when she rushed past him she thought he hid a smile. But she also noted that he frequently turned to watch her as she passed. And when at meals she moved silently through the room, she was aware that his gaze did not content itself with studying her face, but calmly moved up and down her figure, pausing to linger caressingly at her breasts, at her softly rounded hips, up and down. . . . Sometimes his steady regard made her so nervous that she almost dropped the serving dishes, and her face would grow flushed. She sensed, irritably, that Gavin got a certain satisfaction out of knowing he had ruffled her calm. And although she tried to avoid him, he seemed to take a perverse pleasure in interrupting her work, or asking her to do small things for him. Several times in the evening, after she had cleared the dishes, she would see him in the hall and he would ask her to bring him his pipe. Or his gloves. Or his cane.

She had the feeling all these errands were merely excuses to bring her near him, and once she was near, he found ways to make her linger. What did she think of the condition of his gloves? Would that spot come out? Oh, yes, it was merely a trick of the light after all . . . and then he would pull the gloves on slowly, smiling into her wide sapphire eyes.

These encounters angered her, partly because she could feel the physical pull of the man's presence, knowing that he desired her. Once when she stooped to pick up a glove he had negligently dropped, she was outraged to feel his hand brush her bent back. She snapped upright, ready to upbraid him.

"Ah, did my coat brush you?" he murmured. And as the blood rose to her cheeks, he smiled damnably. As if he knew she dared not accuse him of drawing his fingers across her back lest he dismiss her—and worse, as if he knew his touch had aroused tingles all across her spine.

"Will that be all, sir?" she heard herself ask in a choked voice.

He stood considering her, a superior smile on his face. "Yes. For the moment."

She wheeled and was gone, rushing into the kitchen so fast she collided with Cook, who cursed her roundly.

Evidently, Ella, the subdued, mousy little creature who had replaced Reba did not please Gavin, nor did the big ungainly Tillie who had replaced Mary Bridey. Roxanne guessed that he was considering her as a suitable substitute for Mary Bridey in his big square bed upstairs. The thought made her seethe with helpless fury.

Another day, Gavin caught her alone on the stair landing, and when she would have brushed by, he grasped her by the shoulders and whirled her around.

"Why do you dislike me?" he demanded roughly. "Your dislike shines out of your eyes."

Roxanne, who realized full well that she disliked him the more because she found him attractive, shrugged off his hands and drew herself up to her full height. "I don't dislike you. Sir." Her voice dripped insolence.

His dark brows drew together fiercely, and for a moment she thought he was going to strike her. Then his eyes quested down her stiffly upright but luxurious figure, and a smile softened his autocratic features.

"It's no matter, Roxanne," he said. "The day will come when you'll like me well enough."

Well enough for what? she wondered, turning to watch his tall, straight figure disappear down the staircase. If he had any hope of getting her in his bed, he was sadly mistaken!

Nevertheless, she was shaken by the encounter and glad when Gavin departed on a short business trip to Boston.

While he was away, Mary Bridey left. It was a sad leave-taking, with the girl impulsively throwing her arms around Roxanne and weeping. Then Mrs. Hollister came out frowning, and Mary Bridey straightened her little hat and climbed into the horse-drawn cab that was to take her and her few belongings to her new abode. From the cab she turned and waved.

Roxanne stood and waved as long as she could see the cab. It seemed to her heartless that no one accompanied Mary Bridey to get her settled, but Mrs. Hollister hurried Roxanne back into the house, saying there was work to do. Hearing Mrs. Hollister's deep sigh as the door closed, she knew that the housekeeper was really very glad to be rid of Mary Bridey.

Gavin came back from his journey raving about the New England Limited, on which he had made the return trip from Boston to New York. A luxury flyer, it was nicknamed the "White Train" because of its cream and gold cars. A six hour run, Gavin told his father enthusiastically at dinner—amazing time! It had two Royal Buffet Smokers and seven parlor cars laden with tassels and plush, big individual chairs with hassocks, plate glass mirrors, looped silk curtains and draperies and bronze cuspidors! And after sundown its two red-carpeted restaurant cars were illuminated by Pintsch lights and the tables were curtained off from one another by heavy brocade hangings. Ah, it was the last word in luxury!

As she carried away the soup plates, Roxanne imagined dreamily wending her way across those red carpets under the Pintsch lights, clad in Clarissa's peach and cream best, sitting down to eat pheasant under glass, on her way from Boston to New York with . . . there she stopped.

Not with Gavin. Not after the way he had treated poor Mary Bridey!

After supper, when she had cleared away the dishes, Roxanne was passing through the front hall when she became aware that Gavin was standing there alone, pipe in hand. He had been waiting for her, she decided, and almost turned on her heel. Instead, she lifted her chin and started to march past him, but his voice arrested her.

"Roxanne."

"Yes, sir?"

He leaned down as if he would sniff the perfume of her hair, and she flinched away from him.

He kept his voice low, only for her ears, since the door was open into his father's bedroom. "I'm not like Rhodes, tasting every flower," he said, and for a moment so warm was his voice that she thought he was going to reach out and touch her. "I have discriminating tastes, Roxanne. Nothing but the best pleases me."

"Then *I* cannot please you," said Roxanne in a trembling voice, "for I am but a servant in this household."

"Ah, that could be remedied," he murmured.

She gave him a troubled look and hurried by him, sure that his eyes were following her as she moved on up the stairs.

That night, as she sometimes did on warm sleepless nights, she thought about Buck and Julie . . . frail Julie. They'd be married now, trying to make a life together, and Julie would be using up what small store of strength she possessed in Buck's too-eager embraces. For Roxanne well remembered the violence with which Buck's arms had enfolded her, the wild sweet frenzy as their bodies flailed together, straining fiercely there on the Kansas prairie. Julie would be . . . all used up. And yet, in a way Julie was triumphing over the death that too soon would claim her. She was fulfilling her destiny in her lover's arms. Kind, sweet Julie.

Hot tears fell on Roxanne's pillow as she remembered Julie. Tears for Julie, no doubt a few for her lonely self.

Sundays were a respite in the Coulter household. Joab Coulter believed in honoring the Sabbath day and keeping it holy. He barely allowed meals to be prepared on Sundays.

This was a thorn in Mrs. Hollister's side, but it delighted Roxanne, for it gave her a day off.

Sometimes on hot summer Sundays she sauntered out of the Mt. Vernon Place house, pausing to look back at its flat brownstone front so heavily accented by bold cornices above the windows and at the roof, its conspicuous molded trim. Then she would hurry down the wide stone steps and make her way to the Franklin Street Presbyterian Church, which she loved because it looked like a Gothic fortress, and because the stroll down Cathedral Street to reach it was most enjoyable. Or she would walk down Monument Street to Park and attend the First Presbyterian, marveling at its lofty spire, which seemed to pierce the very clouds.

The Coulter family attended the First Methodist Church, which had been designed by Stanford White in 1882. Roxanne greatly admired the simple Romanesque masses of this great structure with its nine-level belltower of Port Deposit granite and its flared conical roof of heavy red tile.

Once, at an appropriate distance, she followed the

Coulters, father and son, to services, finding a seat at the back of the huge oval auditorium.

She did not gain much enlightenment from the sermon, however, for sitting near her were two pert and well-dressed young girls who roguishly snapped and unsnapped the fasteners on their gloves in an attempt to attract the attention of the young men seated in front of them. Roxanne watched this innocent flirtation with amusement until a huffy dark-clad dowager said loudly, "Sh-h-h," and the girls returned to decorum, folding their hands on their laps . . . though their eyes danced. They looked happy and vivacious and as if they *belonged* in these handsome surroundings. Roxanne envied them.

After church she hurried away from the handsome, leisurely crowd. Neither Gavin nor his father saw her, for they were busy shaking hands outside with well-dressed friends, many of whom were fashionable women in big hats with feathers and gorgeous clothes Roxanne longed to own.

But on the way home, her spirits rose. In her first week of employment on Mt. Vernon Place, Roxanne had found an extra key to the main front door and had quietly appropriated it. Now, knowing full well that everybody would be out if she hurried home, she decided she would use that key. Today she would not enter the house "below stairs." Today she would march up to the handsome front door and let herself in for all the world as if she were mistress of the house!

Her key fitted the lock smoothly. She swung the door wide and walked into the cool dark hall dreamily, savoring the moment. She was momentarily blinded by the darkness after the brilliant sunlight outside, and she drifted along the hall imagining herself to be the fortunate Clarissa.

There was a ghost of a sound from the direction of the stairs. Suddenly she found herself swept up into a pair of strong arms, her breasts pinioned against a hard masculine chest, and a warm kiss planted firmly on her protesting mouth.

As she struggled to free herself, she was abruptly

released, and the stranger who had swooped down on her regarded her with a puzzled expression.

"Why, you're not Clarissa!" he cried. "But something much better!"

And to her horror, before she could protest, he swept her up in his arms again and kissed her more slowly, exploringly. His lips were warm and insistent, his tongue impudently probed her parted mouth. She felt excitement mount in her as she strained to free herself from the strong, resolute arms that held her.

Suddenly he set her free. Her heart beating wildly, she staggered back to look at the tall man whose brilliant smile flashed at her as he made her a low bow.

"Not only the key to the house but the key to my heart!" he cried, with a sweeping gesture. "Now tell me, which one of Clarissa's friends are you?"

The flush on Roxanne's already flaming cheeks deepened. Except for his clothes, this striking figure before her might have stepped out of the portrait of the Virginia gentleman at the end of the hall. This undoubtedly was the roving Rhodes Coulter, home from his wanderings. His hair was thick and dark and worn rakishly. His brilliant green eyes were set in a square-jawed face bronzed by wind and weather, and his smile was a brilliant flash of strong white teeth as he stood there in his sturdy seaman's clothes and regarded her with delight, thoroughly enjoying her discomfiture.

"Since you're temporarily tongue-tied by my manly charms, may I offer you a glass of sherry? Unless you'd prefer tea?"

I'm more than tongue-tied, she thought bitterly. He had mistaken her for one of Clarissa's friends, a girl from Baltimore's social set. With her rather arrogant bearing, attired in her own clothes instead of the serviceable gray cambric uniforms with large starched cotton aprons which she, like the other maids, wore, it was an easy mistake to make, she realized. But one which must be corrected and at once. There was the matter of the key, which must not be brought to Mrs. Hollister's attention, lest she be dismissed like Reba.

"I'm Roxanne," she stammered. "I must have got the front door key by mistake. I—"

"You mean you actually *live* here?" His broad shoulders seemed to grow broader, but he did not move aside to let her pass. "Indeed I find the house improved in my absence!"

"I'm a housemaid here, Mr. Rhodes," said Roxanne, her voice still shaking slightly from the impact of that kiss.

"And you know my name?" His green eyes narrowed. "Wherever did we find you, Roxanne?"

"In San Francisco. I worked for your Cousin Hattie."

"No, that was Mary Willis," he corrected her.

"I'm Mary Willis's daughter," lied Roxanne uncomfortably.

He studied her, smiling. "Well, I think we'll just go out for a stroll, Roxanne," he said.

Roxanne stiffened. She did not like the offhand familiarity of his manner; it reminded her that she was a servant in his house. "I'm sorry, sir, I've no time," she said crisply.

"Ah, but you'll go strolling with me, Roxanne," he said softly, taking her arm in a firm grip. "Because I visited San Francisco earlier this year. I went to see Aunt Hattie, and I know that Mary Willis had no daughter."

Roxanne held her breath. She had felt so secure, so safe.

"There's no need to look so frightened," he said. "We'll just go for a pleasant Sunday afternoon stroll, and you can tell me all about it—why you're passing yourself off as an old maid's daughter, for instance?"

Seething, Roxanne perforce accompanied his tall form back outside and down the steps. She walked beside him in silence as he shortened his long stride to match her own. He led her past the cylindrical stone shaft of Baltimore's Washington Monument that dominated Mt. Vernon Place, and down St. Paul past old St. Paul's Church with its uncompleted belltower. As they walked, he kept up a running monologue, occasionally asking her questions which she, lost in thought, did not answer. She did not know how to meet this new problem. Finally, he gave her a keen look and stopped to hire a horse-drawn carriage. He gave the driver directions and helped her up to the cab.

"Stop here, driver," he said at last, and looked pointedly past her. "Ah, there's a sight to loosen the tongue, Roxanne."

"What is it?" mumbled Roxanne, turning to look at a handsome brick and stone Gothic structure with turrets and a fancy cupola that stood behind a high brick wall.

"The city jail," he said quietly, a warning in his tone. "Now tell me who you really are and what you're doing in my father's house."

"My name is Roxanne Rossiter," she said hopelessly. "I'm from Savannah." In terse sentences she outlined how she had gone to Kansas to live with Uncle Josh and Aunt Ada, and—carefully omitting any mention of Buck or Julie—why she had left. A girl friend had helped her escape a forced marriage with an elderly banker, she told him. But on her way east her money had run out. When her seat-mate, intemperate Mary Willis, had died suddenly on the train, she had taken the woman's ticket and the letter and had come to Baltimore, impersonating her in hopes of finding employment and shelter.

"And what of Mary Willis?" he asked.

Roxanne told him of the doctor and how there'd been sufficient money for decent burial. She hadn't stolen the old woman's money, she added hastily, just the ticket and letter.

He was silent at that. After a while he gave her a whimsical smile, and she was again sharply reminded of the portrait of Joab Coulter's father-in-law in the hall. "So a young lady who knows French and who's gently bred is now emptying our chamberpots," he murmured.

Roxanne winced. "I'm serving meals," she said hastily. "Mrs. Hollister discovered I knew one fork from another and could set a table properly."

"Do any but myself know your story?" he asked.

Roxanne shook her head. "Everyone here accepts me as Mary Willis's daughter. I could say I'm illegitimate," she added hastily.

He laughed. "Best to say nothing at all unless you're prodded."

"You'll keep my secret then?" she asked anxiously.

"I've kept the secrets of thugs shanghaied abroad vessels, and remittance men one step ahead of the law, and men dying of the fever in tropical ports far from home—the secret of a slip of a girl should be safe with me."

She felt almost weak with relief. "They plan for me to be Clarissa's maid when she returns," she explained.

"Do they now? Well, that's a good idea. You'll be happier sorting out Clarissa's dainty underthings, I'll wager, than scurrying around weighed down by tureens and platters!"

She smiled.

"I wish I had funds enough to keep a mistress!" he declared merrily. "Then you could laze around all day, Roxanne!"

She lifted her chin and gave him a cold look. "I will be no man's mistress." She stated it flatly. "I will marry and have a house of my own."

"To be sure," he said, delighted at striking this spark.

They drove slowly home. When they drew near the house, Roxanne said nervously, "I'd better get out and go home alone."

Rhodes demurred, insisting he'd take her up to the front door in style. But she grew desperate. "Please, your father will dismiss me if he thinks I'm setting my cap for his son!"

He chuckled at that, but ordered the driver to stop. As she jumped down from the carriage, he caught her hand, held it for a moment while his green eyes looked into hers. "My silence has a price, Roxanne," he said.

"And what might that be?" she asked, stiffening.

"That you stroll out with me on Sunday afternoons,"

he said, smiling into her sapphire eyes. And she relaxed, gave him a gay wave of her gloved hand and hurried away, to let herself in by the servants' entrance.

Now that she'd met him, she understood why Reba had said, *Mr. Joab Coulter likes Mr. Gavin best, but everyone else prefers Mr. Rhodes.* She too preferred Rhodes, and the memory of his kiss stayed with her like a light caress through the day, and there was a dreaminess in her smile as she lay on her pillow that night.

The golden pleasures of first love had been denied her, but perhaps she had found something else.

Chapter 7

Serving dinner to the three Coulter men in the long dining room of the town house on Mt. Vernon Place was an experience. Stiffly erect at the head of his table sat Joab Coulter with Gavin on his right and Rhodes on his left. All so different, Roxanne thought—and yet, in some ways, alike, for they were all dark-haired, tall and forceful. But Joab Coulter had a fanatic's thin face; his son Gavin's countenance was cool and hard and appraising; while Rhodes's devilish green eyes gleamed in a carefree bronzed face, his wicked smile flashing at Roxanne as she assisted Greaves the butler in serving dinner.

Their conversation fascinated her, mainly because they seemed never to agree on anything.

One muggy evening, when a storm was about to break and the air was heavy and breathless, she began to serve from a steaming tureen of delicious Chesapeake Bay oyster stew, but stopped when she heard

Joab Coulter's rumbling voice, sounding as if it had come out of a cavern.

"Don't talk to me of steamships, Gavin," he thundered. "They're a fad. They'll go out of fashion eventually."

Roxanne, curious, served the soup and then busied herself at the big mahogany sideboard in order to listen.

"Father, how can you say that?" cried Gavin. "When you know very well that new French ship, *La Touraine*, is a floating palace that crosses the ocean in seven days! Fifteen courses are served on her dinner menu! Why, I haven't a doubt the next ships built will abandon auxiliary sails altogether."

"Never," said his father flatly, bringing the palm of his hand down on the table hard enough to shake the dishes. "And as to how I can say that, I'll point out to you, Gavin, that they talked the same way about the *Great Eastern*. She was the biggest ship in the world—it cost $300,000 just to launch her back in 1858, and she was a failure, a dinosaur. She'd have ruined her owners if she hadn't been lucky enough to get the job of laying the first transatlantic cable! And what about Collins—going to rival Cunard!"

"He did," interposed Gavin. "The Collins Line's *Pacific* held the record for a steamer for thirteen years—330 miles in a single day's run."

"Pshaw," said his father. "The Baltimore clippers beat that! The *Flying Cloud* logged 374 miles in a day, didn't she? And the *Sovereign of the Seas* once covered 421 miles! And as for Collins's *Pacific*, she disappeared without a trace on her regular run from Liverpool, you'll remember. Blew up in mid-ocean! And how did Collins end up? Forced out, that's how!"

Rhodes was silent, his green eyes flickering as he watched the heated exchange between the two men.

Suddenly Gavin swung on him. "Why don't you speak up, Rhodes?" he cried. "You know as well as I do the days of sail are over!"

Rhodes's smile had a steely quality. "Not for me, they aren't." He said it flatly.

Gavin sneered. "We're losing money every year, and you know it. And why? Because we won't convert to steam, that's why!"

Rhodes shrugged. That simple gesture seemed to madden Gavin. His face turned purple, and he leaned forward belligerently. "You're encouraging Father in this madness," he cried. "We've dropped a packet already and we'll soon be bankrupt, do you hear? Bankrupt! While you're away sailing and chasing skirts in every port, I've been studying the books!" He stopped talking abruptly, flung down his linen napkin and stalked out of the room.

His father watched him exit, then turned to Rhodes. "It's strange," he said. "We agree on nothing, you and I—except one thing: Sail." He looked puzzled. "I can't understand it in Gavin. On all else he's sane."

"Gavin has no feel for the sea or a good ship under him," said Rhodes. "Only a feeling for money." He sighed. "You should listen to him, no doubt. His way leads to success."

His father snorted. "Success! Why, this is a passing fancy, this steam. A few more disasters and they'll turn back to sail! It's clean and it's fast—"

"And unreliable," said Rhodes with a crooked smile. "Mind you—" he held up his hand—"I'm for sail. It's the life I love. But commercially . . ." He shrugged. "Gavin's right."

His father gave him a cold look. "So now we agree on nothing?"

Rhodes grinned. "Perhaps the wine. It's a good vintage. And your selection of housemaids. They're very choice this season." His green eyes followed Roxanne's slender figure as she hurried over to serve them.

"Keep your eyes from the housemaids," said the father severely. "You should spend more time in church and less at the gaming tables. Don't think I don't know about your wild ways. But you've the devil's blood in you, I'm not forgetting."

Rhodes's face hardened. "My grandfather is a sore

point with you," he said sarcastically. "Still it's his fortune that Gavin claims we're losing."

His father's face paled. "Your mother's father was a hard-drinking Virginia rakehell," he roared. "As godless a man as ever walked the earth!"

"He held his own among men," murmured Rhodes, sipping his wine, "and died possessed of a fine plantation and a fortune he made himself."

"A devil," muttered his father. "A veritable devil. He had bastards everywhere!"

"Only in Virginia," said Rhodes with a wink at Roxanne.

The next afternoon Roxanne was sent on an errand into southwest Baltimore. She was to pick up some small items for Mrs. Hollister, who made the happy discovery that Roxanne was not only clever with tradespeople but that she would come back with accurate change. She went by trolley and, her errand being quickly concluded, she decided to take a few minutes to stop and see Mary Bridey.

At the address Mary Bridey had given her, a tall respectable-looking Lithuanian woman wearing a bright red shawl let her in and indicated that Mary Bridey lived upstairs. Roxanne ran up the narrow wooden steps to where a door was open into the upstairs hall—for air, no doubt, to trap the cool breeze that blew through sheer curtains at the windows. And beside those windows Mary Bridey herself sat on a painted rocker, stitching a small patchwork quilt in bright colors.

At the sight of Roxanne she gave a glad cry and dropped the quilt. Hugging Roxanne warmly, her blue-green eyes sparkling, she proudly exhibited her new domain. It consisted of a bed-living room and a tiny kitchen. Gavin had not been *too* generous with the little Irish girl, Roxanne saw, looking around her.

Mary Bridey pointed out her treasures. Her bed, she declared, was "a real Jenny Lind." Pitying her, Roxanne feigned admiration for the cheap button-turned bed, a far cry from the delicate "spool" she had been used to in Savannah. And see, Mary Bridey added proudly, her green-painted washstand had a white marble top! The organdy curtains that adorned her open windows were an extravagance; she had made them herself, and didn't they look nice? And the quilt—she blushed—was for "our bed."

"Has he been to see you?" asked Roxanne at this mention of the bed. After that first discussion they had never referred to the father of Mary Bridey's child by name, but only as "he."

"No." Mary Bridey shook her head wistfully. "Although he's back, isn't he?"

"Yes," said Roxanne. Gavin had been back from Boston for days. Plenty of time to come and see Mary Bridey, she thought bitterly.

"He'll come," said Mary Bridey confidently. "I'm sure he's very busy," she added lamely, and continued displaying her treasures.

Roxanne was further disheartened as the Irish girl proudly pointed out a battered pine "pie safe" with screen wire in the doors and a spindle-back side chair with a mended cane seat, both of which Roxanne recognized as having been discarded by Mrs. Hollister.

Mary Bridey was eager for news of "the house," which Roxanne discerned meant news of Gavin. She listened thirstily as Roxanne told her of the doings of both brothers. When Roxanne asked if Mary Bridey would not like to take the trolley back with her and say hello to the staff (and she hoped, without saying so, confront Gavin face to face), the girl quickly demurred and looked away in confusion. Roxanne guessed that Mary Bridey's new affluence had a condition attached to it—that she stay away from the house and out of Joab Coulter's sight.

"Ah, it will be lovely for you when Miss Clarissa returns," sighed Mary Bridey, changing the subject. "Handling her pretty dresses and scented handkerchiefs and silk underwear—her underwear is all made by the nuns, you know!"

"Reba told me she was hard to get along with," Roxanne said dryly.

"Ah, yes, she's spoiled, but the stories you'll hear! All about great balls and tea parties and spicy scandals. She leads such a wonderful life, does Miss Clarissa. She goes dancing all the time, and when she's on the Eastern Shore—that's where she comes from—she rides to hounds. Imagine!" Mary Bridey's blue-green eyes shone, but Roxanne's eyes were troubled.

Great balls . . . scented silk underwear . . . riding to hounds . . . how did one compete with the Clarissas of this world? Beauty? Roxanne's mirror told her she had beauty. But beauty wasn't enough. Dainty little Mary Bridey had a flowerlike face. And that flower-like face had only got her into trouble.

Roxanne roused herself. "I must be getting back. Mrs. Hollister will wonder what's happened to me."

"Ah, do come again soon," pleaded Mary Bridey. "The woman downstairs barely speaks English, and I'm so lonesome here."

Roxanne promised she would and left, going back down the wooden stairs. In the hall below stood the tall Lithuanian woman in the red shawl. It was her house, Roxanne knew, and Roxanne returned her smile as she left. In the street outside, before she hurried off to catch her trolley, she turned to look back at the shabby yellow brick row house, sand-wiched monotonously among a long line of identical neighbors, and felt resentment at the way Mary Bridey had been treated. Poor Mary Bridey . . . her baby would be born on the "wrong side of the blanket," though she must have come to the Coulter house a fresh-faced colleen full of hope . . . it wasn't fair.

Roxanne had gotten off the trolley and was hurrying home when she saw Rhodes coming toward her, driv-ing a buggy. Drawing up to her he said merrily, "I'll show you the waterfront, Roxanne!"

When she protested that she was expected back, Rhodes said airily, "Nonsense. I'll tell Mrs. Hollister I had a hankering for some soft-shelled crabs and saw you with your market basket. Come along!"

As Roxanne climbed in beside Rhodes, she became uncomfortably aware of the powerful thigh muscles that brushed her own legs while she settled next to him.

"Clarissa's coming home tomorrow," he said. "Then maybe you'll have more interesting things to do."

She smiled at him, listening to the clatter of the horse's hooves, noting how expertly he handled the reins, how gentle but firm was his touch.

"Do you like Baltimore?" he asked. "Have you made any plans for the future?"

"Why, yes," said Roxanne pertly. "I plan to marry a millionaire I've not yet met, and have a lady's maid of my own. And scads of diamonds."

He laughed. "With your face, you could do it!"

They had reached the waterfront and were clattering past a ship's chandlery with picturesque small-paned windows. Rhodes pointed out an Old Bay Line steamer down at the dock. "Overnight to Norfolk," he said. "Clarissa sometimes visits friends in Norfolk."

Roxanne looked at the steamer and yearned to sail on her. She felt a pang of envy for the absent Clarissa.

"Where is Clarissa now?" she asked.

"She's been visiting friends in New York and Boston and buying out all the shops. You can expect to spend hours and hours just sorting through her purchases—if she hasn't lost most of them on the train on the way here!" Rhodes laughed.

He handed her out of the buggy as if she were a fine lady, and Roxanne smiled and pushed back a lock of her fair hair that blew in the salt air. Still playing tour guide, Rhodes indicated here a fine old gaff-rigged sloop in the dredging fleet used for oystering, and there sloops with skipjack rigs. He told her that the growing blue crabs, which were confined in floats, from May to October became the succulent soft-shelled crabs so popular in Baltimore. Everywhere fish were being hawked, and Rhodes pointed out that there were some two hundred kinds of fish native to the Chesapeake. Besides the fishing fleet, there were ships from everywhere, loaded with iron, tobacco—which was the green gold of southern Maryland—and a variety of raw and manufactured products.

"You're from Savannah," he said abruptly. "Did you know that the first steamship to cross the Atlantic sailed from Savannah? It was named for the city, and was financed by Savannah merchants. Why, America's first iron steamship was launched from Savannah."

Roxanne hadn't known that, but she lifted her head a little more proudly at the knowledge. Still . . . her eyes fell on one of the beautiful and rakish Baltimore clippers that rode the Bay.

"One of ours," he said softly. "I don't think I'll like Gavin's world of steam, Roxanne. Even though it's surely coming." His voice grew richer. "Can you imagine what it's like to have the deck of that ship under your feet, Roxanne?"

"Is she the one you returned on from your last trip? When you visited San Francisco?" she asked.

He nodded and frowned. "She's lying around waiting to pick up cargo. The clippers won't hold as much as the steamships will. It's too bad."

Roxanne agreed with him. The fair ship rode lightly as a gull upon the water. How could one compare her with an iron vessel belching smoke?

"But that's not what I brought you here to see," he said, and her interest quickened. "Over there—see her?" His eyes glinted as he pointed out a square-rigged schooner riding the glittering blue waters of the Bay. "The *Virginia Lass,*" he said. "She's not part of the Coulter Line. She's mine. Old, but seaworthy."

"She's lovely. Can we board her?"

"Some other time. I wanted you to see her." He laughed. "She's the only thing my lovely mother left me—except the memory of her smile."

Roxanne cast a look at him. His mother . . . Joab Coulter's second wife, the one the servants called the heiress. Rhodes's voice had softened when he spoke of her.

"Do you have a picture of your mother?" she asked.

"A small photograph of her in my room, but her portrait hangs near the front door."

Ah, she thought. The beauty with the gallant lift of the chin and the sad, lovely eyes . . . Not a happy woman, Joab Coulter's Virginia bride.

"She was lovely," said Roxanne.

"Yes . . . lovely in every way." He sighed. "She left little impress on our household, Roxanne. After she died, he slipped into very rigid ways, but while she lived she was a softening influence on my father."

"Was this her ship?" asked Roxanne, indicating the *Virginia Lass*.

He nodded. "Wedding gift from her father. New and shining then—like herself." He stared fiercely at the wind-battered masts, the wave-battered hull.

"What was he like? Your grandfather?"

Rhodes laughed and the salt wind blew through his thick dark hair, ruffling it. She was reminded of the portrait. "Oh, he was a devil of sorts. Dedicated to women and wine. He made merry hell in his day, but —contrary to what my father says of him—he hurt no one but himself. And my mother loved him dearly to the day she died."

"It must have been hard on her, married to a man who hated her father," mused Roxanne.

"It was," he said shortly. "It was hard on her just being married to my father. What she saw in him I'll not be knowing." There was an almost Irish lilt in his voice when he said that, and Roxanne remembered guiltily how Cook had once whispered that Rhodes had come along late in his mother's marriage, sometime "after she'd hired that wild Irish groom" for her horses. He had nothing of the Coulter look, she realized. Their arrogance perhaps, their dark hair . . . but his eyes flashed in a face that she suddenly realized had a look of Ireland about it—in spite of his resemblance to his maternal grandfather. She studied him now as he stood gracefully beside her, saw that his build was more powerful than that of the man in the portrait, and saw also the lighthearted arrogance of generations of Irish lords, disinherited and brought low, dancing in his reckless smile.

She wondered if Rhodes knew that Joab Coulter was not his father.

"Do you think the Coulter Line will convert to steam?" she asked.

"No." He shook his head. "Gavin doesn't realize what my father's doing, but I do. He's trying to purify the stench of the slave trade from our line! He's too stubborn to make the changeover to steam until enough green seas have washed over our bows to make us clean again! His first wife—Gavin's mother—though a Maryland aristocrat herself, had two sisters who'd married Mississippi planters. They were both ruined financially by the war. Father could have helped them, but would he? Hell, no! It broke her heart and she died. Then he married my mother. She was a free thinker and had never held with slavery, but her father had had slaves on his Virginia plantation, and my father never forgave her for it. He made her miserable as long as she lived. I think it was his way of purifying himself because he'd once been a slaver. Yes, that's what the Coulter Line is founded on, Roxanne—slaving. In fast Baltimore-built clippers. Don't look so shocked. All the world knows it. But you'd be wise not to mention it in Gavin's presence; it's a fact he won't face up to—like many others, one of which is that my father will run the Line his way until the day he dies. Whether he goes broke or not."

"But if he was a slaver," faltered Roxanne, "then how can he—"

"Condemn others for having bought his cargo? Ah, but he repented his sins, Roxanne. And some others didn't—my mother's father, for instance. It's what he has against me—my wild blood that came to me through my mother. Though God knows, it's not so wild!"

Roxanne stared at him. She had never heard him go on like this. She was pleased that he would speak so freely to her; it meant he trusted her.

"It's getting late. We'd better get back," he said and led her off to buy a big basket of soft-shelled crabs. Roxanne climbed back into the buggy, smiling. She felt she had established a closeness with Rhodes; it was the happiest day she had spent in Baltimore.

On the way back she let him kiss her in the shade of a giant elm that grew in a quiet corner of the park. The contact shook her more than she cared to admit. And when Rhodes, pressing his advantage, kissed her again, this time gently probing her lips with his tongue, while his hands sought her breasts, she pulled away and gave him an uncertain look.

He attracted her, but his name was Coulter. And she didn't want to end up like poor Mary Bridey, tucked away in some quiet place to have her baby and be forgotten.

Chapter 8

Clarissa's return was a great event in the household, and for Roxanne everything changed overnight. She was in the front hall when Clarissa arrived, sweeping grandly through the front door on Rhodes's arm. A girl of Roxanne's height and weight, with a fashionable pompadour of dark auburn hair and brown-auburn eyes that almost matched. A laughing, chattering Clarissa, who clung possessively to Rhodes's arm—and whose laughter stopped short when she saw Roxanne.

"You had some luck while you were gone, Clarissa," explained Rhodes, indicating Roxanne. "You got yourself a new lady's maid!" He told her that Roxanne had been Aunt Hattie's maid and companion in San Francisco.

Clarissa frowned. "I wanted to choose my own maid," she said petulantly with a cold look at Roxanne.

She doesn't like the way Rhodes looked at me, Roxanne discerned uneasily. She's afraid I'll compete for him!

"Oh, well." Clarissa shrugged. "She can help carry my things to my room anyway. Roxanne," she ordered, "bring that pile of boxes. You can start unpacking."

Roxanne flushed a little under the peremptory tone in Clarissa's voice. Clarissa was eighteen, only slightly older than herself, but she was dressed in a lavish sheer brown organdy with a hat to match, ornamented with artificial peach roses and a huge peach tulle bow. Her dainty hands were encased in peach kid gloves, and her arrogant stance proclaimed that she owned the earth. Roxanne was sharply aware of the plainness of her own serviceable gray cambric and stiff starched apron. Soberly, she bent to pick up a pile of boxes.

"Here, let me help," said Rhodes.

Annoyed, Clarissa said, "Oh, let her do it, Rhodes!"

Upstairs, Rhodes deposited a stack of boxes beside the stack Roxanne had carried up, and left. Clarissa, peeling off her kid gloves, watched with some dissatisfaction as Roxanne untied packages and put the contents away in drawers. When she ran out of space to stuff things, even in the big walnut armoire, Clarissa said irritably, "Oh, put the box under the bed!"

Roxanne complied, going down on her knees to slide the large carton under the bed. She wondered where Clarissa was going to put all the things in her trunk.

As she undressed, Clarissa carelessly left items of her clothing scattered about the room, which Roxanne then had to step forward and pick up. Plainly it was not going to be easy to work for her.

Stripped down to her "combination" underwear, with its chemise top and light bloomer bottom, Clarissa paused to survey her figure critically in the tall cheval glass.

"I haven't gained any weight," she stated complacently, "in spite of all those wonderful late suppers!" As Clarissa turned about for a better view of herself, Roxanne surveyed her thoughtfully. She saw a girl of her own height with a figure quite strikingly like her own. But Clarissa had a candy-box pretty face with wide, rather vacant eyes of a rich dark brown that matched her thick auburn hair . . . while Roxanne's face was stunning in its beauty and impact. Each of Roxanne's features was perfect—her dark-lashed sapphire eyes, her soft expressive mouth, her sheer peach-bloom complexion, her small firm chin, and her thick and gleaming dark-blond hair.

She saw Clarissa studying her, just as she studied Clarissa. There was irritation in Clarissa's glance, a kind of angry look that said: You are only a servant; how dare you be so beautiful?

Later, from the second-floor stair landing, Roxanne heard Clarissa, freshly clad in peach dimity with a little ruff at the neck and great satin bows at the elbows, telling Rhodes, "I don't know if I'll keep Roxanne. She's very conspicuous looking for a servant and—sort of above herself, if you know what I mean."

"Oh, you mean that insolent look? Well, remember Roxanne speaks French and has had some schooling. She knows her knife from her fork!" Roxanne looked over the banisters and saw him turn to Clarissa as if a new idea had struck him. "Say, there's your chance, Clarissa. Roxanne can easily pass as a French maid."

Rhodes pressed the point. "How many of your friends have French maids? Why don't you dress her up in black silks with white organdy ruffles and take her about with you? You'd be the talk of the town, Clarissa!"

Clarissa considered him doubtfully. "Do you really think so?"

"No doubt about it," said Rhodes in an airy voice.

"Sort of froufrou . . ." murmured Clarissa.

Roxanne turned away smiling then, but she was startled when Clarissa, bent on having a French maid since none of her Baltimore friends had one, suddenly ordered a length of lavish black silk and a lot of white organdy and had her seamstress whip up a concoction that was different from anything Roxanne had ever expected to wear in service.

At Clarissa's command, she tried it on in front of

the tall cheval glass in Clarissa's bedroom: Black silk stockings. Black high-heeled shoes. A gleaming black silk dress with leg-o'-mutton sleeves, a seductive bell-shaped skirt and a ruff of white at the throat. A fluted white organdy apron tied with a big bow in the back and a little tiara-like fluted organdy ruff to wear in her piled-up dark-blond hair. The dress fitted her like her own skin and rustled when she moved. Roxanne studied her reflection in the mirror and thought such an outfit belonged in a music hall or cabaret.

"You can't mean I'm to go out on the street looking like this?" she said, aghast. "Everyone will stare at me!"

Clarissa's faint smile told her that was the idea; she stood entranced, studying Roxanne narrowly—now garbed in her very own idea of what a French maid should look like. "And remember," Clarissa cautioned, "to speak only French. If you can't say something in French, just don't speak at all. I wouldn't want people to know you were a counterfeit."

Roxanne rustled from the room, painfully conscious as she went down the stairs of how the clinging black silk outlined not only her breasts, her dainty waistline, and her softly rounded hips, but clung to the curve of her bottom as well and moved as she moved. The whole effect was so seductive, it looked as if it belonged in a boudoir. She couldn't imagine going out on the street in it.

Striding through the hall below, Rhodes paused to watch her descent with kindling eyes. "Clarissa's done something right at last," he exulted. "You're magnificent, Roxanne."

"I feel ridiculous," she muttered. "Like a dog on a leash—with a diamond dog collar." And walked on past him.

Rhodes laughed heartlessly, she thought—and gave her bottom a familiar pat. She whirled and struck at him. Deftly he avoided her blow and went out whistling, looking very pleased with himself. Roxanne glared after him and rustled out to the cupboards to find a lamp wick.

Later, as she was hanging up Clarissa's clothes, Roxanne noticed something that had not caught her attention before: While Clarissa's wardrobe consisted primarily of peach and pink and ruffles and furbelows —all standard enough in the fashions of the day—every dress had something striking to catch the eye. And every hat as well, for Clarissa's hats were ingenious creations of feathers and ribbons with artfully sweeping brims. Even her gloves were special—they were jeweled, tasseled, scalloped. Roxanne realized that every item in Clarissa's wardrobe had been chosen for its impact on the viewer; the girl's one desire seemed to be to make herself conspicuous and attract attention.

Much to Roxanne's horror, Clarissa's new way to attract attention was to parade around Baltimore with Roxanne following two paces behind her. On these walks, Roxanne found herself carrying Clarissa's fan —which usually matched her costume—a large reticule containing smelling salts, lacy handkerchiefs, visiting cards, Paris powder and perfume, an extra pair of kid gloves, and a white prayer book (for Clarissa publicly affected religious devotion). Often the reticule also contained a romantic novel which Clarissa was borrowing from a friend and must smuggle into the house —an item Roxanne was always glad to see, for she would manage to read a chapter now and then as she straightened up Clarissa's room. In fact, Roxanne might have gotten used to it all, if it had not been for the crowning insult, the parasol. Clarissa wasn't content to carry her own beruffled parasol—and she had one to match each of her afternoon gowns. Instead, Roxanne must carry it, bending forward slightly to hold it so that it shaded Clarissa's pretty vacant face from the sun, her own face red with embarrassment at the amused glances directed at their progress as they paraded through Baltimore's better downtown streets.

All over Baltimore Clarissa exhibited her new toy. Roxanne was stared at and giggled at all over the city. Heads turned curiously to look at her as Clarissa minced and Roxanne rustled sexily by. Clarissa's friends all asked Roxanne questions in French. Her accent, as she answered, was as bad as theirs, but in their ignorance they didn't know that.

Roxanne felt ridiculous on these tours, most of which were journeys to the houses of Clarissa's friends, where she cooled her high French heels in the corner of one elegant drawing room after another, jumping up every few minutes to be stared at as she did Clarissa's bidding—to bring a fan or to take it away, or to pin up a stray lock of hair of Clarissa's artful coiffure that had come loose during animated conversation as the young ladies gossiped, seated around massive sterling tea services.

Had she not been so conspicuous, Roxanne would have enjoyed these journeys, for the houses themselves had enormous individuality: There was the Renaissance-style mansion of the Misses Lyons, where the furniture was all tall, dark and handsome, and the people were uniformly short and round. And the posh abode of Miss Paige, where Roxanne was promptly banished below stairs, to be pursued by an amorous butler around the table in the servants' dining room. And the ornate Greenspring Valley "cottage" of the nouveaux riche Pottersby clan, where one of the handsome Pottersby boys jumped out of a doorway, cried "Boo!" and kissed her as she hurried with a glass of water to Clarissa, who claimed she was fainting from the heat.

As it was, Roxanne hated these excursions. Surrounded by all the trappings of wealth and power, she was made to feel a fool—and worse, sometimes she was made to feel like the legitimate prey of lustful upper servants. She kept her head high and her back stiff and rustled along in her picturesque black silk and white organdy, challenging all comers with her sapphire eyes. Though she hated the trappings which proclaimed her a lady's maid instead of a lady, she tried her best to hide it.

In spite of the embarrassment, there were compensations:

Such as the visits to the glovers.

Gloves were a necessity. Women of fashion wore them even inside the house. They had stacks of gloves. And every formal occasion meant long opera gloves (which the glovers called twenty-button gloves). Some of these long gloves were so tight they were called mousquetaires; they were said to have been adapted from the gauntlets worn by the famous Musketeers. Men wore gloves on the dance floor as well as on the street. Even waiters in restaurants and the servants in wealthy homes wore them to serve dinner. At least at the table one could remove one's gloves and still remain in fashion.

Clarissa made frequent visits to her favorite glover, whose window displayed gloves known as Limerics, of such fine calfskin that even a pair large enough to fit a man's hands could be squeezed into a walnut shell. Roxanne stared, fascinated, at these gilded nutshells when Clarissa decided on them for gifts for the men of the Coulter household.

The glove-making family who owned the shop was named Barrington. The father and elder son managed the small factory in the rear of the shop where the hand-made gloves were produced, while the younger son, Denby, clerked.

When Roxanne entered the shop, Denby's expression became as rapt as if an angel had just come to earth.

Clarissa noted the glazed look in the young glover's eyes, and her voice reflected her irritation as she said sharply she'd like to see some of their newest styles, please.

Denby recovered himself and favored Clarissa with a professional smile. Hastily he produced a half dozen pair of gloves in Clarissa's size—for she was a regular customer of the shop. But even when he came around from behind the counter to help fit a pair of long embroidered kid mousquetaires on Clarissa's shapely arms, his gaze hardly left Roxanne.

Denby Barrington was in his early twenties, above medium height with light hazel eyes and silky brown hair. He sported a drooping silky mustache of which, Roxanne guessed, he was inordinantly fond. His complexion was rather pale—no doubt he did not get outdoors much. There was pride in the way he walked and moved; his was a swinging gait which in a heavier-set man might have been a swagger, but in reed-slender Denby it was rather graceful. There was a suggestion that his coltish build might fill out later to wiry strength. It seemed odd to Roxanne that a man should have such a dainty profession, but otherwise she gave him little thought. She could not help noticing, however, how Denby's hazel eyes followed her as she moved about the shop, rustling in her seductive black silk uniform. Watching him as he fit the gloves carefully on Clarissa, Roxanne decided that he had the manners of a Grand Duke, and wondered if his mother had lovingly pressed those stiff spotless white cuffs, that tall stiff white collar.

"These gloves are so tight they cut off the circulation in my arms," complained Clarissa, flexing her arms doubtfully. "I have a friend in New York whose doctor warned her that if she persisted in wearing such tight gloves she would get varicose veins and hands as red as any kitchen maid's!"

"Ah, but they must be tight so that they will wrinkle properly," pointed out Denby. "That is the famous fashion created by the divine Sarah!"

"Sarah Bernhardt's arms are thin as rails," objected Clarissa. "And mine aren't. I know because I saw her in a play in New York."

"Ah, then we must choose between fashion and health," he declared jovially.

"I should prefer to have both," said Clarissa in a tart voice, fighting a losing battle as she tried to tug off the gloves.

"Here, let me help you." Denby sprang to her aid. "You must remember it takes a good fifteen or twenty minutes to put these on and, if it is a warm day, at least as long to take them off, else you will tear them."

"I'll take the gloves whether they tear or not," cried Clarissa irritably. "Just get them *off*!"

Now that fashion had won, Denby was all solicitation. "You must remember to flutter your hands. It restores circulation," he advised in a serious tone, and Roxanne hid a smile.

Eager to distract the ladies as he wrestled delicately with Clarissa's tightly encased arms, Denby, who was schooled in glovers' lore, told them of gloves that had been made of the skins of snakes and dogs and whales, the fiber of nettles, even the hairy growth of shellfish. Once, spiders had been used to produce enough silk for several pairs of gloves that had been presented to the Royal Society of London. Clarissa, forgetting her discomfort, exclaimed she would love to see a pair, but Denby explained that in captivity the spiders fell to eating each other—and besides it took some seven hundred thousand spiders to produce but a pound of silk for gloves.

Roxanne laughed aloud and Denby flushed with pleasure.

He snapped his fingers at a young female clerk who hovered nearby—Roxanne strongly suspected she was a younger sister—and the clerk hasily wrapped up the three pairs of gloves that Clarissa had selected. Roxanne watched resignedly; it would be her unfortunate duty to have to stretch those gloves onto Clarissa's arms and tug them off again.

Clarissa said she'd come by again when they had a better selection, managing by her voice and manner to snub both shop and owner. Denby looked chagrined, but Roxanne noticed that he rushed to the shop window as they left and watched them walk down the street. She looked back and on an impulse smiled at him. She had liked the young glover; somehow she felt that he did not regard her as a servant but a young lady on whom, if one were encouraged, one paid social calls. Then she wondered in horror if it was the swaying motion of her bottom in the tight black silk dress that he was watching as she leaned forward in her effort to shield Clarissa's face with the parasol. Her face burned at the thought, and she watched the bright leaves that fluttered to the ground with relief. Soon Clarissa would have no excuse for her parasol; she would be bundled up against the cold winds that swept down from the north.

"You should not have laughed in the glove shop," Clarissa reproved her. "It was a silly bid for that young man's attention."

Roxanne yearned to tell Clarissa who was bidding for attention, but she turned away so that Clarissa would not see the contempt in her eyes.

When they got home, Roxanne put away Clarissa's new gloves, assisted Clarissa out of her clothes and corset, combed out Clarissa's hair, straightened the room, and drew the drapes so that Clarissa could enjoy a pleasant afternoon nap.

"Oh, and Roxanne," Clarissa called sleepily as Roxanne turned to go. "You're to help Greaves serve dinner tonight. That new girl—the mousy one whose name I can never remember—cut her hand with the carving knife."

"She's not supposed to carve," said Roxanne, surprised. "Greaves does that."

"I know. The stupid thing was bringing the carving knife and fork to Greaves in her half-witted way when she tripped and fell."

Roxanne shuddered to think that the girl could have been impaled on that long wicked knife.

"So I've told Mrs. Hollister you'll be available until the girl gets that unsightly bandage off. You can change to your gray uniform for serving dinner, Roxanne. Just wear the black when you're at your usual duties."

Roxanne nodded to indicate she understood and went out to change immediately into her gray. It was bulky and stiff, and it made her look heavier, but she got into it with a sigh of relief. At least she did not look like a fancy woman in the sober gray.

There was time enough before dinner for a walk. So Roxanne availed herself of the opportunity, and begging some bread crumbs from Cook went off to feed the pigeons in the park. She liked being outside, feeding the birds in the bright fall weather.

At the park, amid the pigeons, she met a serving maid from the brownstone house next door on Mt.

Vernon Place. A big blond immigrant girl named Anna, who came from Eastern Europe, and who cried in her heavily accented English, "Ach, don't I know you? You vork next door to me!"

Roxanne, still smarting from Clarissa's spiteful comments, was very glad to talk to someone. Anna regaled her with stories of the house where she worked. She'd been there for five years—almost since getting off the boat, she laughed. Her employers, whom she called simply "the family," were away in Europe, and things had fallen apart something awful; the butler was drunk most of the time and the housekeeper was letting things go to wrack and ruin while she slept or read for long hours in the best bedroom. Anna shook her head with foreboding as she imagined what would happen if the family were to return early from their grand tour of the Continent.

Roxanne listened with interest to these revelations and then companionably walked back to Mt. Vernon Place with Anna. Anna's English was fluent, but she had trouble pronouncing her *w*'s.

"I know all about *your* family," Anna volunteered as they strolled along, and Roxanne gathered she meant the Coulters. "Vun of the maids ve had till last summer used to vork over there. I asked her how could she leave a house vith all men—and single to boot. Ven ve have only a married couple and five daughters at our house!"

"There's an unmarried girl at our house too—Clarissa," demurred Roxanne.

The big girl shrugged. "It's only men who count," she stated. "All the girls who vorked at *your* house," she added significantly, "vere after vun or the other. For myself I've alvays fancied the younger vun, Mr. Rhodes—more blood in him, I'd vager, although . . ." She shrugged and fell silent.

Roxanne smiled. "And the girls who work for the Coulters—do they all succeed with the Coulter men?" she asked casually.

Anna gave her an appraising look. "Some say so,"

she murmured. "They also say, in the kitchen, that *you* can take your pick," she added slyly.

Roxanne flushed and fell silent. She hadn't known she was being discussed in the kitchen next door.

When they parted, Roxanne promised to attend an upcoming crab roast with Anna. Though she was well aware it would not be attended by people of any social importance, she told herself she ought to get out more.

At dinner, shuttling back and forth between the dining room and kitchen, Roxanne mused that now that Clarissa was back, the conversation at the dining table had changed. Ships and commerce were no longer discussed. Beautifully gowned Clarissa dominated the table with her rippling laugh and animated gestures. Clad in amber lace or pink silk lined with rustling violet taffeta, a spray of pearls and diamonds in her auburn hair, Clarissa kept the table lively with her sallies. Gavin seemed absorbed by Clarissa, but sometimes Rhodes's green eyes followed Roxanne. At such times, her cheeks flamed and she tried to keep her eyes downcast, for the looks he gave her were not the looks he bestowed on the presumably virginal Clarissa.

Later that evening, as she sat in her mean little room, Roxanne told herself rebelliously that she must get out and mix with people. She must not yearn for Rhodes—whom she could not have on her terms—or mourn for Buck whom she had lost. Over the weeks her feelings about Buck had at least clarified, and she had begun at last to have a certain reluctant understanding of the way Buck had felt about her. Worn out with waiting for Julie and in the immediate presence of death, he had clasped Roxanne's young body to him compulsively. It was not love, it was *wanting.* And in the madness of that wild turmoil of sky and sound she had felt the same thing.

Sitting on the bed, she lit her lamp and realized irritably that she had forgotten to clean it. Its chimney was badly fogged, and she had to give up the idea of reading the novel she had filched from the back of Clarissa's armoire. There would have been hours to read, too, because Rhodes had taken Clarissa to a ball given by plump little Mary Stadler at their Renaissance-style mansion. Roxanne had laced Clarissa up, had powdered her arms the better to ease them into the new long gloves, had combed her pompadour to imitate Gibson Girl lines and had pinned into it a spray of diamonds made in the fashionable Southern Cross constellation design. Around Clarissa's neck she had clasped an equally fashionable dog collar of pearls. And thus attired, in filmy copper-colored tulle, Clarissa had waltzed out into the night with Rhodes.

They would be back later, and Clarissa would be sulky if the evening had not gone to her liking. Roxanne would have to undress her, unlace her, comb out her long hair, put away her finery, turn down her bed, perhaps run down and heat a glass of hot milk for her. And *then* she could return to her own room and sleep till the rattling milk cart woke her in the morning.

Feeling wakeful, she tried to turn her thoughts from lucky Clarissa, whirling about in Rhodes's arms, and found herself remembering Kansas. Strangely, now that she'd left the prairies, she could remember not just the loneliness and the bad times, but other more appealing things: the sweet smell of the mixed prairie grasses, the chunky little meadow mice and the pretty prairie deer mice with their white undersides and big shoe-button eyes.

Ah, well, she was here now and she had to make the best of it, for the present, at least.

Gavin went out of town again, and Rhodes busied himself at the docks—with what matters Roxanne did not know, but he came in late and whistling to dinner, and sometimes missed dinner altogether. Clarissa was very miffed at Rhodes's desertion, for when she had first returned home, Rhodes had squired her about a good deal. At such times she had been exuberant, dismissing Roxanne almost graciously, sometimes even giving her a few hours off. But with Rhodes preoccupied with other things, Clarissa grew bored and petulant and pouted at his lack of attention.

On Monday, Clarissa struck back. A carriage, conveying a dapper young gentleman dressed for a go at lawn tennis, called for her. As Clarissa went out to meet him, wearing a long linen skirt and sporty blouse, Roxanne saw her lift her head airily, sending a triumphant glance up at Rhodes's fourth floor window. But Roxanne hid a smile, for she knew that Rhodes had gone out early. Obviously Clarissa did not.

Roxanne turned away from the window with a sigh, and went to change to her sensible gray uniform, because she had to help big Tillie with the ironing. That morning, Clarissa—indignant that Rhodes had smiled too frequently at Roxanne at dinner the night before—had said coolly, "I've told Mrs. Hollister you would help in the laundry today, Roxanne,"

From the steaming laundry, Roxanne saw Anna next door hanging out clothes, and going to the open window, waved to her. Friendly Anna always made a point of waving, sometimes from the servants' entrance out front, sometimes from a window as she shook out a dust mop. Today, Roxanne was cheered by the sight of Anna. And when Anna slipped over to remind her about the crab roast, Roxanne was glad to affirm her promise to attend.

On Sunday afternoon, Roxanne joined handsome Anna and two burly young men who worked in one of the giant warehouses that were a Baltimore landmark, as they rode in a delivery wagon piled with hay. Along with a giggling crowd of housemaids and delivery boys, they made their way out into the park-like Greenspring Valley, where the crab roast was held. Someone had brought a fiddle, and they square-danced on the grass. Roxanne was sharply reminded of that moonlit summer night in Kansas when she had square-danced in the Smiths' big barn and Buck had discovered her. . . .

The food was delicious, but there were also several kegs of beer and, as it was rapidly consumed, the party grew raucous. All in all, it was a rough affair. Roxanne was glad when the wagons, with everyone singing "The Band Played On" loudly, creaked back into

Baltimore. On the way back, Roxanne found herself desperately resisting the advances of her date, one of the burly young warehousemen, who was roguishly grasping her knees under the hay. When she finally struck at him, he roared with laughter and gave her a bear hug and a smacking kiss on the lips. Her hat fell off as she pulled out of his rough embrace, and she had to scramble for it in the hay, afraid the wind would carry it off. As they turned the corner of Mt. Vernon Place, she bade them all a hurried good-bye, tumbled out of the wagon and fled.

The next week the ever exuberant Anna asked her to attend a clambake, but Roxanne declined. Remembering how Anna's men friends had almost pinched her black and blue, Roxanne explained earnestly that she must catch up on her reading at the Enoch Pratt Free Library.

Anna's eyebrows elevated. "Miss Hoity-Toity!" she exclaimed. "My friends aren't good enough for you, eh?"

"It isn't that," said Roxanne, flushing uncomfortably because Anna had perceived her true feelings. She didn't want to marry a day laborer who got drunk on Saturday nights and beat his wife or landed in jail. She wanted—she looked about her wistfully—she wanted what the Coulters had.

Plus happiness.

Chapter 9

Roxanne was a great favorite with Mrs. Hollister, and sometimes, on days when Clarissa's strident calls were not too intrusive, the older woman asked her to take tea with her.

They would sit and chat, balancing delicate teacups from a lovely set of Bavarian china that Mrs. Hollister spoke of mysteriously as a "gift from a gentleman." The first time Roxanne had entered Mrs. Hollister's bedroom, she had been startled at the luxury of it. Although it was in the servants' wing, it was quite large, a partition obviously having been taken out to make it so. And the furnishings were at least as good as those in Rhodes's room. Even the dainty tea service and linens were, Roxanne imagined, far beyond an ordinary housekeeper's meager salary. Whenever the girl admired anything, Mrs. Hollister always smiled a secret smile and said they had been gifts from "an admirer." Somewhat baffled, Roxanne presumed Mrs. Hollister had had younger, palmier days. Certainly the housekeeper had been with the Coulters for many years, and Roxanne could hardly imagine her receiving an amorous gentleman friend here in the house.

"You are what I might have been," the older woman mused one day, studying Roxanne across her teacup. Mrs. Hollister sighed. "You must be careful to make the right decisions in life, Roxanne." *As I did not*, her tone implied.

When Roxanne inquired about Mr. Hollister, Mrs. Hollister turned to her with the air of imparting a great confidence.

"There *is* no Mr. Hollister," she admitted, looking behind her as if someone else were there to hear. "When I first went into household service, I added a *Missus* to my name for—for protection."

Roxanne's puzzled sapphire eyes wondered silently what kind of protection that would afford.

"From men," said Mrs. Hollister delicately. "From their—advances, Roxanne."

"Oh," said Roxanne, her face clearing. "Yes."

So Mrs. Hollister had never married. Surprised, Roxanne couldn't help glancing at the plain gold band on Mrs. Hollister's plump left hand.

Mrs. Hollister caught her look and fidgeted. "It's a friendship band," she said, twisting it, and decided to change the subject. "I've never given up wearing a bustle," she said. "It does so become my figure, doesn't it?"

Roxanne thought it made her look fat, but she smiled and went on sipping her tea.

"You could have a great future, Roxanne—just as I might have had," said the older woman wistfully. "You could marry a wealthy tradesman. You know Baltimore is full of wealthy self-made men."

"Or perhaps I might marry into one of the wealthy old-line families?" suggested Roxanne dryly.

Mrs. Hollister looked alarmed. "Oh, no, you shouldn't aspire to that," she cried. "You will only come to grief, Roxanne. Gentlemen of the old school—"

"Don't marry serving wenches. So Mary Bridey has informed me."

"Have you seen her?" Mrs. Hollister asked. "How is poor Mary Bridey?

Roxanne nodded. "She's very lonely. I think she would like to see you."

"Oh?" Mrs. Hollister's hand flew distractedly to pat her soft gray hair. "Well, of course I'm very busy right now, but later I'll try to get around to it."

Roxanne thought of Mary Bridey seated on the green rocker, so wistfully asking for news of the "great house," and set down her cup abruptly. "Thank you for the tea," she said. "I must get back. Clarissa will be calling for me, and she'll be angry if I don't answer."

"I suppose you find it difficult to work for Miss Clarissa?"

"Yes," said Roxanne shortly. "Especially," she added, "since she makes me wear these silly clothes."

Mrs. Hollister tch-tched. "I suppose they do make the men look at you," she murmured sympathetically.

"Look at me? When I'm bent forward holding a parasol over Clarissa's empty head, with my bottom swaying in this tight silk dress? Can you blame them if they look? It's providential they don't make remarks! And they probably do after we've passed by!"

"You mustn't feel that way," insisted Mrs. Hollister, obviously upset. "And here in this house I'm sure nobody feels you're—well, *that* sort of girl."

"You mean Gavin and Rhodes are impervious to tight clothes?"

Mrs. Hollister's brows drew together. "You should call them *Mister* Gavin and *Mister* Rhodes," she chided. "We mustn't forget they're Mr. Joab's sons, and entitled to our respect."

"Even when one's bottom gets patted?"

Mrs. Hollister set down her teacup with a little crash. "Oh, dear," she said. "You mustn't—that is, you mustn't—" She was floundering.

"Get involved with gentlemen," said Roxanne quietly, with a level look. "That *was* what you meant, wasn't it? I should look for new money, not old?"

"Exactly." The older woman sat back and smiled, serenely unconscious of the irony in Roxanne's voice. "That way everything will work out just fine."

"Thank you, Mrs. Hollister, for the tea," said Roxanne again, and went off to help Clarissa dress for another excursion about the city.

The day was a particularly galling one. The bitterness of her position swept over Roxanne as she sat angrily at attention in the drawing room of a turreted Victorian mansion, her lap weighed down by a large reticule—from which she was constantly called to produce lozenges, a fan, fresh gloves, headache powders, smelling salts, handkerchiefs. Clarissa did not really need any of these things; she was just showing off before her handsomely gowned friends and enjoyed making Roxanne jump about.

Later, back at the house, Clarissa said petulantly, "You forgot to speak French when I asked you if the carriage was outside!" Roxanne's lips tightened as she bit back an angry answer. She caught the tumble of petticoats Clarissa flung at her with an irritable "Here, put these away. I don't know why my room is never tidy!" Roxanne yearned to tell her why, but instead she addressed herself to folding the lacy petticoats into a neat stack and forcing them into the already bursting drawers of Clarissa's big marble-topped dresser. At that point, she didn't care if they ripped. Luckily they did not, and she closed the drawer.

Still upset, she was clumsy at dinner and broke a platter. Cook glowered, and Greaves sighed and said Mrs. Hollister would deduct the cost from Roxanne's salary. Fuming now at what she considered a gross injustice—Cook should have told her it was scalding hot!—Roxanne rushed out after clearing the dinner dishes and took a fast walk, hoping the exercise would cool her hot blood. The evening air did cool her hot cheeks, and rounding the corner, she met Rhodes returning home late. He came to a halt when he saw her, and she told him rather tartly that he'd missed dinner—again.

He shrugged. "I'm in no mood for dinner anyway." He ran a hand through his dark hair and clapped his hat on again. "I'll walk with you, Roxanne." He joined her and together they strolled down past the Peabody.

He studied her as they walked along. "And now that you've been with us a while, have you decided what you want to do?" he asked quietly.

Still smoldering from Clarissa's jibes and the injustice at dinner, Roxanne's fingers clenched. "I want money—and power!" she choked. She could have added more; she could have said: *I want the feel of silks on my body and a carriage of my own with a smart team to take me where I want to go—instead of just tired feet!*

"Do I detect a note of rebellion?" Rhodes sounded amused.

Roxanne ignored that. "And jewels," she added resentfully. "And fine clothes. And"—she brought her fist down on her gloved hand—*"I'm going to have them!"*

"Such things don't mean much to me," he mused.

"That's because you've always had them!" she flashed.

"Perhaps." He turned to her with a smile. "And how do you propose to arrive at your heart's desire?"

"I don't know," she admitted sullenly.

"The marriage route is the usual one, I believe," he said. "A rich marriage—'fortunate,' I think they're called."

"Yes. I suppose so." She took a deep breath, stopped, and looked up at him, her sapphire eyes big and wild. "Rhodes—would you marry me?"

He stopped too and grinned down at her lovely reckless face. "Well, I'll take you to bed and discuss it."

She flushed. "I said *marry*."

He threw back his big head and laughed. "Not today, Roxanne. I'm not ready to be tied down to any one woman. And when I do marry," he added softly, "she's going to want me—and not just what I can give her."

Roxanne's flush deepened. "I didn't mean, *will* you?

I meant *would* you? Would any man of wealth and position marry a servant girl?"

He shrugged. "It's been done."

"Name someone you know who's done it," she challenged.

He frowned. "Well, I just don't know of anyone, Roxanne, but—"

"That's what I mean," she cut in, eyes blazing. "What you suggest is practically impossible—it doesn't happen."

He reached out and fingered a strand of her hair that had come loose from her piled-up coiffure. "Nothing is impossible," he murmured, "to a girl with hair of gold and skin like silk."

But was that really true? she asked herself. To her, all doors seemed firmly closed.

His gaze was soft, and he could have taken her in his arms, for at that moment the street was empty and they stood well into the shadow of a building. But he did not. She almost wished he had—it might have cooled this angry fever in her blood.

"I'll walk you home, Roxanne," he said. "I've decided to find a bit more excitement tonight than my father's house affords."

Saloons, she thought. Gambling. Women. All those things his father criticizes him for enjoying.

"You don't find life on Mt. Vernon Place exciting enough?" she challenged, studying him.

His strong masculine face, his jaw very square in the light from the street light, his green eyes smiling down quizzically into her own made her pulse quicken. She knew her question had sounded inviting, and something perverse in her had meant it to be so.

Again he reached out and toyed with a tendril of her gleaming hair. "So lovely . . ." he murmured, and sighed. "If I played games with you. I'd be tempted to go too far, Roxanne. There's a softness to your skin that heats a man up. And then you're bent on marriage. . . ."

She quivered at his touch but, stubbornly, she did not refute his statement that she was bent on marriage.

Of course she was, she thought rebelliously. Wasn't every girl?

When she did not speak, his smile faded and his hand fell away from her hair. "So tonight I'm pursuing more commercial joys around the bedpost. And I plan to get drunk as a skunk."

"Why?" she demanded, feeling deflated.

"Because every damned thing that could go wrong went wrong today," he said. "Getting cargo for a clipper these days is one hell of a business."

Bidding her good-bye at the servants' entrance, Rhodes strode on down the street, his broad shoulders swinging jauntily. Still breathless, Roxanne let herself in and made her way past storeroom doors to the back stairs that led to the kitchen. She was always a little breathless when Rhodes was around. It was so easy to imagine him taking her in his arms, and herself melting against him. It was hard not to continue the daydream to see herself in a long white dress, walking down a church aisle with him; to see him slipping that dress down over her bare shoulders on their wedding night and feasting his eyes, his hands, his lips, on her nakedness. Whenever Rhodes chanced to look at her, her very skin felt feverish, and she shied away from brushing against him if they passed in the hall.

Rhodes seemed to be aware of his effect on her, and was amused by it, she knew. And now he was off "to pursue commercial joys around the bedpost"—which meant fancy women, of course. Why should that concern her? But to her annoyance she felt a wild, unreasoning jealousy at the thought of those women he held in his arms, whether they were the trollops of Baltimore or sloe-eyed beauties in foreign ports; she envisioned sultry creamy-skinned wenches with limpid dark eyes begging him to take them, China dolls and lovely Malaysians, exotic Spanish beauties waving indolent fans, flirtatious French girls or bright-eyed Scottish lasses, all pursuing or pursued by him. She was jealous of them all.

But she didn't want to become one of those girls. And so she waged a losing battle with her heart.

Chapter 10

Clarissa had naturally wavy hair, so Roxanne was spared vexing sessions with a curling iron. But it was her duty to wash the young woman's daintiest silk blouses and underthings, and she found this a chore because Clarissa was invariably critical of her efforts.

Mary Bridey had been wrong; Clarissa never confided in Roxanne, never discussed with her life on the Eastern Shore or what happened at the many balls and parties she attended. Aside from a grumpy, "That stupid Sam Harrington stepped on my foot!" or "I'm sure Mary Stadler is using the same dressmaker—she was wearing a dress exactly like mine in a different color!" Roxanne seldom heard comments from Clarissa about her doings.

Roxanne reported this to Mary Bridey on one of her visits, and the little Irish girl seemed surprised. "Sure and Miss Clarissa must not like you," she blurted out, "for she was always telling me about them!"

"Oh, she doesn't like me," agreed Roxanne with a

laugh. And realized that Clarissa, who loved to show off, must have enjoyed preening before the less fortunate Irish lass, who had given in too easily.

More and more the lazy Clarissa found it convenient to send Roxanne on errands rather than go herself. Roxanne dropped visiting cards at the homes of Clarissa's friends, picked up parcels in department stores, carried scented notes about Baltimore—Clarissa "regretted" or Clarissa "would attend." But they were duties Roxanne loved. She enjoyed being out in the bright fall weather, walking fast amidst the crimson and gold and scarlet leaves that swirled through the air around her before they fell at last to form a rich-hued carpet on the ground.

She hated her ridiculous garb, and as soon as she was out of sight of the house she would take off the starched sheer apron and the tiara-like ruff from her hair, stuff them both carefully into the large reticule she carried, smooth back her dark-blond hair in embarrassment lest anyone had seen her do this, and with her color a little higher march on. In her rustling black silks, and with her warm shawl pulled around her shoulders, she looked as if she might be in mourning for a loved one.

Sometimes her errands took her past Barrington's, the glover's establishment. She knew the glover's younger son Denby was wistfully mad for her, and it gave her oft-deflated ego a boost to saunter by and see him look out, yearning for her with his hazel eyes.

Often, he called someone from the back to take his place at the counter and hurried out of the shop to either join her for a short stroll or try to persuade her to come back into the shop. There, under the guise of showing her some new gloves—tasseled ones, jeweled ones, hand-painted ones—he managed to touch her hand, and his boyish face would flush darkly, and he would begin to stammer.

Roxanne liked that. It gave her a feeling of power—she who was so powerless to change her circumstances, whose very survival depended on the will of others.

Whenever she could slip away long enough, Roxanne also visited Mary Bridey who, now that November's winds were blowing, spent her days with her unwieldy body huddled in a shawl, rocking, rocking. After that first confidence on Mt. Vernon Place, they had never mentioned Gavin by name. Roxanne had guessed that he was not a frequent visitor, but still she was shocked when Mary Bridey mentioned that no one from the "great house," as she insisted on calling the Mt. Vernon Place house, had been to see her.

"No one?" cried Roxanne indignantly.

"Only you," admitted Mary Bridey wistfully. With a defiant lift of her head, she moved her now ungainly figure aside to display a Windsor cradle made of maple and pine and painted green like the chairs and table. "The milkman sold it to me," she said. "Isn't it dainty?" She touched the cradle lovingly. " 'Tis for my little one. Won't he look fine in it?"

"Maybe you'll have a daughter," smiled Roxanne, "and *she'll* look fine in it."

"No, it will be a boy," said Mary Bridey confidently. "Olga, the Lithuanian woman downstairs, says I'm carrying my baby high and that means it will be a boy. She says you can always tell! I'm due at Christmas," she added. "My baby will be a Christmas gift—and then I won't be alone any more."

Roxanne's eyes misted over at the brave way she said that, and when she left she hugged Mary Bridey impulsively. "Let me speak to him," she pleaded. "Let me ask him to come to see you."

"No, you mustn't." Mary Bridey straightened her thin shoulders. Her voice was stern. "If—if he wants to see me, he'll come. And if he doesn't . . ." Her voice broke. "Well, after all, 'tis my own child, all mine, and nothing can change that."

"It makes me so angry," said Roxanne huskily.

"Sure and you must not feel that way," chided Mary Bridey in her gentle voice. "I am luckier than so many, Roxanne. I have a place to live until I have my baby—a nice place." She looked around her as if trying to convince herself of her good luck. "And I don't have to work and wear myself out." She twisted her fingers together. "I could be working twelve hours a day. Like my sister did in Ireland before she bore her first. There's a woman next door whose husband does nothing but drink all day, and she works twelve hours every day. And *she's* pregnant with her fifth."

Roxanne bit back the bitter words that rose to her lips. She supposed Mary Bridey really was better off gloomily waiting to give birth in these meager rooms than working twelve back-breaking hours a day.

For that matter, she supposed she must consider herself lucky, too, for Mrs. Hollister was not nearly so hard to work for as some of the other housekeepers that Anna next door had described to her. And thank fortune she was working and not out on the street, like the loose-lipped, tow-headed young girl she had seen picking up a sailor on the wharf yesterday. She shuddered as she remembered that thin face, those vacant feverish eyes.

Clarissa, of course, was another matter. The girl was infuriating to work for. But Roxanne was unwilling to face up to the question of why she did not leave, simply walk out and take her chances in a rough and tumble world. For then she would have had to face the answer: Rhodes.

The day after her visit to Mary Bridey, Gavin, watching her from the landing as she carried some newly-ironed petticoats upstairs to Clarissa's room, asked, "Are you happy here, Roxanne?"

Roxanne, her arms held stiffly out before her so as not to wrinkle the petticoats, paused to stare at him. The almost possessive look he gave her irritated her.

"I suppose I'm happier than Mary Bridey," she said sullenly.

His eyes narrowed. "Ah, so that's why you always look past me these days," he murmured, and let her pass.

That afternoon Rhodes, in an exuberant mood, came home early and caught Roxanne in the downstairs hall. He came up from behind and swung her around to give her a resounding kiss. Roxanne, forgetting for the moment that she was holding out for marriage, melted in his arms and returned his kiss with fire and fervor.

Now when she went on errands for Clarissa Rhodes caught up with her and accompanied her on her rounds. On those occasions he would often take her for short forbidden excursions, sightseeing around the city. Once, he took her to see the square Gothic tower of the Independent Fire Company, which Baltimoreans knew affectionately as Old Number Six, another time, to the huge multi-buildinged complex of Johns Hopkins Hospital.

"A man should know his terrain," he declared. "And a woman too. Even though," he added roguishly, "her main stamping ground may be the house."

Roxanne tossed her head at that, but she always enjoyed these encounters, for they added to her fund of knowledge about the city she lived in. Of course, often she had to hurry back and quickly don her apron again and invent some likely excuse for being so late. Still, she found it exciting just to be with Rhodes, matching her shorter steps to his longer ones, feeling the restless drive of the man with the reckless eyes and flashing smile.

"Aren't you afraid to be seen in public with me?" she asked rather pertly one day. "Your father might hear about it and cut you off!"

"No," he said quickly. "I think I'd always take the consequences of your company, Roxanne."

And as if to prove it, the next night when she strolled out for a walk after dinner, he came up behind her and caught her arm jauntily and took her to a music hall.

Roxanne tapped her feet to the music as a man in a straw boater and a striped jacket and white trousers did a soft-shoe dance around a bored-looking brunette beauty who rested her plump white arms on a folded parasol while he sang in a high falsetto about "a bicycle built for two." Then the girl onstage kicked up her heels and her skirts, and they did a fast dance into the wings, to the accompaniment of laughter and applause.

Roxanne loved it. She had not been to a music hall before, and she found the lights and the gaiety entrancing.

Afterwards, Rhodes hired a hack and they went clip-clopping along in the clear cold air.

"Your father would have disapproved of this, wouldn't he?" she asked. "I know Clarissa hides her novels. She's afraid he'll see them and forbid her to read them."

Rhodes, who was leaning back with his arm lightly around her shoulders, turned on her and said with a surprisingly bitter laugh, "My father's morality? Oh, yes, let's talk about that. It's a very mixed up thing, his morality. He's eaten up by guilt feelings. Though why it came over him so late is hard to understand. He was brought up on the edge of the law—*his* father had an office on Lombard Street and built and sold fast ships. Pirate ships, if you want to be specific. And slavers. And hired captains to operate them. Those ships had to be not only fast but cheap, in case they had to be scuttled, cargo and all. Not that anyone *wanted* to scuttle the cargo, you understand; it was black gold in those days—but they preferred scuttling to going to jail. As a young man my father sailed out as second in command on a slaver, and then he was made captain of his very own slave ship."

"It's hard to believe," murmured Roxanne.

"He wasn't running slaves to the United States then. He was buying them in small lots from the slave markets on the west coast of Africa and selling them in Cuba or South America, Brazil was still buying then."

He stopped talking, his lip curling.

"And what happened?" demanded Roxanne.

"After he got rich, he got religion," sighed Rhodes. "He turned his back on what he'd done and set out to criticize others. So because Gavin's mother was a Marylander and her father an abolitionist, Gavin is a saint! And because my mother was a Virginian and her father was a slave owner, I'm a sinner! That's an example of his thinking these days."

Roxanne could see the injustice of that. She tried to lighten it by saying, "And are you? A sinner?"

"Aren't we all? But I'm no worse than Gavin and, maybe," he muttered, "not as bad."

Certainly not as bad, she thought, remembering Mary Bridey. And then, regretfully, But still his brother. The thought was still with her when he ordered the hack to stop and wait for them while he took her strolling in the park. At a shady, romantic spot he bent to kiss her. When she responded too warmly to his kiss, his arm tightened about her, his tongue pressed past her parted lips, and she felt with shock one of his hands toying with her breast. The touch was electric. It shook her. Reeling with emotion, she pushed him away, said thickly, "No, Rhodes. No."

"You're sure?" he asked, his fingers tracing a fiery path down her spine. "You're sure you want me to hold some other woman in my arms tonight?"

She stared at him, her eyes dark, taking that in. *Another woman . . . when it could be her. Oh, no, she didn't want other arms to hold him, ever!*

But . . . he was a Coulter, Gavin's brother, and look where that road had led for poor Mary Bridey!

"Yes," she choked. "Any arms you choose!"

"That's plain enough," he said, and took her home.

When they alighted, he did not try to kiss her, and she knew that she had wounded him. He was very cool and correct with her for the next couple of weeks, and—to Clarissa's delight—squired his impetuous auburn-haired cousin everywhere.

Roxanne decided that Rhodes was just trying to make her jealous—and she *was* jealous, abominably so. A few days later, she ran across him in the hall and he paused to talk. "I see you so seldom . . ." she said, looking up at him through her dark lashes.

"I don't want a woman with a price tag, Roxanne. Especially if that price tag is marriage," he replied crisply, and tipped his hat to her and left.

She could hear him on the walk whistling the old sailors' ditty, "The Maid of Amsterdam." She knew the words because Rhodes often sang it, and now she flushed to hear the taunting notes:

> "I'll go no more a roving with you, fair maid,
> Since roving's been my ru-i-n!"

Chapter 11

December had come, wintry and unusually cold for generally mild Baltimore. The great clipper *Clarissa* had long since sailed, but Rhodes had not sailed with her. He lingered in Baltimore, and Roxanne hoped that he had stayed because of her.

Gavin was moody. She knew from dinner table conversations that he was trying to negotiate a loan for the shipping line. His father's health being poor lately, this duty fell to Gavin. Rhodes took no part in it, insisting that he was thinking of taking the *Virginia Lass* out on a voyage. He had begun provisioning her, but there was no talk as yet of a cargo. Roxanne wished she could sail away with him.

At the handsome Mt. Vernon Place house, plans were under way for Christmas, but which members of the family would be home for the holidays was still in doubt. For Gavin planned a trip to Boston to get financing if their Baltimore sources failed them, and restless Rhodes might sail at any time. If the men left, Clarissa announced, she herself would accept an invitation to spend the holidays on the Eastern Shore; and Joab Coulter, whose step was less steady these days and who looked unusually pale, did not raise his voice to say she could not go. Roxanne wondered if the old man would have to spend Christmas alone, cut off from all the members of his family.

When she mentioned this to Mrs. Hollister, the housekeeper only smiled brightly. "But *we'll* be here," she chirped in a happy-sounding voice. A remark that made no sense to Roxanne.

Clarissa had put on a little weight during the fall, and now, as she tried on the new gowns she had had made to wear to the balls of the yuletide season, she was irritable. Her irritation took the form of storming at Roxanne. Clarissa insisted Roxanne lace her steel-boned corset tight enough to keep her waist its usual size and then complained bitterly that Roxanne was hurting her. Ignoring Clarissa's endless scolding, pulling harder, Roxanne laced Clarissa's corset tight enough to trim her waist to the desired size. By dint of a long shoehorn she forced Clarissa's feet into fashionable round-toed high-buttoned shoes a size too small. And powdered her arms and delicately tugged the skintight mousquetaires onto Clarissa's protesting arms. Sometimes she felt that dressing and undressing Clarissa was probably more exhausting than spending a whole evening at a ball.

Early in December, Roxanne had begun buying gifts, for she felt obliged to give Christmas gifts to all the staff, and her earnings were meager. And now that the weather was so cold she found it necessary to invest ten dollars in a warm blue wool winter suit, which had a fashionable bell-shaped skirt and just a suggestion of a train. A lovely new blouse to go with the suit cost another precious three dollars. She had hoped to buy herself a novel or two for Christmas, but realized she would not have enough money once her gifts were purchased.

For Mrs. Hollister she bought a pompadour comb for twenty-nine cents. For Greaves, a tall detachable linen collar, which cost a quarter. For Ella, whose hand had never healed properly and whose work Roxanne and Tillie tried surreptitiously to do, she bought a box of candles, knowing they would be welcome at her home—Ella took everything she could home to her big impoverished family. For Lizzie and Tillie, Roxanne bought a box of fancy toilet soap—fifteen cents each. Desperate—for she still had Mary Bridey's gift to buy and her money was fast running out—she bought a peck of bright red apples for thirty cents and shined them on a linen napkin; these apples she could distribute to the stableboys and grooms and assorted part-time help who might be there during the holidays.

Shortly before Christmas, Roxanne made the cold journey through biting wind-whipped streets to visit Mary Bridey, and found the Irish girl busily stitching a layette. Roxanne had brought along her gifts of a soft woolen blanket she had found in a downtown department store for thirty-five cents, and a dress length of pretty green calico which she had coveted herself and considered a great bargain at six cents a yard.

Mary Bridey exclaimed joyfully over her gifts, saying her room was cold and what a difference a warm blanket would make! And what a lovely dress she could make from the calico! She added guiltily she'd been so busy making the baby's clothes that she did not have Roxanne's gift ready yet.

"That's no matter," smiled Roxanne. "But I stopped by with these because Clarissa's planning such a round of gaiety that she'll probably keep me busy every day until all hours right through New Year's, so I might not see you till after the baby's born."

But Mary Bridey looked so sad and disappointed that Roxanne promised to come to see her the Sunday before Christmas, and when she did—in a driving snow that frosted her hat and lashes—she thought Mary Bridey was looking very pale.

"Have you seen the doctor?" asked Roxanne uneasily, brushing off snow.

"No. I'm to have a midwife," explained Mary Bridey, helping her.

"You don't look too well," murmured Roxanne. "Perhaps you *should* see a doctor. . . ."

"No, I've just not been sleeping well lately. Worrying, I guess." Mary Bridey tried to smile but didn't quite manage it.

Roxanne thought she had reason to worry, about her future and the future of her unborn child.

"You're not to worry," she said stoutly. "I'll help you." And Mary Bridey's eyes brimmed with tears.

For Roxanne's coming, Mary Bridey had set the green painted table with her festive best, and cooked a chicken. Roxanne protested at this effort, but Mary Bridey, again serene, pooh-poohed her protests. And indeed some of the color came back to her thin cheeks as she told Roxanne that Mrs. Kaunas, the woman downstairs, was learning English so they could converse. The Lithuanian word for Christmas meant "log evening," when the huge Christmas log was burned, Mrs. Kaunas had explained, adding that the tree downstairs would be trimmed Lithuanian fashion with straw bird cages.

As Roxanne drank tea out of the cheap unmatched cups, she determined that as soon as she could, she would buy Mary Bridey a proper china tea set, using the girl's birthday as an excuse to give it to her. She ate only a wing of the tasty chicken Mary Bridey had prepared for them; chicken, she knew, cost seven cents a pound and she suspected that Mary Bridey had scrimped for this occasion.

Roxanne insisted on washing the dishes and stayed until dusk. Then she made her way home over the icy streets, leaning against the biting wind, and told herself bitterly that no man was worth what Mary Bridey was going through.

On the street outside the Coulter house she passed Rhodes, just coming out the front door, and her sapphire eyes softened. He looked so big and hearty and sure-footed as he ran jauntily down the icy steps, smiling at her as he passed. Perhaps, she thought, perhaps there were exceptions. . . .

Well before Christmas, Denby Barrington was emboldened to leave a gift for Roxanne at the house: a pair of gloves, the new slip-ons, of creamy kid. Roxanne wondered if she should accept them; she decided not to do so would hurt Denby's feelings.

So she dropped by the shop to thank him, and together they went strolling down the wintry streets through a lightly falling snow that covered dirt and slush and turned Baltimore into a white wonderland where children pulled their sleds and tossed snowballs from mittened hands. The snow piled up on Denby's hat and frosted Roxanne's lashes and shawl—for she hadn't yet been able to afford a winter coat.

As they walked, Denby entertained her with the story of Lafayette's visit to Baltimore in 1825. In his honor, the debutantes of Baltimore had worn long gloves with his likeness painted on the back. Lafayette had steadfastly refused to kiss his own painted image, to the dismay of the young ladies in the receiving line, whose gloved hands had gone unkissed.

Denby looked as if he would like to kiss Roxanne as he said this. He bent close to her in the shelter of an icicled doorway, but a careening delivery wagon, skidding on the icy street, threw a splatter of slush their way and they jumped nimbly out of its path. The moment was lost.

At the Coulter house, feverish preparations were in progress for a gala Christmas season. A large wreath of holly was hung on the door. Rhodes had provided mistletoe on the chandelier in the front hall, and there were branches of evergreen everywhere—drooping over the mantels, the pictures, the clocks; there was even a long rope of laurel looped over the banister to the second floor.

Their tree, which was placed before one of the tall windows of the second-floor drawing room, was a large, pleasant-smelling cedar. The staff decorated it with apples and cranberries and popcorn strings and painted pine cones, and topped it with a gilt paper angel. Clarissa frowned at this country-style trim and added her own more sophisticated decorations: expensive oranges, tiny, elegant silver trays and baskets of sweetmeats, candy eggs and gilt gingerbread, and some fancy little cakes she had Roxanne select at the baker's and then suspend by colored ribbons from the branches. Roxanne being the most adept at tying fancy bows, this duty fell to her alone, and she spent hours climbing up and down a stepladder, attaching these goodies to the tree under Clarissa's watchful eye.

In the kitchen a major effort was going on: not only a huge turkey to be stuffed and roasted, but all sorts of puddings and hot breads, and mince pies. The candies had all been made earlier, and the fruitcakes, having been made last January, were now considered sufficiently aged and were being taken out of the tin containers in which they had reposed all year wrapped in linen napkins, to be sliced paper thin and served with wine.

Mousy little Ella's hand had never healed properly, and just before Christmas she hurt it again, this time on the apple peeler. Roxanne, exhausted from pouring Clarissa into and dragging her out of her clothes, knew that meant she must help serve Christmas dinner.

On Christmas Eve the staff—already exhausted by the extensive preparations—exchanged their little gifts at the kitchen table, after they finished their pudding. Roxanne was touched at their gifts to her, for they were all the sort of thing a young girl would wish to have—dainty soap, hair combs, hairpins, a linen handkerchief. She smiled her thanks at them all.

But she was surprised when Rhodes—from whom she had expected no gift—stopped her in the deserted hall to give her a small package. "Not so blue as your eyes," he murmured, and when she unwrapped the gift box he had given her, she found an ornamental hat pin of pale blue enamel set in gold and studded with seed pearls.

She looked up at him, confused, to find him studying her with a strange expression in his green eyes.

"Blue is for purity, isn't it?" he asked, smiling.

"No," she said. "That's white."

"Oh?" His voice was caressing. "Important difference. . . ."

As she stammered her thanks, he added, "I have something else for your hat—to wear only when I'm around." From behind him he brought out a sprig of mistletoe and gravely affixed it in her pomadour. She waited, her senses tingling as, slowly, he drew her toward him, smiling down into her eyes. Her own eyes were large and bright as he clasped her to him, and his gentle kiss was long and lingering. And upsettingly thrilling.

She drew away, shaken.

"Remember you're saving yourself for marriage," he observed coolly and turned away. "Merry Christmas," he flung over his shoulder. "I'm off to visit the flesh-pots in the town."

With a pounding heart she watched him go, and jumped as she stuck her finger on the beautiful hat pin.

It looked lovely when she tried it on her hat before the cracked mirror in her room. And made her feel quite fashionable and wealthy. But the wealthy feeling was as nothing compared to the tremulous joy she had felt in Rhodes's arms.

With a frown, she took off the hat and stared into her own eyes in the mirror. They looked scared. Rhodes and she were fencing, and he was playing a waiting game. Now she asked herself, could she hold out?

Christmas Day dawned early for the staff. They were up long before sunrise, dusting, polishing, scraping, peeling, kneading. The kitchen was a beehive of activity from which they all came and went, for Clarissa had generously offered Roxanne's services to Mrs. Hollister.

The servants all gossiped about the gifts the Coulters had given each other. Roxanne was gratified to learn that while Gavin had sent Clarissa a Venetian hair net made of gold thread and mother-of-pearl from Boston, Rhodes had given Clarissa a hat pin of moonstone with a twist of gold. Privately she did not consider it nearly as attractive as the one he had given *her*, and was delighted. The absent Gavin had ignored the staff, Rhodes gave them all small gifts, and Clarissa gave Mrs. Hollister a fan and Roxanne a small lace collar. Joab Coulter gave his family checks in varying amounts and the staff small amounts of cash in sealed envelopes. Roxanne was very gratified to receive this small Christmas bonus, for it meant she could soon buy Mary Bridey the tea set she had in mind.

Clarissa spent a lot of time opening—and exclaiming over—gifts from her friends: an assortment of silver combs and Paris powder and scented notepaper and handsomely framed photos and fancy bottles of cologne. Roxanne hovered in the background, to take away the wrappings. But there was one large bouquet of hot-house roses, which arrived when the family were all gathered round their tree, that caused Clarissa to flash Rhodes a look of triumph. The roses were from an admirer and designed to make Rhodes jealous, Roxanne guessed. If so, they were lost on Rhodes, who was deep in serious conversation with his father. Clarissa frowned and thrust the roses at Roxanne with a curt command to put them in water.

Although Gavin remained in Boston, both Clarissa and Rhodes ate Christmas dinner at home with Joab. Mrs. Hollister complimented Roxanne on the table setting and peeked in, smiling, to watch the family enjoy their groaning board. The dinner began with Chesapeake Bay oysters and a rich soup, followed by black bass and broiled salmon. Then Greaves staggered in with the thirty-five-pound turkey on its huge silver platter, and Joab himself carved the bird with much ceremony. Roxanne had assisted in the preparation of the oyster stuffing, and its hot spicy aroma reminded her she'd been too busy to eat all day. There were candied sweet potatoes with marshmallows, tasty asparagus, quince preserves, pickles, aspic of lobster, a huge variety of hot rolls—and dessert was a flaming plum pudding in a footed silver bowl also triumphantly carried in by Greaves, while Roxanne trailed behind him carrying a baroque silver pitcher filled with thick hot wine sauce.

Roxanne, shuttling back and forth to the dining room, noticed that Clarissa only picked at her food and watched Rhodes pensively. Joab never ate much. Only Rhodes did justice to the dinner.

Afterward the staff enjoyed the same dinner, except for the wine, for it was a tradition at the Coulters' that on Christmas Day the servants should eat as well as their masters. Roxanne learned from Mrs. Hollister that this was an innovation of the Virginia Lady, Rhodes's mother.

On Christmas evening, having got Clarissa dressed and muffled in satin and furs for her latest ball, Roxanne slipped away, carrying a basket laden with all sorts of goodies from their Christmas dinner carefully wrapped in a linen napkin. Mary Bridey might not have their company, but she would certainly enjoy some of their dinner!

It had begun to snow again, lazily flaking down on the already white sidewalks, and the gold of the streetlights picked out groups of cold, red-nosed carolers, their heads wrapped in stocking caps and shawls, singing "God Rest Ye Merry Gentlemen" and "Hark, the Herald Angels Sing." Roxanne found herself blithely humming the ancient carols as she hurried along, the basket on her arm, looking into the brightly lit windows of the houses that displayed Christmas trees decked with popcorn and candy, and revealed happy children playing with newly received rocking horses and china-headed dolls.

How different was this Christmas from the last, she mused. Last Christmas she had been snowbound on the Kansas prairies, trapped in a cheerless house with sharp-faced Aunt Ada, looking out through frosted panes at a white undulating wasteland, wishing vainly for spring to come. Now she was walking in a new blue suit and the heavy shawl she had purchased with her own money, down the snowy streets of a great eastern city, carrying a basket of Christmas goodies to a friend. She smiled and her heart lightened.

It was with a brisk step that she arrived and knocked at the front door of the plain little brick row house.

After a time the door was opened by Mrs. Kaunas, the tall Lithuanian woman, who looked scared. "Bad

. . . very bad," she whispered, and motioned upstairs.

Roxanne flashed a look at her and flew up the steps where a grayhaired midwife answered her knock. "I don't think there's nothing I can do," she whined. "The baby won't come, it won't."

Fearfully, Roxanne stared past her. On the bed lay Mary Bridey, looking pitifully small. Her face was wet with perspiration, her hair hung damply to her face, and there were dark circles etched by pain under her eyes. Bravely she smiled at Roxanne.

"Mary Bridey." Roxanne dropped her basket and hurried over to her friend. "When did the pains begin?"

"I don't know," mumbled Mary Bridey. "Hours ago."

"Where is the doctor?" asked Roxanne impatiently.

"She called *me,* miss. She didn't call no doctor," interposed the midwife. She sounded vaguely indignant.

Mary Bridey's light damp fingers touched her arm. "I was trying so to save money, Roxanne. Sure I'll be needing it when the baby comes." Her voice ended in an anguished screech as she writhed on the bed, her body arched in pain.

Appalled, Roxanne watched as the agony subsided and Mary Bridey once again lay limp and perspiring and silent on the bed.

"Her's weakening," observed the midwife knowingly, rolling her eyes. "The baby will have to be took, that it will, since it ain't comin' natural."

If the midwife was right and the baby was lodged, they'd break Mary Bridey's pelvis bone in the delivery. That meant she'd most certainly die.

Galvanized into action, Roxanne cried, "I'll get the doctor. Where's the nearest one?"

"Corner house," mumbled the midwife. "That way." She pointed.

Roxanne sped from the room and downstairs to the snowy street. The plump little doctor in the house on the corner did not like to be wrested from his Christmas festivities with his family, but Roxanne's white face and broken-voiced pleas to come quickly changed his mind. Snatching up his black bag, he puffed along beside her, snapping questions.

From the street they could hear Mary Bridey's screams. The screams had ceased as they went up the stairs.

Hands twisted together, Roxanne stood back as the doctor examined Mary Bridey, who now lay exhausted and only half conscious. Roxanne wondered how anyone could be so cruel as to leave the little Irish girl to go through this alone.

"She's very weak," he said over his shoulder to Roxanne. "The child is lodged. I'll have to use instruments."

"Oh, no!" cried Roxanne.

He turned to give her a fierce look. "If I don't, this baby will surely die! It's a choice between the mother and the child!"

"Mary Bridey," cried Roxanne. "Tell him—"

From the bed the Irish girl raised a hand to quiet her. "Do . . . whatever you must, doctor," she whispered. "I want my baby to live."

Roxanne closed her eyes.

"Have you had any experience with this sort of thing?" asked the doctor.

Roxanne opened her eyes and shook her head.

"Then get out. Wait in the hall. Hester will help me." He indicated the midwife. "Hester, you should have called me sooner," he said grumpily.

"I didn't want to interrupt your Christmas," muttered Hester. "Bad enough I was called away from my family on Christmas Day, without you bein' called away too, Doctor."

Roxanne sat on the stairs while the thing was done. She pressed her hands to her ears to blot out Mary Bridey's agonized screams, and sobbed in sympathy. Silence came and Roxanne blessed chloroform. Rocking back and forth in misery, she railed inwardly at fate for letting this terrible thing happen, at all the Coulters for their hard hearts, and most particularly at Gavin, who must be made of stone. She blamed herself for not coming sooner, she blamed the stupid midwife for not calling the doctor, she blamed the doctor for not finding some better way . . . some sure way to save both mother and child.

Mrs. Kaunas offered her a cup of hot coffee, but Roxanne waved it away. Finally, the bedroom door opened and the midwife beckoned her inside. "No hope for either one," she mouthed at Rozanne.

Roxanne hurried past her. Limp and weak, Mary Bridey lay on the bed while the doctor tried vainly to staunch the bleeding. The Irish girl's thin face was very white, and growing whiter as her life's blood flowed away. "My . . . baby?" she whispered.

Roxanne cast a look at the doctor. He frowned and shook his head. Her gaze fell on the sad little bundle on the table. She moved her body so Mary Bridey might not see it and clasped the Irish girl's thin white hand in a firm reassuring grip. "Your baby's fine," she said sturdily. "You have a lovely son, Mary Bridey."

"You'll . . . tell him about the baby?" Though Mary Bridey's voice was a wisp, Roxanne had no doubt who was meant by *him*.

"He sent you word, Mary Bridey," she lied gently. "That's why I came. He was called away, but he sent word he loves you and he's coming for you."

"Oh, Roxanne . . ." Mary Bridey's tired half-closed eyes opened wide for a moment and their expression was glorious. "Is it really true?"

"Really true," said Roxanne, who'd been taught all liars went to hell. There was no hell so deep she wouldn't find some way to comfort Mary Bridey now. "He loves you, Mary Bridey. He always loved you."

The lashes fluttered down on Mary Bridey's thin white cheeks, the soft mouth no longer moved. A few minutes later, the doctor came and held a mirror to her lips. Roxanne looked away.

"She's gone," he said quietly, and disengaged Roxanne's fingers that still clung to the dead girl's hand as if to give her life. A little cry burst from Roxanne and she crumpled up.

"I was called too late," said the doctor severely, as if her cry was an implied criticism. "I should have been called weeks ago. There was nothing anyone could do. The baby was lodged—I had to break the pelvis bone." He looked at Roxanne's suffering white face and sighed. "Perhaps you could tell me where her family is, so they can be notified to make funeral arrangements. Hester tells me the woman downstairs won't be much help."

"They're somewhere in Ireland. I—I don't know where."

He pondered that. "I understand she was unmarried and had no money."

"That's true, but—I'll pay for her burial," said Roxanne staunchly.

The old doctor gave her a kindly look, which took in the cheap shawl and ready-made suit. "And have *you* any money?" he inquired.

Roxanne bit her lip. "I'm employed," she said stiffly. "I could make payments."

"No one will give you credit," he said. "Better let me handle this."

So gentle Mary Bridey, with her flowerlike face, would now be buried with her stillborn child in a pauper's grave. Roxanne felt sick. Through her tears, she cast a last look at that pale thin form and fled. On the way out she almost tripped over a chair on which were piled the bright patchwork quilt and the length of green calico Roxanne had given her. Roxanne swallowed. Those were the last bright colors Mary Bridey had ever seen. While the world made merry, she had died among strangers.

On the stairs Roxanne paused. Her heartsick gaze took in, through the open door downstairs in which the Lithuanian woman was silhouetted, the Christmas tree, trimmed with little straw bird cages, and the big fireplace where a Yule log burned bright. Log Evening . . . poor Mary Bridey's bright young life had burned out before the Yule log became an ember.

Mrs. Kaunas awkwardly patted Roxanne's shoulder and muttered something in her own tongue and then, eyes bright with tears, nodded upstairs and said in her thick accent ". . . like my own daughter."

At that Roxanne's own tears spilled over.

"Did he ever come to see her?" she choked.

"Who?" Mrs. Kaunas asked, puzzled.

"Gavin—Mr. Coulter."

"No one came. Only you."

Shaking her head, Roxanne turned away.

Out in the snow she trudged along, her numbed arm still carrying the basket. Unseeing, she marched past houses with lighted windows and Christmas holly on the door. Past a raucous group of carolers drinking hot rum and loudly singing "Deck the halls with boughs of holly," she hurried. On a downtown street she gave her basket of Christmas goodies away to a child who was selling paper flowers on a corner and looked hungry. The child eagerly pulled aside the napkin and sniffed. She gave Roxanne a blissful look and happily trotted home to share it with her family.

Roxanne could not bring herself to return to the Mt. Vernon Place house—home of the Coulters, of Gavin. She walked the streets until she was exhausted, and if Gavin had been there, she would certainly have done him bodily harm.

Grim-faced, staggering with fatigue, she reached the house as church bells were ringing. The servants were still up, making merry in the kitchen. Someone—Greaves, she guessed—had bought wine. Avoiding alike their proffers of wine and their questions, so as not to sadden the only party they were allowed all year, she hurried up the stairs, threw herself on her bed and wept for her sweet friend who had found death in Baltimore.

Chapter 12

The ice storm that sang and crackled and screamed after midnight, making cold creep in through the windowpanes, had left a frozen fairyland by morning. The trees were iced to miracles of crystal. Delicate icicles hung from the windows and fell to the glittering sheet of ice on the street below.

Taking a pan of salt to sprinkle on the front steps, Roxanne hurried outside eager to see all this beauty, but she slipped on the top step and hurtled painfully to the bottom. She managed to get up and went down again on its glittering surface. It was like walking on oiled glass. On her third try she stayed on her feet, retrieved the pan and brushed the salt across the steps, finishing the job she had been sent to do.

As she straightened up, listening to the musical tinkle as icicles snapped off in the bright sunlight and the icy coating of blowing branches cracked under the strain of the wind, she saw on a nearby bough a little frozen bird. For a moment, she stared at it and then, walking carefully, hurried inside, her happiness quenched.

Life was like that, she told herself fiercely. A frozen world where you couldn't keep your footing . . . where those you loved . . . died.

Somehow she got through that numbing Christmas week, with everyone around her busy and jolly, with Rhodes coming in late filled with holiday toddies, bawling out Christmas carols, and Clarissa in velvets and furs and jewels off to her endless parties and balls. Gradually, Roxanne's perspective was restored, the hurt partly healed. Mary Bridey's death had made her realize how fleeting life was. In her grief, she yearned to be comforted in the arms of a lover, and she also realized with force that once missed opportunities were forever gone, that the eyes that smiled into yours today would smile into another's tomorrow if . . . if you were fool enough to let them go.

She was thinking, of course, of Rhodes.

Gavin returned around the middle of January, but she could not speak to him. Keeping her eyes averted she pretended not to see him much of the time. It was the only way to hold her job, she told herself grimly, for she could not have brought herself to be civil just yet.

Ella's hand worsened and became infected. Mrs. Hollister said she would have to replace her, but Ella cried and said all her seven brothers and sisters depended on her. So Mrs. Hollister sighed and kept her on. Roxanne was glad, even though it made double duty for her and Tillie, who surreptitiously helped Roxanne do most of the jobs that Ella, with her painful bandaged hand, could not do.

February came and big Tillie announced that she was leaving soon to be married. Her husband-to-be, who worked on the docks, planned to leave the seashore and take her with him back to his father's little cottage in southern Maryland's tobacco country. As a wedding gift, Roxanne gave Tillie several rolls of wallpaper to brighten her bedroom there—they cost a nickel apiece, and Tillie was very grateful.

Ella's hand had mended at last, and she worked doubly hard to make Mrs. Hollister want to keep her. A big plodding immigrant girl who barely spoke English had applied for Tillie's job. Her world was changing, Roxanne thought; only Clarissa remained constant.

Rhodes was still readying the *Virginia Lass* for sea, and Gavin had gone to Boston again.

On one of her many errands for Clarissa, Roxanne passed Barrington's, and Denby ran out of the shop, evidently hoping to walk along with her. He was eager to see her again, but she put him off. Disappointed, he retreated, and she went on alone barely noticing either his presence or his absence. Her thoughts were only of Rhodes.

It was hard holding Rhodes off these days, for she had begun to desire him with an earthshaking force. When their hands met, when their eyes locked, what passed between them was sweet and almost painful, and it rocked her to her very toes.

She lived in constant fear that she would give in to him, that her insistent body would overpower her mind, and that she would become his mistress. And lose him finally, as Mary Bridey had lost Gavin? It was a thought not to be borne. She wanted Rhodes passionately, but she wanted him forever, held to her firmly by a narrow golden band, third finger, left hand.

At night she dreamed of herself in a drifting bridal veil, her face gleaming pale through the lace, and beside her Rhodes—tall, proud and self-confident, firmly taking her to wife. . . . Always the dream broke and faded, and in its place came vague nightmares where cold winds pursued her, and sometimes she woke and felt that cold clutch around her heart.

Casual, debonair and teasing, Rhodes seemed blithely unaware of the devastating effect he had on her, of the way he could rock the very earth beneath her feet just by the touch of his hand.

Soberly, she regarded her face in the mirror in her room, one bright February morning. What mattered a pretty face if it did no more than attract a man only to lose him? What mattered a sweet body if it were never clasped in the arms of a chosen lover?

Something fierce and elemental stirred in her. Love came before marriage, she told herself defiantly, just as justice came before law. And what were a few words spoken over her, after all? Rhodes was *hers*, hers by natural right—her chosen mate. And she would take him and hold him. Forever.

How to do that, she asked that lovely face that brooded back at her from the mirror. The answer that came back to her was purely feminine, old as Eve:

She would make him want her so much that he could not bear to lose her. She knew she had a beautiful body. She knew that Rhodes desired her. And she would use that beautiful passionate body of hers to fan the flame of his desire into a forest fire. He would hold her, caress her, savor her sweetness. His strong hands would cup her chin as his green eyes looked deep into hers finding love and affection there. His strong hands would cup her delicately molded breasts as his head bent so his lips could tenderly nuzzle them. Oh, how she would respond to him! Her eyes gleamed with anticipation. He would find her not a cringing virgin, but a woman of storm-swept passions.

He would find her . . . not a virgin at all.

For a moment the thought shook her—but only for a moment. Rhodes did not seek virginity in a woman—he was off to the fleshpots of the town, hadn't he said? For the moment she would push marriage from her mind. She was content to be his mistress, to share his life.

With a sigh she leaned on her arms and smiled at that lovely face in the mirror. The face smiled back winsomely. *Tonight*, she told herself. Tonight, she would melt into his arms and the flame would burn so bright he would forget all other women and desire only her.

She would bind him to her with passion.

All day she thought of it, blundering through her work, dropping things, forgetting tasks. Clarissa was astonished and indignant when Roxanne actually stepped on the hem of her train, tearing it. She whirled about and screamed at Roxanne, but Roxanne hardly heard her. Her head was awhirl. Tonight she would be held in the arms of her lover and taste the golden pleasures of love, one by one. She could hardly wait. When at dinner she dropped the heavy soup tureen on the kitchen floor—fortunately it didn't break—and all the staff stared at her aghast, she blithely ignored Mrs. Hollister's scolding and Cook's shouted curses. Tonight . . . tonight she would be his, her heart sang. And after tonight everything would be different. She would belong to Rhodes. She would go where he went. She would follow him to the ends of the earth. And what would soup tureens matter then?

After dinner, she changed into her blue suit and the new ruffled blouse, brushed her hair till it gleamed and pinned it up carefully. Rhodes had gone up to his room to dress, she guessed, for an evening on the town. A roistering evening, as it seemed all his evenings were these days. When she heard his light step descending the stair, she stepped quickly out of the shadows of the servants' wing and confronted him on the landing.

He looked very imposing tonight, she thought, with his black three-button cutaway coat which fit his arrogant shoulders so jauntily. Black trousers encased his narrow hips and long muscular legs and broke slightly over his feet. A frosty expanse of white shirt, a vest and a tall detachable collar that reached to his square jawline completed the ensemble. In his tie was stuck a horseshoe tiepin with a single ruby. Smiling, his green eyes considered her too.

"You're looking very fetching tonight," he murmured, and sweeping off his hat, he bent down to kiss her. "Ah, Roxanne, Roxanne," he sighed, his voice muffled deep in her piled-up hair, "must you be so set on marriage?"

If she had had any doubts, as he took her in his arms, they were swept away. Take tonight! her heart cried. Forget your scruples and your fears—take tonight!

She stirred in his arms. Her voice was dreamy. "Rhodes . . . Rhodes, I want you to take me to the *Virginia Lass*."

He held her off from him in surprise. "Now? To-night?"

She nodded, her sapphire eyes burning blue in the gaslight. Her voice was soft and caressing, light as gossamer. "Because it's your ship, Rhodes. I want to belong to you *there*."

For a moment he gazed into those sapphire eyes for confirmation. It was there in her steady blue gaze.

He needed no further encouragement. Downstairs and out the front door he swept her, and into his waiting carriage. He shook the reins and wheeled the horse around the corner, and they reached the docks at a gallop. He's hurrying before I change my mind! thought Roxanne, amused. As if I would! With a luxurious sigh, she leaned her body against him, cuddling into the warm circle of his arm. Her thoughts had a bright glaze, just as the buildings they clattered by seemed to have a glow in the moonlight. This was so right, so right. . . . She loved him, she would not deny him. He was hers by natural right—as she was his; so it would be.

Roxanne was trembling as she stepped into the little rowboat and saw, at anchor across the glittering dark water, the tall furled sails of the *Virginia Lass*, riding in the fitful moonlight. She was aware of Rhodes's compelling gaze, from eyes brilliant yet shadowed in his dark face. As he rowed, his strong muscles rippled beneath his coat, attesting to his powerful physique. When they arrived at the ship, he "ahoyed" the watch and helped Roxanne up the ship's ladder.

On deck, she looked about her dreamily. A lovers' setting, she thought: the creak of the great ship, so eager to be off and away, its tall masts casting their lean shadows across the clean-scoured deck. The salt wind blew tendrils of Roxanne's fair hair around her face. It was unseasonably warm for February, a false taste of spring to come. Here in the sighing winds, as she listened to the faint creak as the ship rode restlessly at anchor, the voice of her heart was louder than the voice of her conscience, the voice of reason. Her joy fluttered and expanded as the sails would billow when the tall ship took to the sea, and around her the anchored ships were mysterious hulking shapes in the night, spice laden, bound for romantic lands.

She smiled up at Rhodes, a slow lovely smile, and in silent answer to those hot green eyes that held hers, took out the pins from her hair, letting it cascade around her shoulders in pale moon-washed loveliness. She looked up at him with parted lips, and the midnight sky was no deeper than the depths of her eyes.

"Roxanne," he said in a husky voice, and gathered her to him. His lips brushed her ear and her shining hair, wandered over her high arched brows and touched her long silken lashes, caressed her hot cheeks, and found her lips in a long lingering kiss.

That kiss had in it tenderness and love—the love of a man for his mate. Roxanne felt that tenderness, that yearning reach out to her through the gentleness of his caressing lips, the warmth of his embrace, and she surged toward him with a broken cry, flinging her arms around his neck. Her knees felt weak. Here was the lover she had waited for, here to take and hold her.

"Rhodes," she whispered. "Rhodes."

"Let's go to my cabin," he murmured against the perfume of her hair.

"Yes. Oh, yes."

Snapping out a curt order to the watch, Rhodes swung her up in his arms and smiled down at her. There was a glory in his face tonight, she thought. As if he felt it too, this sweet wild magic that had enveloped them. And she was content to rest in those arms, to feel against her breast the strong rhythmic beat of his powerful heart. She felt the buttons of his coat dig into her soft flesh as with long strides he carried her to his cabin, kicked open the door with his foot and took her inside.

The cabin was lit only by moonlight. And in her heart she felt she had been carried across a threshold—

just like a bride in a trailing white veil. Her breath sobbed in her throat as she felt her body being gently lowered onto his bunk. With a broken sigh she relaxed and let his lips blot out reality as he lowered his body onto her own.

His hands were moving now . . . caressingly. Along her pulsing white throat, across her tingling bosom. He was unfastening the lacy ruffles at her throat and undoing her bodice. Her trembling hands reached up to help him and he laughed deep in his throat, a triumphant laugh that thrilled her. Now his hands were questing inside her bodice, finding her breasts, which sprang to vibrant life at his touch. She lay there quivering as those strong hands caressed her, aching for him, dreamily expectant of the moment when he would take her and make her his own.

She sighed and closed her eyes and gave herself up to love.

Suddenly, there was a noise outside the door and Rhodes's head went up sharply, to listen. Her own eyes snapped open as she heard running footsteps and a pounding on the cabin door.

"Mr. Rhodes!" It was Greaves's voice, sounding excited. "Mr. Rhodes, it's your father, sir. He's been taken bad, and the doctor's been called. Mrs. Hollister said I should find you, sir, and I didn't know where else to look—"

With an oath, Rhodes landed on the cabin floor with both feet, fastening his trousers as he did so. "Wait here," he muttered. "I'll be back."

"No." Confused and shaken, Roxanne sat up. She did not want to be left on the ship to wait and wonder. They had been so close . . . her heart still beat too fast. Had Greaves waited only a little while, their love would have been consummated and then—then she would have waited for him anywhere. But now she knew this cabin would seem cold without him. "No, I'll go with you," she said hastily, her feet finding the floor as she fumbled with her bodice.

"As you like," he said tersely. "Hurry."

With nervous fingers, embarrassed now, she managed to dress while Rhodes waited impatiently. "You're dressed," he said. "Come on."

"My hair!" she cried. "I can't go out with it streaming down like this!"

"Let it go," he said impatiently. "You can pin it up on the way home."

"Yes, all right," she said. After all, his father might be dying.

Greaves was apologetic. He did not seem particularly surprised to see Roxanne. Her face flooded with color as she realized that Greaves—and probably the rest of the staff—already believed her to be Rhodes's mistress. They got into the small boat in which Greaves had rowed out to the ship.

"I hope we're in time, sir," Greaves said anxiously. "Mrs. Hollister thought we should hurry."

"What happened?" demanded Rhodes. "He was all right at dinner."

"It happened later, sir. He had these sharp pains around his heart, sir, and he called me and said, 'Greaves, you'd best get the doctor,' and clutched his chest. The pain got so bad he could not speak, sir."

Rhodes cursed under his breath. "I hope you went for the doctor first," he cried, "before you came looking for me?"

"Oh, yes, sir." Greaves bobbed his head earnestly. "I brought the doctor to the house myself, and then Mrs. Hollister said I should find you, sir. I asked at one or two of your regular"—he coughed and gave Roxanne an unhappy look—"and they said you might be here, sir," he added weakly.

"You did right, Greaves," approved Rhodes. "Here, man, give me an oar and we'll get there faster."

Ashore, they hurried into the carriage that had brought them, while Greaves returned in the horse-drawn hack that he had hired. Roxanne rode beside Rhodes in silence, her heart a shambles. Now she was pressed against him. His arm was thrown carelessly around her and her right breast rested tinglingly against his forearm. Every time the carriage jolted over the uneven street she felt her breast bounce against him, felt the slight pressure as he held her more securely. She was half suffocated with desire—and with something else: anxiety. She was convinced that Joab Coulter was not Rhodes's father—whether he knew it or not—and somewhere, dimly, she perceived a threat in that: a threat to Rhodes.

They found the place in turmoil when they arrived. The whole household was up and gaslights burned everywhere, announcing something extraordinary had happened. Mrs. Hollister, pale and distracted, met them at the door.

"Doctor's with him," she reported, and then her voice broke. "Oh, Mr. Rhodes!"

"There, there, Holly." Rhodes patted the housekeeper's plump shoulders and the little woman collapsed against him. "He's a stout fellow; no need to cry over him yet."

She gave him a look of such trust and confidence that Roxanne was moved. Then Mrs. Hollister stepped back, dabbing at her eyes. "You'll want to go in to see him," she said more calmly. "Mr. Gavin's there."

Rhodes said sharply, "Gavin's back?"

"Yes, sir. He arrived right after you left."

Rhodes's eyes narrowed.

As if hearing his name mentioned, Gavin came out of the room. He looked tall and very elegant. His arrogant gait was arrested and his eyes widened as he saw Roxanne standing close beside Rhodes, her ruffled collar askew, her blouse unevenly buttoned, her hair in disarray and long blond streamers of it cascading down the shoulders of her blue suit. Startled comprehension flooded his face, and Roxanne's own face turned a guilty scarlet that he should see her this way. She wanted to run upstairs, but she also wanted very much to know if Rhodes's father was going to die. If he died, it could make a difference, overturn everything. Rhodes would be his own man then. He would be free to marry her, if he chose. For she knew that Joab Coulter would consider Rhodes's wild life climaxed in shame if he married one of the housemaids, and that he would disinherit him without a qualm.

So she stood, disheveled but reluctant to move, while Rhodes strode into the big bedroom and shut the door behind him. Greaves motioned to Mrs. Hollister that he wished to speak with her, and the housekeeper accompanied him into the long dining room and shut the door.

That left Gavin alone with Roxanne in the front hall.

"How—how is he?" she asked.

"Well enough," said Gavin. "He'll survive. But it gave us all a bad scare. *Angina pectoris*, the doctor says; he must keep out of the cold winter winds."

She gave a sigh of relief. Whatever she'd been thinking, she didn't want the man who called himself Rhodes's father to die.

Now Gavin advanced upon her, his eyes narrowing. Roxanne stood her ground defiantly. She belonged to Rhodes; Gavin might as well face it.

"I might have known," he murmured heavily, looking down at her with angry eyes. "Rhodes. . . ."

She lifted her chin.

A smile twisted his saturnine features. "Rhodes is a ladies' man," he mused in a low contemptuous tone. "I always have company matters to keep me occupied. What chance have I to compete against him?" She flinched as Gavin reached out and gently fingered a golden strand of her hair. "I hoped to waken that look in your eyes myself, Roxanne," he murmured sadly. "I am away too much, though I thought your prim self-righteousness would make you proof against him. But I see I was wrong—you've been able to forgive my brother his little indiscretions."

Some warning bell tolled within her.

"What . . . indiscretions?"

His dark brows elevated. "Why, poor Mary Bridey, of course."

"Mary Bridey?" she whispered incredulously.

"Of course," he said. "I found the poor girl a place to stay because Rhodes had left her in the lurch. But

Mary Bridey was Rhodes's paramour, not mine. I thought you knew that by now."

She felt as if she'd been slammed into a stone wall. Rhodes . . . it was Rhodes who'd seduced Mary Bridey, who'd gotten her in the family way and let her have her baby alone, let her die alone. . . . She remembered that Mary Bridey had never actually named the father; they'd always delicately said *he*. But Mary Bridey had said wistfully, "And he's back now, isn't he?" She hadn't meant Gavin back from Boston—*she'd meant Rhodes back from the seven seas!* It was so plain, and it struck Roxanne with such force that she swayed. But when Gavin reached out to catch her, fearing she might fall, she brushed away his hand and stared at him, stunned.

"I've upset you," he muttered. "Come with me into the dining room, Roxanne. That door could open, and my father mustn't hear what I've got to say."

Mechanically her feet carried her into the dining room. Her world seemed slanted, crooked, the pieces of her life slipping crazily this way and that. It couldn't be true, she told herself wildly, that Rhodes—Rhodes, who was everything to her—had callously seduced and then deserted that sweet little Irish girl. Why, he was—he was directly responsible for Mary Bridey's death!

She was dimly aware that they were in the dining room now, that she was leaning against the hard edge of the table and Gavin was speaking.

"Get hold of yourself, Roxanne," he said in a concerned voice. "I wouldn't have broken it to you like this. I thought you knew. Everyone else does. Do you want some brandy?"

She shook her head numbly.

"When I saw you standing there looking rumpled, it came over me: Now he's gotten her too. . . ."

She flinched, her mind in turmoil. "I'm not his mistress, if that's what you're thinking," she choked. "We haven't—I've never—" she floundered and broke off before the light that flared up in his eyes. "I'm sorry," she mumbled, "for the way I've treated you. I thought—"

"Ah, I'm well aware what you thought. It isn't the first time I've let people think ill of me on my brother's behalf. But you . . ." There was a bittersweet note in his voice now. "I wanted *you* to think better of me than that, Roxanne."

She stared at him, her heart only half-accepting what he was saying. "Your brother should take the consequences for his own deeds," she said bitterly.

"Like enough you're right," he said indifferently. "But I'm older, and Rhodes—well, in some ways he's more like a son to me than a brother. I've always felt responsible for him. And since my father insists on regarding Rhodes as the devil himself, I try to shield Father from knowledge of certain—ah—transgressions."

"That's very decent of you, Gavin," Roxanne said, her blue eyes dark and unhappy.

He looked troubled. "I've talked rather freely to you, Roxanne. I wouldn't want this to go any further. No—" He held up his hand sternly at her indignation. "No, let's not worry about my reputation. It is what it is. But if Rhodes crosses my father one more time with his merry ways . . ."

"What then?" she asked alertly.

"Even I wouldn't be able to shield him," he sighed. "Father will disown him. I wouldn't want that to happen, Roxanne."

She subsided, biting her lip. "Your father is right about him!" she said reluctantly. "Rhodes is a devil!"

The smile that broke over his face was like sunshine. "I suppose I wanted to hear you say that," he admitted.

"The truth should always be known," cried Roxanne, and caught herself up short. Wasn't she too living a lie? And didn't Rhodes have the power to bring her house down at any time? Ah, but she had harmed no one, she told herself. She'd merely taken a ticket and a letter the owner would no longer be needing, and assumed another woman's identity for no evil purpose. But poor Mary Bridey . . .

She seethed inwardly, hands clenched. She could hardly wait to accuse Rhodes!

"Say nothing to Rhodes," warned Gavin sternly, guessing her intention. "You'll only bring out his nasty side. It won't change anything, but he'll be angry that I told you. He'll storm about and make a loud scene—oh, you've never seen him that way; he's putting his best foot forward now. But a stormy scene right now could kill my father."

"I'll wait till he's away from the house!" cried Roxanne.

"No, he'll only come looking for me and the result will be the same. Promise me, Roxanne!"

Her face was haggard. She wavered.

"Promise!" he repeated sternly.

"All right, I promise!" she cried hoarsely and flung away from him.

He stood and watched her go, a melancholy half smile upon his face.

Upstairs she threw herself down on her narrow bed and wept . . . for Rhodes, for young love, for all that could never be.

And then she sat up and dried her eyes and stared into the dark, hugging her arms around her, and a coldness such as she had never known closed around her heart.

After a while she heard Rhodes's step on the stair, heard his soft knock, and when she didn't answer, his insistent "Roxanne."

"Go away," she said harshly.

He hesitated, and then after a moment she heard his retreating footsteps.

She lay there, shivering, wanting him, staring into the dark, and all the while that icy cold feeling gripped her heart.

Chapter 13

The next morning Roxanne, tired and heavy-eyed, brushed by Rhodes as if she did not see him. He frowned.

"Roxanne, I *had* to return last night!" he cried. "My father could have been dying!"

"What you do is your own business," she said crisply. "And no affair of mine."

He regarded her with a puzzled look, but she had no intention of explaining. How dare he act so innocent!

Gavin strolled by. "Are you keeping Roxanne from her work again?" he asked in a bored voice.

Rhodes straightened up, an angry light appearing in his green eyes. "Not any more," he said curtly, and turned on his heel and left.

Roxanne wondered if, now that she no longer noticed him, Rhodes would sail away. But even there she was wrong—that he had not remained in port for her sake was obvious, since he continued to stay even though she ignored him.

Clarissa's complacent manner indicated that she felt Rhodes had stayed because of *her*. And he did begin to squire Clarissa about more often, but Roxanne noted that he had a preoccupied look about him.

On a fine winter day when the weather was crystal clear, as Roxanne helped Clarissa dress to go out with Rhodes, Clarissa unbent a little and began talking to her—as she had once doubtless talked to Mary Bridey.

"New York," Clarissa said, turning to view her reflection in the mirror, "is the only place to live, Roxanne."

"Why?" muttered Roxanne, her fingers busy tying a grosgrain bow at Clarissa's elbow—which presented a moving target.

Clarissa shrugged loftily. "Oh, it's all *there*, Roxanne—Delmonico's and the shopping, the theater and all those wonderful mansions that line Fifth Avenue."

Roxanne finished tying the bow and stepped back. "Do you think you'll get there?" Normally she would not have asked, but Clarissa was in an expansive mood today.

"Oh, yes," said Clarissa confidently. "Rhodes will take me there. He'll have everything—after he's inherited, of course," she added hastily.

Roxanne stared. "But what about Gavin? Do you mean his father won't leave Gavin anything?"

Clarissa shrugged and gave Roxanne a sulky look. "Well, I don't know why he should," she said. "Rhodes's mother was the heiress—not Gavin's. The Coulter shipping fortune was really built with her money. Of course it will go to Rhodes!"

Because you want it to, surmised Roxanne shrewdly, her lips curling in a slightly contemptuous smile. "I thought Rhodes's father didn't approve of him," she murmured.

"That's only temporary," said Clarissa airily. "He'll approve of Rhodes—after he marries *me*."

Roxanne could see that he might. After Clarissa had gone, Roxanne sat and stared out the window at the wintry street, and her face was sober. Clarissa had an impeccable background, with ancestors who'd come swashbuckling into Maryland in earliest days. Clarissa's people, who now lay buried beneath moss-covered stones overrun with myrtle and ivy, had walked under the Wye Oak—and in their day they had ruled their corner of the earth.

What chance had a dispossessed child of the Old South against the fortunate Clarissas of the world? All she had to offer was a pretty face. . . .

Suddenly Roxanne lifted her head and frowned. That was nonsense! She was as pretty as Clarissa—prettier! She had as good an education and better manners. All she needed was an equal chance!

But . . . how to get that equal chance, that was the problem.

Later that week, Denby came by to deliver, personally, five pairs of the new slip-on gloves Clarissa had ordered. At the door, he asked for "Miss Roxanne, Miss Clarissa Calvert's personal maid." He handed the gloves to Roxanne with much ceremony in the front hall. Roxanne, whose hands were still damp from washing out Clarissa's dainty French underthings, would have asked him to sit down on a rosewood chair, but Greaves was watching with raised eyebrows from the open door of Joab Coulter's bedroom.

"I would like very much, Miss Roxanne, to see you again," Denby said in a low intense voice.

She was touched. "As you can see, I do not have a front parlor in which to receive callers," she said wryly, remembering Kansas and Mr. Witherspoon.

"I would be very pleased to call for you in a carriage," Denby said gravely. "And to take you any place you desire. A play perhaps? A vaudeville show?"

Roxanne, who never went anywhere except on trolleys or on her own feet now that she had broken with Rhodes, smiled at him.

"I should like that very much," she said slowly.

Denby's face lit up radiantly. "Tomorrow night?" She nodded.

And so the lady's maid and the glover's son began

doing the town in the evening. Denby was good company; he strove to be. His quips were from the latest musical comedies. The tunes he hummed were the hits of vaudeville. He told Roxanne proudly he had gone to New York last winter to buy some materials for his father's shop, and while dining at Luchow's he had seen the famous actress Lillian Russell and the big spender Diamond Jim Brady. He told her Lillian Russell pedaled down Fifth Avenue on a silver bicycle, and that she owned hundreds of pairs of gloves, some single pairs of which cost more than a whole year's wardrobe for an average woman.

In a hired carriage, Denby took her to see Fort McHenry, whose five-pointed design had given it the name "the Star Fort." The fifteen stars and fifteen stripes that had flown over it in 1814 had inspired Francis Scott Key to write "The Star Spangled Banner." They dismissed the cab and walked in Druid Hill Park, which had been the great estate of Nicholas Rogers.

On the way back, under the pale winter sun, Denby tried to kiss her. Roxanne resisted, and instantly he dropped his arms.

"You must forgive me, Miss Roxanne," he said earnestly. "I was carried away by your beauty: It goes to a man's head, it does."

"That's all right, Denby," she said, smoothing her skirts. "I just—"

"I know," he interrupted, with a look of great wisdom. "You must save your kisses for the man you marry. I understand."

That was not what she had been about to say. She had not kissed Denby because she was not sure how she felt about the young glover.

But she was guiltily sure of how she still felt about Rhodes.

Her mind was concentrating on that when Denby said, "I would like to take you to church on Sunday, Miss Roxanne, and bring you home with me afterward, to meet my family and have Sunday dinner with us."

Roxanne muttered a preoccupied yes, just as if he had asked her to go to a concert. Much later she realized that if he wanted her to meet his family, it probably meant that Denby was going to propose. She considered making an excuse but decided it would hurt his feelings; she'd have to let him propose and then say no as gently as possible. He had her regard—but only as a friend; somehow she must make that clear.

Sunday dawned clear and cold with a slushy snow on the sidewalk. Denby called for her in a hired carriage, but he did not take her to the small church near his home that his family attended. Instead, beneath a gray sky he took her to the flashier Mt. Vernon Place Methodist Church. Its exterior was of native greenstone, which Denby—ever ready with a fact or statistic—told her came from the Bare Hills Quarry of Baltimore County. Roxanne looked up at the contrasting reddish sandstone of its great arch and rose window and tall gingerbready spire, and made appropriate admiring noises, though she had attended the church before.

Denby looked pleased and together they went inside to hear the sermon. Roxanne prayed for Mary Bridey, wherever she might be, for Julie and Buck—and for her own soul for leading Denby on, a man she never meant to marry.

When they came outside, Denby handed her into the carriage with aplomb. As they rode toward his home, Roxanne mentioned the White Train, which Gavin had described, and relayed Gavin's description of its wonders.

"*I* will take you riding on the White Train, Roxanne," cried Denby in a vibrating voice, his face flushed. "I know you see me only as a person whose family has a flourishing business, but someday I am going to be very rich. I will have my own shop and I will take you anywhere you care to go."

Her throat closed up at this boyish declaration, and she patted Denby's hand. She felt like a traitor, in love with rakehell Rhodes and riding along primly in a jouncing carriage beside Denby.

From their expressions it was easy to tell how his family felt about her. Denby's father, a square sturdy quiet man, obviously liked her. As did Denby's older brother, whose admiring eyes followed her about. But the women—Denby's mother and two sisters—were set solidly against her. They were all slender and had pale hazel eyes like Denby's, and their smiles seemed pasted on their hostile faces.

At dinner, which was served in the small comfortable dining room of the large apartment they occupied over the shop, Denby's mother pursed her lips and inquired about Roxanne's family. Roxanne suddenly realized with a jolt that she was Roxanne Willis to these people, and said vaguely they were from San Francisco.

"*That*," said Denby's mother heavily, giving Roxanne a penetrating look over the stewed chicken, "is a very long way away." Her scathing tone indicated that it was too far away for Roxanne's antecedents to be properly checked. Roxanne was painfully aware that while she, with her people's genteel plantation background, might look down on those who lived over shops, they looked down on her as a lady's maid and not good enough for their son.

It was at once apparent that Denby was the darling of his mother and sisters. The youngest, he was definitely a pet, and all deferred to his whims. His older brother seemed reconciled to this, and his father, sturdy and quiet, seemed to care little about what went on. All the men lit pipes or cigars after dinner, making the living room blue with smoke.

On the way home, Denby told Roxanne that his father had insisted on both his sons smoking, since he had heard it would help them avoid the dreaded consumption from which two of his uncles had died.

"And your mother and sisters?" wondered Roxanne, who had not heard of this before. "Doesn't he fear for them also?"

Denby gave her a shocked look. "Ladies don't smoke,

Miss Roxanne!" he cried. "Why, I read in the papers that a woman was arrested for smoking on the streets of New York!"

Denby read tabloids, she knew. His conversation was sprinkled with such trivia.

Masterfully, he drew the horses to a stop on a side street and asked Roxanne if the blanket tucked around her skirts was warm enough. Roxanne nodded.

"Your mother and sisters don't like me," she murmured, in an effort to forestall what she guessed would be a proposal.

"That does not matter to me." He looked intensely into her eyes. "What matters is, do you like me, Miss Roxanne?"

"Yes, of course I do, Denby, but their opinion should matter to you. They love you very much."

He made an impatient gesture. "They think I'm a baby! Always giving me advice, fussing over me! Miss Roxanne, I think you know why I brought you to meet my family, what I'm going to ask you."

"Yes," she said hopelessly, beginning to feel the cold creeping in around the blanket over her knees. She shivered.

"You're cold!" he cried, and put an arm around her.

"It is cold," said Roxanne, feeling desperate. "Denby, I think we should drive on. The horse must be freezing. He should be stabled."

"The horse?" Denby gave her an odd look. "I'm asking you to marry me, Miss Roxanne. To share my life."

"You're very sweet, Denby," she said slowly. "But—but I'm not ready to marry anyone just yet."

"I'll wear you down!" he cried. "I'll bring you flowers and take you dancing! I'll sweep you off your feet!"

At just that moment one of the new conveyances, an automobile, roared up the street behind them, and their horse snorted and began to prance with fear. The automobile backfired and Denby was hard-put to keep the horse from panicking. As it passed, Roxanne saw there were four people in it, two men and two women. All were laughing gaily.

In the back seat, leaning back with his arm around a pretty girl wearing a beaver-trimmed hat and muff, sat Rhodes.

Roxanne's cold fingers clenched in the white kid gloves Denby had given her. Absorbed in their laughter, the auto-riding merrymakers had not seen the couple seated in the carriage.

Impulsively Roxanne threw her arms about Denby and kissed him. Taken by surprise, he dropped the reins and clutched her. His lips were warm, almost tremulous. At last she pulled away, her face flushed, and saw that he was pale and shaken.

"Miss Roxanne," he stammered, "does this mean . . ."

Sanity came back to Roxanne. Denby was nice; she must not hurt him.

"Take me home," she said gently. "We'll talk again later, Denby."

Looking blissful, Denby delivered her to the Coulters' house. She slipped away quickly before he could kiss her again.

Chapter 14

Roxanne began using excuses to avoid seeing Denby: headaches, other pressing engagements, work. She knew it was craven of her, but she just couldn't bring herself to break his heart by telling him they could never be more than friends.

Now, because she was avoiding Denby, she found herself in the house more. She felt trapped there, weighed down by the overwhelming presence of the Coulter men: Rhodes—silently demanding; Gavin—waiting; old Joab—disapproving and querulous.

Rhodes's light flirtation with Clarissa had ended, and Clarissa was back with the numerous swains she had dated before. They called for her at the house, in surreys, in buggies, even in the new noisy horseless carriages. When Clarissa was home, she flounced about and was short-tempered with Roxanne, ordering her around, finding fault. Roxanne, preoccupied with her own problems, went about her duties mechanically, hardly noticing Clarissa's bad temper.

Rhodes left her alone. He spoke to her pleasantly as he passed; occasionally, he smiled at her—and on those occasions she turned away lest he should read desire in her eyes. At dinner his eyes sometimes followed her about.

Clarissa noticed this and was piqued.

"Don't lace your waist so tightly," she scolded Roxanne. "It makes you look too—too conspicuous at dinner."

Roxanne was astonished. "But I don't lace at all," she protested. "I don't even own a corset!"

Clarissa stared. And then her expression grew resentful. "I wouldn't feel dressed without my corset!" she cried passionately, and ordered Roxanne to help out in the laundry.

As the days passed, Roxanne realized that Rhodes had not given up his courtship of her—he had only postponed it. Apparently he was convinced that her rejection of him was based on pique at being so nearly bedded and then abruptly routed out and returned to the house. He courted her in a dozen merry ways: with a quick good-humored smile and a cheerful word as he passed; by being thoughtful of her at dinner and other times—even coming up to her in the street to help her in with her heavy market baskets; by tipping his hat and stopping his carriage for her, or catching up with her in the park and walking along talking to her, even though she kept her head down and marched along in silence.

Evidently his plan was to wear her down—and it was working.

Looking into those reckless green eyes that seemed so candid and open, she found it harder and harder to believe that Rhodes had callously left Mary Bridey to die while he distributed Christmas gifts. There must have been some misunderstanding, she told herself. Was it possible that Gavin had found Mary Bridey her new place and had not acquainted Rhodes with that fact? Was it possible that Rhodes, returning, thought Mary Bridey had departed for places unknown? Could the poor girl have sat and waited for a lover who would have come, but had no idea where to find her?

All these excuses she found for Rhodes—and more. It was possible, she told herself, that he never knew about Mary Bridey's condition at all. Perhaps no one had told him. Would he then be so to blame?

But her heart was reluctant to know the truth, so she did not do what she could have done without breaking her promise to Gavin—she did not ask Greaves or Cook or Mrs. Hollister. Instead she kept a brooding silence, and each day softened toward Rhodes.

She was on the point of forgiving him when one night, she heard the footsteps that Mrs. Hollister had warned her about.

It happened after a day in which Clarissa had been particularly difficult. Roxanne had gone to bed exhausted right after clearing up the dinner dishes. She had hurried up the back stairs to the second floor in order to avoid Rhodes, who might be lingering in the hall waiting for her. She'd had no mind to see him tonight, for tired as she was, she was afraid she might give in to him, rest her head on his shoulder, close her eyes and let him comfort her.

When she awoke it was dark, and she realized it was late, for the moon was high. Outside her door, coming from the direction of the stair landing she heard stealthy footsteps.

Roxanne sat up alertly. That was not Rhodes's bounding step or Gavin's precise one on the stair. Greaves would have no reason to come upstairs this time of night, nor the other servants. The footsteps were going up to the fourth floor, of that she was certain. She lay there wondering. One of the maids, no doubt, summoned to an evening's frivolity in a big square bed on the fourth floor. But *whose* bed, Gavin's or Rhodes's?

Surely it could not be two-hundred-pound Cook or Jane, the heavyset unattractive Lizzie, or the plodding girl who had been hired when Tillie left to be married. Ella, perhaps? Though mousy, little Ella had definite possibilities; her clothes were shapeless, but she might have a pretty figure under them—who could tell?

An hour passed as Roxanne lay there sleepless, and then she heard the stealthy footsteps coming downstairs again. Her curiosity overwhelmed her. She had to know which maid it was; then tomorrow she could begin to watch and decide which bed the girl had slept in.

Quietly, she eased her door open and on bare feet tiptoed up the dark steps from the servants' quarters to the main landing.

Clarissa, her auburn hair a tumbled mass about her shoulders, was coming down the stairs. She was wearing a very fetching nightgown, the top of which was undone to reveal most of her breasts in the gaslight. When she saw Roxanne she clutched her trailing satin and lace dressing gown about her, and for a moment her eyes widened in horror; then she got control of herself.

"What are you doing up?" she snapped. And before Roxanne could answer, "Get to bed!"

Silently Roxanne turned away, but her world was cartwheeling about her head. Reba had said she would bet Clarissa had tried out Rhodes's big square bed! No doubt Clarissa was planning to make sure that Rhodes stayed with her, as she herself had thought to do. Or that he took her with him when he left.

Dull pains knifed through Roxanne's heart at this new treachery. Rhodes, merry Rhodes, was dallying with Clarissa in his bedroom by night even while by day he pursued Roxanne. Oh, she had been right about him—right!

Roxanne clenched her fist and a sob escaped her. How she hated herself for loving him. Why couldn't she hate him—instead of eagerly waiting each day to see his face?

As she crawled back into bed she thought she heard the front door open. And then light footsteps on the stairs—Rhodes's footsteps. No, it must be Gavin, she told herself. Clarissa would not have slipped up to Gavin's room when she was madly in love with Rhodes.

The next night Rhodes came into the dining room just as Roxanne finished cleaning up. Nobody was around, and although she tried to avoid him, he moved too fast and blocked the kitchen door with his big body. She turned about to go the other way, but he caught her lightly by the shoulders.

"Roxanne," he murmured.

She flinched away from him and stood stiff and immobile in his grip with her head turned away. But his lips caressed her hair, found her ear, worried it. He pressed his teeth lightly into her earlobe, and she heard him chuckle.

"Don't," she said sharply and drew away from him. "I don't wish to be one of your women!"

He spun her toward him merrily, so that she was brought up against his strong chest. "Ah, now, don't tell me there's someone else," he chided. "Not, for instance, my brother Gavin?" His face clouded a little when she didn't answer. "I'm a far nicer fellow," he said softly, his index finger exploring her neck, wandering down her bosom.

"That's a matter of opinion," said Roxanne haughtily, slapping his hand away and trying to struggle from his grasp.

Though his hands dropped to his sides, still he blocked her way. "Then it *is* Gavin . . ." he murmured. "Surely you're not thinking that Gavin's the marrying kind?"

"And why not?" she demanded.

He sighed. "Foolish Roxanne," he said. "Gavin will marry for advantage. He's got the future of the company to think of."

"You're wrong," she said flatly, just for the pleasure of contradicting him. "You don't know Gavin at all."

He stared down at her flushed rebellious face. "Perhaps I don't," he muttered. "Let's hope so." And turned on his heel and was gone.

Roxanne stared after him, frowning. Rhodes had the annoying trick of sounding sincere. And even though she knew she couldn't trust him, her heart gave that the lie. She opened the kitchen door violently and almost banged into Lizzie, who looked amazed at the grimness of Roxanne's expression.

The encounter—although it had shaken her physically as any contact with Rhodes always did—had made her think seriously of Gavin for the first time.

Why should she not marry him? she asked herself coldly.

He had not asked her, of course, but that seemed a minor matter in her present furious state. She was well aware of the intense light in Gavin's eyes when he looked at her, of the way his eyes followed her about.

Later in the week, Roxanne woke and again heard footsteps—this time creeping down from the fourth floor. At the third floor stair landing they stopped abruptly. Time passed—too much time. Roxanne sat up on one elbow and frowned. People didn't walk halfway downstairs in the dark and just stand there. Could Clarissa have fainted? Feeling a tingle of alarm, Roxanne slipped out of bed, moved on silent bare feet to the door, opened it soundlessly and crept into the hall.

Downstairs she heard the front door close, heard Rhodes's light step taking the stairs up two at a time. She could see that the gaslights on the stair landing were lit, but burning low.

Standing in the darkness of the servants' wing, Roxanne saw Rhodes pass by. His step faltered and he uttered a low, surprised "What the devil—!" His eyes were riveted on something before him which now moved into Roxanne's view: Clarissa, half undressed, looking sleepy-eyed as if she had just crawled out of bed, gave him a provocative look and with a rebellious toss of her head disappeared down the hall into her own rooms. It was glaringly clear to Roxanne that Clarissa had seen Rhodes arrive—perhaps by looking through Gavin's window—and had hurried down and waited for him to come upstairs. She had wanted him to see her—undoubtedly to make him jealous.

Roxanne shrank back into the darkness, and after a moment Rhodes went on up the stairs. The next morning his face was expressionless as he greeted

Clarissa at breakfast; Clarissa gave him back an angry look and spat out a good morning.

Clarissa's strategy had not worked.

And now Roxanne understood that it had been Gavin into whose bed Clarissa had crawled that first night. She had made him a substitute for the disinterested Rhodes.

The showery April days passed, and Clarissa's temper was as changeable as the weather. When, one day in late April, Gavin again left for Boston on another of his business trips, Clarissa swept the entire contents of her desk to the floor in a fury. As a result, Roxanne spent half a day trying to get the ink from the gilt and crystal inkwell out of the carpet.

Rhodes was seldom around these days. He was busy at the dockside, Roxanne knew, for on her strolls she had sometimes seen him there, talking to seamen, supervising the loading of ships' stores on the *Virginia Lass*. She wondered idly where those furled sails would take him when at last they billowed to the wind: the spice islands, the South Seas, Tahiti, the Caribbees?

When he was at home, he constantly clashed with his father. At dinner, Roxanne heard the older man criticize Rhodes's behavior bitterly: he had been seen gaming last night, at a brothel the night before.

Once after dinner she heard Rhodes growl at Gavin, who was temporarily back in town, "Who could be telling him these things? Has someone been set to spy on me? Or is it you, Gavin?"

Gavin shrugged. "What would it gain me to spy on you? I've enough on my hands holding the company together."

"Oh, is that what you're doing in Boston so much these days? I wondered."

"If you took more of an interest in the Line's financial affairs, you'd know without my telling you what I've been doing in Boston!" retorted Gavin hotly. "You'd do well to listen to what Father says—else he may fling you out without a cent!"

Gavin went on upstairs, and Roxanne, in the front

hall, was about to brush by Rhodes when he grasped her by the shoulder.

"What have *you* got against me?" he demanded angrily. "I've done nothing to you and yet—by God, this whole household is mad! My father rails at me, and sets spies on me! I'll be glad to sail away from Baltimore!"

Roxanne considered him coldly. "Clarissa is the answer to your problems, Rhodes!" she said, taunting him, and he let go of her and stamped away with a curse.

It had not been announced, but it was soon understood that Clarissa would marry Gavin. Knowing looks were exchanged among the servants; they whispered, nudging each other. Oh, Miss Clarissa was a smart one, they agreed, going to goad Mr. Gavin into setting an early date for the wedding!

Roxanne, remembering how stricken Clarissa had looked that first night as she had tiptoed down from Gavin's room, was sure that Clarissa had started the affair to make Rhodes jealous, but it had gone too far and now she was committed to Gavin.

Whether this bothered Rhodes, Roxanne could not tell. The *Virginia Lass* was being outfitted and a mast replaced; Rhodes was leaving soon, everybody knew that. He seemed upset sometimes when he looked at Clarissa, and drummed his fingers and frowned. Perhaps he really was jealous, Roxanne thought, and wondered why he had not improved his fortunes by marrying this heiress who had so hungered for him. *That* would have made him independently wealthy and got him out from under his disapproving father's thumb.

In any event, Clarissa was very nasty to Rhodes, making sarcastic, cutting remarks and then flouncing off with a withering look. Roxannc supposed a woman scorned—especially a woman as spoiled as Clarissa—would always find defection hard to forgive.

Rhodes had another violent quarrel with his father—this one over his roistering in the town. It happened one day after dinner when Rhodes was about to go out. Joab Coulter stood in his bedroom door glaring at

Rhodes. They had words, and Joab told Rhodes, in a voice that seemed to boom forth from a cavern, that he would burn in hell for his follies, and then slammed the door.

Roxanne, who had come out just at the end of this exchange, watched Rhodes's discomfiture unsympathetically. He turned to find her cold blue eyes on him and jammed his hat on his head.

"No doubt you're right, Roxanne," he said bitterly. "Ambition is the wisest course. You and my brother Gavin have something in common. You both believe a wealthy marriage is the answer to everything." He studied her, eyes narrowed. "Perhaps it is!" he muttered, and swung on his heel and left.

Chapter 15

Spring was late in Baltimore that year—damp, and sometimes the winds were biting. Several of the staff came down with colds, and even Clarissa, usually in blooming health, complained of a sore throat. The doctor was promptly called, to make sure it wasn't diphtheria, a dread disease. But he pronounced Clarissa's complaint laryngitis, and recommended rest in bed and a sweet-tasting alcohol-based cough syrup.

Clarissa pouted, saying she wouldn't stay in bed! Especially since those new people, the Staffords, were giving that great fancy dress ball tomorrow night! But when tomorrow came she had a high fever, and in the afternoon she was forced to admit that she was unable to attend. She sat up in bed to pen a note conveying her regrets to her hostess, and to the young gentleman who was to have escorted her.

"And this?" Roxanne asked, holding up the invitation to the ball.

"Throw it away!" screamed Clarissa, falling back

against her pillows and pulling the covers up around her. "And get out! Talking to you makes my throat hurt!"

She reinforced her last remark by coughing, and Roxanne, with the invitation on its creamy vellum and the two scented notes on monogrammed paper in hand, went down to bring up Clarissa's costume from the laundry, where Ella was pressing it.

Roxanne took the billowing, gold-spangled, creamy satin ball gown from flush-faced Ella, who'd just finished it and who murmured, "Ain't it beautiful?" in an envious voice.

It was indeed, thought Roxanne, staring down at it as Ella arranged its folds over her outstretched arms.

"Cook says it's meant to be a queen's dress, and that Miss Clarissa will wear a white-powdered wig with it."

"It's a Marie Antoinette costume," explained Roxanne. "She was a queen of France who was beheaded. They wore powdered wigs and beauty patches of black court-plaster on their faces then."

Roxanne held the lovely costume lightly over her arms as she went up the stairs, dreamily wishing *she* were attending the ball tonight.

At the third floor landing, she paused. Why should she not attend the ball? In her hand was the invitation which was to be presented to the footman at the door. In her arms was Clarissa's ballgown. And in her room—for a last curling and combing—was the big powdered wig Clarissa meant to wear with it.

Thoughtfully she looked down at the costume. In mask and wig, she could present her invitation—and who would know she was not Clarissa? The Staffords were new to Baltimore; as to the others, no one knew what Clarissa was wearing to the ball. She could slip out! If the servants saw her, they would assume Clarissa had decided to go to the ball after all and think nothing about it. And it was not a gown Clarissa would be wearing again soon. It would be promptly packed away in a box for use at some future ball. Why, Clarissa would never even know she had worn it!

Roxanne's eyes sparkled. She would do it! She would attend the ball!

Swiftly she turned down the steps into the servants' wing instead of going into Clarissa's rooms. She spread the lovely dress out on the bed and proceeded to comb and curl the wig. She would leave them there. If Mrs. Hollister should chance to enter her room while she was out, she would assume Roxanne was repairing some spangle that had come loose, or a seam that Clarissa had burst.

On light feet, Roxanne journeyed across Baltimore and delivered the note of apology to the boring young gentleman who was to have squired Clarissa to the dance, then home again to get ready.

Later that afternoon, Roxanne slipped into Clarissa's darkened bedroom, past her sleeping form, and got a pair of sheer silk stockings. Clarissa had so many that one pair would never be missed. She also took the gold kid ball slippers Clarissa was to have worn which were just a trifle large but could be lined with something, a piece of muslin perhaps. And Clarissa's dainty ivory fan and the satin purse she had planned to carry. Recklessly, Roxanne decided that she would be in no deeper trouble for going the whole way than half. So she picked up the satin cloak Clarissa had planned to wear over the costume and crept out.

Back in her room she realized irritably that she had forgotten the black satin mask and returned for it. As she opened the drawer, Clarissa awakened.

"What are you doing, blundering about?" she demanded. "You've waked me—oh, my throat hurts."

"I'm sorry," said Roxanne blandly. "I was putting some of your things away." As she spoke, she picked up not only the mask but a pair of Clarissa's mousquetaires; prudently she did not select the new ones—for once worn nothing would make such tight gloves look new again—but a pair Clarissa had worn before.

"Bring me some hot milk," ordered Clarissa, holding her throat. "And some of that cough syrup."

Roxanne hurried out with the things tucked in her apron, and stopped by her room to leave the mask and gloves before she ran downstairs to fetch the hot milk.

While Clarissa drank it, Roxanne opened a drawer and idly pulled out some of Clarissa's lovely underthings.

"What are you doing?" asked Clarissa.

"These need mending," explained Roxanne. "Some of the lace has come loose."

Clarissa nodded indifferently. "Take this glass away and let me sleep," she said in an irritable voice. "I don't want to be disturbed tonight at all—it will only make me furious to wake up and realize others are dancing!"

It would make her even more furious if she woke up and realized just *who* was dancing—and in her gown, thought Roxanne. When she took the empty glass away, she had beneath the lacy undergarments a bottle of Clarissa's Paris perfume, her Paris powder and big swansdown puff.

"Sleep well," she said gently.

"Oh, go away," said Clarissa in a rude voice.

Roxanne departed triumphantly to consider her treasures. After dinner, she lugged hot water up to her room and took a bath in a small tin tub she had borrowed from Mrs. Hollister.

At last, powdered, perfumed, luxuriously gowned as a mock-queen, Roxanne inspected herself in the mirror with satisfaction. Her color was high—she had no need of rouge spots. Her sheer silky skin gleamed through its light dusting of perfumed Paris powder, and her huge satin skirts moved seductively as she walked. The costume's decolletage was very daring, cut so low the nipples of her high rounded breasts almost peeped out; she had been surprised that Clarissa had had it cut so low. But when the dress was being fitted, Clarissa no doubt had intended to make Rhodes, who was also going to the ball, jealous by wearing that revealing decolletage while being escorted by another man.

A slight froth of off-the-shoulder lace almost met the tops of the tight white kid mousquetaires. Roxanne had spent all of twenty minutes urging them onto her well-talcumed arms, and feeling those arms going numb, she practiced fluttering her hands the way Clarissa did, while waving the filagreed ivory fan. The effect was very fetching.

Her bodice was tightly molded in lace-appliqued satin spangled in gold, and from her waist a huge lace-appliqued cream satin skirt billowed out, its hem and train gorgeously spangled. When she lifted the train, a lacy touch of Clarissa's borrowed underwear showed beneath it, as well as Clarissa's golden ball slippers, now padded to fit Roxanne's more slender feet.

With the white powdered wig firmly anchored to her own dark-blond hair, the black satin mask shadowing her sapphire eyes, and a bit of black court plaster artfully calling attention to one flushed cheek, she could have been mistaken at a distance for Clarissa. Only the more perfect molding of chin and neck gave her away.

Regally she moved to the door—and paused. This was the part she dreaded most—sneaking out of the house.

The servants had gone to their rooms early, for it had been a hard day in the laundry. Rhodes and Gavin were presumably out. Joab Coulter was safe abed. Taking a deep breath, Roxanne hurried down the front stairway, meeting no one. Down the front hall, out the front door—she had made it!

On the steps she paused and looked about. There were no hacks for hire clattering by as she had hoped there would be. She walked rapidly down the street, her satin cloak clutched about her, and managed to flag down a horse-drawn hack in the next block.

The driver was not too surprised to see a masked Marie Antoinette step out of the glow of the street light into his cab, because masked balls were all the fashion, and kings and queens and knaves and potentates all rode—sometimes even in backfiring automobiles—up to the lighted doors of Baltimore's great houses.

Roxanne had remembered to drop some money into

Clarissa's satin purse so that when the hack swung up before the Staffords' handsome Victorian mansion, she was able to pay the driver. Her heart was beating wildly as a hired footman handed her out of the hack. Roxanne hesitated, wishing that she had not embarked on this venture. But at that moment, a large party spilled out of two just-arrived carriages, and Roxanne melted in with them, surrendering her invitation to the footman and gliding through the downstairs hall of the Staffords' handsome home. There, a maid took charge of the ladies, ushering them into a room where they were divested of their cloaks and where they could leave their purses. Many took their masks off and inspected their faces in the mirror—Roxanne did not. She turned and drifted out, mingling with the guests. In the great white and gold ballroom which the Staffords had just finished decorating—indeed they had given this ball to show off its magnificence, almost as recent as their own—she was immediately claimed for a dance by a harlequin-costumed young man.

Roxanne recognized his voice. It amused her that she knew the man she was dancing with—although he did not know her. It was a young dandy with an unmistakable pale yellow mustache who often called at the house and took Clarissa driving. She was claimed next by a sturdy musketeer and then a pipestem-legged Robin Hood complete with bow and arrow. The musketeer she thought she recognized, although she could not be sure. After that she danced with strangers who merrily tried to guess her identity while, laughing, she supplied them with false clues.

Then, across the crowded ballroom, she saw Rhodes. Even in costume and masked, she recognized those broad shoulders, the poise of that leonine head, that swinging gait.

He was wearing the uniform of a colonel in the Confederate Cavalry. His belted gray coat was double-breasted and trimmed with gold braid, which also ornamented his cuffs. His collar was gold, and a stripe of gold ran down his blue trouser legs. Roxanne noticed that the coat fit him too tightly and the sleeves were a shade short, and decided that the uniform probably had belonged to that Virginia gentleman, his rakehell grandfather.

If so, it would certainly have infuriated Joab Coulter to see Rhodes wear it.

As her current partner, a bandy-legged Henry VIII, danced her toward that corner of the room, Roxanne gave Rhodes an enticing smile. Tonight, she told herself wickedly, she would play the part of flirtatious Clarissa to the hilt—she would even ensnare Rhodes, and then leave him wondering who she was. Malicious laughter welled up inside her. Tonight the man with the roving eye would be led on, and then thrust callously aside, even as he thrust others aside!

Ah, he had seen her! She saw him peer through the dancers for a better look at her. Shortly, then, he made his way to her side and bowed and asked her for a dance, and she was well content. For she was sure he could not know she was wearing Clarissa's costume—after all, Clarissa had so many, and this was a new one. And certainly he would never associate this lavish Marie Antoinette disguise with the servant girl in his household.

Returning the smile of the masked cavalry officer, Roxanne melted into his arms. She danced enticingly close—close enough to cause raised eyebrows about the room.

Rhodes gave her a narrow penetrating look, but soon smiled down at her. She was well aware of the view her low-cut dress afforded of the tops of her round pearly breasts.

"Might one be permitted to guess who you are?" he asked.

Roxanne shrugged carelessly, but realized that he would recognize her voice. "One might," she whispered, and touched her throat. "Laryngitis."

"Ah," he said. "Laryngitis. Or perhaps you think I would know your voice?"

She shrugged again, swinging about to the music. "I have never been to Baltimore before. I am here visiting relatives," she whispered.

"Then perhaps I had best claim you for all your dances before you take wing and depart," he said humorously.

"My dances are all promised to others, but perhaps you can cut all my suitors down with your cavalry saber!"

He considered her, half smiling. "And for you, indeed I might." There was a rich timbre to his voice as he said that, and Roxanne regarded him vengefully. Damn him for being so attractive, for making her heart beat faster, for making her remember what it was like to be held in his arms.

She felt shaken and irritated when he bowed and left her to be claimed by another. She saw him dancing next with Clarissa's friend, Mary Stadler, who was not wearing a mask, and who seemed quite taken with him. Roxanne recalled unhappily that the Stadlers were very rich.

The evening wore gaily on. Roxanne danced, she drank champagne from a frail stemmed glass, she ate a late supper beside a man who had often paid court to Clarissa. Twice more she danced with Rhodes, who smiled down at her almost tenderly.

"Are you having a good time?" he asked.

"I attend many balls," she whispered airily.

"I am sure you do," he said soberly, and waltzed her around again.

Suddenly it came to Roxanne that there would be an unmasking at midnight. A quick look at the ornate French clock on the white marble mantel told her it was five minutes to twelve. Horrified, she realized that although most of the guests might not recognize her, and she could easily give a false name and claim to be an out-of-town guest someone had brought along, Rhodes would certainly recognize her, and so might some of Clarissa's friends who had conversed with her in their schoolgirl French.

She made a quick excuse to Rhodes about a broken heel, and, Cinderella-like, hurried away through the glittering crowd to claim her cloak and purse before she metamorphosed back from reigning queen to servant girl.

A servant helped her into her cloak, and as she went into the front hall, still masked, she saw Rhodes, who must have followed her. His mask discarded, he now stood at his ease with his booted feet planted on the marble squares of the hall, smiling at her.

She tried to pass him.

"A last dance!" he protested. "You cannot leave before the unmasking—I must know your name."

"My throat hurts," she whispered coldly. "I must go home."

"Without an escort?" He looked about him.

"I came without one. He was—detained by business."

"Then perhaps I will serve?"

She glared at him. "You have great effrontery, sir," she whispered. "A lady may dance with a gentleman at a ball, but she need not recognize him afterward."

Though it was true enough, it was also an insult, but it did not faze Rhodes.

"Then perhaps we can strike a compromise," he said thoughtfully. "A stroll through the garden, and then I will see you into a hack and you can go home without my ever knowing who you are!"

That suited her well enough.

Eyes snapping, she strolled beside him through the damp garden in the cool spring night. Around them, the tulips were already out; daffodils and hyacinths would soon be blooming. At the sundial he paused and peered down into her face. "I can't see your eyes in the shadow of that mask," he complained. "Take it off."

She turned her head away from him. "No," she whispered firmly.

"In that case," he said, "I shall kiss you with it on."

And before she could turn and flee, he had seized her and pressed his warm mouth down upon hers. As always, his touch was electric, shaking her to her toes. Unwillingly she relaxed against him, quivering at his touch, while he explored her lips, quested past them with his tongue. His fingers too were questing beneath her cloak. She felt their fiery trail move lightly down the back of her neck, move along her shoulders and trace designs across her bosom. Then he was stroking lightly the tops of her round white breasts, exposed by the low decolletage of her ball gown. She gasped as his probing fingers eased into the cleavage between them. Atingle with a medley of sweet sensations that almost overwhelmed her will, Roxanne wrenched herself away from him with a ragged sigh.

"I know who you are," Rhodes murmured as he let her go.

She stood frozen.

"You are Clarissa Calvert," he said, and his wicked smile flashed. "I saw your costume as it was brought downstairs to be pressed—and I would recognize your perfume anywhere. You were supposed to go to the ball with Phil Worthington, Clarissa. Why the devil didn't you?"

"I am *not* Clarissa Calvert," whispered Roxanne heatedly.

He laughed. "Then we'll prove or disprove that right now," he said, and reached for her mask.

Roxanne was quicker than he. Having anticipated what he would do, she had reached behind her and with her gloved hand pulled down a slender tree branch, which she released so that the thorny branch snapped whiplike across his face, drawing blood.

As Rhodes flinched back with an oath, she gave him a hard push and, turning, ran down the garden path to disappear into the boxwood maze. She could hear him pursuing her, feet pounding over the gravel, sometimes just on the other side of the dense tall shrubbery. Her breath rasped in her throat as she twisted and turned, but she kept going and eventually found herself clear of the maze on the other side of the big garden.

She did not dare to try to find a cab now. Rhodes might come out of the maze at any time and catch her, but she had to go home! And somehow, to get rid of her gloves, for the thorns had pierced them and drawn blood from her hand as well as from Rhodes's surprised face. She hoped darkly that she had marked him well! But this gown must be got home and somehow smuggled back into the sleeping Clarissa's room, along with the rest of her finery. She herself must appear to be both surprised and sleepy if Rhodes came thundering in and woke up Clarissa.

It was not too far to the Mt. Vernon Place house, if she cut through the park. She guessed Rhodes would spend some time looking for her before he went home, expecting her to work her way around front to get a cab. She hoped only that her gold slippers would hold out as she pelted through the park.

In the dark, deserted park she thought she heard running footsteps behind her and stopped to hide in some bushes. The footsteps came no closer, but it was some time before she dared to emerge. Now she was frightened that Rhodes might have reached home before she did.

But if he had, she reasoned, even if he had burst in on Clarissa, he would have found her in bed and pooh-poohing any idea that she had been at the ball. Clarissa never knew where her things were. It would take her some time to get sufficiently organized to search for her costume. With good luck, Roxanne could still make it.

The street was empty on Mt. Vernon Place as Roxanne sprinted toward the servants' entrance. Halfway there, her foot collided with a can with a string tied to it that some child must have been playing with in the street, and it bounded down the steps with a loud clatter. Shuddering, Roxanne shrank back against the brownstone building to find the key she had tossed into Clarissa's purse. The key fitted into the lock readily enough, but the door did not respond to her pressure.

In the excitement of her escapade, she had forgotten that at midnight, when he went to bed, Greaves threw the heavy bolt on the servants' entrance. She was locked out!

In panic, she ran out into the street and stared

desperately at the building. The tall downstairs windows were all locked from the inside. The basement windows were covered with iron bars. There was no chance of getting in from the back; the door to the laundry was barred right after dinner. Her short career as Cinderella was over; now the piper would have to be paid. If she pounded for Greaves, he would let her in, of course, but he would surely inquire as to her costume and undoubtedly feel it his duty to mention it to Mrs. Hollister tomorrow. Clarissa would hear about it and she would lose her job! Jobs were almost impossible to find, and there were always a dozen eager immigrant girls waiting for every position.

Standing in the glow of the streetlight she searched feverishly through the small satin purse that matched her gown. Clarissa had intended to go to the ball, so perhaps—her search revealed not only a lace handkerchief and some throat lozenges, but also the front door key! In triumph she held it up and looked at it in the light cast by the streetlight. Deliverance! Scooping up her skirts, she hurried up the stone steps. As she reached the door, she heard an upstairs window close and prayed it was not Clarissa, wakeful and looking out the window to see *her* wig and *her* gown about to enter the house.

With great care Roxanne turned the key around in the lock, eased the door open and shut it behind her as quietly. The hall was dark; only the light from the street lamp outside filtered in through the fanlight above the door. Again lifting her skirts, she tiptoed past Joab Coulter's closed door and up the dark staircase, feeling her way.

On the second floor landing she paused to listen. No one was about. No sound broke the thick dark silence, for the gaslights in the hall had long since been turned off.

With a deep sigh of relief, feeling her way in what was now total darkness, she climbed slowly up the stairs to the third floor landing. Once there, she would only have to steal down the three steps into the servants' wing where she would be safe! She would remove her costume in her own room. Clarissa slept like a stone; she could slip in there and replace everything and tiptoe out again unnoticed.

With these thoughts on her mind, Roxanne felt her way up the dark staircase. Around her the big house was very quiet, waiting, listening.

She had reached the third-floor landing when she thought she heard something just ahead and paused, her eyes dilating suddenly as she stared into a pool of darkness that seemed to waver.

Something . . . someone was there!

Tensing, she opened her mouth to scream. A hand was clapped over it, the mask was snatched from her face, and she was gripped in a vise-like embrace and borne to the floor of the stair landing. The back of her head struck the wainscoting as she fell. Although part of the force of the blow was absorbed by her powdered wig, which was knocked askew, she was still stunned by the impact so that for a moment her head swam and blackness engulfed her. When consciousness returned, she was gasping. Hot lips were clamped over her own. Fighting for breath against that demanding mouth, she heard the rip of fabric as her dress left her shoulders and eager possessive hands roamed her soft flesh, roughly tearing the fabric away.

As she flinched and tried to pull away, the grip—she now realized her body was being held to the floor by a pair of strong masculine legs—tightened, and a voice that was hardly more than a growl commanded: "Quiet!" And with it a wrenching pressure on her arm that made her gasp in pain.

Crushed, half suffocated, in utter terror, she fell silent, struggling for breath as her attacker, whose hands had been massaging her bared breasts with almost painful violence, now became more gentle, his touch more caressing as he deliberately probed her sensitive nipples. Her senses came alive at his new gentleness, and tiny needles of feeling darted in all directions from the touch of his fingers. In shame and horror she felt her body respond, heard what she thought was a triumphant chuckle in his throat as he pulled up her skirts with a sudden savage jerk, tearing her petticoat, and ripping the fabric of the silky panty-legs savagely, his hot fingers thrusting through the gap between her thrashing thighs, while with a terrible desperation she fought to free herself.

But there was no escaping him. His hands, his strong body, were everywhere, pressing down on the hard floor, holding her powerless. And now she felt his male hardness press against her thighs as almost viciously he drove in deep, deep. She felt his body react in surprise at the ease of his entrance, and even in the storm of her emotions she thought: *He is surprised that I am not a virgin.*

As if angered by that, he seized her even more violently, and she felt within her a punishing, leaping hardness that almost drove her breath from her. A silent scream tore from her tortured suffocated throat, as with a kind of controlled violence he thrust deep and rhythmically. Moving with more authority now, he became more gentle as his own passion mounted. With each sharp thrust she fought within her a leaping flame that threatened to engulf her, a tingling surge of feeling that mounted, finally sweeping all before it as, pressed in a close heaving embrace, her own wild nature burst forth and she responded to him fiercely. Again she could feel his surprise and a new almost triumphant gentleness as he caressed her.

Finally, it was over and, hot with shame, she knew a new horror: his fingers caressing the pulsing column of her throat tightened studdenly, cutting off her breath altogether. She fought with desperation then, fought for her very life, kicking and clawing, trying her best to strike at him, even though he kept her arms painfully pinioned. Desperately, she tried to mark him. If he was going to kill her, at least let him bear her marks! But she was unable to, and as her breast heaved with effort, the fingers around her throat constricted still further. A dizzy blackness settled down over her and the world drifted away into the dark.

Chapter 16

Fighting her way up from the pit, from a stifling blackness, Roxanne regained consciousness. Her throat ached. As she touched it with her fingers, she winced at the pain. She opened her mouth but could not speak. She tried to rise and fell back, a violent pain shooting through her head as she moved. She felt along the floor with one trembling hand, trying to get a purchase again in order to rise, and her hand touched something soft. She recoiled at first. Then recognizing the feel of soft linen, a handkerchief, her fingers closed around it almost gratefully—a known object in a dark world. Finally, she remembered where she was. On the third-floor stair landing.

Only she wasn't.

Still clutching the handkerchief, she tried to get up, but her head bumped into a wooden protuberance overhead and she fell back with a groan. She reached up and her fingers sought the obstacle, felt along it—a shelf. Holding tightly to the edge, she managed to rise and pull herself forward, only to fall up some steps and bump into a door. She turned with a gasp, slamming her face into a pile of folded linen sheets.

She knew where she was at last. She was in the big linen closet that opened off the third-floor landing. After she had passed out, her attacker must have dragged her in here and closed the door!

Clutching the handkerchief, Roxanne turned and struggled painfully up the steps and through the door, still stunned by the violence she had suffered. She tripped over her torn skirts and almost fell as she staggered down the dark stairs into the front hall.

The handkerchief she held up to the light that came in from the fanlight above the door bore the initials *R. C.*

Rhodes Coulter.

With a sob, she clenched it in her hands, and rage gave her strength. A wild moaning scream rose from her hurt throat as she staggered toward Joab Coulter's door and slammed her fist against it, again and again, making the very timbers rock as pain splintered through her knuckles.

The door flew open and Joab Coulter appeared, a maroon velvet dressing gown hastily thrown over his bony night-shirted figure—only to fall back at the half-dressed wild-eyed apparition which confronted him.

"Your son—*your son*—raped me just now!" Roxanne gasped. And thrust the handkerchief toward him.

Examining the handkerchief, he saw the initials. He looked at Roxanne, her crazily-angled wig and her torn dress which, before his appalled gaze, she snatched around her. He did not immediately notice that it was a torn ball gown. His face was very pale.

"Rhodes," he said dully.

"Yes!" She clutched her hurt throat. "Rhodes!"

Joab made a gesture as if to sweep the cobwebs from his eyes. He seemed lost in thought, standing there somewhat like a tall scarecrow, not fully comprehending, as he gazed at Roxanne's shaking form. Gradually a great cloud gathered on his face.

"Rhodes!" he roared. It was a cry of rage.

As if in answer, the front door opened and Rhodes

stood there, resplendent in his Confederate uniform. His face, cruelly scratched by the thorny branch, was streaked with blood. He glared at Roxanne—then, as if realizing her condition, his eyes widened.

"What has happened?" he demanded.

Fury overwhelmed her. "Don't ask me what has happened!" she cried hoarsely. "You know what you did! You knew I wouldn't give in to you like Mary Bridey and so you hid on the stairs and almost killed me to work your cruel way on me!"

"Rhodes," cut in Gavin's voice behind them, "is this true?" And Roxanne swung around to see a horrified little group standing on the stairs: Gavin in street clothes, looking aghast; Mrs. Hollister wearing a little nightcap; Ella and Jane in shapeless cotton wrappers, looking awed. Lizzie was nowhere to be seen; she slept soundly. Greaves, sleepily pulling on a jacket, was just coming down the hall from the dining room.

"Of course it's not true," snapped Rhodes. "An over-eager wench has torn her clothes and set up an alarm to get herself a husband, can't you see that?"

Anger so engulfed Roxanne that she felt dizzy and weak from it. She felt as if her head would melt. She raised her arm to strike him down, to wipe the lie from the cruel mouth that had uttered it. Even as she did, he caught her by the wrist and said in a soft savage voice, "What devil's game are you playing, Roxanne? Don't tempt me further. I've half a mind to thrash you now—don't goad me into it!"

His father's voice interrupted him. "Where were you just now? And what's that you're wearing?"

"Outside walking about," said Rhodes irritably. "And as you know very well, it's my grandfather's Confederate uniform."

Roxanne clenched her hands. "He's lying," she gasped. "He—raped—me! And—I—want—him—*charged!*"

Joab Coulter's deepset eyes never left his son's face. "Is it your intention to hang?" he roared. "Or do you mean to marry this woman?"

Rhodes gave a bitter laugh that flicked Roxanne as

if a whip had licked a raw place. "I've no intention of hanging, I can assure you. And as for marrying this woman, I had thought of it, but I'd not marry her now if hell froze over!"

"You'll do as *I* say!" howled Joab Coulter, and suddenly, as he took a step forward, he gasped and his big body sagged. Rhodes, leaping forward, caught him before he could fall to the floor.

"Get the doctor, Greaves!" barked Rhodes. "This lying wench may well have killed him with her accusations!"

The world blurred red before Roxanne's eyes, but as she swayed, someone caught both her hands, held them firmly. It was Gavin; in a moment she saw his face swim toward her through the mist of her fury.

"Roxanne," he said softly. "Steady." He held her there, while she shook. "Greaves, after you've called the doctor, bring Mr. Colfax," called Gavin. As if from a great distance Roxanne heard the door close and Greaves's hurrying feet clatter down the steps outside. "Get her some brandy," muttered Gavin to Ella. "Quick!"

Ella ran into the dining room and emerged with a cut-glass decanter and a glass into which she splashed some of the liquid. Gavin held it to Roxanne's trembling lips. "Steady now," he encouraged. "Don't faint, Roxanne."

Roxanne felt the hot liquid burn down her throat. "I'm not going to faint," she mumbled.

"We should get you upstairs," Gavin said. "Mrs. Hollister, now that Rhodes has taken Father into his bedroom, perhaps you could—?"

Roxanne resisted Mrs. Hollister's urging hand on her shoulder. "Do not try to dissuade me, Gavin," she said grimly. "I am going to charge your brother with rape."

He shrugged. "That is up to you, Roxanne."

She was vaguely surprised that he did not defend Rhodes as he had before over Mary Bridey.

"Go on upstairs with Mrs. Hollister," he urged. "She'll put you to bed."

Roxanne waved the housekeeper away. "There's more you should know," she said coldly. "I am not Mary Willis's daughter. My name is Roxanne Rossiter, and my grandmother lived in as good a house as this one—better—before Sherman burned it to the ground on his March to the Sea!"

Gavin stared at her. "Are you saying you *impersonated* Mary Willis's daughter?"

"She had no daughter. She died on the train coming here, and I took her ticket and the letter she was carrying from your father—I was desperate for employment."

Gavin looked surprised and oddly pleased. "I always thought you were . . . different," he murmured. "But why tell me this now?"

"Because it will all come out when the police get here."

"Ah, now," he said thoughtfully. "Impersonation . . . theft . . . You and Rhodes could end up in the same jail."

"I don't care!" she cried passionately. "He raped me, and I want him brought to justice!"

Gavin seized her hand. He seemed magnificent tonight, triumphant in some strange way. As if he had jousted with devils . . . and won.

"Trust me," he whispered. "Say no more of this for now. My father's in a bad way. I have to go to him." He indicated the bedroom door. "But tomorrow I'll see what's to be done."

Roxanne bit back the violent words that rose to her lips, the demand that something be done *now*! Furious tears frosted her lashes.

"Trust me," he said again, in a compassionate voice, and pushed her gently toward the stairs.

Roxanne sagged back against the newel post as the front door opened to admit the doctor, who lived only two doors away. Nodding to Gavin, he hurried in and bustled toward his patient's door. When Gavin followed him into the bedroom, Roxanne moved heavily up the front stairs. Halfway up she heard the front door open again and paused to see another hastily dressed gentleman hurry in. She recognized him as John Colfax, Joab Coulter's lawyer. She wondered if he were here to swear out a warrant for Rhodes's arrest? Or perhaps to make marriage arrangements?

Roxanne struggled up the stairs toward her room, clutching the long streamers of torn fabric about her. On the stair landing, which was awash with light from the gas lamps that had been lit, stood Clarissa in a peach satin dressing gown, her face very white.

She recoiled at the sight of Roxanne.

"I . . . heard," she muttered. "And you were . . . wearing *that*?"

Roxanne looked down dispassionately at the ruined gown. In the light of what had happened to her, wearing somebody else's dress to a party seemed enormously inconsequential. "I wore it to the ball," she said tersely. "I went in your place. You can dismiss me for it."

But Clarissa's mind was not on dismissal.

"And you were attacked . . . wearing *my* dress?" The words were torn painfully from Clarissa.

Suddenly Roxanne understood Clarissa's surmise. Her own face went white and she swayed against the wall.

Roxanne had gone to the ball in Clarissa's place. And in Clarissa's place she had been attacked. No wonder Rhodes was angry! He had been thwarted. If she had been Clarissa, he could have claimed he was drunk and gallantly offered to marry her at once. But she was a servant girl . . . one to whom he had been attracted, it was true, but a man in his position didn't marry a servant.

Fury so all-encompassing it shook her very being consumed Roxanne suddenly. And in that moment she swore that if she lived, she would get even with Rhodes. Someday, somehow, it would be done. She would bring him down.

Her hatred of him gave her skin a kind of glow that kept her warm as she moved back to her room, but there she sank down weeping, exhausted. She was sure she was covered with bruises. But no wound she had suffered was half so great as the deep searing wound to her pride, to her self-esteem, and yes—although she would not at the moment admit it—to her heart.

For Rhodes, who had held her heart in his keeping, had seized her, had used her roughly for his pleasure, taken her against her will—and without love. *Without love* . . . that hurt the most.

She started at a knock on the door. It was Gavin.

"Do you need anything?" he asked, through the door.

She mumbled "No," and he went away, even his walk sounding tired, dejected.

Poor Gavin . . . he had tried so hard to shield Rhodes, and now there was no longer any way to shield him. Tomorrow the world would know Rhodes for what he was. Tomorrow there would be police and questions and—she shuddered in horror—they would ask her things, personal things. She bent her head and sobbed. Rhodes had brought her to this! And to think, for a while she had loved him!

Jane, looking sympathetic, brought up buckets of hot water, and Roxanne scrubbed herself mechanically, wincing as she touched bruises that already were darkening to purple blotches. Pulling on her coarse white cotton nightgown, Roxanne sank down onto her bed and hugged her shoulders miserably, shaking with a kind of cold that was not external. But she could not sleep.

She kept going over and over in her mind the horrible events of the evening. How could Rhodes have been so vile?

The sound of raised voices filtered through to her from downstairs, and she decided to sneak out to the landing to see what was going on. Had poor old Joab died? Were Gavin and Rhodes quarreling?

She tiptoed barefoot down the stairs and stood in the shadows on the second-floor landing, listening.

The men were standing outside Joab Coulter's bedroom door: Rhodes and Gavin, their faces white; the lawyer, looking uneasy.

"It's a deathbed will, Rhodes," cried Gavin. "Of course it will hold."

"My father can't cut me off with a dollar!" cried Rhodes. "His fortune—this whole damned house—came to him from my mother! How dare he!"

"There's the matter of the young woman—" began the lawyer.

But Rhodes jumped in with, "Damn the young woman! Roxanne's lying! Can't you see that? She came here pretending to be Mary Willis's daughter with *this* in mind—making one of us marry her!"

Roxanne stiffened, her anger almost causing her breath to stop.

"That's not important now, Rhodes," cried Gavin.

"The devil it's not!" shouted Rhodes.

"The important thing is that father's changed his will and left everything to me. Now I can—"

"I told you, my father can't do that! I'll have my share back. I'll have you in court, Gavin. I'll break that will!"

Gavin straightened, seemed to grow taller. His voice took on the chill of ice. "If you do, you'll do it from jail," he said silkily. "The girl Roxanne has complained against you. She says you violated her. Your life will be at stake if you're brought to trial for it!"

Angrily, Rhodes faced Gavin. "And who'll help her bring her complaint? You, my brother? You, who always wanted to inherit the Line so you could have the pleasure of converting it to steam? Oh, I see it now—you two connived against me! *You* told her to rip her clothes and cry rape!"

"You're no brother of mine!" thundered Gavin in a fury. "And my father realized that at the last—that's why he cut you out of his will!"

Rhodes's face was very white and strained. "No brother of yours? What do you mean by that?"

Gavin's voice had become a roar. "I say your mother cuckolded my father with her Irish groom, who was running from the law when he landed on these shores! I say no Coulter blood flows in your veins! That's what I say! That's what I'll tell the world if you try to break this deathbed will! And then I'll see you jailed for what you've done to Roxanne!"

Rhodes leaped forward and grabbed his brother by the throat. The muscles in his powerful neck corded, and the broadcloth over his shoulders bulged as he shook Gavin vengefully. "Brother you may not be," he said through clenched teeth. "But your blood will run nicely red across this carpet for saying it!"

The lawyer grasped Rhodes's arms, crying at him to desist, but with a fierce gesture Rhodes shook him off. Gavin swung at him and missed. Then Rhodes flung Gavin from him so violently that Gavin hit his head against the far wall and slithered down it, insensible.

At that moment Rhodes, standing in the hall below Roxanne, presented a perfect target for her. She grabbed the nearest object, lifted her arm and threw a heavy bust of Plato down at Rhodes.

Rhodes looked up and saw her. For a moment, hell looked out of his eyes. Suddenly, with the quickness of a cat, he ducked as the heavy marble flashed through the air and crashed to the floor beside him.

"Hellcat!" he flung at her and strode out through the front door, slamming it behind him with such force that a pane of the fanlight broke and the glass shattered on the floor.

"He's a violent man, violent," said the doctor, shaking his head.

"All the Coulters are violent," the lawyer said grimly, turning to survey Gavin's inert form. "Of course, it's possible that, as Gavin says, Rhodes isn't a Coulter. Come, you'd better see to Gavin. He's taken a pretty heavy blow on the back of the head where he connected with that wall."

With tear-blinded eyes, Roxanne staggered back to her room. *Hellcat*, he had called her, this man who such a short time before had held her trapped in his arms, exploring all her secrets.

May he rot in hell! she thought vengefully, and the tears that she had managed to hold back before burst forth in a shower of grief, rage, heartbreak and humiliation.

Chapter 17

In the morning Roxanne got her bruised body out of bed, donned her gray suit and went downstairs intending to get the police herself. At the foot of the stairs, she met Mrs. Hollister, who was wearing a black dress, her eyes red with weeping. The plump little housekeeper blocked Roxanne's way determinedly, saying she didn't know where Roxanne could be going at this time of morning.

Roxanne said crisply that she was going for the police, since no one else had.

Oh, dear, said Mrs. Hollister, distressed. And at a time like this, with a death in the house. Couldn't it wait?

Roxanne gave her a withering look.

Mrs. Hollister took a deep breath and said smoothly that with Roxanne so upset last night, she had not mentioned it, but she herself had heard a cat crying outside just after midnight. Thinking it might have been run over by a carriage, she had gone downstairs and out the servants' entrance to look for it. When she had returned she must have forgotten to lock the door, for while everyone was in an uproar downstairs she had gone back to check, and had found it standing open.

Roxanne gave her a stubborn look. "If the servants' door was standing open, it was because Rhodes left it so in his hurry to get out and rush in again by the front door!"

"Oh, no, that couldn't have been," corrected Mrs. Hollister quickly, her eyes very wide and blank. "I heard all that noise downstairs, and I ran to the window of the second-floor drawing room before I went downstairs. I myself saw Rhodes coming down the street."

Roxanne, remembering now the servants' entrance had been locked and bolted against her, felt sick. But she knew that she was beaten. The police—everyone, in fact—would prefer to believe that person or persons unknown had slipped into the house and attacked her and slipped away again—rather than have to charge a prominent citizen's son with the crime.

Mrs. Hollister gave her a pleading look, her lips quivering.

Suddenly Roxanne understood. It was *loyalty* she was seeing, family loyalty! All those lovely things in Mrs. Hollister's room. The lingering looks Mrs. Hollister had been wont to give her employer, and now her deep black mourning garb. Mrs. Hollister had been Joab Coulter's mistress. He had given her those things! No wonder she had added a *Mrs.* to her name, to make her seem more respectable. Perhaps Joab had no longer desired her when he grew old and his rheumatism bothered him, but he had kept her well.

And she had been grateful! Naturally the loyalty and gratitude she felt toward Joab had spilled over onto his sons. That explained why she had been so anxious to get rid of Mary Bridey, so eager to cover up anything that went wrong. Loyalty—loyalty to her lover!

Roxanne stared at Mrs. Hollister for a speechless moment, comprehending all that. It explained, too, how the housekeeper had felt about *her*. Mrs. Hollister had wanted Roxanne to marry well, but at a secondary level, not in the Coulter family. And to bring charges against one of the Coulters was, to someone like Mrs. Hollister, unthinkable.

Roxanne swept past the housekeeper and almost collided with Greaves, who was carrying a large black funeral wreath to affix to the door. "I will send for my things," she flung over her shoulder.

Gavin, a band of black crepe on his sleeve, came out of his father's bedroom in time to hear that. "Why, where are you going, Roxanne?" he asked, dismayed.

Roxanne gave him a twisted smile. "Mrs. Hollister has just told me she was a witness to Rhodes's innocent arrival last night. It seems the family must stand together against outsiders."

Gavin dismissed frightened Mrs. Hollister with a wave of his hand. "There's no need for witnesses, Roxanne. Rhodes has disappeared."

"Disappeared?" she repeated stupidly.

"The *Virginia Lass* has up-anchored and sailed away. God knows where Rhodes has gone or if he'll ever be back."

She stared at him, stunned. Whatever she had expected, it was not this. Rhodes was gone!

"So it would be stupid for you to go to the police," he said. "They'd only ask you a lot of embarrassing questions, and it wouldn't amount to anything. They can't punish a man they can't find."

Roxanne's rebellious heart saw some sense in that; she had dreaded the questions the police would ask her.

"It will make no difference between us, Roxanne," said Gavin earnestly.

"I can't stay here." She shivered.

"I'll take rooms for you with a lady I know. She's elderly. It's quite a nice place."

"And why," she asked wearily, "would you do this, Gavin?"

"Because I want you beside me, Roxanne." Gavin's voice was caressing. "This is no time to discuss it, with my father lying dead on the other side of that door, but—I want you to think about me, Roxanne. About us."

"But what about Clarissa?" she asked. "Doesn't she expect you to marry her?"

He frowned. "The court will appoint me Clarissa's guardian, but no marriage will take place. Clarissa is immature; she needs seasoning before she will make any man a good wife."

And in the meantime, Roxanne couldn't help thinking, *you* will have charge of her fortune, just as your father had.

But his words had made her heart beat faster. She was well aware of how Gavin felt about her. And in her present rebellious mood, fiercely angry at Rhodes, not knowing how to strike out now that he was gone, she wondered what it would be like to marry Gavin. To queen it over the big house on Mt. Vernon Place. Let Rhodes hear about that! How it would gall him!

So she smiled seductively at Gavin. "You are right," she agreed. "You need a more mature woman at your side." She gave her hair a graceful pat, knowing full well the gesture caused her ripe figure to be outlined against the morning light.

His eyes kindled, but he made no move to touch her. "You're so lovely, Roxanne. . . ." His voice was hoarse. For a wild moment she thought he was going to seize her and crush her in his arms, but he seemed to take a fresh grip on himself, and only a faint tremor in his voice betrayed him. "I only want you to ask your heart if you feel as I do."

She stared at him. It was a simple declaration; it sounded sincere.

"I don't ask for an immediate answer," he said hastily. "I only want you to think about me, Roxanne."

She studied him. And studying him, she made up her mind. She needed no smiling lover who'd be gone with the dawn. She needed a man she could trust, and depend on. She smiled. A cold smile. Gavin was so trustworthy, so certain of his way. So . . . so different from Rhodes, who was everybody's darling and careless of his path through life.

Yes, Gavin would do nicely.

There was the sound of a carriage arriving, of footsteps outside, people come to offer their condolences.

"I will make the arrangements today," Gavin promised hastily as he answered the door. Roxanne gave him a thoughtful look and climbed back upstairs to pace the floor of her little room restlessly. All day downstairs, people came and went. But true to his word, in the afternoon Gavin took her in a carriage to her new quarters.

"Everything is taken care of," he told her as they alighted in front of a handsome but run-down red brick Georgian mansion. "Mrs. De Quincy is a widow, somewhat hard of hearing. She lives alone, and will be glad to have someone occupying her second floor."

He took her into the high-ceilinged house, past a jumbled collection of family heirlooms, and introduced her to Mrs. De Quincy. The woman, a vague, fluttering, white-haired old lady in a long purple silk gown, cupped her hand over her ear and said "Speak louder." Then shouted that she was delighted to have Roxanne; since her late husband had died, said Mrs. De Quincy, she'd had the most delightful people upstairs. Roxanne understood this to mean that she habitually took in roomers.

Gavin, who had to hurry back, bade Roxanne farewell at the door. "Right after the funeral I'm leaving for Boston," he told her. "If there is anything you require, ask Mrs. De Quincy or send for Mrs. Hollister. I will leave them instructions. I will be gone for a while. You understand, I must wait a decent interval." She nodded, watching him from beneath sooty lashes. "And when I come back, I will have something to ask you, Roxanne."

He pressed her hand and was gone. Mrs. De Quincy's maid, a stalwart black woman, gave Roxanne a disapproving glance and lumbered upstairs with her bag.

Roxanne assumed that the maid disapproved of aristocratic Mrs. De Quincy taking in roomers.

Upstairs, the maid swung the door wide on her spacious new quarters, light and airy, with big windows and handsome drapes. The furnishings were pre-Civil War and very elegant. Roxanne couldn't help contrasting this place with Mary Bridey's shabby quarters. But then, she reminded herself, Gavin had been doing that for Rhodes—and perhaps reluctantly. These rooms were for the woman he would one day make his wife.

For she had never doubted that Gavin's declaration was a proposal of marriage, and the luxury of her new surroundings reinforced that belief. She walked about bemused. A drawing room—she had a drawing room! And a small formal dining room and a very large and elegant bedroom with a tall marble-based pier glass and furniture of rosewood and satinwood. There was a dressing room as well but no kitchen. Roxanne discovered she did not need one. Her landlady maintained an excellent cook, and the maid brought her meals up to her three times a day, on a giant footed tray of antique silver.

Roxanne was amazed at Gavin's solicitude.

She was even more amazed when, a few days later, a clever little French dressmaker arrived to measure her for several handsome gowns, showing her fabric samples and some magazine illustrations from which to make her selections.

Roxanne chose an elegant beige walking suit, almost the color of her dark-blond hair. It was tailored, and the belted skirt was cut in many gores, lined with gold silk, and had a little train. With it she would wear a soft, high-necked, overhanging blouse of lingerie material with deep insets of handmade lace. She also chose a princess-style tea gown, gored from neck to hem, in a deep blue silk that almost matched her sapphire eyes. It was lined with light blue taffeta, which gave it the fashionable froufrou rustle. And, daringly, a low-cut white satin ball gown that fell off the shoulders, exposed the upper half of her round white breasts, and was caught at the shoulders with sprays of rhinestones. It would fit her like her own skin to the hips, then swirl into a bell shape with a rather long train. She looked at it dreamily. With a higher neck and sleeves it might have been a bridal gown. . . . She roused herself from her reverie, and turned to the dressmaker.

"These will be sufficient for now," she said.

"But Mr. Coulter said you were to have as many as you like," cried the dressmaker in distress. "I have many more to show you!"

Roxanne shook her head.

The dressmaker looked unhappy. "When I come for your fittings," she said, "Mr. Coulter has authorized me to bring hats and veils and underthings and shoes and stockings and gloves for you to choose from."

"Very well," said Roxanne. "But I have a favorite glover. All my gloves must come from Barrington's." And she sent the woman on her way.

Hot on the heels of the dressmaker arrived a note from Mrs. Hollister, who asked if she might call later in the afternoon. The gray-uniformed maid who brought the note was a girl Roxanne had never seen before, a pretty Russian girl who, when asked if she spoke English, said "Soon," with a flash of white teeth.

Roxanne gave her a sympathetic look. The girl was her replacement in the Coulter household, no doubt. Anxiously, she stood inside the hall door awaiting Roxanne's reply.

Roxanne agreed to receive Mrs. Hollister that afternoon at two o'clock, realizing that the girl might suffer if she didn't. Mrs. Hollister might well believe she hadn't delivered the message properly.

Promptly at two, Mrs. Hollister arrived, wearing deepest black. Roxanne received her coolly; she had no love for the woman who had cast off Mary Bridey and had lied to save Rhodes from her own just vengeance. The plump little housekeeper looked around her, apparently surprised at such sumptuous surroundings, and stammered out what she had come to say: that they all missed Roxanne at the Mt. Vernon Place house.

Roxanne inclined her head regally—after all, she might soon be giving Mrs. Hollister her orders for the day—and inquired about the staff.

Cook was fine, she was told. Greaves, unfortunately, had a stiff back from lifting a heavy trunk for Miss Clarissa. Lizzie was stepping out with the milk-cart driver—a widower, old enough to be her father; what she saw in him, Mrs. Hollister couldn't imagine.

And Tillie and Ella?

"Tillie and Ella—" Mrs. Hollister hesitated—"are no longer with us. We have hired two new girls to replace them."

"Why have you dismissed them?" cried Roxanne in rising indignation. "What had they done?"

Mrs. Hollister bit her lip. "Mr. Gavin replaced them before he left for Boston. It was because—well, because of what happened to you. He didn't want gossip spread."

And Cook and Greaves and Lizzie never gossiped . . . while Tillie and Ella might.

"That was cruel of Gavin," Roxanne said slowly.

"He did it to shield you," cried Mrs. Hollister. "He gave them both two weeks pay and a reference."

Roxanne's lips twisted. "The one who brought your note was very pretty. And the other?"

Mrs. Hollister sat straighter. "Both are very pretty. Mr. Gavin likes pretty women in his household." She paused for a moment, but then said solicitously, "Mr. Gavin wanted me to bring you anything you needed from the house. Blankets, linens, dishes."

"The rooms here are handsomely furnished," said Roxanne. "And my landlady's cook and maid provide well for my needs."

Mrs. Hollister looked relieved.

Had they heard from Rhodes? asked Roxanne in spite of herself. The woman looked surprised. No, they had not, she said. Mr. Rhodes had disappeared off the face of the earth, it would seem. His father had punished him by disinheriting him; surely—

"Joab Coulter was not Rhodes's father," said Roxanne, and the other woman started. "You knew that," she added brutally. "Why pretend with me?"

Mrs. Hollister took a deep breath and straightened. "Yes." She stated it coolly. "I knew. You see, I met Joab"—she no longer called him "Mr. Joab"; the cards were on the table now—"I met Joab when I was only fourteen. I was the daughter of one of his ship captains, and I met him when he came to inform me that my father had been washed overboard in a storm. Since I had no means of livelihood, he assured me that he would give me employment in his household as a chambermaid. Ah, he was so handsome then. . . . Before I was fifteen he took me to his bed—he was a widower, with a little boy . . . Gavin." She spoke the name softly, as if he were her own son. "A year later he married Amanda Rhodes and we all moved to Mt. Vernon Place. At first I thought my heart would break, knowing he was up there in the bedroom with her—they occupied Miss Clarissa's rooms then. But after a time I realized he did not love her, that indeed he hated her, had only married her for the wealth she brought him."

Mrs. Hollister looked down, picking at the black lace that trimmed her black silk dress. "At first it gave me joy to see him tear at her, make her weep with his accusations. And then"—she looked up at Roxanne and her chin lifted—"and then I came to feel sorry for her and to love her. Amanda was a good woman, full of heart. I think she knew about me, that I shared his bed, but she never let on, and she was kind to me. When she hired her Irish groom—and I think he had not been a groom before he came to us, but an impoverished gentleman—I was glad for her. The light came back to her eyes and she was happy for a time. Then he was killed in a stable fire. And she lost heart altogether. Later when Rhodes was born, she came to life again and all her love was lavished on her son. That left Joab for me—and I took what was mine. Three rooms were combined to make my large back room on the third floor. Joab gave me gifts, did everything to make me comfortable. Of course, Amanda died, but even then I understood that he could not marry me—not a housekeeper; he had his reputation to think of. But we lived together as man and wife after the shades were drawn."

"And Rhodes never knew about his real father?"

"No, and I don't think Joab ever knew either. Certainly *I* didn't tell him, although I surprised Amanda and her lover one day in each other's arms. And I never let on to Joab; I kept her secret well—except for Gavin, who surprised it out of me one day. In a way, I guess you could say I was Amanda's friend."

"And it was because Rhodes was her son that you lied and said you'd found the door to the servants' entrance unlocked?"

Mrs. Hollister bobbed her head. "And I'd do it again, Roxanne. I owed it to her, not to let her son suffer—for she could have thrown me out of the house, you know. Joab would not have stopped her. He'd have set me up elsewhere, but I'd have seen so much less of him. . . ."

Roxanne stared at this woman of divided loyalties. It must be hard to be Mrs. Hollister. She sighed. "I understand why you did it, but it goes no less hard with me. I'll not try to undercut you with Gavin, Mrs. Hollister. I think he needs you."

To her surprise, tears filled the other woman's eyes. "They're like my own sons," she choked. "I've mothered them since they were little."

"I am glad you came," said Roxanne as Mrs. Hollister rose to go. "It's nice to understand at last."

"It isn't a bad life," said Mrs. Hollister earnestly, patting Roxanne's hand. "If I had it to do over, I'd do it all again." Her face broke up. *"Oh, I miss him so,"* she murmured, and fled.

As Roxanne watched her go, a plump little figure in rustling black silk, her eyes were bright with compassion. Joab Coulter had been many things, most of them bad, but he had had the staunch love of one woman, and according to her lights, he had been good to her.

But Mrs. Hollister's story had upset Roxanne, and

she hurried out of the house, which seemed suddenly oppressive, to take a walk. She strode down the street, noticing the gardens filled with flowers. For it was almost May and Baltimore was abloom.

She paused and sighed as she found herself in front of the handsome brick house at South and Gay Streets where young Betsy Patterson had been wooed and won by that glittering nineteen-year-old gallant, Jerome Bonaparte. Napoleon had put a damper on his youngest brother's marriage soon enough, and dark-haired Betsy had had to retreat via England to her native shores, Napoleon having refused to recognize the marriage. How sad it must have been for Betsy, proud daughter of a self-made merchant prince of Baltimore, to happen upon Jerome years later (then King of Westphalia) while he was strolling in a Florence museum with his second wife . . . his queen. Once Betsy had aspired to be his queen.

Roxanne shrugged. Daring Betsy had gambled for an empire and lost, but . . . she herself might gain a shipping empire. Her eyes grew dreamy as she cast a last backward glance at the elegant mansion, the walled garden overrun with flowers. Perhaps like Betsy she would someday dance the night away with a man of glamor and fortune. Perhaps, when Gavin returned, *she* might join the wives of Baltimore's merchant princes—Pattersons, Carrolls, Calverts—and give dainty teas and lavish balls. . . .

But her feet dragged.

Suddenly Baltimore had become an alien city. She longed for Savannah with its moss-draped live oaks and its leisurely ways. She longed for her lost girlhood, her lost innocence, a time before she had become the pawn and plaything of men. . . . Sometimes, as she passed a magnolia tree, she imagined herself back home among the scented creamy blossoms, the chinaberry and mimosa with its lacy foliage and blossoms like powder puffs, with the scent of a wild honeysuckle overrunning the gardens—a young carefree Roxanne lolling in a hammock in the summer shade or playing with a favorite kitten.

The picture faded. She was here in this ironclad city that had once been circled by walls, that might as well be a walled city now, so firmly did it shut her in.

She must wait for the day Gavin returned and took her to wife.

Gavin had promised.

She must wait.

Chapter 18

All of May and part of June Gavin lingered in Boston. He was not a man given to writing, and Roxanne did not hear from him. Waiting in her spacious surroundings with nothing to do, Roxanne chafed.

In her loneliness, she turned to Denby.

The young glover brightened when she strolled into his shop, but grew sad again as he told her that his father had died two weeks before. An automobile had run him down in the street at dusk one day. His skull had been fractured. Roxanne murmured condolences.

"I would have sent flowers if I had known," she said sincerely. Denby gave her a wistful smile; he seemed rather subdued today. "We closed the shop for a day out of respect for my father," he said. "But now it's business as usual. Though I'll be happy to slip out for an hour and walk you home."

She nodded her assent, and he called someone out from the back workroom as he joined her at the door.

Impulsively, when they neared the De Quincy house,

Roxanne, let Denby kiss her. She thought, resentfully: *If Gavin doesn't want things like this to happen, he should be here*! Denby asked to see her again and she agreed. She told herself she was comforting him for his father's death, but in her heart she knew it was untrue. She needed his warm admiration, his sunny compliments to bolster her against loneliness and to steady her sadly flagging self-esteem.

On a warm day Denby borrowed a bicycle built for two from a friend and they pedaled with a hamper into the country for a feast of cold chicken and soda pop and sandwiches. Seated on newspapers—the "funnies," which had made their debut in a New York paper the year before and to which Denby was passionately addicted—on the damp ground, Roxanne munched the fried chicken Denby's mother had prepared for them. She listened as Denby told her that his older brother was getting married at the end of the month. The brother also wanted to expand the shop and become competitive by making a cheap grade of gloves. Denby twirled his silky brown moustache fiercely. He disagreed; he wanted to continue to cater to the carriage trade. Roxanne smiled at him indulgently. Intense Denby, with his aristocratic bent, would always wish to cater to the carriage trade.

Denby called for her frequently at Mrs. De Quincy's decaying mansion. He took her to a music hall, and out to dinner. On a Sunday afternoon he rented a rig and they drove through the narrow winding roads of the lush Greenspring Valley, admiring the new homes going up there—large villas, gigantic "cottages," Tudor-style mansious. But he did not take her to his home.

Once he took her to a fair, a dusty, crowded, cheerful place. They rode the big ferris wheel and walked through the sawdust, ate cotton candy and visited a gypsy fortune teller in a tent.

"You will go far," the gypsy told Denby, and he looked pleased.

When Roxanne turned away, saying lightly, "I don't want to know my future," Denby seized her hand and said, "Ah, tell us. What of Roxanne?"

Frowning, the old gypsy woman bent over Roxanne's hand. "Your fate will be decided in a city with seven hills," she said at last.

"Cincinnati!" crowed Denby, who had once visited a cousin there.

"Rome!" exclaimed Roxanne, remembering that Baltimore's "best" families often made the Grand Tour.

Neither of them remembered that San Francisco was built on seven hills.

Several times Denby asked her to marry him. Always, she patted his hand with a sigh and turned him down. She liked Denby, but she did not love him. And she had promised Gavin she would wait.

Mrs. Hollister called again—this time, upset—to tell Roxanne that people had noticed her going about with the young glover; some of them might tell Mr. Gavin and then he'd be upset.

Roxanne, who thought that might well be true, thanked Mrs. Hollister coolly and the woman departed.

That afternoon when Denby took her out, she made a point of having him drive slowly by the Mt. Vernon Place house. Mrs. Hollister came out just as they were passing, and Roxanne nodded serenely. The housekeeper colored and scurried back into the house.

She did not call on Roxanne again.

For some reason Mrs. Hollister's warning had stirred Roxanne's loneliness again, and she found herself thinking about her grandmother's home in a kind of heartsick way. In wistful daydreams she walked again beneath overhanging live oaks with drifting beards of the mysterious gray Spanish moss, climbed the dunes, amid blowing grasses and rustling palms, of windswept Savannah Beach. But it was not the sultry soft-voiced southern city for which she yearned the most, and sometimes at night, tossing restless on her big square bed, she admitted it. It was her lost girlhood, her old carefree life, her sure confidence that when she grew up everything was going to be all right. It was for that she mourned.

She tried not to think of Rhodes, wherever he might be. But she found herself thinking of him anyway, and wondering what arms enfolded him now. She imagined him reclining on long verandahs, a tall drink in his hand, his long legs propped on the railing. Beside him sat a sloe-eyed beauty, while in the distance the *Virginia Lass* rode at anchor. At other times she saw him sprawled on the moonlit coral sand of countless palm-fringed islands with countless golden-skinned sirens lolling in the lazy circle of his arms.

She hated herself for these imaginings, but they would not go away. Even though she reminded herself of how lustfully and evilly he had used her. She would be revenged on him one day! she told herself, hands clenched, dry sobs wracking her throat. And when she had brought him down, this bitter yearning would turn to sweet contemptuous laughter, this ache in her heart would cease . . . and she would no longer love him.

At the end of May, Denby's older brother got married. Roxanne did not attend the wedding—was not invited, in fact. She gathered there had been a hot family discussion over her exclusion, for Denby's face flamed and he looked self-conscious when he muttered the news to her.

In mid-June, Gavin returned to Baltimore and came to call. It was a hot, sultry day with the promise of rain—a day Roxanne would always remember.

He arrived impeccably dressed, looking tall and serious. His face was more angular than ever; Roxanne was reminded of a hunting animal on the scent. She had decided in advance what her attitude would be when he returned: she would be cool, mocking, restrained—let *him* pursue.

As she let him in, she said, "I was beginning to think you'd taken root in Boston and were never coming home."

He stood there surveying her from head to foot, and Roxanne was glad she was wearing her elegant new beige walking suit.

"I missed you," he said abruptly, and bent to kiss her. She turned her head slightly to present her cheek to him and beckoned him to a rosewood chair. His keen eyes narrowed and he squared his shoulders slightly, as if deciding this might be a difficult business after all. They made small talk while the maid brought tea. Then Gavin sat at his ease, balancing his cup, his gaze admiring the picture Roxanne made as she poured the tea.

"I had forgotten how beautiful you are," he murmured. "You light up the room. It is all I can do not to sweep that teaset aside and take you by force."

She smiled at him over the teapot, but her gaze was level. "There is no need to send Mrs. Hollister to see me again."

He frowned. "I don't understand. I sent Mrs. Hollister to see if we could make you more comfortable—I left those instructions with her before I went to Boston."

"I think you sent her to make me realize how fortunate was my lot."

He sat back and smiled broadly. "How penetrating you are, Roxanne. Yes, I will admit that crossed my mind too."

"But you see, Gavin, I have no intention of growing old as a handsome housekeeper in your handsome house—taking orders from your wife, whoever she may be."

"*You* will be the wife of my heart." His voice was deep as he said it, and for a moment her heart stilled. She had begun to think he was playing her false, he had stayed away so long.

He put down his cup and, walking purposefully around the small tea table that separated them, leaned down to sniff the perfume of her hair. "So lovely . . ." he murmured. He took her chin with one finger and smiled into her eyes.

"So you've often told me." Her voice was composed. *Now it's coming*, she thought, her grip on the chair arms tightening. *The proposal. And I will say yes.*

"I want you to be happy, Roxanne," he said huskily. "I want us to be together."

She smiled, waiting.

"We are so right for each other," he added, touching her slender forearm, his fingers moving caressingly along it to her shoulder. She did not resist, but sat proudly, looking into his eyes. In her heart was a terrible tumult as, unbidden, the memory of Rhodes's smiling face returned to haunt her. "I have an old dream," said Gavin. "It is a dream I have had as long as I can remember: to make the Coulter Line foremost in the world. To do that we must convert to steam. It will take a large bankroll."

"You have control of Clarissa's money," she pointed out boldly.

"It is not enough." He sighed.

"And all that your father left you."

"My father died in debt," he said bitterly. "He was pig-headed, stubborn."

She had not known that. Somehow she had imagined inexhaustible funds behind the facade of wealth the Coulters presented.

"Do you like your rooms?" he asked abruptly.

She blinked. "They are very nice," she said cautiously.

He cast a restless look around him. "I could have the furniture brought over from Rhodes's room, if you like." He turned and gazed at her full in the face; his eyes were inscrutable. "Or you could move back into the house," he said.

Her arms gripped the chair. "Gavin," she said, puzzled. "What are you offering me?"

His intense expression deepened until she felt herself held like a snake by those eyes. "I offer you my heart," he said. "Which you have had from the first moment you walked into the house."

"And—?"

"Try to understand, Roxanne. I need financing. It will take a vast sum to change the Coulter Line from an out-of-date hodgepodge of sailing craft to a modern steamship line—"

"Gavin," she interrupted in alarm, half rising from her chair. "*What are you trying to tell me*?"

"That I love you," he said. "And that I was married in Boston ten days ago."

A dizzy feeling swept over Roxanne.

"*Married*!" she cried. "While I sat here waiting for you?"

"It will make no difference between us," he said desperately.

"*No difference*?"

"Roxanne, try to understand," he pleaded. "The Foster Iron Works is a huge enterprise—and Janice Foster's father owns a bank as well. It will be enough. And then, Roxanne, you and I—"

"Can have a backstairs relationship? Is that what you have in mind, Gavin? You can say good night to your wife in her front bedroom and creep up the back stairs to mine?" Her voice was so bitter he flinched before it.

"I did not mean that!" he cried.

"It does not matter what you meant," she shouted. "I have had enough of the Coulters—you *and* your brother!"

"Rhodes is not my brother."

"Brother or no, you are cut from the same bolt of cloth! You are as bad as he! No, you are worse! I will have nothing to do with you, do you hear?"

He straightened to his considerable height. He looked angry. "I would remind you," he said, "that you are very young and that you have no resources of your own. If you leave here, you will end up elsewhere in the very way you describe—or on the street. Remember that what you have, *I* have given you. That very dress on your back—"

It was the wrong thing to have said. Flushed with rage, Roxanne drew herself up too. "Since this dress belongs to you, I will take it off! Here and now!" she flashed. And grasping the throat of her soft lingerie blouse, she tore it straight down, pearl buttons flying. She tugged off her jacket and threw it at him.

Gavin was alarmed at the wildness of her gestures. "Roxanne, please," he cried, "you are not Mary Bridey. I would not treat you as a chambermaid, but as a lady!"

She stood stonelike as slowly that filtered through her skull. *I would not treat you as a chambermaid. . . .*

Suddenly a great white light seemed to burst over her. It fixed Gavin in its blinding glare. "Mary Bridey *was* your girl," she whispered, eyes widening. "Not Rhodes's—*yours. You* got her in trouble and left her to die alone! And lied to me to turn me against Rhodes!"

He shrugged, looking sullen. "What does it matter now?" he asked. "What has she to do with us, Roxanne?"

"To do with us? When I might have married Rhodes? *You* drove us apart by lying about her!" Her voice rose in passion. She ran to the fireplace, seized a poker and brandished it. "Get out!" she screamed. "Out of my sight!"

Prudently, Gavin retreated to the door. She gave him a hard push and slammed it after him.

"Roxanne." He knocked on the door, beseeching her to open it. "Roxanne, let me try to make you understand. It is only for a while. We—"

For answer she flung the heavy poker at the door with such force that it almost split the door panels. There was a silence on the other side and then the sound of footsteps going down the stairs.

Breathing hard, Roxanne stood where she was and looked at the wall. But she did not see it. Instead she saw a kind of blackness that represented the future Gavin offered her.

For a bitter moment she thought of Rhodes. Rhodes was forever lost to her, his bright image tarnished. For, whatever forces had driven him, even if she had goaded him past reason, she could never forgive him for that cruel attack or for rejecting her later. A sob tore from her throat. Gavin had done much more than dupe her with his lies—he had destroyed Rhodes for her, and for that she could never forgive him.

And now, if she did not do something, she would have to bend as a willow wand to Gavin's will.

She brought her clenched fist down on the back of a rosewood chair with a blow that numbed her fingers. She would not let it happen!

With trembling hands, she pulled on her best pair of white kid gloves, almost splitting them in her haste, jammed her hat on her head, pulled her coat on over her torn blouse. Then more slowly, she took all of them off, and with a thoughtful expression stopped and combed her hair carefully. She dressed herself in the gray suit Julie had given her, the gloves Denby had given her for Christmas—both a bit shabby from much wear—and hurried down to Barrington's. She took with her nothing of Gavin's.

Denby was working alone and late. He was about to close the shop, but stopped in surprise when the bell above the front door tinkled to announce a customer. He looked up from arranging a display of tasseled and beaded gloves to see Roxanne in the doorway.

Her eyes still bright with the fury she felt inwardly, she gave him a brilliant smile—and her gloved hand, which Denby bowed over and kissed with all the grace of a diplomat.

"Denby," she said bluntly, "do you still want to marry me?"

Joy leaped in his eyes. "You mean it?" he stammered. "You'd marry me, Roxanne?"

"Yes. On one condition: That you will take me far away from here. I will marry you when we reach wherever we're going."

Denby stared at her. "Wherever we're going?"

"Yes. You once said you'd like to open a shop somewhere else. Have you changed your mind?"

He shook his head and his voice was hoarse. "I've not changed it. And I've been thinking of removing from here because the shop's too small for both my brother and myself. He's offered to buy my share. But marry me here, Roxanne, and then I'll take you wherever you wish. With you beside me I can do anything."

She frowned. "No—no, Denby. There's something you don't know. My name isn't Willis—it's Rossiter. I was born in Augusta, Georgia. I ran away from—from a difficult situation with relatives out west and assumed the name of another woman. Gavin Coulter knows that and he could prosecute me for impersonation and for stealing Mary Willis's ticket if—"

"Hush." Denby took her in his arms, cradled her. "It doesn't matter, Roxanne. I don't care what your name is. And—" he held her off at arm's length and his boyish smile flashed—"I'll take you back to Augusta where you were born! That's where we'll go!"

"Oh, Denby, would you?" Caught up by his exultant mood, she agreed that Augusta seemed the answer to everything.

"I'll take you home now," he said, "and in the morning we—"

"No," she said on a note of desperation. "I'm not going back there, Denby. Not ever."

"But your things!"

"I've brought them all." She indicated the little valise Julie had given her. "All that really belongs to me is in here. Don't—don't make me wait to marry you, Denby. Pressure will be brought on me to change my mind. I don't know what I might do."

He looked alarmed. "We'll be married tonight!" he cried. "We'll find somebody who'll marry us tonight!"

There was one more thing. Before she married him, she must tell him she was not a virgin. She drew a deep breath. "Denby, there's one other thing you don't know about me. I—"

"I don't want to know," he said grandly. "I don't care if you robbed a bank or shot the governor!"

"It's nothing like that," she said. "I—"

He silenced her with a kiss. A very long kiss. She felt her blood stir a little.

"Roxanne, believe me." Suddenly dark and intense, Denby's hazel eyes looked deep into her own. "I don't care what your name is or what you've done. I love you anyway."

She smiled at him, a timid newly-trusting smile. *I love you anyway*. Denby had immediately won her heart by saying that.

"Give me an hour, Roxanne. I've got to get some money and pack a bag—and we'll be off."

Alone now, Roxanne leaned against the counter and closed her eyes.

She had made her decision, and she was committed. To Denby.

She would be his wife.

Book II

The Reckless Woman

Part One:

Augusta, Georgia
1896—1897

Chapter 19

Roxanne stared out the grimy window as the train roared south through perfumed meadows and swaying trees. But the coal-fired engine carried its own scent, as well as hot cinders and smoke to blacken the breeze. The last time she had ridden a train, she mused, she had been a hunted woman; now she was a bride with her wedding night behind her.

Yesterday's events drifted like smoke through her mind: waiting for Denby in the shop. The hour had lengthened to two and she'd begun to wonder if Denby had changed his mind and was afraid to tell her. Something in her had brightened at the thought but it was immediately quenched. From upstairs she had heard occasional loud voices. Finally, Denby's mother, a paisley shawl clutched around her, had burst into the room.

"It isn't right! It isn't decent!" she cried. "Getting married in the night like this, sneaking off as if you're ashamed!"

Denby was right behind her. His face was flushed. "Mother," he cried sharply, "Roxanne's going to be my wife; you might as well face it."

Dismayed, Roxanne saw Denby's whole family pour into the room behind him. His pale-eyed sisters lining up like spitting cats beside his sobbing mother. Behind them his older brother, looking uneasy, and his new wife, looking horrified.

"If you go with that woman, you'll never come back!" cried his mother hysterically and burst into a storm of tears.

Traveling grip in hand, Denby stood in an agony of indecision, looking uncertainly from his mother to Roxanne. Roxanne realized then, if she had not before, that Denby, the youngest, was tied to Mama's apron strings—and now that he wanted to break away he was finding those apron strings forged with gold and tears.

"Come on, Roxanne," muttered Denby hoarsely, and grabbed her by the arm. Over his shoulder he called to his older brother, "Wire me the bank draft in Augusta—I'll write where to send it. And where to send my trunk."

Then they were out in the June night. Roxanne stopped. "Denby," she began uncertainly, "are you sure you want to—"

"I'm sure," he said roughly, and hurried her away.

They boarded the train, ate in the dining car, and sat up in the coach all night, talking. When the train reached Richmond in the early morning, they got off and waited for the Court House to open so they could get a marriage license. Roxanne, unsure of the law, lied about her age. She said she was twenty-one. The clerk grinned. They were married by a sleepy Justice of the Peace whose wife played the wedding march off-key on a squeaky organ.

They spent the day wandering around hilly Richmond, the old Confederate capital at the headwaters of the James. With Denby, Roxanne admired the Ionic columns of the State Capitol—a shining white temple for which Thomas Jefferson had sent a plaster model from France. When they strolled about Church Hill, Roxanne sighed over the Corinthian portico of the Church of the Confederacy, with its memories of Jefferson Davis and Robert E. Lee and a war that had cost her people all they had. They visited Chimborazo

Park, named for a mountain in the Andes, which during the Civil War was the site of the world's largest military hospital.

In the afternoon Denby took her shopping on Broad Street and over Roxanne's protests bought her so many new clothes they had to purchase a small hand-trunk to carry them. She noticed that Denby grew increasingly edgy as the day wore on. *He's afraid to go to bed with me*, thought Roxanne uneasily.

They registered in a mellow old red brick hotel, and Denby's voice almost cracked as he fiercely asserted they were man and wife. The desk clerk hid a smile at the newlyweds and beckoned a cheerful black porter to carry their bags upstairs. Roxanne dressed carefully in the lovely new ready-made peach tea gown Denby had bought her. It was princess cut with triangular insets of matching peach lace that reached down a long bell-shaped skirt to a hem which culminated in a little train. It was a very hour-glassy dress; and Roxanne, her hair piled up luminously atop her head, her dainty chin carried as high above her white throat as any Gibson Girl's, saw heads turn as she and Denby came down to dine in splendor in the sumptuous hotel dining room. Denby beamed around him expansively. He was enjoying the homage paid to Roxanne's beauty.

When they were seated at the table, Roxanne wondered if she should tell Denby now that she was not a virgin. She stared at the silver bowl of roses that decorated the table and decided not to. Perhaps—perhaps he would be so inexperienced he would not know the difference. Her face burned at the thought.

"Are you too warm?" cried Denby. "Tomorrow I will buy you a fan."

Roxanne shook her head. "It's close in here," she murmured.

He looked around him. "The overhead fans are going."

Roxanne studied the menu. "This is terribly expensive," she muttered. "Do you think we should—"

"Nonsense." With a masterful gesture, Denby interrupted her to order Oysters Rockefeller, roast beef and wine from the white-jacketed black waiter who took their order. "We're going to have the best, Roxanne—nothing but the best. My brother is going to send me a bank draft for half of my share; he can't raise it all, but he'll send the rest next year. I'll open a shop and you'll wear only the finest gloves, Roxanne—all the women will envy you."

Roxanne gave him a wistful smile. Denby was so enthusiastic. She hoped it would work out as he said and that he would succeed, whether other women envied her or not.

They lingered long at their dinner, and afterward, drinking champagne. Roxanne guessed that Denby was getting up his nerve. At last, he paid the check and rose, squaring his shoulders and swaggering a little. Meekly Roxanne accompanied him. When they reached the door of their third floor room, he unlocked it and then swung her up in his arms, carrying her over the threshold with a flourish.

As he kicked the door shut behind them, Roxanne closed her eyes. That closing door had shut out Rhodes forever, she told herself. She was Denby's now; she belonged to him.

Denby stood her on her feet and gave her an uncertain look. With their backs to each other they undressed: Denby donning a nightshirt that reached to his knees, Roxanne slipping on a soft batiste nightgown with a white satin drawstring at the top that ran through embroidered holes about the round low neck.

Denby still had his back turned when Roxanne slipped into bed. Although it was a hot night, she instinctively pulled up the sheet around her neck. Denby turned and looked relieved to see her covered up. He drew back the sheet on his side and got in gingerly.

Roxanne turned toward him, her wide sapphire eyes regarding him solemnly. "Aren't you going to turn out the light?" she asked.

Embarrassed, Denby leaped out of bed and put out the light. In total darkness he got back into bed. The heat was stifling.

"If you raise the shades," suggested Roxanne, "the moonlight will come in."

Again he rose with alacrity, and in a moment the oppressive heat was relieved by a cool breeze through the screen. The room was now flooded with moonlight —a soft caressing light that turned Roxanne's dark-blond hair, spread out on the pillow, to gleaming silver, and made her eyes dark silvered pools. A man could drown in those eyes.

Roxanne saw Denby needed help. She gave him a tender smile and brushed away the sheet. With delicate fingers she pulled the satin drawstring that held up the top of her batiste gown. As the loosened material slid away from her shoulders and exposed the pearly hills of her breasts and the white valley between them, she heard Denby draw in his breath sharply.

"Roxanne . . ." he murmured and bent down to kiss her lips. She found it a sweet virginal kiss, and twining her slender hands around his neck, she drew him slowly to her. As their bodies met, a little sob of joy escaped him and he clasped her fervently to him.

Roxanne's cheeks were wet with tears. It was wonderful to know she meant so much to Denby.

Wonderingly, his hands explored this vision that had come into his bed, and Roxanne felt her body respond to him as she held him fast and he murmured incoherent endearments into her hair.

And then he was clutching her with clumsy boyish passion, straining fiercely until, his passion quickly spent, he flung away from her and lay panting beside her, staring up at the ceiling. Roxanne, aroused but unfulfilled, stirred restlessly and gave him a troubled look. He sighed and turned his back. Moments later she heard his breathing grow shallow, rhythmic.

Denby was asleep.

Roxanne gave him a fond look, and told the tumult in her passionate woman's body to be still. Turning over on her side, she tried to sleep. But aroused as she was, sleep did not come till morning. When she woke, sleepily opening her eyes, she saw that Denby was already dressed in the clothes he had worn yesterday and was standing with his back to her, feet wide apart, hands clasped behind him, staring out of the window.

As she moved, the bedsprings creaked and he turned. She saw that his face was crimson and upset.

"Roxanne, you aren't—" He swallowed. "You weren't—"

"A virgin," she finished for him.

"Yes!" He said it loudly, giving her an accusing look.

Roxanne stared at him in consternation. She sat up in bed and the covers fell away to reveal her soft rounded form. The top of her gown, with the satin drawstring opened, revealed one pink-tipped pearly breast. She was oblivious to her state of undress. Pushing back her shining disheveled hair, she regarded Denby with large serious blue eyes. "I thought—I thought you loved me enough for it not to make any difference," she said finally.

An agony of doubt and torment crossed Denby's face. "You should've told me," he muttered, turning away. And then, as if the question were wrenched from him. "Who was it?"

"Does it matter?" she asked wearily. "I was *attacked*, Denby. It wasn't my fault."

He turned to gape at her. "Who?" he whispered.

"I don't want to think about it," she said. "It was long ago. In Kansas."

"What happened?"

She thought about that. How could she explain? The tornado making death seem near and close . . . Buck's tortured *need* to hold a woman in his arms . . . her own loneliness that cried out for a lover . . . Julie Smith's emaciated face with its steady candid gray eyes swam before her accusingly. "I can't talk about it," she said, muffled. And then after a while, when he remained silent, "If you think I've cheated you, Denby, we can call it off."

"*Call it off*?" he cried. "How can we call it off? We're *married*, Roxanne!"

"We can be unmarried!" she snapped. "Oh, Denby, what does it matter? The only question is, do you still want me?"

When he was still silent, she got up in her thin nightgown and walked to the window to stand beside him letting the cool breeze blow the flimsy material about her waist and thighs. She sighed and, turning, brushed his arm with the tip of her soft breast. Denby jumped as if stung.

"Yes," he said hoarsely. "I still want you."

She looked up at him, and her expression was very solemn. "I was wrong not to tell you, Denby. I suppose I thought—I thought you loved me enough so that it wouldn't matter."

He gripped her shoulders. "It *doesn't* matter!" His voice rang.

"Oh, Denby." She moved forward into his arms and wrapped her arms about his neck. Her voice was husky. "I promise to be such a good wife to you. I promise to be faithful, Denby."

Now thoroughly aroused, his eyes burned down into hers. "I believe you, Roxanne," he said simply, and swept her up against him. He walked with her to the big bed and fell upon her hungrily, tasting the sweetness of her body as if he were starving. As he clung to her, she felt his tears fall on her cheek.

Roxanne, dry eyed and shaken that she should mean so much to Denby, held him fiercely. *I will be faithful,* she promised him silently. *You were the only man I could turn to when everything went wrong. You stood with me against your family, and now you have forgiven me for this. Whatever happens, Denby,* her heart swore, *I will never betray you.*

She caressed Denby with a new tenderness, rubbed her soft cheek against his to dry the tears born of his emotional struggle, murmured endearments against his ear, molded her body willingly to his, pressed her hips upward, straining toward him sweetly, and felt the breath expel from his lungs in a moment of bliss.

Denby, who had been so shy and hesitant last night, was now suddenly a wolfish lover, demanding, almost overbearing in asserting his marital rights. He held her in a grip that hurt—but she forgave him for it, and even smiled later when she looked down at the dark places that marred her white arms and shoulders, remembering the fierce passion that had driven him.

He loves me, she told herself. He is inexperienced in these matters. He was carried away and forgot that I am not made of leather like the gloves in which he takes such pride, but that I am made of flesh and bruise beneath rough fingers.

She did not know then that they were but the first of many bruises, to her flesh—and to her heart.

They lingered no longer in Richmond, but dressed and hurried to the train. And all the way south on the train, Denby—now exuding self confidence— chattered excitedly about what a wonderful place Augusta was. He'd never been there of course, but he'd heard all about it from a friend who'd been in the brickmaking industry. Clay products were very big in Augusta, he informed her importantly. And textiles.

He didn't have to tell her that textiles were important. She knew that Augusta had been one of the capitals not only of Georgia but of the old cotton kingdom. But it was not Augusta's mills or its railroads or its prosperity that quickened her heartbeat.

She was going home to Georgia. Back to the lovely, leisurely town of her birth, a town that sprawled along the river that flowed down to Savannah and the sea, a river down which she'd traveled as a little child, holding fast to her mother's hand.

Denby was taking her home.

She was so grateful to him she lavished affection on him, and he swelled up with pride at these attentions, believing them a tribute to his prowess as a lover.

In that he was mistaken. Roxanne found him sadly lacking as a lover. He did not stir in her the white-hot passion which she had vaguely expected to find in marriage. Although she would not admit it to herself, she was not enamored of him, and his clumsy love-making only served to emphasize that fact.

But he had forgiven her the loss of her virginity and now he was taking her home to Georgia!

She could forgive him a deal for that.

Chapter 20

With his choice of Augusta, Denby was well content. Its mild climate, its ten-month growing season, its mills and manufactories and railroads all pleased him. And while he busied himself looking for a shop, Roxanne set out to explore a city of which she had only the vaguest memories.

On wide gracious streets she found the graceful Georgian and neoclassic homes of the "Old Money," lovely homes that had been here when "Lighthorse Harry" Lee retook the city from the British in 1781, houses that had been brilliantly lit with candles and aswish with crinolines and satin knee breeches to greet visiting George Washington in 1791.

She passed the mansard-roofed, turreted and gingerbread-bedecked Victorian mansions of the "New Money" that Denby worshipped. Out of the Confederate debacle, Augusta had survived as an industrial city, a trading and railroad center where the soot of industry and puffing locomotives blackened the creamy magnolias. Here the clamor and bustle ruffled the leisurely ways of the Old South. Roxanne would have preferred the old ways; Denby, she knew, preferred the new.

Later she found herself passing a house she vaguely remembered, and paused to read a small sign of polished brass set into a mossy brick wall: *Mrs. Barton's Academy for Young Ladies.*

Roxanne smiled. Here was the school where her mother had taught when they lived in Augusta so long ago. Roxanne had never believed Aunt Ada's story that her mother had been dismissed by the headmistress because the woman's husband took a fancy to her. Impulsively, she went through the iron archway opening in the high brick wall and rang the bell. To a black manservant in a white coat who answered, she identified herself and asked for Mrs. Barton.

As she waited she looked around her. The reception room with its regal fireplace and white wainscoting, both of which she remembered, were just the same. But . . . something was missing: the sound of girlish laughter, the light footsteps of the young. The school seemed to have shut down.

When an autocratic-looking woman leaning on a cane came into the room, Roxanne realized that she had made a mistake in coming. The woman took a long keen look at her visitor and an expression of intense dislike crossed her face. "You wanted to see me?" she snapped.

"My mother taught here," explained Roxanne. "I remembered the school as I was passing by and . . ." Her voice trailed off under that almost menacing stare. "And I thought I would call," she added bravely.

Her hostess remained standing. She did not give an inch. "I closed the school this year," she said coldly. "I should have taken down the sign."

Roxanne flushed. Looking past the imposing woman standing before her, she saw a framed photograph on a marble-topped walnut table. A photograph of a man with a wicked smile and the eyes of a rogue. He would have been considerably older than her mother, had she lived, about the age of the woman before her. Mr.

Barton, she guessed—the man with the roving eye. Now, looking into the headmistress's face, she knew Aunt Ada's story was true. She could almost feel animosity seething in the elderly woman. And although she realized that animosity was not really for her, but was because she looked so like her mother, it still made her very uncomfortable. Quickly Roxanne took her leave, her cheeks burning, and made her way rapidly down the street. In the future, she determined, she would give Mrs. Barton's residence a wide berth.

In her walks about the city, Roxanne also tried to avoid the busy port facilities on the Savannah River, for the river steamships and the tall white sailing ships reminded her too much of Baltimore . . . and Rhodes. He and Gavin had been cut out of the same bolt of cloth, she told herself savagely, and the devil with them both. But her mind unbidden conjured up pictures of Rhodes as she remembered him—strong and lighthearted and laughing. Rhodes, looking down at her with kind keen eyes, making her thrill to his touch. Rhodes the way he had been before . . . before he had lain in wait for her on a dark stairway and scarred her life. Somehow remembering Gavin did not hurt so much, although she had been willing to marry him, had indeed intended to marry him. But Rhodes . . . ah, the memory of him hurt.

Resolutely she put Baltimore behind her, that town that had broken her heart.

She called on her mother's friends, all the names she could remember. She found few of them left. Some had died, some had moved away, some were unaccountably cool.

One old lady whose name was Jessamine Willoughby, and who lived alone in a vine-covered brick house sadly in need of repair, received her warmly.

"I knew your mother well," she told Roxanne. "A lovely child, and you are just like her, my dear. I hope you have made a good marriage."

Roxanne told her that she had married a glover, and that they hoped to open a little shop here in Augusta. The old lady gave her an understanding nod, but Roxanne could not tell whether she approved or not. She served Roxanne tea in delicate Spode cups in a room with cool slanted light, where beautifully made interior shutters kept out the direct sunlight. Roxanne listened to Miss Willoughby's soft Southern voice and smiled into those faded eyes. Sitting here so correctly in a parlor in the town of her birth, she felt she had indeed come home.

Although Roxanne knew she had been exploring a city with a storied past, Miss Willoughby made Augusta come alive for her. "Lord Oglethorpe," Miss Willoughby explained, "established the town as a fort and named it for Princess Augusta—mother of England's George III. An Irishman had first settled it. In 1763, a treaty between five great Indian nations and four Southern governors was signed." She went on enthusiastically, "George Walton, who signed the Declaration of Independence, lived here, and on Rocky Creek is a dam built by Eli Whitney, who so transformed the life of the South."

The elderly woman was pleased with her verbal tour of the city and Roxanne encouraged her to talk. And so they spent a most enjoyable afternoon together.

When Roxanne left, promising to come again soon, her hostess made one remark that puzzled her.

"You will need help here," she said. "Let me think about it and we will talk about it when you come again."

Roxanne refrained from asking what Miss Willoughby meant, thinking it might be just an old lady's eccentricity. In any event, she could clear it up when next she visited her.

But she had no chance, for when she called again the following Thursday there was black crepe on the door, and a weeping servant informed her that "poor old Miss Jessamine" had died of a stroke. He added that her body was being sent back to Atlanta to be buried in the family burying ground.

Miss Willoughby's death saddened Roxanne. She had honestly liked the old lady, and knew her to be one of the town's social old guard. It would be harder for her and Denby to get established here socially without the sponsorship of someone like Miss Jessamine Willoughby.

She had no idea then just how hard it would be.

But in the meantime, she was hopeful, and things seemed to be going as planned. Denby found a vacant shop. The price was a little high, but the location justified it, he assured her, for it was on a small street just off the main artery. On the first floor a spacious show room fronted the street, and behind it were two large well-lighted workrooms. Best of all, there were rooms above the shop suitable for their living quarters. This would allow them to keep the shop open longer hours, locking the door in the evening but coming down if a customer rang the bell. Roxanne was a little daunted at that; she had not really anticipated interrupting dinner to hurry down and sell a pair of gloves. But Denby insisted they must make every sale they could. Every sale worked twofold, he assured her earnestly—it enriched them, and it kept their competitors from flourishing.

When they went from their hotel to inspect Denby's find, and Denby saw Roxanne wistfully eyeing a white-pillared mansion on the way, he squeezed her hand. "Never mind, we'll have one of those too one day," he said.

As she turned to him, her blue gaze softened. Maybe she could never love Denby as a wife should, but help him she certainly would. Together they would make this glove shop a success!

Roxanne climbed the wooden stairs that opened from the shop's back entrance and studied the rooms above the shop: a large front room, a kitchen and bedroom behind. Plain and hard-used, but she would make them livable. With determination, she took off her hat and donned an apron. After a couple of days of scouring, the floors gleamed and the windows sparkled. She resisted Denby's eager desire to rush out and buy fine furniture, realizing it would take time for the shop to succeed and they would need the money for other things. A kitchen table and chairs, a stove and an icebox, a bed and bureau, a branching hatrack and small pine wardrobe, a sofa and two chairs in case of callers: that was enough, Roxanne insisted firmly. Later on would come thick rugs and silver tea sets and rosewood tables and antimacassars and dainty loveseats and delicate china. Later, when they could afford them.

Luckily, she was able to find in the town a cheap set of dishes most of whose cups had been smashed in delivery. And since Augusta was a textile center, she found some inexpensive but good printed cottons for curtains. She splurged on a fine white linen tablecloth and some old silver spoons of a rose design that she fell in love with when she passed a shop window. But those were her only extravagances, and she promised herself she would make that up out of the household money by economizing. Her dish towels she made herself out of a long bolt of linen cloth; she made even her soap. She was determined not to waste Denby's money; he was trying too hard to get started.

Her acquisition of the spoons had cost her more than the purchase money, however, although she did not know it. As she left the shop with her package of spoons, she was observed by one of the leading Augusta socalites, Mrs. Randolph Forsythe.

Thinking of Augusta only as the city of her birth, where her roots should be, Roxanne had not realized that she was returning to the stronghold of her memorable mother's deadly enemies. Her mother's beauty had impressed the young swains of her day, to the chagrin of their womenfolk, and her mother had chosen for herself another girl's intended, a very wealthy and influential girl's intended. Aunt Ada had been right: Roxanne's father *had* fled the city with his bride to avoid not only the horsewhipping Aunt Ada had mentioned, but to escape the animosity of his jilted former fiancee. That jilted former fiancee was middle-aged now and twenty pounds heavier, but she was not so old she had forgotten how it felt to be left standing at the altar while her erstwhile groom fled the city with her best friend. The fact that she had since made a brilliant marriage and was no longer "that poor little

Canfield girl who was jilted" but instead the wealthy Mrs. Forsythe, whose influential husband was being groomed for governor, somehow did not matter. Mrs. Forsythe turned pale on the street at the sight of Roxanne, recognizing at once the mirror image of the girl who had been the cause of her misery. At that moment all the bitterness of that long ago time came flooding back, and Mrs. Forsythe got unsteadily into her waiting carriage, returned to her magnolia-shrouded mansion, shut herself in her white and gold bedroom, and wept for two hours. At the end of that time she began to make inquiries about the girl she had seen who "looked so like . . . so like. . . ."

When she learned that Roxanne was married to a young man from Baltimore who was seeking to establish himself in the glover's trade in Augusta, Mrs. Forsythe's eyes gleamed. Here at last was her chance to strike back at the woman who had caused her such heartache. Quietly, she let it be known among her numerous relatives and even more numerous friends that Roxanne would not be received at her home. Her two married sisters took up the cudgel with *their* friends. Mrs. Barton, the spiteful headmistress whose husband's affections Roxanne's mother had unwittingly captured, heard of it and joined the whispering campaign of the Forsythe connections. Amongst them, they blanketed Augusta with aspersions on Roxanne's character and hints about her "bad blood," and—with knowing shrugs and raised eyebrows—added the damning comment that she had "married down." An informal boycott was agreed upon, the assumption being that if nobody patronized Denby's shop, he would take the hint and go back to Baltimore "where he belonged."

These ladies would see to it that Roxanne's lot was hard.

When in late August Denby opened for business, the gentry did not stream, as expected, into his shop. Puzzled, Denby rearranged his window displays, had his new sign regilded, and waited.

By nature energetic, Roxanne asked Denby if she could not work in the shop. He agreed reluctantly; she could supervise the clerk he had hired while he supervised the glovemakers in the workrooms. Business picked up a little after she started working there, for Roxanne managed to attract a few passing gentlemen by her beauty, gentlemen who were willing to purchase a pair of gloves in order to talk to the possessor of such a face and such a figure.

On one occasion, Denby hurried out of the workroom and the male customer, realizing that Denby was Roxanne's husband, swiftly grabbed his gloves and left. When the clerk Roxanne was allegedly supervising tittered over this, Denby gave Roxanne a sharp look. After that incident Denby started popping out of the workroom almost every time the bell over the shop door announced another customer. It was painfully obvious to him that these smiling gentlemen who bowed so low to his wife were interested in more than gloves.

Fiercely jealous, Denby pounced on this; he smoldered for a while and then one day exiled Roxanne to the rooms over the shop. Let the hired clerk take care of the customers; he would not have Roxanne flaunting herself before the public, he fumed. Roxanne reminded him that his own mother had worked in his father's glove shop when they started. Denby would not listen. He informed her angrily that times had changed. Roxanne sighed and trudged upstairs. She had encountered his unreasoning jealousy before.

That night when Denby came to bed, he stood in the lamplight looking down at her alluring body in its delicate white nightgown.

"Take it off," he said shortly.

Roxanne stared up at him, puzzled. Slowly she drew the nightgown up over her head, so that she lay naked before him.

"That's better," said Denby and seized her roughly, almost pummeling her as he thrashed around the bed. Roxanne was still gasping from that bout when, bruisingly, he took her again. And afterward thrust her away from him almost contemptuously. His manner said plainly, *That's good enough for you.*

Roxanne was hurt and bewildered.

When she woke the next morning, her whole body ached, and she winced when her shoulder moved on the pillow.

After Denby had gone downstairs, whistling, to work in the shop, she took off her dress and studied the bruises he had given her the night before.

Then she sank down on the bed in despair.

He wants to hurt me, she decided. He desires me but he cannot forgive me for being as attractive to other men as I am to him.

She found it a disquieting thought.

Roxanne was also puzzled by the conspicuous absence of the carriage trade from their shop—and by the coolness of her reception in general. People she thought should have welcomed her with open arms as her mother's daughter returned, did not. In fact, they did not welcome her at all. At first she wondered if by living above their little shop they had transgressed the aristocratic code of the South. But no—others were doing it.

Then one morning as she strolled in the park, it all became blindingly clear.

It was early, and as she strolled along, a gentleman in a morning coat, much the worse for drink, tipped his hat to her familiarly and said in a befuddled voice, "Well, if it isn't the young lady all the hubbub's about!"

Under normal conditions, Roxanne would have ignored him and swept on. Now she turned and said sharply, "What hubbub?"

He waved his gloved hand vaguely. Obviously, he had slipped and fallen somewhere on the damp ground, for his glove was muddy. "That's right," he murmured. "Wasn't to tell. All hush-hush."

"*What* is hush-hush?" cried Roxanne.

"All that about you . . . the glover's pretty wife who's come back looking just like her mother—and set all our good wives buzzing. Out to ruin the poor glover, they are!" He leaned dizzily against a tree. "Do you think you could tell me the way to Bacon Street?" he mumbled in a plaintive tone. "I live there."

"I will *take* you to Bacon Street," announced Roxanne angrily.

She seized the arm of the gentleman in the morning coat and marched him the short distance to Bacon Street, where she leaned him against his own doorbell. A well-dressed woman in her thirties—obviously his wife—threw the door open and gave ground in surprise as her husband lurched past her. Then she stood and glared at Roxanne.

"I have brought your husband home to you," said Roxanne in a cold voice. "He is in sad need of a new pair of gloves. I suggest you buy them from Denby Barrington."

She whirled on her heel and was gone, leaving the woman staring after her venomously.

If any further push had been needed to insure her social downfall, that did it. The woman was Mrs. Amalie Stone-Fellowes, and her wandering husband was a scandal in the town. Her curious neighbors, peeking through their lace curtains, had seen Roxanne's arrival with the errant Mr. Stone-Fellowes and promptly assumed the worst. The story spread like wildfire through aristocratic Augusta—further proof, it was said, of the type of woman Roxanne was. Mrs. Stone-Fellowes seethed.

Now Roxanne had acquired a third bitter enemy who wished the new glover to take his store to some other town.

Two had been enough.

But at least Roxanne finally understood the nature of her problem. If only Denby would let her work in the shop! There she could perhaps charm wealthy gentlemen into buying gloves surreptitiously for their wives. Women used stacks of gloves. It was not unusual for a lady of pretensions to take forty pair at a time to be cleaned.

To be cleaned! She could wash and clean gloves upstairs. Surely Denby would not mind that! And it would supplement their too-meager income. When Denby came upstairs after a fruitless day, she broached the subject and Denby promptly vetoed it. He went on to criticize: the dinner, the biscuits were burned again; Roxanne's hairstyle, too conspicuous; the color of the curtains, too bright. His mood was waspish.

It stayed waspish, for business got no better. Oh, he sold a pair of gloves now and then: to women who could only afford cheap ones, to men needing work gloves. But that didn't meet the payroll or the rent. And the carriage trade, which he had so confidently expected, and which indeed was the proper market for his fine handmade gloves, stayed away.

Denby began to find fault with Roxanne all the time, bitterly criticizing her. Her walk was too seductive, her glance was too bold, her clothes fit her too tightly—only harlots displayed their figures in this manner.

"And society women!" shouted Roxanne, driven to rage. "These are the clothes *you* bought for me, Denby. You thought them perfect at the time. My hair is the same too. What has changed you?"

His young face, once so boyish, was suddenly haggard and old. He buried his head in his hands and groaned. "Oh, God, Roxanne," he cried despairingly. "What am I to do? My gloves are the finest in town. Why don't they sell?"

Roxanne was afraid to tell him. "Perhaps if I started working in the shop again?" she suggested tentatively.

"No!" shouted Denby, and flung out of the apartment, to return late and befuddled by bourbon.

Denby placed a large ad in the *Augusta Chronicle and Gazette*. Even that did not help much.

Before the winter was over Roxanne knew it had all been a mistake; she should never have married Denby. She had, she realized, left her heart in Baltimore. She had given it to a rogue. Now she would have nothing, nothing.

But that was not Denby's fault, she told herself sternly. In his blundering way she was sure he loved her. And although she did her best to simulate ardor, to make her response to him as warm and loving as he could have wished, she felt that he sensed his own inadequacy in the bedroom and her counterfeit response, and she wondered if that could be the basis for the jealously he so recklessly displayed.

About Denby she now felt very guilty. His glove shop—never flourishing—was slowly dying. And his enthusiasm for it, once so bright, was waning too. She had brought him here to this lovely city, so staunchly aligned against her. And here he would leave his father's fortune, dissipated for reasons he did not understand. He would go under, working frenziedly.

It made her cry sometimes at night, for pity.

Denby heard her crying and made wild efforts to make amends, believing her tears were due to his treatment of her. He bought her a gold locket on a little chain to wear around her neck. She knew he could not afford such expensive gifts and yearned to ask him to take it back. But so happy was he to clasp it around her neck that she choked back the words and, instead, threw her arms around his neck and wept in earnest.

Denby, touched by this display of emotion at his gift, strutted around the shop for several days.

Until a conspicuously handsome Army major dropped by. This major had formerly stopped by the shop several times and bought gloves he did not need solely to feast his eyes on Roxanne and to try somehow to win her favor. Now back in town, he inquired of Denby if she was there, and insisted he would purchase his gloves from nobody but Roxanne. Stiff-necked with jealousy of the handsome major, Denby told him Roxanne no longer worked in the shop and added loftily that the shop was flourishing and he was hiring an assistant clerk. It was such an obvious bald-faced lie that the major laughed in Denby's face, turned on his heel and left.

That night Denby flung wild accusations at Roxanne: She had encouraged the major, she had led him on; why else would he insist on buying his gloves from nobody but her?

It was useless to reason with him. Denby stormed out of the house in a passion. Roxanne spent the hours awaiting his return staring at the celing in the darkness and seeing before her a bleak future. She could not find the heart to blame Denby for these outbursts, which had become more frequent. She knew he was worried almost to panic because his business was not catching on.

Denby came home very drunk, stumbled through the door and plunged at her in the bed. When she eluded him by leaping up, he bellowed at her to return. Roxanne stood trembling with indecision by the window, uncertain whether to bolt for the downstairs or return to bed—and a bruising evening of lust.

She was spared a decision by Denby himself, who passed out.

Chapter 21

Spring came to Augusta, bringing with it cascades of flowers but no new business. Then summer arrived, and carriages, filled with laughing ladies, their parasols and their escorts, heedlessly clipclopped past the little glover's shop. A winter storm had damaged the sign—it had not been repaired. Nor were thc window displays changed any more. No new ads appeared. But though his temper flared up regularly, Denby held on.

His boyish expression had changed. It had become sullen and bitter. His lips often wore a twisted sardonic smile, and his voice was seldom free of a tinge of sarcasm when he spoke to Roxanne. Geared only to success, failure crumpled Denby.

Had she not felt so deeply to blame for his present condition, Roxanne would promptly have left him. As it was, she stayed and took her anger out in long exhausting walks that wore through her shoes but enabled her to keep a civil tongue in her head when Denby raged at her.

On a beautiful summer Sunday, Denby's temper peaked for the first time in public violence. It happened on the way to church. They made a handsome couple, Denby and Roxanne, strolling in the shade of the dark green waxy-leaved magnolias: Denby with his tall stiff collar, leaning on the horsehead-tipped cane he affected; Roxanne like a swaying flower in peach silk with a long bell-shaped skirt and a little train her white-gloved hand held up carefully as she walked.

Almost at the churchyard, a flamboyantly dressed stranger with handlebar mustaches paused to smile at the handsome figure Roxanne cut in the clinging peach silk that outlined her lissome figure and heightened the gold of her hair.

With his hair-trigger temper, Denby took exception to that admiring smile. His boyish face contorted with rage, and he struck the stranger a smart blow on the shoulder with his cane. The stranger, who was considerably more muscular than Denby, paled and struck Denby a blow that measured his length on the dusty sidewalk.

A little murmuring crowd gathered. Roxanne cast an appealing look at the stranger, who turned and marched away. As Denby got up, she dusted him off with her gloved hands and a lace-trimmed handkerchief.

"We can't go into the church—everyone will stare at us," she whispered. Denby gave her a glazed look. She wasn't sure he even heard her.

Sick at heart, Roxanne took her defeated champion home.

There he accused her of flirting. He flung his gloves at her.

White-faced, Roxanne burst out of the house almost running. She charged ahead blindly—anywhere, just so it was away from him. Her hands trembled. Not only was her husband's business venture in ruins; her marriage—frail at best—was being destroyed.

She clenched her hands so hard the bones hurt, and bent her head with a sob. She had brought him to this, she told herself in agony, through her wild desire to leave Baltimore. *It was all her fault.*

On a hot night when he had sold no gloves all week, Denby broke down suddenly and wept in her arms. She held him, crooning to him, rocking him. And then she said, "Listen to me, Denby. We must leave here. This town isn't right for us."

"Of course it's right for us," he said in a smothered voice. "It's where you were born, isn't it?"

"Perhaps that's *why*," she said reluctantly.

Denby sat up. "What do you mean?" His voice was harsh. "What is it you haven't told me, Roxanne?"

"My mother . . . made enemies here," she explained. "Bitter enemies. I never realized how bitter. And we have inherited them, Denby." Her mouth twisted. "I suppose it's my birthright. I look just like her, you know."

"So-o-o!" Denby sucked his breath through his teeth. "That's it! I knew there had to be something . . . and you seemed to have so few friends." He grasped her by the shoulders, shaking her. "Why didn't you tell me, Roxanne? Why?"

Her voice was muffled. Tears were streaming down her face. She was glad it was dark and he could not see them. "At first I didn't know," she said. "And then . . . I suppose I was ashamed."

He released her shoulders and moved to the window. She could see his slim body silhouetted there in the soft Southern night. His whole stance looked beaten. *"Your enemies,"* he said bitterly. "And I didn't know you had any."

Her voice sounded wooden to her own ears. "They are my inheritance," she said. "They came with my face and figure that you admire so much."

"You're a hard wench," he said spitefully.

"I am what men have made me," she retorted. And suddenly she was not as sorry for Denby as she knew she should be. He had helped dig his own grave. He had refused to let her use the beauty of which he was so proud to make new friends, to attract new customers to the shop. She could have done it, if only he had let her!

"Apparently," he sneered, "I got much more than I bargained for."

"You got more than you deserved!" flared Roxanne. And then, because she knew that was unfair, "I'm sorry," she said shortly. "You're driving me to say things I don't mean. Let's talk about it tomorrow."

He turned away from her with an oath, and she could hear his quick ragged breathing.

"Denby," she sighed. "If only—"

Snarling, he sprang at her and she gave a little cry at the violence of his attack. He took her entirely without respect, as he might take a reluctant harlot—and with punishing force. She felt hurt and ashamed.

But by morning, when Denby went downstairs to mind the shop looking haggard by the pale morning light, her guilt returned.

My fault, she thought dully. Denby could have made his way in Baltimore, sheltered by his family. Perhaps he could have made his way in a neutral city. But she had led him deep into her home ground to the stronghold of her enemies, and he might well die of it. Take that incident with the gentleman who had smiled at her on the way to church. Denby had caned him and, though the man had contented himself with knocking Denby down, others might not be so charitable. There were those who would thrash Denby or even kill him for such incivility.

She began to feel afraid for him. She did not love him, but she felt responsible for him, for his predicament, for this unfortunate change in his boyish personality.

Her sapphire eyes were dark with foreboding these days. By early July she knew things were approaching a crisis. Denby, once so neat, now seldom shaved. He had turned into a human powder keg of raw emotions. It would all have to be resolved—and soon.

It was resolved in a way so bizarre that in her wildest dreams she could not have foreseen it.

On a hot July day Denby rushed upstairs during

business hours. He was livid with excitement. "Roxanne," he cried joyously, "I've sold the shop!"

Roxanne was so startled she dropped a plate she was washing and stared at the broken pieces in consternation. They had very few plates; she could not afford to break any.

"Pack up, we're leaving!" Looking young and carefree again, Denby threw his arms about her and gave her a resounding kiss.

Roxanne disengaged herself and stared at him, stunned.

"Back—to Baltimore?" she asked faintly.

Denby laughed and shook his head. He thrust a newspaper into her hands. The headlines leaped out at her. "GOLD! GOLD!" they shrieked. "BIG STRIKE IN THE KLONDIKE! MINERS ARRIVE IN SAN FRANCISCO WEIGHTED DOWN WITH NUGGETS!"

"It's our chance, Roxanne," Denby cried eagerly. "Hurry and pack. We're off to the Klondike!"

Clutching the paper, Roxanne read. The *SS Excelsior* had pulled into San Francisco yesterday, and wire services had flashed her arrival around the country. For the *Excelsior* had carried a load of ragged, roistering, happy miners—and millions in gold, pure gold, placer gold, wrenched from the subarctic's rugged northern wastes.

Roxanne looked up when she had finished reading. Denby was watching her with sparkling hazel eyes. Not since Baltimore had she seen him look so animated.

"You're not a miner," she protested. "It's wild country up there, Denby. You know nothing about—"

Grandly, he waved her protests aside. "They're scooping gold out everywhere up there, Roxanne. All we have to do is get there and pick it up—that's all we have to do!"

Without realizing it, he echoed the sentiments of many who believed the Klondike's gold lay ready for easy taking—and who would break their hearts and lose their fortunes seeking it.

"But the cost—how much did you get for the shop, Denby?"

He frowned. "Five hundred dollars—cash. And I threw in our furniture. So there's little to pack. I'm going downstairs now to dismiss the staff."

Roxanne gasped. So little! Why, the inventory of gloves alone was worth much more! But there was a madness in Denby now, and she sensed that he would brook no argument.

"Don't you understand?" he cried impatiently as she hesitated. "We've got to get there before all the gold is gone!"

"Then why not leave me here? You could travel faster alone and—"

"And leave you to the men who've been ogling you ever since we came to Augusta?" His voice became a sarcastic whiplash. "I'll not leave you alone and unprotected, Roxanne!"

Roxanne sighed. By now she knew the full sweep of Denby's jealousy.

There was no stopping him. To the Klondike they would go.

She didn't realize then that they were going to be part of a great migration. All over America—indeed all over the world—men had resigned from their jobs in banks, in livery stables, in soda shops, in mills; clerks had jumped over counters and left their wages behind; housewives and farmers, watchmakers and confidence men, cowboys and confectioners, gamblers and preachers—all were united in one endeavor, a grim determination to reach the Klondike before all the gold was gone.

Even as Roxanne packed, others were taking trains, ships, bicycles—or galloping away on fast horses—all with only one thing in mind:

Gold. Yellow gold.

Part Two:

The Race for the Gold
Seattle to the Yukon
1897–1898

Chapter 22

The same afternoon that he sold the shop, Denby, wild with excitement, called Baltimore on Mr. Bell's wonderful new invention, the telephone. Hurriedly explaining about the gold strike, Denby told his bewildered brother to send the rest of his share for the Baltimore shop to Seattle. By evening, her clothes and her treasured spoons hastily packed, Roxanne had bade the staff good-bye (Denby had generously given everyone a month's severance pay) and departed for the railroad station with her husband.

Once again she found herself on a train, headed this time for the far Northwest. At almost every stop someone bound for the gold fields got on. Husky young men, in the main, with a daredevil look in their eyes. By the time they reached Chicago there was even a "'Klondike Car," decorated with miners' picks and jars of nuggets, and filled with talk of the Klondike, that *Thron-diuck* of the Indians which meant "hammer water." About her swirled animated discussions of "diamond hitches" and freakish mining equipment.

To Roxanne all this talk of gold was unreal, but she found the midsummer trip north glorious, a riot of shimmering green trees and tall corn swaying in the breeze and scented meadows filled with flowers. When the train reached Chicago, she promptly fell in love with the windy city on the lake. Denby gave her no time to enjoy it. A feverish restlessness possessed him. They must get on. At each stop, he leaped off to buy a newspaper, scanning it for the latest news of strikes and riches.

Roxanne watched him in amazement. Denby was a changed man. Overnight he had reverted to the carefree young dandy she had married. Of course, before, his conversation had been full of the glover's trade; now it was studded with glaciers and pack ice, placers and moose and the midnight sun—and always gold.

By night he forgot his race for the gold and was again an ardent, if incompetent, lover. He held her in his arms with the old enthusiasm, and Roxanne, clasped in those arms, heard his heart beating fast, as if it were paced to the click-click of the rails. She felt his heavy breath on her cheek and heard him utter words of love she had not thought to hear from him again after her bruising experiences in Augusta. Absently she stroked his head, as if he were a child. But when his lovemaking was over and he slept soundly beside her, she stared wide-eyed into the dark, wondering what would become of them.

In Chicago the Klondike car had picked up a newcomer: a tall man, pale and whipcord lean, somberly dressed in black. A dark-haired man with a bleak face and wintry gray eyes that flashed silver in the sun.

When those silver eyes found Roxanne and rested on her lazily, Roxanne met his gaze and stared back, fascinated. She thought she had never seen a face so hard or so reckless. There were bitter lines about his thin, straight mouth. His name, she learned, was Case—whether first or last she did not know; he seemed to have no other. Before the train reached Minneapolis, some of the passengers were calling him "the Hard

Case" under their breaths, but no man called him that to his face. There was something hellish in the gray eyes that forbade it. Roxanne soon discovered why Case's lean face was so pale. After Case got on the train, the poker games—held for light stakes up to now—became a serious business and the stakes rose even higher. Denby had begun to play cards to pass the time on the train. Sometimes he won; sometimes he lost. It worried Roxanne.

Westward they sped. At Mandan, North Dakota, they crossed the muddy Missouri. Since Denby was too absorbed in his game to notice the crossing, Roxanne wandered out by herself to the observation car and stood on the little open-air platform at the rear to view the river.

Standing there alone, she felt eyes boring into her back and turned to see the tall gambler regarding her from the door. He must have excused himself from the card game, she realized. And followed her? The thought stained her cheeks with color.

He lounged in the doorway, his tall figure filling it for all his supple leanness, and watched her thoughtfully with eyes the color of tarnished silver. As tarnished as his reputation, she thought. His mocking bow spoke of better days, and the reckless bitter smile that flashed across his face told her he held his life none too dear. As the wind whipped his coat aside, she saw with a little thrill of alarm that he had a derringer stuck in his belt—and it did not look new. She had the feeling its small deadly muzzle had spoken, and would speak again. Here before her stood a sinister man of whipcord and steel, like none other she had ever met. A man with a shadowy past—and no future. Somewhere someone would dislike those hands that were too clever with the cards, and would shoot him down.

"Excuse me," she said, and moved to brush by him.

He did not stand aside. "Stay awhile, Mrs. Barrington," he said easily.

He was very close. The train jolted and, suddenly off balance, she was flung into his arms. As those arms closed around her, supple and hard as steel, she felt a sudden stab of electricity, and in her head a warning sounded.

He held her a moment too long and his hard face softened when he let her go. His smile was mocking. "I've wanted to ask you why you're making this trip, Mrs. Barrington," he said. "And I doubted I'd hear the truth unless we were alone."

Still shaken from their exciting contact, Roxanne lifted her chin. "I'm seeking gold like everybody else."

"Allow me to doubt it." His eyes narrowed.

She shrugged. "Denby wants to go."

"Ah, yes. Denby."

Something in his voice irritated her. "And why should he not go?" she asked with asperity. "Is Chicago any better?"

"I am not from Chicago, Mrs. Barrington."

"Where then?"

He shrugged. "Everywhere. Nowhere."

She gave him a withering look, hating him for being so damnably attractive. "Even *you* must have been born somewhere."

"Ah, yes, but so long ago I've forgotten it."

"But you are going to the Klondike to dig for gold," she pointed out. "Are you so much better prepared?"

"Oh, I'm going. But not to dig."

No, she'd known all along he was going there to do what he did so well—to deal the cards on a green felt table and rake in nuggets instead of chips.

"You're blocking my way," she said crisply, giving him a cold look.

"I would never do that." His tone was ironic, but he stepped aside with another mocking bow and let her pass.

Feeling almost as if she'd had her clothes torn off as he watched her leave, Roxanne hurried back to the Klondike car, her color unusually high. The lean gambler exerted a physical pull on her senses that frightened her. She gave Denby a guilty look, but apparently he had not noticed her absence. A few moments later, Case slipped back into his seat and resumed his play. He did not glance her way, but she was uncomfortably conscious of him all the evening.

A hundred miles later, as they roared into the Badlands, Roxanne wondered if even the Klondike could be more desolate than this. Around her rose naked walls of rocks and empty slopes—a scar upon the lovely countryside. She was cheered by seeing far up on a bluff the castle of the Marquis de Mores, a famous French adventurer. She turned to call Denby's attention to it, but he had wandered away. Across from her she met Case's hard gaze and turned away, her heart pounding uncomfortably. She kept expecting him to try to speak to her again, but he did not, although he continued to devour her with his eyes as they crossed Montana. She found him disturbingly attractive in a sinister way and her heartbeat quickened whenever she met that intense silver gaze. Determinedly, she kept her back to him, staring out the window at the awesome landscape, as the train climbed up beyond Helena and snaked through a mile-long tunnel. They rolled through Spokane, crossed the impressive Cascade Range and the Columbia River and, finally, chugged into Seattle. They had made the trip from Minneapolis in three nights and four days.

Seattle was a "hot town," they'd been told, and so it proved to be. Roxanne had never seen so many saloons and bars in her life. The hilly city on Puget Sound was literally bursting at its seams. Daily, every kind of conveyance brought people into the city, and the trains were always jammed. On the waterfront the shipyards resounded to the noise as a "Klondike fleet" was hastily thrown together. Advertised proudly as floating palaces, these ships would make the four thousand two hundred-mile round trip and sail right up the Yukon to Dawson City. Denby told Roxanne they couldn't afford to wait for that luxury. Along with other impatient souls, he rejected the rich man's route and chose instead to enter the Klondike by the nearer back door, sailing up the inland waterway and crossing the mountain passes to the high lakes that fed the headwaters of the upper Yukon. From these lakes the current would sweep their boats down to Dawson and the Land of Gold.

Roxanne hardly cared. She had spent some time wondering whether Case, who had kept so close to Denby during the train ride, would lose interest in them once they reached Seattle. With mingled excitement and dread, she observed that when they checked into the Globe Hotel, Case was right behind them. "Close to the docks," pointed out Denby. "Well recommended." She wondered if Case had recommended it.

While Roxanne unpacked, Denby prowled the stores of Klondike outfitters on Front Street. He was chagrined at the prices, which had doubled and tripled overnight, and came home to tell Roxanne indignantly he'd been charged a dime for his regular five-cent cigar.

Worse, he'd discovered all sailings were booked for the foreseeable future. What few tickets there were had been bought up by scalpers, who were offering them for exorbitant prices. He'd found a man who had two tickets but wanted fifteen hundred dollars apiece for them—ten times their worth, Denby fumed. Roxanne's heart sank; she didn't know how much his brother had sent him, but she was sure Denby couldn't afford three thousand dollars for their tickets.

That evening Denby told her he was going to play poker with the boys. She knew that meant Case. She'd seen the men seated around a table already playing cards as she passed his room.

Denby came back late, looking dispirited, and stumbled into bed without touching her. She presumed he'd lost.

The next day she strolled about hilly Seattle, admired the view from Queen Anne Hill, the blue lakes and bluer skies, and studied the suddenly overworked shipyards of Puget Sound, where the noise of hammering never ceased. All the tired old tugs and scows and paddle-wheelers were being refurbished to make the trip to Alaska. Many of them didn't look seaworthy even to her landlubber's eyes.

At the docks she ran across Case. He was standing,

tall and somberly dressed, beneath the wheeling sea birds, his gray eyes studying some far distant spot. A moment later he turned and saw her. Feeling breathless, Roxanne watched him approach.

"Mrs. Barrington." He made a formal bow, but the gaze he bent on her was anything but formal—it was hot and penetrating. Roxanne's blood pounded in her ears. He was so damnably attractive, she could feel herself blushing.

"Have you—have you been able to book passage to Alaska yet?" she asked, when the pulsing silence between them became unbearable.

"My ticket was waiting for me when I arrived. I wired a friend to pick it up for me."

"That's what we should have done," said Roxanne in a breathless voice. "But we didn't know anybody here. Which ship is yours?"

"The *North Star.*" He indicated the best-looking steamer of the lot. "She leaves tomorrow."

Roxanne's eyelids fluttered as that steady gaze returned to hold her fast. "How nice to have friends. . . ."

"My friend picked up two tickets," he said dryly. "She was going along with me, but then something else came up, so she's left me with one to spare."

She! So his friend was a woman. . . . Her unruly heart pounded indignantly. She forced herself to think of Denby, desperately prowling the steamship offices. "Would you sell your extra ticket?" she wondered.

Case smiled—a flashing smile that lit his hard face like winter sunshine breaking across the ice. Boldly those metallic gray eyes traveled from the top of her head where her jaunty little sailor hat perched atop her hair, gleaming gold in the sunshine, down her lovely face, pausing at her luminous blue eyes, caressing her cheek where the color came and went beneath her sheer skin, past her slightly parted, expectant lips. His gaze continued down the white column of her throat that pulsed slightly under this inspection, on across the gentle swell of her young breasts and past them—moving slowly along her narrow waist and softly curving hips to her elegant legs—now outlined in her long-skirted suit by the strong wind from Puget Sound.

"I'd *give* you my extra ticket, Mrs. Barrington," he said softly, in a voice that left no doubt as to his meaning, "if you'd share my stateroom."

Looking up into his dangerous face, the thought of what sharing his stateroom would entail went through her almost like physical pain. Under the pressure of those steady eyes, her clothes seemed to disappear, her hat to float away and her hair, loosed miraculously from its pins, to cascade joyously about her suddenly naked shoulders. She imagined herself swaying toward him, clad only in a silky gown, filled with desire. Saw herself melt into those lean arms, saw herself pressed against that lithe, hard body. Then her gown too floated away as their naked figures, clasped in passion, toppled slowly toward the bunk.

Her senses rocked—then righted themselves as reality returned. She was standing on the Seattle dock with both feet planted firmly on the boards. She was a married woman and this man before her was deep trouble. Cheeks flaming from fear that he might have seen an answering glow burning deep in her own eyes, she said hastily, "I meant—for my husband."

Case threw back his head and laughed. "No, I'd planned to share my stateroom with something softer than a husband." His narrow gaze continued to study her flushed face. "But I wouldn't mind wagering the ticket, Mrs. Barrington. You might tell your husband that."

He bowed again and left her. Roxanne, her heart thudding, stood on the wind-whipped waterfront and watched him go, a lean somber figure moving rapidly away from her . . . just as tomorrow his ship would depart from her, moving out into the broad Pacific. Her hands clenched at the thought of his leaving. She didn't want him to leave. She walked about, trying not to face the truth, trying to let the brisk salt wind cool her hot cheeks. But before she left the docks for her hotel, she had admitted it to herself, told herself it was only because she found her nights with Denby so—so unsatisfying. Whatever the reason for it, the truth was there before her as she hurried along: She *wanted* the lean gambler from nowhere, wanted him desperately.

As she walked, she recalled what he'd said about wagering his ticket. Was he saying he'd allow Denby to win the ticket because of her? Pack Denby off to the Klondike while he missed the boat and lingered in Seattle . . . with her? She looked down in hot mortification at the thought and found that her hands were shaking. She twisted them together to steady them.

Her thoughts pricked at her. Why shouldn't she let this happen? More than Case wanted to linger in her arms, Denby wanted passage to the Klondike. Why should she not give him his heart's desire?

She was still fighting a fierce internal battle with her turbulent emotions when she got back to her hotel room and found Denby lying on the bed, his arms folded behind his head, staring at the ceiling with a disgruntled expression.

"Roxanne, did you know people are even *stealing* tickets to Alaska?" he asked moodily. "Just like they've stolen all the dogs in this town to use them pulling sleds up there."

"I know." Roxanne took off her hat and tossed it on the dresser, smoothing her hair, studying her reflection nervously in the mirror. "I ran into that man you gamble with—the one called Case." Her voice was casual but it had a ragged edge. "He told me he has an extra ticket on the *North Star* and he's going to wager it." She swallowed. She could hardly believe she had actually said it.

Denby sat up, his face alert. "Case told you that?"

She nodded. "At the docks just now."

"The *North Star* . . . Roxanne, that's a big steamer." He got up and walked restlessly about. Roxanne watched him miserably, wondering if she'd done the right thing.

Denby was very quiet at dinner. With a worried frown, Roxanne observed his resolve build. She almost threw her arms around him and begged him not to go when he announced shortly after dinner he was going down the hall to play cards with the boys.

After he left, she climbed into bed. Too restless to read, she lay in the dark while unbidden thoughts of Case, of his vigorous, sinister, totally-male charm, played in her mind. Now she knew what it was to desire a pirate or a highwayman. The feelings of all those women in the novels she had read were suddenly clear to her. She wanted Case because he was dangerous and he was *there*. She lost herself in glorious imaginings of Case's warm, lean body next to hers. She sighed and moved gently in the bed, her flesh atingle with yearning. Down the hall, she told herself dreamily, he was dealing out the cards. He was losing his ticket to Denby, thus arranging Denby's departure, and their lover's liaison. In guilty happiness, she drifted off to sleep.

She awoke to the sound of the door opening. Denby staggered in, the light from the hall illuminating his haggard face. She didn't have to ask him to know that he had lost.

"Oh, God, Roxanne, I lost a thousand dollars," he muttered, and flung himself onto the bed, his shoulders shaken by uncontrollable sobs. When she tried to comfort him, he shook her off. Jumping up, he grabbed a whiskey bottle from the dresser and began taking big gulps of the fiery liquid. "I stayed till the last, Roxanne, trying to win it back—but I couldn't. The game's over and I'm down a thousand. And there's no chance to win it back, because tomorrow morning Case is sailing on the *North Star*." He gulped more liquor. Finally, turning up the bottle, he poured the remainder of its contents down his throat. Roxanne watched him in alarm, expecting him to have a heart attack. Instead he threw the bottle at the wall, where it crashed with a report that made her jump.

"Damn Case," Denby muttered thickly. "I think he cheats!" And stumbled to the bed and swayed dizzily. Roxanne leaped forward to break his fall. With difficulty she got him turned over, got his feet on the bed, got his shoes off; he was dead to the world. Perhaps, she thought bitterly, it was better this way. Then he wouldn't have to face the consequences of what he'd done until morning.

But for herself, she knew a blackness of the soul. She felt used, tricked, cheated. And guilty. There was no excuse for what she had done. Between them, she and Case had set the trap that had destroyed her husband.

Bitterly she stared at Denby, lying passed out on the bed. He looked young and helpless and defeated. Out of a black rage, she clenched her hands achingly. Damn him, Case had used her! Used her to destroy Denby! As if she hadn't done enough to Denby in Augusta. . . .

Her fury mounted until it throbbed in her head. She began to pace distractedly. Fool that she was! Case had played with her. Oh, he had known the devastating effect of his masculinity on her, had seen her response flare up in her eyes. He'd never meant to send Denby away so that he could stay in Seattle with her—he'd only meant to lure Denby into his poker game so he could win a thousand dollars!

Damn him! On a gust of rage, Roxanne pulled on her clothes and, with hell in her heart, stormed down to Case's room, striking the door a vicious blow with her fist.

Case answered her knock attired in a white shirt open at the front, and dark trousers. Behind him the room was empty. The players had all gone home. Only a table littered with chips, glasses, and bottles and surrounded by straight chairs betrayed that they had been there. Over one chair were draped Case's vest and coat. She guessed that he had stayed up to pack for the morning, when his ship would weigh anchor for the Land of the Midnight Sun.

To her utter fury, he did not look at all surprised to see her. His unsmiling poker face exhibited no emotion as she spun past him into the room. With one violent sweep of her arm, she cleared the poker table—bottles, glasses and chips all flying into a litter of broken glass on the floor. She whirled to face him, panting.

He was watching her with a little smile on his dark lean face. "Quiet, you'll wake the hotel. Remember your reputation, Mrs. Barrington."

She dashed toward him, her arm upraised to strike. That arm was caught in a grip of steel, held fast. Her brilliant eyes smoldered up at him as his amused face came close to her own. "You tricked me!" she cried wildly.

"Tricked you?" Case's dark eyebrows rose. "Your husband fancies himself a gambler, Mrs. Barrington. He wagered a thousand for a ticket worth fifteen hundred—and lost. That's all."

Bitter and contemptuous, Roxanne's laugh rang out. "I might have known you'd say that—a man like you!" She jerked free and turned to go.

His lean body blocked her path. "It was my way of bringing you to me," he said softly.

She caught her breath and looked up at him, this man who was leaving for Alaska in the morning. Complex, cold, calculating, he stood before her. His white shirt sleeves were rolled back, and she could see his lean forearms. The top buttons of his shirt were unbuttoned to reveal a hard, muscular chest. Those tarnished silver eyes bored into hers.

. . . my way of bringing you to me, he had said. And here she was. Feeling the pressure of his steady gaze, the force of his strong relentless will. Desperately she wanted to hate him, but as she stood there so close to him she could feel her anger being swept away, lost in the hot fire of another emotion. They faced each other in the dim light, a man and a woman, silent, rapt. Theirs was a confrontation of wills as they stared at each other—and in the end her eyes were the first to drop. Her lashes wavered and fell to make dark wings across her soft cheeks. She stood uncertainly, hands clenching and unclenching, her round breasts rising and falling with her ragged breathing.

"Roxanne." His voice was low, compelling. "Look at me."

Scarlet, she turned her head away. He took her slender shoulders in his hands, and she shivered at the contact with those strong, delicate fingers—fingers whose sensitive touch could differentiate between the thickness of two cards or feel the spots on the dice as he rolled them out on a green felt table. "Roxanne." Again that coaxing voice caressed her. "Look at me, Roxanne."

Against her will, she found her head tilting upward and her eyes, now big and dark and distrustful, looked into his.

"I must go," she said hoarsely.

"Oh, God, you remind me of someone else," he muttered. "So long ago. . . ." And clasped her to him almost roughly and buried his face, in a sudden fierce gesture, in her hair.

Roxanne's whole body trembled. There, pressed against him, for a terrible moment another man's face stormed through her consciousness. But it was not Denby's accusing face that rose before her—it was Rhodes's. Rhodes whom she had loved so wildly, and who had betrayed that love in Baltimore.

With a sob, she relaxed against Case as his grip tightened possessively about her. Tingling, she felt his hands moving over her body, felt her dress loosened suddenly, felt it eased down around her shoulders, slid down over her hips.

"I never meant—" she whispered.

"Hush," he said. "Don't talk." And set his mouth over hers, rendering speech impossible.

Roxanne—accustomed only to Denby's inept love-making—responded throbbingly to that kiss. For the first time in so long, she was being held in a man's arms—not a boy's. A dangerous man, whose kisses scorched her and whose fingers seared her white skin as they traveled exploringly against her silk chemise, fumbling with the ribbon that held the top of it. The bow gave and the satin ribbon slipped away easily. His deft right hand came into fiery contact with her breasts as he brushed aside the top of her undergarment impatiently. She felt her skin prickle as the silk slid down her back and came to rest on her hips.

His lips left hers as he fitted a hand around the

small of her back and with his other hand brushed away her silky slip so that it rustled down to the floor.

"No," she said, recoiling. "No, I—"

"I understand why you came. You want your husband's losses made good. I am prepared to give you that."

"But I'm not—" She stopped, feeling dizzy. What had she been about to say? That she was not a harlot? But was she not behaving like one? Her price was merely higher.

A hot wash of shame flooded over her, flushing her pale skin, and she could not meet his eyes. For he had reminded her of Denby's existence, something she had for the moment forgotten. Yet . . . she had wronged Denby by delivering him into Case's hands, and now she must make that right. What other way was there? She must set aside the consideration that she was doubly wronging him by what she was about to do. This was the only way to get the ticket for which Denby had gambled a fortune and lost.

Case stepped back and looked at her, as she stood, her garments tumbled at her feet, like Venus rising from a foam of cloth and silk. His silver eyes flamed to molten metal as they traveled boldly up and down her figure, naked except for silk stockings held by pink satin garters and high-heeled satin shoes. His avid gaze rested tenderly on her straight slender shoulders, her pearly pink-tipped breasts and hand-span waist, her softly rounded hips and tapering elegant legs. He reached out a hand and touched lightly, experimentally, the soft silky triangle of dark-blond hair between those lovely legs. Roxanne quivered and felt her stomach muscles contract. In sudden panic she would have turned and run then—no matter what the cost, but he swept her up against him, crushed her lips and breasts exultantly against his hard muscular body, and a breathless moment later they were on the bed.

"Let me help you get these off." His hand shivered down her thigh, snapped a satin garter softly. The impact of that snapping garter rocked her senses, already swimming. She clung to him as, with a low laugh, he pulled off her shoes and eased the satin garters down around her legs. And then the stockings, ever so slowly, his hands exploring as he went.

Gossamer, they floated after the shoes to the floor, and with easy grace he lowered his body onto hers, felt her flinch when his belt buckle cut into her stomach.

"My belt," he muttered, tearing it off.

"At least," she murmured, "you aren't wearing your derringer."

The belt and pants followed the shoes and stockings to the floor.

"I don't need a gun to defend myself against women," he said.

Her sapphire eyes dreamed lazily up at him. "You might," she murmured.

He laughed again, a chuckle deep in his throat. Then his fingers were tracing across her resilient body, his clever hands exploring its pink-tipped hills and pale translucent valleys. Her whole being seemed to flame up as his hands moved, and she writhed and swayed toward him, clasping her hands around the back of his neck, pushing away the collar of his shirt, fiercely ripping the remaining buttons.

Sliding his arm beneath her, he raised her toward him and kissed her eyebrows, her hair, her cheeks, her nose, her mouth, her throat. His lips slid lower, down her pulsing throat and across her heaving bosom to nuzzle the soft tingling tips of her breasts. Eyes closed, lashes lying dark upon cheeks rosy with heightened color, Roxanne responded to his ardor recklessly. Forgetting Denby, forgetting the world. Once again she was held in a man's arms, a vibrant, exciting, dangerous man who would be gone tomorrow . . . a man whose arms would never hold her again.

With the desperation of the damned, she clung to him, every sense astir, the blood raging through her veins. And Case, sensing the passion he had aroused, reveling in it, suddenly abandoned his teasing explorations and gripped her to him in a hard embrace. As his manliness made its strong, savage entrance, a little moan escaped her, and she flung herself violently against him. Their bodies fused in a fierce embrace. For a long, splendid moment everything surrounding them throbbed and receded and burned. Her blood sang in her ears and a great joyousness filled her.

Then his lean body left her, flinging itself away to lie panting beside her. Her stomach muscles tightened as she felt his fingers glide over its satin surface, and her eyes flew open to see that he had turned on his side and was leaning on one elbow looking down at her. Somehow during all of this he had removed his shirt, and seeing his long pale body stretched out beside her, she blushed.

"You're very young, aren't you?" he asked thoughtfully.

"In years . . . I suppose so."

He laughed, a low chuckle. "Much the answer I'd have given myself some years ago."

She wanted to know. "The—the woman who was going to sail with you. Is she—?" She hesitated.

"Is she what?"

Reluctantly the words were forced to Roxanne's lips. "Your wife?"

"No, she's a madam. I broke her out of jail, where she'd no business being, and brought her to California. Since I gave her the money to set up in business, she's grateful to me."

"So you're running from the law?"

"Not running exactly. Just keeping ahead."

Her eyes were large and dark as she thought about that. "Why was she in jail?"

"She was framed by a jealous lover. They used me to frame her and I felt responsible for getting her out."

Roxanne gave him a sweet trusting look. His answer had pleased her. "They call you the Hard Case," she murmured. "I think they're wrong."

He sighed. "No, they're right. I take what I want. If the prey is wary, I lay traps. Just as I laid a trap for you."

"You didn't trap me," she said soberly. "I—I wanted you, Case." She could not meet his eyes when she said that. It seemed so shameless, lying there naked in bed beside him.

They were silent for a while.

Then, "How could you have married him?" he asked suddenly. "That green boy?"

Roxanne turned large, honest blue eyes toward him. "Because he was willing to take me as I was—and love me anyway," she said simply.

He stared at her. "I suppose that's reason enough," he muttered. "There was a girl once, a long time ago. I wish I'd taken her as she was!"

"What did she do to you?"

"She moved in with my best friend while I was away. I came back and found them together. I didn't find out until much later that she was dying and she knew it . . . maybe it would have made a difference."

With a stab, Roxanne remembered Buck in Kansas . . . and black-haired Julie Smith. "We all die," she said in a sad, smothered voice.

"Eventually," he agreed. "My own chances aren't too bright, right now. There are three men after me, waiting to gun me down. Not to mention the long arm of the law."

"Is that why you're going to the Klondike, Case?"

He nodded grimly. "Nothing else would lure me to that frozen icebox. But there's no law up there to speak of, so I've been told." He rose, began to dress. "It's nearly morning. I want to be on board before the crowd arrives." The watching law, she thought. "I wish I could give you that ticket, Roxanne, but I sold it for fifteen hundred dollars."

He did not have the ticket. Then she had given herself for nothing! But no . . . Her emotions in a turmoil, she realized he was giving her money!

Scarlet with humiliation, she watched him count out one thousand five hundred dollars, lay it carefully on the night table beside the bed.

"I'd add five thousand to that," he said, "if you'd go with me."

Did he think he could buy her? Anger poured over her. She sat up, her naked figure as lovely as a water sprite's, and with a violent gesture swept the money to the floor. "I'm not for sale," she cried bitterly.

"I never thought you were," he said quietly, his eyes flickering as they roved over her beautiful naked body and flushed angry face. "I was telling you I'd buy that half of my stateroom back—even if it cost me five thousand dollars—if you'd go with me and share it, Roxanne."

She stared at him. He really meant it. He'd pay five thousand dollars—a fortune!—just for the pleasure of her company.

Her anger cooled as suddenly as it had been born. But she remembered that she was a married woman and she shook her head slowly. "I'm not going to the Klondike, Case. Denby won't have enough money to take us both. But—before I take this money, Case, tell me—did you cheat Denby?"

He shook his head. "No, he lost it fair and square. Gambling takes a cool head, and Denby hasn't got one."

She sighed.

"Ah, Roxanne," he said, leaning over and moving his lips gently down the curve of her neck and across her breasts. "Come with me to Alaska. I can take care of you far better than he can."

Come with me. . . . It was a siren song. Roxanne looked up for a yearning moment into that dark intent face above her, the deep eyes that promised so much. Then her back stiffened and she looked away and tried to still her aching heart. She had done enough to Denby, brought him enough ill fortune. Lifting her head, she looked back at Case, faced him bravely. "I don't want to go to the Klondike." Her voice was defiant.

He straightened up and studied her and his hand stroked her pink nipples once more. He sighed. "But somehow I think you will," he said softly. "You're too pretty for a man to leave in Seattle." His smile faded. "Do you want to see me off?"

"I can't," she said reluctantly. "Denby might wake and find me gone."

"What are you going to tell him," he asked her curiously as he tossed his remaining things in an open bag, "about the money?"

"That you had a change of heart," she said.

He laughed. "Only a woman would think of that."

She saw now that the rest of his bags were packed. "I'll see you in Dawson City, Roxanne," he said.

She lay there and watched him go, her body rich with memories of the hour just passed, wanting to linger lazily on the white sheets where they had clung together and somehow given each other life—and hope for the future. Her thoughts grew dark and brooding as the door closed, and for a treacherous moment she almost called him back. Her heart wanted to cry out, "Wait, I'm coming with you. I'll share your stateroom—and your life."

But she could not do that to Denby. Not to the man who half a lifetime ago had said, *I love you anyway.*

After a while she got up and dressed. Through the sounds of morning she walked dreamily back to her room, remembering the yearning look in Case's eyes just as her body remembered his lean, rock-hard embrace.

Wrong? Oh, yes, it was undeniably wrong but—she stretched her arms and back deliciously—how wonderful it had been, and all too short . . . to last a lifetime. For now she would go back to Denby and his brief, irresolute bouts of lovemaking. At least, she thought, she would have made amends for causing him to lose his money. And with luck, Denby would never know how it had been regained.

Quietly she let herself back into her room. Denby still lay in a drunken stupor. She bathed and climbed into bed. The money she left on the floor as if it had been stuck under the door. Wild thoughts hammered through her head. There was still time . . . time to leap up and find Case, to go to the Klondike with him. She put her pillow over her head, trying to smother her disloyal thoughts, and finally drifted into a light, restless sleep.

She was waked by Denby, who was standing by the

door, dull-eyed and holding his head with one hand. In the other he had the stack of bills he had scooped up from the floor. "Where did this come from?" he was asking.

"Where did what come from?" muttered Roxanne sleepily.

"This money by the door."

Roxanne sat up and stared. "*What* money by the door, Denby?"

He waved it at her. "This stack of bills," he said wildly. "Where did it come from?"

"Your gambler friend must have shoved it under the door. Perhaps he had a change of heart, Denby. Perhaps he wanted to teach you a lesson—not to gamble."

Blinking, Denby stared down at the money in his hand. "Why would he want to do that?"

"Who knows?" Roxanne yawned. "Gamblers do quixotic things."

"How would you know?"

"I read it in a book."

Denby snorted and then grasped his head and groaned. "Well, I'll find him and damn well ask him why."

"No, you won't," said Roxanne looking at the glaring sunlight coming through the window. "He sailed on the *North Star*, remember? It's past noon, and she left port this morning."

Denby stared at her and then with kindling eyes at the money in his hands. He counted it excitedly. "Fifteen hundred—I only lost a thousand to him. He must have been drunk!"

Roxanne shrugged. "Perhaps he can't count."

"But this means—Roxanne, I was only short five hundred! I can buy our tickets now!"

Roxanne's eyes widened. "You mean you had enough money for your own ticket all along?"

"Of course. I was only gambling to get enough money to take you along."

Roxanne stared at him. Then suddenly she began to laugh. Bending her head to touch her knees, she sat there in bed and rocked and laughed until the tears rolled down her cheeks. It was not for Denby's passage to the Klondike that she had sold her honor—it was for her own!

"I don't see what's so funny," said Denby stiffly.

Roxanne dried her eyes. "No, there's nothing funny," she gasped. "I'm just hysterical. Pay no attention to me, Denby."

In the afternoon, having drunk a large glass of juice and somehow fumbled into his clothes, Denby took Roxanne and swaggered down to the docks to buy passage at scalper's prices on a grimy tub up the inland waterway to Dyea. From there they would go overland, scaling the snowy Chilkoot Pass to the high mountain lakes that flowed into the upper reaches of the Yukon. Then they would drift with the current downriver to Dawson City, where the Klondike River met the mighty Yukon.

Their ship was leaving in two days, but Denby steadfastly refused to buy what was considered a proper outfit. He invested in a bare minimum of supplies. "We'll buy ours at Dawson City," he said blithely. "Only those who travel light will get there before winter sets in. You wouldn't want to spend the winter trapped in the snow somewhere, would you?"

Roxanne admitted she would not. Her mind was only half on what Denby was saying. She wondered what he would do if he knew how he had gotten his money back—and the price she had paid for it. She thought of Case, the man with the silken touch and the hard body, and wondered if already he had forgotten her. Although she had been reluctant to make this trip to Alaska, she no longer felt that reluctance, and she knew it was because of Case. *I'll see you in Dawson*, he had said.

Her heart swelled. She promised herself she would see him there.

The Yukon 1897—1898

Chapter 23

Everything and anything that would float shuttled back and forth to Alaska in the fall of 1897: tugs and sailing sloops, coal barges, side-wheelers and scows and pleasure yachts; ancient freighters and long-condemned derelicts patched up and set afloat. The vessel Roxanne and Denby found themselves on was one of the latter, and one of the worst equipped of this astonishing flotilla to brave the inland passage north to the land of gold.

Named the *Clara V*, she was a decrepit coal carrier that had been condemned some three years before by the U.S. Government. The Klondike strike inspired her owners to seize the opportunity to convert her. With amazing swiftness they had set her afloat, and sweating carpenters had worked round the clock to rough in berths for passengers—which could later be ripped out in Alaska and sold by the board foot. To the amazement of the six hundred passengers, wood shavings had been sprinkled over the floor—to obsure the fact that coal dust had not been swept out. In this grimy setting, with hay and every type of mining equipment piled high on the deck, the passengers were wedged in ten to a cabin. They were lucky—below decks two hundred horses were sandwiched in so tightly they could barely move and, maddened by their confinement, went into a screaming, whinnying, kicking, biting frenzy at each blast of the ship's whistle. Crates of several hundred yelping dogs—bought and stolen, whose present owners mistakenly believed they would prove good sled dogs—completed the cacophony of sound accompanying them as they left Seattle. The rails were lined with eager would-be prospectors attired in business suits, natty tweed shooting jackets, brand new mackinaws and, occasionally, Paris gowns. Many would not return alive.

This floating bedlam did not travel alone. The *Clara V* had two ships accompanying her—one an overcrowded and ancient side-wheeler which did not even boast a ship's compass; the other a square-rigged brigantine with a leaky hull which depended on continuous pumping to stay afloat. Even so, among the many odd rigs heading for Alaska, these were not particularly worthy of remark. Roxanne, driven on deck by the unbearable stench below, looked helplessly at tents pitched in lifeboats and asked herself what she was doing here. The small crowded dining room only could accommodate fifty passengers at a time, and so some six sittings were required to serve a meal. Due to lack of storage room slabs of meat were hung from the dining room ceiling and on gusty days when the ship rolled, the passengers rubbed against hams and cured meat—their future dinners. In these overcrowded conditions, everybody slept in their clothes for the whole voyage and starvation began to seem quite possible.

Ravenously hungry, Roxanne and Denby found themselves waiting with the rest outside the dining room door, snatching food from the trays being carried in. Roxanne's arms were not long enough to make this venture very successful, and Denby was no good at it.

But it was there they made their first real friend on shipboard—a pleasant young blond giant, named Leighton Clarke, whose long reach conveyed badly cooked pieces of fried chicken to his hungry friends, as well as to his own smiling mouth.

Leighton fascinated Denby because he declared that his brother had made the trip to the Klondike some ten years before by river steamer. He fascinated Roxanne because he was a great golden giant of a man. It was easy to imagine Leighton as an early Anglo-Saxon swinging a broad-ax, standing resolutely astride a narrow bridge and striking down the advance guard of an opposing army. With his thick blond hair and beard and ruddy skin, he braced himself against the ship's rail, which looked too frail to hold him. Turning his blue eyes on them, he spoke—in a cultured voice that had just a touch of a British accent—of his family now residing in Washington, D.C. They had traveled all over the world, Leighton said, and he picked up the accent during the years when his father, a career diplomat, was attached to the American Embassy in London. Eventually a walloping gift by one of his great aunts to a presidential campaign had gained for Leighton's father a full ambassadorship, from which he had since retired in glory, and now he resided in a yellow brick Georgetown mansion near Dumbarton Oaks.

Leighton told them he had been traveling idly up the coast from San Francisco with no fixed destination in mind when the news of the Klondike strike came, and he had joined the rush out of a sense of sheer adventure. Roxanne enjoyed his banter. Except for snatching food from passing platters, he was scrupulously courteous to all, and he regaled Denby and Roxanne for long hours with stories of his life in the world's great capitals. When Roxanne asked why he had not followed his father's footsteps into the diplomatic corps, Leighton shrugged and evaded the question, but for a moment there was sadness in his fun-loving blue eyes. She guessed that he might be sowing his wild oats, but would return one day to become ambassador to some romantic country. It was fun to imagine him as a diplomat in a silk stovepipe hat and cutaway coat, bowing to queens.

Whenever the ship put into port, Leighton was there gallantly offering his arm to Roxanne as she went down the gangplank. She marveled that Denby was not jealous and supposed it was because he was so intent on gold. Stopping at the ports of call was a matter of annoyance to the impatient Denby—and indeed to most passengers—eager to get on before the early northern winter chilled the landscape.

At Vancouver they lost one of their small flotilla: the brigantine, badly loaded, capsized and had to be towed into port for repairs. Now they were two ships, struggling up the inland waterway, their passengers in a deadly race with the ice that would freeze the northern rivers bank to bank and shut the Klondike off from the world outside. The passengers grumbled, got jumpy. They were crowded and miserable and had good reason to be afraid.

Roxanne found her fellow voyagers to be a mixed bag. Seven ministers from New England were among them, balanced by a number of hard-eyed gamblers and confidence men who stared boldly at Roxanne and caused Denby to redden with anger. A madam from Chicago and her girls flounced about the boat in ruffled beribboned taffetas and hats with veils, their red lips curving with delight at the very mention of the name Dawson—where, each one was convinced, droves of rich tired miners waited, eager to pile buckets of nuggets at the toes of their high-buttoned shoes.

The madam, who was named Josie Mawkins, noticed at once the sapphire-eyed blonde the male passengers called merely The Beauty. One day when Denby was occupied elsewhere, Josie swished up to the rail beside Roxanne, laid a gloved hand lightly on Roxanne's arm and said shrewdly, "With looks like yours, you could travel first class. You know that, don't you?"

Roxanne pretended to misunderstand. "Traveling

first class wouldn't matter much on this ship, would it?"

"You know what I mean," said Josie, giving her a hard look. "That husband of yours doesn't look flush to me. Hear he's got no outfit, just some luggage. Now *I'd* outfit him for you when we reach Dawson, and start him out after gold, if you'd see things my way."

Roxanne stared at her.

" 'Course you'd find it easy to pay me back in Dawson, whether he struck it or not," explained Josie complacently. "Miners would sure fight it out for a chance at you—you'd have more gold than you ever saw."

Roxanne, nonplussed at this direct offer of a gilded life, was momentarily unable to frame a suitable reply. As she stared at the madam, it came to her that the brown eyes she was looking into were kind eyes—cynical, worldly-wise, but kind just the same. "Thank you," she said ruefully, "but I've got a jealous husband. He onced caned a man just for smiling in my direction on the way to church."

"That," said Josie bleakly, "is a crying shame." She patted Roxanne on the back. "Let me know if you ever change your mind."

"Thank you," said Roxanne. "I'll remember."

She was smiling as Josie left, thinking, if Denby could have heard that conversation, he'd have had apoplexy. She went back to viewing the shoreline, for in spite of the overcrowding, she found the voyage through the green water fascinating. Below soft banks of clouds, almost unbroken forests stretched to starboard. Now and then an Indian village broke the shoreline and she saw bright totem poles rising majestically among the burial houses. Sometimes, in the distance, she spotted high-prowed Indian canoes skimming the waters, their brilliantly decorated hulls dimmed with seal oil and soot. Playful schools of porpoises gathered around the ship and, once, a group of killer whales.

Roxanne's enchanted gaze ignored the tumbledown cabins of Wrangell and instead looked with delight at the dangerous beauty of Wrangell Narrows, where tall dark firs were reflected in the water against a backdrop of majestic snow-capped peaks. In spite of its dilapidated appearance, Wrangell did a thriving business—especially in liquor. Many passengers purchased "medicinal" liquor here, having been warned that Alaska was "dry."

Once through the Narrows—so treacherous they could be negotiated only by daylight, they moved beneath flights of ducks and screaming seagulls to the bustling town of Juneau, set on a knoll and backed by an almost perpendicular mountain. There they stretched their legs on the boardwalk and looked across the channel toward Douglas Island where the mighty Treadwell Mine, reputed to be the largest gold mine in the world, was situated. The storekeepers warned them there would be problems in landing the enormous amount of gear that now weighted down the ship, but no one listened. All were eager to push on.

Roxanne knew that the golden giant, Leighton Clarke, had more than a casual interest in her. It was revealed in a sudden intentness of his casual blue gaze, in the way he maneuvered to be near her. But Leighton had a delicacy in these things; his manner was impeccable. And since Denby apparently was not jealous of Leighton, Roxanne relaxed—she found Leighton's company very pleasant. She decided that she might like the Klondike after all.

The boat had barely cleared the harbor at Juneau when their sister ship, the limping side-wheeler, blew up. Her passengers had had no idea that, contrary to regulations, she was carrying dynamite. In the resulting fire, Leighton proved to be a hero. Making off in one of the hastily launched boats to rescue the sidewheelers's passengers, he returned to the burning ship again and again; once to open crates so that the terrified dogs in them might swim in one long frightened streak to shore and safety. Roxanne felt sorry for the side-wheeler's passengers and did what she could to help. When the stranded adventurers had to be left at Juneau, there was much weeping and cursing on their part. Denby was unsympathetic, muttering that this misfortune had cost them a day; he feared they might be iced in. Roxanne, giving Denby a withering look, turned her blinding smile on the smoke-blackened giant who had come back from saving the dogs.

The *Clara V* now had her own troubles. Because the coal she had taken on at Juneau was unevenly loaded, she listed perilously to starboard. She threatened to capsize as soon as the wind came up. All the passengers took part in trying to right the vessel. It was not until they reached the Lynn Canal that they discovered the lazy crew had left most of the coal in Juneau—they were out of fuel. While the terrified passengers ran about in a driving rain, the *Clara V* drifted broadside into a three-masted schooner. The apoplectic captain of the schooner pulled out a rifle and bellowed at the *Clara V*'s captain to come out and meet his doom. Somehow the ships were pried apart. The schooner limped on. And the *Clara V*—the crew having rigged makeshift sails—lumbered along behind. The passengers took heart—they were almost at their destination.

Though the voyage had been a nightmare, none of them realized how lucky they were to have made it at all. Other ships in the raffish flotilla beating up the coast had run aground, foundered and sunk in fog or simply disappeared without a trace.

When the ship reached Dyea, anchoring well offshore in the dangerous mountain-bound harbor with its twenty-foot tides, Roxanne was appalled at the way they unloaded. Small lighters transported the freight to Dyea's shallow flats. But the horses were simply lifted on slings and dumped over the side into the water to flounder ashore as best they could. Lumber too was tossed over casually, while the owners figured out how they could maneuver it ashore. Bales of hay were handled in the same manner, bobbing on the incoming tide. Surely the hay would be ruined, Roxanne thought, and the horses, if they made it through the icy water, would starve! Even the small boats that took the passengers ashore could not make it all the way.

Leighton leaped out into two feet of water and gallantly carried Roxanne to shore while Denby splashed along behind.

From the jumble on the soggy gray beach, alive with shouting people and yelping dogs and wet neighing horses, they rescued their baggage and moved on to the tent city of Dyea. There they waited while Leighton bargained with several of the short broad-shouldered Chilkat Indians about helping them to carry their tents and supplies. Roxanne noted with interest the thin sweeping mustaches on the stolid broad faces of the men and the cosmetic blackening on the women's faces.

Up Trail Street into the winding river gorge they followed their silent packers, camping on the way until they reached Sheep Camp on a plateau at the timberline, thirteen miles inland. Beautiful and deadly and untamed, wild Alaska lay around them.

From Sheep Camp they could view their immediate objective—Chilkoot Pass four miles away. To cross it they would scramble and slide over slippery glaciers and rock ledges dangerous with ice, and Roxanne would need the stout boots she had purchased in Wrangell. The first obstacle to get around was a boulder so large it was called Stone House; following that, passage was through a narrow gorge to a flat ledge called the Scales—and then the ascent, an almost impossible thirty-degree incline up the snowy face, a notch in the rugged and lofty white hills that horses could not negotiate—only men could. Leaning over the pass as if peering down to watch their progress was a three hundred-foot tall glacier, diamond white in the sunlight, a tower of ice held up insecurely by the twin granite peaks that guarded the pass. Its frightening size and insecure suspension fascinated Roxanne, who half expected to see it come tumbling down into the valley, sweeping them all before it. Everything they owned had to be heaved and struggled to the top of this white monster and carried down the other side. Even with help it took several days. Had they carried a ton of supplies apiece, which the Canadian Mounties later required, and no packers, it might have taken forty days to haul it all to the top of the pass.

Later fifteen hundred steps would be hacked in the solid ice and a single file of men, bent double under heavy packs, would lockstep up it in a swearing, sweating line. But right now it was a hodgepodge. They floundered up—and slid down.

At night, wet and ravenous, they stayed in a hastily constructed board hotel at Sheep Camp. Its lone twenty- by forty-foot room was quickly filled in the evening with a wild motley crowd of wet and dirty men who charged in and paid their seventy-five cents in advance to eat beans and tea and bacon in relays. At night everyone unrolled blankets, hung their socks and shoes on the rafters above, rolled up a coat for a pillow and fell asleep exhausted in their clothes. New people arrived daily. On the second day two of the new arrivals were women.

Roxanne was glad to see them. Aside from the proprietor's wife, who slept with him behind a calico curtain in one corner of the room, Roxanne had been the only woman in the group since they left Dyea.

The women were Mary Jane McManus, a shoe clerk's wife, who with her husband had sold all they owned and headed for the gold fields. And Marjorie Rawson—"Call me Marge"—a big stalwart black-haired woman who wrung Roxanne's hand and declared she'd flung her last half dollar in the surf at Dyea and was here to make her fortune or bust. Talkative Leighton, the only man around who topped Marge in height, stared at this Amazon as if he didn't believe what he was seeing, and was stunned into silence. Roxanne took to Marge Rawson at once and, while Mary Jane followed her husband around in a wistful way, Marge and Roxanne talked. Marge had a huge load of supplies that would take her many days to haul up the steep pass. Once, as they stopped breathlessly to talk at Stone House, Marge surprised Roxanne by giving her a keen look and asking, "That marriage of yours for real? Or just livin' at it?"

"It's real," sighed Roxanne, listening to Denby

swear in the distance as he floundered after Leighton, who was weighed down with a three hundred-pound pack.

"Hm'm." Marge considered her. "That one wants you, you know."

"Who?" asked Roxanne, knowing full well.

"Leighton Clarke, that's who. You gonna take him up—on his offer?"

"He hasn't made me an offer," said Roxanne.

"He will," predicted Marge. "And then," she added significantly, "you might have to make a choice."

Roxanne thought, too, that events might come to that, but she hoped to put the dilemma off as long as possible. Regretfully, she bade Marge good-bye at Sheep Camp, just before they made their last climb over the Chilkoot Pass. Struggling over that white escarpment, Roxanne once again looked up with a shudder at the tremendous glacier that hung poised above her, guarding the pass. The day was cloudy, and the glacier's huge insecure mass, so brilliantly white in the sunlight, was a beautiful mixture of gleaming turquoise and translucent sapphire. Denby floundered on after the packers, but Leighton, pausing beside her, observed that the glacier was the color of her eyes. As he spoke, a deafening report issued from deep within the glacier and they both froze, expecting the huge mass to shatter and hurtle down on them. But the monster remained poised above them and the noise degenerated into a sound somewhat like distant cannon rumbling, as if down deep the very mountains were locked in war.

Galvanized into action, Roxanne and Leighton hurried away from the summit and followed Denby and the packers down ten miles to the shores of beautiful blue Lake Lindeman. There they paid off the packers and pitched camp. Immediately Leighton and Denby began building a rakish boat, whipsawing the shoreline timber at a speed that wore Denby out and made him collapse under his blanket every night while Leighton sat and smiled at Roxanne. They talked of many things across the campfire as they ate their ptarmigan stew and canned milk.

At last, raising a mast and fashioning their tent into a sail, they boarded their craft and moved it out onto Lake Bennett. Crossing the difficult shallows below the lake, they fought to keep from going aground. The swift current of the deep Whitehorse River carried them down to Miles Canyon, where they made camp and consulted the map of sorts they had purchased at Juneau. Ahead lay the notorious Whitehorse Rapids, twisting down a canyon some seventy-five to a hundred feet wide.

Against Denby's wishes, Leighton decreed that almost all the supplies should be unloaded and backpacked down the grassy path that led to the foot of the nearly mile-long rapids. Roxanne would walk. He and Denby would shoot the rapids alone.

From the bank Roxanne watched as the bucking boat, now minus its sail, whirled out into the wild white water. She could see Denby's frightened face and Leighton's laughing one as their craft rushed on. The boat plunged ever faster, sometimes disappearing entirely into the foam that closed over it like long white fangs, sometimes seeming to leap up out of the water, rearing and tossing. Roxanne screamed as she saw them hurtling on a collision course toward a huge boulder that stood in midstream—and almost collapsed with relief when they barely missed it, shooting past it like a bullet and charging on until at last they bobbed through the high-ridged crest to safety.

The skeletons of wrecked boats below the canyon, where they reloaded, bore mute testimony to the danger of the voyage. But the only damage sustained by their party in running the rapids was to Roxanne—she discovered two days later that she had somehow lost her precious spoons.

The floundering over the pass, the trip down from the high lakes, the portage had all taken time, and the fierce northern winter was fast setting in. Past fog-shrouded banks they slid, watching the geese fly south. For fresh food, Leighton brought down a goose or two with his rifle. But even though she was hungry, Roxanne hated to see the beautiful birds drop from the sky. Chunks of ice floated ominously down the Yukon now, and sometimes they heard a thunder that came not from the clouds but from the pounding hooves of the caribou herd as they fled this soon-to-be-ice-bound land. Once their boat was nearly capsized by a great herd of caribou that plunged into the water near them to swim to the opposite bank.

But it had all taken time—too much time. The flaming colors of September, with fiery birches and gold-orange aspens and purple-red buckbrush, had turned to gray as the Yukon Valley forests lost their leaves and the morning winds lashed hillsides powdered with frost. The days had shortened markedly, and along the river banks ice formed and broke off as the little streams that fed the river froze solid and the water level dropped. The river was filled with floating chunks of ice when at last they reached Dawson.

The landing was full of shocks. They arrived in time to see dozens of discouraged men climbing the gangplank of a small river steamer to depart the town. From the bank a wild-eyed man in a black hat waved his arms at them and howled, "Get out while you can! Go back! There's no food here. Go downriver to Fort Yukon or you'll starve!"

Denby was for sticking it out in Dawson. But Leighton, taking a quick walk through the crowded boom-town streets and asking questions in the ramshackle stores, shook his head. The three of them managed to buy tickets on one of the last boats to make it out of Dawson before the ice closed down the river traffic.

"Does this mean we're going home?" demanded Roxanne incredulously.

Leighton shook his head. "It means we'll winter in Fort Yukon."

Denby brought his fist down in anger on the ship's rail as he watched Dawson disappear through the ice cakes behind them and they rounded Moosehide Bluff. He looked as if he wanted to cry.

Their trip to Fort Yukon was nightmarish. "Conceived in hell," one grumpy passenger described it. Gamely, the crowded boat fought her way through floating ice until the ice jammed her rudder. When her captain managed to get her to shore, she was immediately walled in by ice. The passengers eyed each other in alarm, wondering if they'd have to walk to Fort Yukon.

But they had a bit of luck. From the coast a warm chinook wind melted the ice in the channel. For almost twelve hours they made good headway and the passengers drank liquor—always plentiful somehow—and sang boisterous songs. Suddenly their songs were hushed. In the distance came a rising roar—of moving ice bearing down on them.

"The river's freezing," said Leighton grimly.

No one went to bed that night. In darkness black as soot, while the water seemed to rise, the current speeded up, hurtling them along. Then, suddenly, the avalanche of ice reached them. Crashing, rending, like some giant beast it roared down upon them. The little steamer was whirled about and trapped in a narrow canyon between walls of ice. White-faced, hanging onto the rail to keep her footing, Roxanne felt the reverberations as blocks of ice smashed against the hull. The noise was appalling. Around Roxanne people were praying. Suddenly the steamer was snatched upward—held in the grip of ice that a moment before had been churning, frothing water. In that short space of time the Yukon River had frozen bank to bank.

Dawn presented a terrible sight. Other boats that had followed them were smashed, their occupants nowhere to be seen. The river was like a miniature mountain range, full of jagged, upended ice blocks, some as large as houses, frozen into immobility. As far as the eye could see up and down the Yukon, nothing moved.

Somehow they got to Fort Yukon, floundering over

the surface of the icy river, sinking into the snow along the banks. They felled trees and made roaring bonfires and shivered and starved. It was sixty-seven degrees below zero. All around them, branches of trees were exploding as the sap froze, making a perpetual cannonade, when they finally trudged into Fort Yukon.

And there they spent the winter.

It was a winter Roxanne never liked to think about, even years later. Crowded and quarrelsome, the prospectors were jammed around red-hot sheet-iron stoves, eating short rations provided by the hunters who now and then ventured out during the short winter days and bagged an occasional moose. Wedged on the floor beneath one of the bunks, which were built three tiers high to accommodate as many as possible in the cramped cabin, Roxanne sometimes found herself dreaming of Seattle and the wicked wonderful night she had spent with Case. She shivered as she remembered the silken feel of his smooth gambler's hands on her body, the surging response that she had not troubled to hide and that had delighted him. She wondered now, had Case made it to Dawson? She remembered how one ship had blown up, how others were stranded partway on the journey. And there were all the terrible things that could happen to a man in Alaska. She had heard that many new arrivals had died on the trail or drowned in the rivers.

No, Case was alive, *must* be alive. He'd be sitting at a green felt table with stacks of chips before him, dealing out the cards, his hard face looking just as it had in Seattle. . . .

And sometimes, on the darkest nights, when the wind howling round the cabin shrieked and penetrated the chinks, when the temperature outside dropped to seventy degrees below zero, she thought of Baltimore. Then the cold she felt had nothing to do with the savage blizzard outside. She thought of Rhodes, who had broken her heart, and sometimes, at the edge of sleep, his green eyes still seemed to be smiling down into hers. She felt—not the lighthearted ecstasy she felt when she thought of Case—but something deeper, something hurtful, a kind of essential hunger that would never be assuaged. At those moments she sometimes reached out for Denby, forgetting that the women were herded together on one side of the room, the men on the other. Then she would bury her face in the rolled-up coat that served as a pillow, and dry sobs would wrack her slender body. But morning would find her dry-eyed and ready to do her share of the back-breaking work that had to be done in order to stay alive in Fort Yukon.

Leighton helped break the monotony of life there. Crouched beside a sheet-iron stove in the evenings, he entertained them with stories of life in Paris, London, Rome. Through his eyes Roxanne wandered London's foggy streets, heard Big Ben chime, rode through Hyde Park greeting friends, attended a Paris Beaux Arts ball where women wore only high heels and fans, roamed the Coliseum with its dozen of cats, and fed the pigeons in St. Peter's Square. Through his eyes she saw a glimmering of something else: a gracious way of life with an international flavor she had not known at the Coulters' Baltimore town house.

How could he bear to leave all that? she wondered.

Even in the daytime, Denby hugged the stove. But she and the golden giant would go out on good days into the stinging arctic air, walking in the new-fallen snow on the snowshoes Leighton had rigged for them. They walked and looked at the jagged surface of the frozen river, at the gale-lashed trees in the pale grayness of the short winter days—and occasionally Leighton shot a white hare. They would flounder back and shake themselves off like dogs, making wet patches on the floor where the snow from their clothing melted, and join the others sitting about the plank floor or—exhausted—curl up and try to sleep.

On days like that Roxanne wondered why Leighton made no move toward her. She was puzzled by him. His eyes told her he wanted her, but when they were alone, he never made any move to possess her. It was as if he blew hot, then cold. The winter wore on, but she couldn't figure him out.

Then one day the weather was surprisingly nice after a fresh fall of snow, and she and Leighton were trudging through a wonderland of lacy white branches against a silver gray sky, when they stopped by mutual consent on the bank of the frozen Yukon. Here they were far from the fort, and there was a stillness around them as if even time stood still. Their breath was frosty on the chill air. A ptarmigan took wing near them and an icicle broke from a tree branch, falling to the ice with a bell-like tinkle. Clad in her makinaw, long wool skirt and boots, Roxanne leaned against a tree trunk and let the red woolen shawl she was wearing over her head fall down around her shoulders.

As if he could not help himself, Leighton leaned down and covered her soft mouth tenderly with his own, wrapping her in his big arms. Her lips warmed beneath that gentle pressure, and she gazed up at him with troubled blue eyes as he suddenly pulled away from her.

His voice was husky. "I shouldn't have done that, Roxanne. It was treacherous of me," he muttered and stalked away, leaving Roxanne struggling to catch up with him. But her heart, which had felt frozen by the long winter, lightened. What Marge had told her back in Sheep Camp had been true after all. The golden giant loved her. For a treacherous moment she wished he were not quite so honorable, wished that he had crushed her in his arms and made a nest for them in the snow. Her cheeks grew hot thinking of it. She wrapped her shawl around her head, and they tramped back together, but she could not meet Leighton's eyes as they reached the fort, where Denby waited disconsolate by the fire.

That was the only time during the whole long winter that Leighton took her in his arms, and by spring she was convinced that his honor was too strong—he would never touch her again.

With the coming of spring the ice broke on the Yukon, and, except for floating chunks and occasional ice jams, the river's channel was clear again. As if they were one body, the whole heterogeneous mass of humanity that had wintered in Fort Yukon was on the move again. Denby and Roxanne and Leighton made it upriver with the others, back to the town they'd fled so precipitously the fall before—Dawson City.

They found Dawson agog with war news. During the time they had been at Fort Yukon, the battleship *Maine* had been blown up in Havana harbor, and the United States was now at war with Spain. They also found Dawson girding itself for a different kind of onslaught, of staggering proportions. Five thousand people were reputed to be camped on the shores of Lake Bennett, waiting for the thaw, at which time they would surge downriver into Dawson. Another five thousand camped at Lake Lindeman and along the upper Yukon. Countless thousands already were attempting the White Pass and the Chilkoot, and there were lines of river steamers crammed with eager stampeders heading up the mouth of the Yukon. All this in addition to the ragged hundreds who, like their own party, had been stranded below Dawson the previous autumn.

The Klondike 1898—1899

Chapter 24

Once again they were in Dawson. This time, instead of facing starvation in the chill subarctic night, they faced starvation in the long subarctic day.

Their money had run out. Leighton muttered something about a check from a trust fund that was sure to come and stalked off into the forest to hunt. Meat was as good as cash in Dawson, with its inpouring hordes. Denby gave Roxanne a helpless look, and she returned it.

They were walking about the unprepossessing shack town of Dawson worrying when they heard a shout: "Hey, Roxie!"

Roxanne turned to see big Marge, her face split with a grin, bearing down on them. She had just got into town, having spent the winter camped with thousand of others on the shores of Lake Bennett. But *she* had made money all winter doing laundry and, after buying dogs and sleds, had started downriver before the ice broke. She had some bad moments on slushy ice, but she had made it. She and a new husband, acquired on Lake Bennett and married to her by a real preacher—'course they had no license, but she guessed it was legal. Anyway, they were living together fair and square! Marge gave a shout of laughter that caused passing miners' heads to turn.

Roxanne turned to meet the new husband. He was a shy little schoolteacher from Oregon with a shock of iron-gray hair and a surprisingly sweet smile, who gave his big bride a look of pure adoration. Roxanne wanted to laugh at their incongruity and to cry at their simple and obvious love for each other.

"How are you and Denby making out?" Marge wanted to know. "And where is that big feller?"

"Leighton has gone hunting," said Roxanne.

"Gold or moose?"

"Moose."

"Right sensible of him." Marge nodded her head. "That's what you should be doing too, boy!" She slapped Denby forcefully on the back and he looked pained. "You found any gold yet?"

"We just got here," explained Roxanne. "And the fact is, Marge, we can neither go nor stay—we have no money."

"That's bad," Marge said. "Dawson's an expensive town, sure enough. Didn't take but one look to see that! Me, I'm establishing a laundry. Got me some soap and a fire-builder!" She gave her husband a jovial poke in the ribs; he winced and grinned. "You want to come to work for me, Roxanne? All the miners for miles around'll bring their dirty long johns in just for a look at you!"

Roxanne cast an apprehensive look at Denby. "Yes," she said before he could object. "That is, if you can put us up. We have no place to live."

"You will have! I'm sure not stayin' in Dawson though. I'm goin' where the action is! Out to Bonanza; them's the boys has got the gold to afford to get their long johns washed."

"Bonanza's twenty miles away," said Denby, looking interested.

"The twenty most traveled miles in this part of the world, I'd wager," said Marge. "And all of them'll be beatin' a path to my laundry when we get it started."

Roxanne smiled at Marge. Before Marge had holloed at them, she'd been considering trying to find Case. It would have been a bit difficult since ladies didn't enter saloons and she could hardly send Denby on such an errand. Now she was saved from begging Case's aid, but was almost sorry. She'd wanted to see the gambler again. Those stolen moments in a Seattle hotel room had lingered in her memory and had kept her going when Leighton's bright smile was absent. Leighton was a man of family who hobnobbed with the wealthy when he wasn't out slumming with adventurers. But Case . . . Case was like herself, tossed out on the tide of life to sink or find his way, and the rough seas had tarnished not only his eyes but his heart and soul. She felt a kind of kinship with Case that she had never felt with another human being.

Denby cheered up when Marge cried in her big voice, "Well, let's all stay at a hotel tonight, seein's we've got to rough it in the morning goin' out to Bonanza!"

The hotel left much to be desired, but it was luxury after their cramped life at Fort Yukon and their miserable journey upriver to Dawson by boat. Morning found them ready to gulp down flapjacks and maple syrup greedily and make the trek to the Bonanza diggings in good style. That journey took them up the Klondike River. Marge had tossed her head disdainfully at Dawson City, built on a swamp and standing like a street marker at the junction of the Klondike and the Yukon. "Carnival kind of town," she muttered. "Out where they work, that's where men'll want their laundry done!" Marge led the way to Bonanza, selected the site, negotiated with the owners and supervised the building, ordering her husband and Denby and Roxanne around with equal good nature.

"She's sure bossy," grumbled Denby.

"She's feeding us," said Roxanne. "Where would we be without her?"

Having no answer to that, Denby subsided. But he drifted away once the laundry got started and there was constant heavy work to be done. He heard rumors of gold strikes: on the Stewart River, the McQueston, the Pelly. When he got word of a new strike, he was happy for a day or two. He'd make love to Roxanne—short unsatisfying romps when she was so tired she almost went to sleep in his arms. And with his arms about her, he'd coax her to stake him with the money she'd earned. It was a sure thing this time—it was always a sure thing. He'd rush out on wild goose chases that took all the money Roxanne earned. They always came to nothing. Denby would come back tired and disheartened and in a bad temper. He never mentioned seeing Case, for which Roxanne was thankful. She supposed shrewdedly that Denby was afraid that if he saw Case, Case might want his money back.

Between excursions of prospecting with Denby, Leighton packed in moose meat to pay Marge for his room and board and laundry—and for staking him on his trips with Denby. When the big man was there, he carried huge tubs of water and firewood for Roxanne. In the long subarctic days when it was still daylight at midnight, work on Bonanza and nearby Eldorado went on back-breakingly around the clock, and Leighton worked tirelessly to help her. Roxanne was grateful to him. Sometimes, stirring the boiling water with a long stick, she was so tired she could drop. Into that boiling water she thrust an endless tangle of shirts and trousers and long johns stiff with prespiration and dirt. Marge's laundry did a thriving business.

Soon the weather grew pleasant. Brier roses perfumed the valleys, and the lupins blanketed the upland slopes with violet hues. Everywhere amid the rocks, berries were ripening—raspberries, cranberries, currants and blueberries. Roxanne's work was now a gasping, perspiring business. The afternoon temperatures sometimes soared so high that she had to stop and fan herself; her worn clothes clung to her wetly. On the hills the snow melted fast, forming thousands of gurgling little rivulets that seemed to rise from the earth itself and that cascaded down into now dense subtropical vegetation. Nearby on Bonanza and Eldorado, men sluiced and worked back-breakingly with shovels to wash free the yellow gold from the frozen muck of last winter's diggings. This spring cleanup would establish whether a man was rich or poor. Gossip swirled about—some people expected to realize as much as three hundred thousand dollars from the frozen muck they'd dug out last winter.

Roxanne, struggling with the big tubs, fighting mosquitoes that buzzed in thick clouds, her lovely face flushed as she stirred clothes into the boiling water in the midsummer heat, was cynical. Stories, she'd learned, grew big in the Klondike as every man tried to outbrag the other. But plainly some had struck it rich; she saw men toting bags of gold, and Marge was paid off in nuggets. Sometimes they tipped Roxanne in nuggets. All the miners liked her. Some of them were even a little in love with her and followed her wistfully with their eyes. The Dawson blond, they called her, as if Dawson weren't full of bright blond fancy women, and other shades as well—black, white and brown. By night Roxanne fell into bed so tired she could not move, sleeping under only mosquito netting. Denby rarely made love to her anymore. On the boat and at Fort Yukon life had been too cold and too public. Here at Big Marge's in the midsummer heat, he was sulky because he'd found no gold.

Eventually, Case heard that Roxanne was there and came out to Bonanza to see her. Unlike the grubby bearded miners, who looked as if they'd slept for a season in their clothes, Case was trim and clean-shaven, his white shirt snowy against his somber dark suit. Even his boots shone. When Roxanne looked up and saw him standing there, she almost dropped her heavy washtub. He didn't offer to help her with it. Instead he leaned against a tree and looked her up and down. "Hello, Roxanne."

Slowly she set the tub down and straightened up. "Hello, Case."

"Why didn't you look me up?" He sounded almost

angry. "You wouldn't have had to do *this.*" He nodded contemptuously at the tub.

"It's honest work," sighed Roxanne, irritatingly aware of her worn skirt and mended blouse and damp tumbled hair.

A bitter little smile played around his mouth. "So that's it," he said. "Still the unbendable little housewife."

Roxanne cast a sad look around her at the slippery mud, the long clothes lines. "I wouldn't call it homemaking," she said.

His eyes narrowed. "I'm at the Last Nugget, Roxanne." She knew the place—one of the biggest saloons in Dawson with gambling day and night. "Why don't you come back to town with me and let me show you around Dawson?"

The thought of going with him tugged at her. "Ladies don't go into saloons," she murmured.

Case laughed. "Ladies don't come to the Klondike," he said. "They may start out as ladies, but by the time they reach Dawson, they're women! Come on, that isn't your reason."

"It's Denby," she admitted. "He's out on the Pelly, and I wouldn't want him to hear when he gets back that I'd gone into town with you. You see, Denby doesn't know—about us."

Case gave her a mocking look. "Isn't it time he found out? You can't spend your life washing clothes on Bonanza Creek!"

She thought she owed him an explanation."I've got to get Denby on his feet—somehow. I keep hoping he'll discover gold."

"So you can leave him?"

Her already hot face flushed still darker. The thought had crossed her mind. It was one thing to leave a down-and-out husband, quite another to leave a prosperous young miner.

Case gave her a thoughtful look. "Then *I* hope he discovers gold too, Roxanne. Suggest to him that he might strike it rich at the Last Nugget."

"No—I don't mean *that* way, Case." Her voice was

hurried, embarrassed. "That would be—" She stopped helplessly. Denby had to make it honestly—not by being hoodwinked by her lover into believing he had a winning streak at cards. "Did you bring your laundry?" she asked weakly.

Case gave her a blank look. "Did you think I came out here twenty miles to bring you some dirty shirts?" he asked bitterly. "You can come in to town when you're damn well good and ready, and we'll talk!"

He stalked off.

Roxanne watched him stride away up the muddy creek bank, and part of her heart went with him. The wild reckless part that wasn't owned by Denby or anybody else. The part of her that wanted to wear beautiful clothes and fine perfumes, to strike out alone and make her way in the world of men—in saloons or anywhere else. Lord, she'd heard girls with half her looks were getting a dollar a dance for a one-minute waltz in Dawson! But she knew what Denby would say about that.

With a sigh, she went back to stirring the clothes in the tub and tried not to remember that reckless night in Seattle, the feel of Case's strong hands on her body, driving her to heights of frenzy and desire. She pictured him as she had seen him then, lean and naked, his dark face very close, every cell of her being wanting him, aching for him. And the little laugh he had given as finally he took her, possessed her, made her his own.

Her face was hot from more than the steam of the cauldron she was stirring. There was a cauldron in her heart too, and one day it might burst its bounds and fling her toward Dawson City and the man with tarnished silver eyes.

In the meantime there was Denby, who had gone with Leighton to explore the Pelly River basin, to see if they could find gold. Desperately she hoped they'd find it. Then she would be free!

Someone else came out from Dawson to see her that summer. It was Josie Mawkins, the madam from Chicago she'd met on the boat. Somehow Josie had gotten her "young ladies," as she liked to call them, over the Chilkoot Pass without any broken legs, and now she was set up with "the hottest place in Dawson," by her own boast.

She found Roxanne working outside, her head draped in mosquito netting against the thick clouds of mosquitoes, stirring clothes in a boiling hot tub with a stick.

"Well, it's you!" laughed Josie, lifting the veil of mosquito netting that draped her own hat and peering at Roxanne. "I heard about this great-looking Dawson blond that had set all the men on Bonanza Creek plumb wild, and I came out prospectin' myself to see if I couldn't lure the girl into my establishment. What's that you're doing? Laundry?"

Her voice was so incredulous that Roxanne, pushing back a damp lock of hair from her perspiring face, laughed.

"But a girl with looks like yours don't have to do laundry! You don't have to waste that bosom and those hips and those fiery eyes and that bright smile on washing clothes!"

"It's a living," said Roxanne grimly, giving the clothes a poke.

"So's shovelin' dirt in a smoky hole on Bonanza Creek," countered Josie, slapping at mosquitoes. "But men like Case at the Last Nugget rake in a lot more gold and don't get their hands so dirty."

Roxanne looked up sharply at this mention of Case. Had Case sent Josie out to call on her?

Josie sighed. "Sure I can't persuade you to come into town and get all flossied up?"

Roxanne smiled at her and said softly, "I have a jealous husband, remember, who believes he's going to strike it rich."

"Well, *his* way is chancy," argued Josie. "*My* way is sure. No matter who gets rich out of this here gold strike, I'm bound to. So would you, if you'd come and work in my house. Think it over, Roxanne, dearie. The offer's open. Anytime."

Chapter 25

Knowing for certain that Case was in Dawson changed things for Roxanne. Before, she had worked doggedly, staking Denby, wishing he'd strike gold so she could leave him without feeling guilty, but now she worked herself into insensibility each day to keep from thinking about Case, from remembering.

The miners who patronized Big Marge's laundry mainly for the pleasure of viewing the Dawson blond found a change in her, a preoccupation. But they still came and clustered around, paying the price of new clothes to have their old ones laundered, just to watch the beautiful girl at work.

Marge's laundry did a thriving business all year. Not only would miners pay the price of a new shirt just to get an old one washed, but the blazing fire at Marge's hearth that next winter (wood mainly supplied by Leighton, who stayed there too) made her cabin the warmest on Bonanza Creek. It was heated, too, by the crowds of warmblooded miners eager to help Roxanne stir the dirty clothes or take them out and hang them on a rope slung between two poles—all the trees in the vicinity having been cut down for rough lumber or firewood. Outside, the clothes froze immediately and were delivered flat and stiff—but clean—to their owners, whose business it was to thaw them out. Sometimes they paid extra to have it done for them at Marge's hearth.

That fall, Marge, cannily realizing there was gold in Roxanne's popularity, hired men who had run out of funds to construct a log addition to her cabin, in which she set up a kind of boardinghouse. Coffee and moose meat sandwiches and sometimes cranberries and ptarmigan stew were served by day, but by night rude cots were set up to accommodate half a dozen men—usually those who chose to sleep there rather than return through the sub-zero murk to their own cold digs. Behind a curtain at one end dwelt Roxanne and Denby. Behind a curtain at the other end dwelt huge, exuberant, energetic Marge, and her self-effacing husband.

Roxanne often had occasion to thank God for Marge. For without her that winter would have been unbearable. Even at Aunt Ada's she had not worked so hard. And here the air had a bitter bite that went through her much-mended clothes more fiercely than the worst of Kansas winters. Here her eyelashes froze, and the wind whipped her like a painful lash. On one terrible day at sixty degrees below zero she took some boiling water outside to pour into a miner's cup and it froze as she poured it. As she stumbled back to the door half frozen, crying in fury, her tears froze on her lashes.

Because Case was in Dawson, Roxanne kept away from the town. Seeing him might have weakened her newly-affirmed vow to be a good and decent wife to Denby. Wearily she mended and remended her worn clothes, helped Marge fix moose meat sandwiches and tended the tubs. On clear days when a pale sun shone briefly in the skies, she sometimes ventured out on the snow with Leighton as she had at Fort Yukon.

Most of the time they all huddled miserably inside, trying to keep warm. And the half dozen men who sheltered each night in Marge's commodious cabin would look at Roxanne with hunger in their eyes.

When Denby grumbled about their fate, Marge told him grimly that they were the lucky ones. Look at those scurvy-plagued miners on Bonanza and nearby Eldorado, wrapped up in all the clothes they owned, gnawing frozen slabs of bread by candlelight. Look at them, working all night in this frozen hell, stoking bonfires on their claims so next day the granite-like soil would be thawed enough to dig into.

But when those grubby miners reached bedrock in those smoky holes, countered Denby wistfully, the white gravel they found was laced with gold. Marge gave him a derisive sniff. *Here*, she argued, they had buckwheat cakes every morning, poured from a crock kept from freezing by setting it by the hearth at night and replenished all winter; Denby didn't know when he was well off. Marge emphasized her words by slamming down a pot of coffee and stomping off to the tubs.

Rumors reached Bonanza Creek that winter of a strike in Nome. Most people scoffed. Nome! Roxanne shivered. Nome was even deeper into the frozen north. Thank God she didn't have to go *there*.

By the time that terrible frostbitten winter was over even Denby had had enough. He only bobbed his head in unhappy assent when Roxanne told him she had saved enough money for their passage back to Seattle.

Roxanne asked Leighton if he planned to return to Washington. No, he told her, he would never return to Washington; he planned to spend the summer exploring the vast Koyukuk River basin; perhaps he would even winter in the north before returning to the outside, as all the Klondikers called the rest of the world. She appreciated Leighton's penchant for exploring far places and regretfully wished him luck. She would miss the friendly giant.

Marge said it wasn't right for them to spend their last days in the Klondike out on lonely Bonanza

Creek. Declaring that Roxanne had washed her last long johns—except Denby's—her laughter bellowed. She said she was taking them all into town on a spree —her man could mind the laundry for a spell. They'd stay at a hotel. After all, the ice was melting. Any day now it would break and the first river steamer would come hooting around Moosehide Bluff, and Roxanne and Denby would be going back aboard it. For herself, she was staying. This was a big wild country, just right for her and her man. They'd grow up with it. She'd bought up five gold claims; this summer she'd have men working them. In time she'd be a rich woman and when she went back outside, she'd have a carriage and maybe a "livered" driver. Roxanne smiled at Marge's happy mispronunciation of "liveried" and hugged her warmly. More than anyone in the whole frozen world of the Klondike, she'd miss Marge.

Into town they went, dressed in their best, to put up at one of Dawson's best hotels, the Astoria, a jerry-built frame two-story building that Roxanne hardly preferred to her corner of Marge's two-room cabin. They ate out at restaurants where supplies were running low, awaiting the breaking of the ice. All the town's businesses were girding for the spring onslaught. Soon the river would be full of boats, Roxanne was told excitedly, and the town would be overflowing.

Fools, she thought dispassionately. Imagine wanting to come *here*!

"Town won't hold 'em," was Marge's cheerful comment.

Roxanne was astonished to learn that a railroad now ran from Dyea to the head of the canyon and an aerial tramway reached to the summit—all those weary miles they had plodded on foot. Even Marge stared when they were told that entire steamboats had been taken, section by section, over the summit and reassembled on Lake Bennett.

"Maybe you and Denby oughta stay here, Roxie," ruminated Marge. "Soon this'll be the biggest city west of Winnepeg."

Roxanne smiled at Marge and shook her head. Her mind was made up, but she looked around her more thoughtfully at the burgeoning town. Dawson's only sidewalks were wooden, its buildings were a jumble of clapboard and rough plank and log topped with stovepipe chimneys, and hastily painted signboards abounded. All was a great jostle and bustle as sled dogs and horse-drawn wagons ploughed through deep-mired streets past clomping bearded miners wearing wide-brimmed hats and boots. Behind this sprawling shack town rose the rugged hills. And beyond those hills ran cold deep rivers, hardly explored, up which men crept in tiny rafts and canoes, searching for the yellow metal that would buy them everything.

Roxanne looked around her at this alien landscape, this raw boom town that had meant to her only back-breaking work and harsh primitive living, and was thankful she was leaving it. *Home*, she thought, with a little thrill. *Home to the States*. The thought warmed her more than the newly-hot northern sun, more than Marge's happy shouted quips.

The day the ice broke with a grumbling roar, there was a general cheer on Front Street, and when the shrill whistle of the first river steamer was heard coming around Moosehide Bluff, the whole population surged toward the waterfront, Roxanne and Marge and Denby and Leighton among them.

The steamer brought news: America had won her war with Spain. But her other news could not wait for docking. From her decks even before she docked came hoarse voices calling, "Gold! Gold in Nome! Bigger strike than the Klondike!"

From the waterfront crowd came a great exultant roar. Men who hadn't struck it rich on the Yukon—and that was nearly everybody—howled and tossed their hats in the air at this news of a second chance. Gold in Nome! They jumped up and down; they waltzed the nearest woman or each other about, they shouted and howled and terrified the dogs, who ran away yelping.

Roxanne, separated from her party as men poured

off the overcrowded steamer, found herself pushed back along Front Street by the moving masses. She stepped into a doorway to let the crowd go by, standing on tiptoe to try to find Marge or Denby or Leighton among the throng.

Standing, peering into the crowd, she saw Rhodes.

She froze to immobility, not certain she had seen aright. Yes, there he was, as tall and formidable as ever, swinging along Front Street. He was casually dressed, his coat flung carelessly over one arm, his white shirt open at the neck. The sun glinted on the silver band of his dark wide-brimmed hat, shadowing the deeply bronzed face that moved alertly from right to left as he walked, his deep green eyes keenly studying his surroundings. Roxanne, feeling suddenly stifled, saw that he had lost none of that air of reckless confidence, none of the pantherish grace she remembered from Baltimore. She swayed dizzily. Rhodes—*here*!

She might have turned and run, but just at that moment he looked in her direction, and his bright smile flashed. Roxanne stood rooted, wishing she were anywhere but here. His step quickened as he shouldered his way through the crowd toward her. When he reached her, he swept off his hat in an exaggerated bow. He looked just as she remembered him, handsome, arrogant, very sure of himself. And for some reason triumphant.

"This is my lucky day, it seems," he said. "My first day in Dawson, and I walk right into an old friend."

She had not dreamed that seeing him would hurt her so. Her tormented heart was thudding in her chest. Somehow she got out an answer, was relieved that her voice had a light, almost indifferent ring. "Old friends we're not. What are you doing here, Rhodes?"

"I thought I'd drop in on the Klondike. The *Virginia Lass* is anchored offshore—didn't want to risk her on the river trip."

From the crowd, somebody jostled Rhodes. As Rhodes turned, a bearded miner's baritone rang out, proudly telling a little knot of newcomers, "You don't have to go to Bonanza to see the Dawson blond, boys

—there she stands in the doorway, one of the sights of the Klondike!"

Roxanne crimsoned. Rhodes could see the speaker was indicating *her*.

"So *you're* the Dawson blond," Rhodes said, amused. "I've been hearing glowing reports of your beauty all the way upriver."

Bitterly aware of her worn dress, the patches on her sleeves, she said, "Well, now you know the reports were unjustified."

"On the contrary." His lazy smile wandered over her lovely body. "You wasted no time after I left, Roxanne. I heard you got married."

"Yes."

He glanced at the sea of men who ogled her as they passed by. "And your husband lets you out alone?" he asked. "Faith, he's a fool to do it with a flirt like you."

Bright anger flooded her. He'd used her, raped her, cast her aside—and he still had the gall to needle her. "Denby has struck it rich," she lied airily. "We're off to San Francisco to spend the money."

He looked at her sharply, his eyes noting the worn dress.

"Where I'm to buy an all new wardrobe—jewels, furs," she added hastily.

"Of course." He was studying her, looking for chinks in her bright new armor. She preened before him, hoping to make him suffer. He'd cast her aside, but now she was rich! It was a lie, but it didn't matter. Making him *think* it was true was all that mattered.

To her horror, one of the miners who frequented Marge's laundry chose that moment to emerge from the crowd. He tipped his hat to her. "Well, it's pretty little Miss Roxie," he said. "Them shirts you laundered for me is the whitest yet. Never thought nothing would get this muck off them, but your little hands sure done it. It was a lucky day for Marge when she hired you, ma'am!"

"Thank you, Mr. Mayberry," said Roxanne in a

stifled voice. Bright color flooded her face as he departed.

"I presume," murmured Rhodes politely, "you launder as a hobby?"

"It's better than working for the Coulters," she said evenly.

His sunny green gaze lost its warmth. "What a lovely winter you must have spent—washing clothes in this climate." He laughed. "Almost as pleasant as mine. The *Lass* was frozen in the ice in the Bering Sea."

"I'm glad you enjoyed it," she said sweetly. "May I wish you many more of the same?"

He studied her. "You've grown bitter, Roxanne."

"Just older."

"No, hardly that." He considered her gravely. "Just harder shelled."

And who made me that way? she wanted to scream at him. You! You and your deceitful brother!

"There was a day," he mused, "when you were soft as the summer breeze. I see all that is far behind you. Have you the courage to have a drink with me? Or does your ladylike spirit keep you out of these dens of iniquity?" His gesture took in the saloons that lined Front Street.

Suddenly she blamed him for all her troubles—all of them. Rhodes had known she loved him, and he had used her vilely. Her hatred of this powerfully built man who stood before her, cool and insolent and infinitely desirable, flamed up like a torch, to give venom to her words. Her level gaze was unwavering. "I wish I were a man," she said through her teeth. "I'd gun you down right here and now for what you did to me in Baltimore."

"Then it's fortunate you aren't," he said coolly. "For I'd be forced to defend myself, wouldn't I? And you might end up on your back in the mud." His insolent gaze moved down from her angry face, past her panting round breasts to her supple waist, down past her hips to the skirt-hem she was holding up with one hand to avoid trailing it on the muddy boardwalk, revealing a pair of worn but dainty boots. "Of course, you could always kick me to death with those," he mused.

Her teeth clenched painfully in her soft lower lip. "Stay out of my way, Rhodes—and out of my life."

"Tell me where you're staying," he said.

Roxanne stared up at him, at his smiling face looking down at her. He hadn't heard her at all. He thought he could pick up where he'd left off in Baltimore—pick up, that is, where he'd stood *before* he'd raped her! Out of her fury at his smugness, came a plan. She would bring him down! She forced her stiff lips to smile—an attempt at coquetry. She could see it puzzled him.

"I'm staying at the Astoria." She tried to sound gracious. "You'll find it's the best in town."

"Good. I'll check in there before I sight-see. Could be we'll run into each other."

"I doubt that," said Roxanne, still smiling brightly but with an edge to her voice. "I have a husband now, remember?"

"As if I could forget!" he said lightly and bowed again. "Nice to have seen you, Roxanne."

He melted into the stream of passing miners and was gone. Roxanne, still rigid with shock, stood there breathing hard. After a moment she got hold of herself and plunged out into the crowded street, pushing her way through men who, delighted to be shoved aside by a pretty girl, laughed and called to her as she passed.

Straight to the swinging doors of the Last Nugget she rushed, almost lunging through them. There was hell in her heart as her head swung around, surveying the room, and she was panting from fury. The big room was floored with rough boards and filled with tables. Across from her stretched a long mahogany bar over which a huge painting of a reclining naked woman beamed, and nearby stood a player piano. The bartender looked up from polishing his glasses in surprise, doubtless because everyone else had gone down to meet the first river steamer. Roxanne faltered a moment, then started defiantly across the room to ask the bartender where she could find Case. She didn't need to ask. He was clattering down the stairs.

Midway down the stairs, he saw her. His head came up alertly and he strode toward her, lean and graceful, his shirtfront gleaming white against his somber clothes, his boots shining as if he had just polished them. "At last," he murmured. "At last you've come to town. . . ." His dark face was split by a flashing white smile.

She moved toward him, her reckless face lovely and almost as dangerous as his own. "I want a favor, Case," she said. "I am prepared to pay for it."

"Ask."

She found it surprisingly hard to say. She smoothed back her dark-blond hair nervously and looked down at her hands.

"Bartender, two whiskeys," called Case over his shoulder, and pulled out a chair at one of the wooden tables for Roxanne. "Did you hear about the gold strike in Nome?"

"Yes, they were howling it from the boat. Will you be going to Nome?"

He shook his head. "No. Dawson's Canadian soil, but Nome—that's U.S. Could be they'll be looking for me up there—if there's any law in Nome, which I doubt. Anyway, I'm well set up here. . . ." He paused as a sinewy dark-haired girl in a yellow satin negligee trimmed in black lace sauntered down the stairs toward the bar. Well set up . . . Roxanne saw what he meant. Case ignored the girl, was silent as the bartender poured their whiskeys. "This will buck you up." He handed one to Roxanne.

She took a quick swallow of the fiery liquid and choked. Case gave her a grim smile. "Two winters in the Klondike and you haven't learned to drink?" he marveled.

"The first winter we were stranded in Fort Yukon," she gasped.

"Same thing," he said. His gaze caressed her. Roxanne turned to look at the girl.

"Her name's Yvonne," Case said imperturbably. His face was dark and inscrutable.

Roxanne turned away from Yvonne's murderous glare.

"A long time ago," she said, choosing her words, "a man did me a great injury. The day has never gone by that I have not wanted to be revenged on him."

His eyes widened at the controlled savagery of her tone.

"I saw him again today. Here in Dawson. I—want to ruin him, Case. I want to destroy him as thoroughly as he destroyed me."

For a long time Case sat regarding her. "What did he do to you?"

"Does it matter?" she asked wearily.

"It might."

"He raped me—on a dark stairway." Her laughter was brittle, forced. "He thought I was somebody else."

Case toyed with his glass. "I see," he murmured dryly. "The ultimate insult. Raped—by mistake."

She felt angry color stain her cheeks, but she kept her voice steady. "If you will do it, Case, I will be *very* grateful."

"How grateful?" There was a whimsical turn to his mouth.

She swallowed and lifted her chin defiantly. "I—I will spend the night with you, Case. Just as I did in Seattle."

He nodded. "Sounds fair enough. What is it you want me to do?"

"Denby and I are leaving on the river tomorrow morning for San Francisco. He—the man said he was just sight-seeing, so he probably plans to leave on the same boat. Only I don't want him to catch that boat, Case. I want someone to waylay him in a dark alley tonight and roll him—take his money and his ticket. I want him to have to spend a couple of miserable years here in this frozen hell, broke and unhappy—as I have. I want him to suffer, Case."

"The way your hand is shaking you're going to spill that drink."

Roxanne set the glass down with a clatter.

Case's smile was mocking. "You'll have forgiven him by spring."

Roxanne's splendid sapphire eyes turned their full glory on him, wide and beautiful with anger. "If I stayed here—which I'm not going to," she said in a hard voice, "by spring I might decide to kill him myself."

Case chuckled. He leaned back and smiled at her expansively. She couldn't read the look in his eyes. "You're sure you wouldn't rather I killed him?"

A shudder went through her. "No."

"Too bad," he murmured. "I could pick a fight with him and shoot him down, but rolling a man in an alley . . . that isn't my style. Still, for the reward that's offered . . ." He reached out and his fingers idly stroked her wrist. From the bar the girl Yvonne flung her a venomous look.

Roxanne's voice hardened. "If you won't do it, I'll get someone else."

"In that case," he said with a wintry smile, his silver eyes flashing, "you can count on it. What's the name of this man you hate so much? And where is he staying?"

"His name is Rhodes Coulter." It was strange to hear that name, which had sung through her head on so many occasions, on her lips again. "And he said he was checking in at the Astoria—the same place we're staying."

Case continued to stroke her wrist. She felt the skin prickle lightly at his touch. "You're sure you can get away tonight? I'd hate for you to miss your boat, Roxanne."

He meant, she knew, that he'd come and drag her off the boat if she didn't pay up. Her mouth tightened. "You don't think I'd welch, do you?"

"Life has made me cautious where women are concerned," he said gently.

She gave him a withering look and took back her wrist. "Call me when it's done," she said and rose. "I'll be in Marge's room."

"Big Marge, the laundress?"

"Yes, she's staying at the Astoria too. Ask for her. And bring some kind of identification, something you've taken from Rhodes so that I'll know you got the right man."

"My friends are very efficient," smiled Case. "I'll bring you his wallet—minus the money, of course; that will go to pay the hired help."

"It's a deal," she said, looking directly into his eyes. She felt slightly dizzy from so much pent-up emotion. "I must go now," she said abruptly. "They'll be looking for me and they mustn't find me here."

The girl in the yellow satin negligee moved toward Case as Roxanne hurried out.

Denby and the others were combing Front Street, looking for her. She told them the crowd had swept her down Front Street and she'd been trying to fight her way back; she must have missed them in the crush. They accepted that.

When she could get Marge alone, she said, "Marge, I need a big favor. I want you to pretend to be sick tonight, so I can stay with you."

Marge stared at her. "I take it you won't *really* be staying with me?"

"That's right."

"What're you up to, Roxanne? This sounds like trouble."

"It's—personal, Marge. Something that flared up out of the past. I don't want Denby to know."

"Some man . . . yes, I can see you wouldn't want Denby to know. Not if you plan to go on livin' with him." Marge sighed. "Oh, well, you can count on me, Roxanne."

She saw Rhodes again at dinner. He came in while they were eating in the hotel's rough-hewn dining room. He had changed to a dark suit and sported a ruby tie pin. He looked very fit, and very handsome. He bowed deeply to Roxanne.

Roxanne glowered, and he did not approach them, but took a table across the room.

"Who is that?" asked Denby sharply, setting down his fork.

"Who is who?" asked Roxanne indifferently, attacking her moose steak.

"I think he means that man who bowed to you," said Leighton.

"Nobody bowed to me," said Roxanne. "He must have been bowing to Marge."

They had to be content with that.

All through dinner, Roxanne could hardly eat—even though the table was loaded with delicacies just off the boat, fresh onions, fresh-cooked turnips, things the miners hadn't seen all winter. She kept her head lowered because every time she looked up she found in her line of vision either Denby's suspicious face or Rhodes's broad smile. She noted Rhodes had ordered the best dinner the house afforded and seemed to be enjoying it. Obviously he had not fallen on hard times. *He* hadn't spent the winter struggling with frozen laundry! There he sat at his ease, his dark hair shining, calm and well fed. She hadn't known she could hate a man so much. She yearned to take her plate and throw it at him with all her strength.

After dinner Marge complained that she wasn't feeling well. Roxanne announced piously that she and Denby should go to bed early since they'd be leaving in the morning. Denby looked upset. Later, in their cubbyhole room, he muttered something to the effect that he'd thought to look about the town with Leighton—last chance. Roxanne asked him to wait till she saw how Marge was first, he might have to go for the doctor. When she came back, she declared that she'd better stay with Marge, who was having pains around her heart and refused a doctor. She told Denby to go on to bed when he came in, she'd be with Marge. She turned to leave.

"Don't you want your nightclothes?" asked Denby.

Roxanne shrugged. "I won't be needing any. Her bed is too narrow for two. I plan to sit up on a chair all night." She marveled that she could lie to Denby so coolly.

He actually looked relieved; she presumed he was looking forward to a last toot on the town with Leighton.

In Marge's room, Roxanne fretted. What if Case's henchman hadn't been able to lure Rhodes into a dark alley? Perhaps Rhodes had gone to bed early, then he'd be on the boat tomorrow and out of Case's reach. Sitting on the bed, Marge darned a pair of stockings and watched her.

Roxanne jumped when there was a light knock on the door.

"That'll be *him*," said Marge grimly, and Roxanne gave her a guilty look as she opened the door.

Case was waiting in the hall. He looked very jaunty and very dangerous, his tall frame lounging against the wall.

"Come in," said Roxanne quickly, and he stepped inside. Marge sat up in surprise when she realized who it was. Everyone in Dawson knew the lean gambler by sight. Case nodded to Marge.

"Does this satisfy you?" He handed Roxanne a black leather wallet with the initials *R. C.* chased in gold. "There's plenty of identification inside. He's a big fellow, broad shoulders. Tall, dark hair, green eyes, strong build. Wearing a black hat with a silver band."

She nodded wordlessly and without looking at the wallet, stuffed it into her purse.

"Did you—did you have trouble?" Her lips were dry.

Case grinned. "Took four good men to get him to the ground, but they did it. Fought like a wild man. You ought to see what they look like; he damn near killed them."

"And Rhodes?" She moistened her lips.

"They held him down and poured a Mickey Finn into him—he's sleeping it off at Kate's Place—the boys took him there."

A sporting house . . . they had taken him to a sporting house. Where no doubt he'd be right at home, when he woke up. Only, she thought grimly, this time he wouldn't have any money to spend.

"Then he's all right?" she said.

"Only bruised," shrugged Case. "And sleeping like a baby."

When he woke up, he'd be stranded in Dawson and he'd have to claw frozen earth out of a smoky hole to make a living—at least until he could get money from the outside. And that would take a long time. It was revenge enough.

"There's just one thing more," she told Case grimly. "I want you to get one of the girls at Kate's Place to tell him that this was Roxanne's revenge. I want him to know I did this to him. Promise me, Case!"

"Honor bright!" Mockingly he held up his hand. "You must hate this poor devil!"

"I do," she grated, her fists clenched. "Oh, I do!"

"And now for *your* part of the bargain," he said, eyes narrowing. "Shall I escort you back to the Last Nugget? This place isn't quite luxurious enough for me."

Marge, who had been a fascinated listener, now opened her mouth. "Well, I'll be!" she muttered. "I'll be!"

Roxanne gave her a haggard look. "If Denby comes, don't open the door. Tell him you're better, and I've gone to sleep and you don't want to wake me."

Marge nodded, but Roxanne saw her shaking her head as she left, and heard her mutter, "The Hard Case—who woulda thought it? I'll be!"

Chapter 26

To hide her face, Roxanne put on a hat with a veil, which she'd borrowed from Marge. Downstairs through the deserted lobby—for all the action was in the saloons at this time of evening—and out into the brief subarctic night, she followed Case. Her heart was in turmoil. It was all madness. Rhodes, pounded to the street and silenced with knockout drops, was lying in some sporting house. Denby was tearing up the town with Leighton celebrating his last night in Dawson. And she, who had been brought up a Southern lady, was slipping through the jostling crowds on Front Street, one hand carefully holding up her dress to keep from muddying the hem. And at her side was the most dangerous man in Dawson, whose reputation for skill with cards and with his famous derringer had preceded him to the Klondike.

None of it could be happening to her. She was bound to wake up.

Through the swinging doors of the Last Nugget

they went. The noise was deafening. Roxanne was dimly aware of a crowded room where stomping miners applauded a high-kicking girl with a rouged face and wild, flying black hair. A girl in spangles and black mesh stockings who kicked her high heels and yelled out a song to the accompaniment of the rinky dink piano. Fancy women in gaudy clothes were sandwiched among the miners, laughing raucously, drinking straight whiskey from the bar. The room was blue with cigar smoke, and the very floorboards vibrated to the din.

Her head whirling, Roxanne let herself be led through the crowd by Case. Someone turned and caught sight of her sumptuous bustline. Too drunk to care about consequences, he gave a loud yip of delight and reached for her veil. Case knocked his arm away and reached for his derringer. For a moment a pair of befuddled drunken eyes peered into that dark deadly face, identified him and turned away. Case shrugged and, sticking the derringer back in his belt, pulled Roxanne along after him. Plainly tonight he was not a fighter but a lover.

Her cheeks burning under the black veil, Roxanne walked up the flight of stairs that so many fancy women must ascend with their lovers-for-an-hour. For most of the bars had rooms upstairs that were simply brothels. Looking down at the floor in numbed mortification, she followed Case along an upstairs corridor to a big room that overlooked Front Street.

Case closed the door and locked it after them, lit a lamp, went over and drew the blinds and turned to face her. He looked narrow and tall and limber and intensely alive. She took a deep breath and slowly reached up and took off her hat and veil, tossing them to a table.

She was aware that she was in what was probably the most luxurious room in Dawson. The furniture was mahogany and it matched—except for the bed, which was very fancy and made of gleaming brass.

"Had everything here brought up from San Francisco," said Case, noting her glance around the room. "This bed—best in Dawson. You won't have slept in one like this since you left the States. Not," he added, smiling, "that I intend you to sleep."

Her fingers brushed the fabric of her skirt. They felt stiff. She hoped he wasn't going to stand there and watch her undress. Well, even if he did, this was her deal—he had already done his part.

He sensed her nervousness. "Would you like a drink?"

"Yes," she said desperately.

He waved her to a chair and she watched him pour the liquor—expensive, strong—splashing into the glass. He moved toward her in long strides, and she took the glass from him with a hand that shook slightly. He touched its rim to his own. It made a small clinking sound that set her nerves on edge.

"To us," he said softly. "And to tonight. It may be all we ever have of each other."

His gaze was sober as he said it, and she lifted the glass to her lips, mesmerized by the pressure of those intense eyes so close to her own. She took a quick gulp of whiskey, and as the hot liquor scalded down her throat she choked.

Case laughed and, leaning over her, touched her cheek. She froze to waiting stillness, clenching the glass in her hand. It was as if Seattle had never been, as if he had never held her in his arms, as if they were strangers again. His fingers moved down her cheek idly, slipped along her jawline, played briefly with her earlobe and a lock of her hair that had come loose, and moved down her neck. She shivered as his fingers reached the base of her neck and slipped beneath the collar of her dress. As deftly as a woman, he had the top buttons undone and his hands roved exploringly across her bosom, across her shoulders, easing the fabric down.

She felt tension rising in her. And with that tension, a need to postpone the moment that he would take her. Desperately she tried to keep him talking.

"Was—was breaking that woman out of jail your only crime in the States?"

"No." His deft fingers had found her upper breasts. "I killed a man."

She took another quick drink and choked. "Why?" she gasped.

Somehow even as she coughed more buttons had come undone. His competent fingers were moving more swiftly now. Impatiently they had released the ribbon that held the top of her chemise, and it slid down softly, leaving her breasts bare and gleaming pale in the lamplight. He bent his head low over her shoulder, nuzzling her hair while his fingers lightly stroked her breasts. Her breathing came faster.

"Would you like the light out?" he murmured.

"No. Why did you kill him?"

Case's head came up. From very close, he looked into her eyes. For a moment she believed he saw through her, to some dim vision from the past. He spoke slowly, meditatively. "He drew a gun on me, claimed I'd cheated him in a game. He was going to kill me, but I was quicker." His dark face softened. "It was long ago. Let's not talk about it."

"No."

"You have things to forget too, Roxanne."

"Yes." Oh, God, yes, she had things to forget. . . .

Suddenly she clung to him.

"Make me forget," she whispered.

His lips found hers then, a swift sweet pressure, and his hands clasped her waist and lifted her up so that she was standing. With one arm around her, while his lips and tongue gently probed her mouth, he finished undressing her. First her dress slid away, then her petticoat, billowing lightly to the floor, leaving her body deliciously free and yielding in his arms. Eyes closed, she swayed against him.

His lips left hers, and she opened her eyes to see him smiling down at her. With a lithe gesture he swept her up, carrying her to the big brass bed and laying her down upon it gently, so that only her feet with their muddy boots hung over. Gently he removed them. Beneath were silk stockings—mended but still silk.

He sat down on the bed beside her. His hands gently caressed the silk of her stockings. "These are the same garters you wore in Seattle," he murmured. "Pink satin."

"They're the only pair I own," she said ruefully. "Worn out, like all my stockings. This is the best pair I have left."

"The stockings may be worn," he said, "but the legs are the best in town."

She closed her eyes and turned her head from him as he lightly caressed her inner thighs and eased down her stockings. Through half closed lashes she saw him stand up abruptly and remove his clothes—all of them. She kept her face averted from his long aristocratic body, and all her senses snapped awake as he bent toward her and gently fitted that long hard body to her own soft yielding one.

His hands seemed to be everywhere, caressing her tingling nipples that hardened ecstatically at his touch, moving fierily along her spine, tracing a flaming path across the silken skin of her stomach and her rounded buttocks, tingling their way along her inner thighs. Gently but strongly he entered her, moving with pulsating rhythm. Tension mounted in Roxanne. Aching desire flamed up, trembled to waiting stillness, flared up again.

She felt swept up and passionately, recklessly alive in a way that she had never felt with Denby. It was Seattle all over again—but better.

And then, knowing her response bespoke a white heat of passion, he took her fully, wildly, letting his own passion drive him. Tender explosions flowered swiftly within her, and subsided only to explode again. A wild sweet ecstasy overwhelmed her and lifted her up and up into a dream world. They drifted together through a passionate interlude of clinging bodies, agonizingly close, drinking deep of fulfillment.

And after, they lay together in silent, naked peace. Her bare hip touched his and his right arm cradled her shoulders. Downstairs, the honky tonk piano tinkled while a hoarse young female voice wailed out a sentimental song about a woman wronged. Downstairs, there were stomping feet and applause. It all seemed so far away.

Roxanne turned to the man beside her with a dreamy look. "I think I love you a little, Case."

His gaze was wistful and tender. He rested a gentle hand on her satiny breast, caressed it lovingly. "No, but I wish you did."

She sighed. "How can you tell that?"

"You enjoy me as a lover, but I don't think you quite approve of me as a man. Otherwise you wouldn't have stayed away all winter out there on Bonanza Creek."

She smiled lazily. "I'm here now."

"Yes." He bent to plant a kiss on a pink nipple. "You're here now." Roxanne was silent, her breath coming fast and shallow.

He lay there fondling her in silence. Then suddenly on a gust of passion he took her again, and they strained together in wordless wonder at this bright flame that gripped them, exalted them, consumed them, and then cast them back panting and spent.

He lay beside her looking up at the ceiling. "I'd leave the Klondike for you, you know," he said. "I'd take my chances in Nome or anywhere you wanted to go."

Her heart lurched. It was a tempting offer. "Anywhere, Case?"

"Anywhere." It was a solemn declaration.

She lay there imagining it. Traveling the world with Case. Cities as she had never seen them—gambling halls, dance halls. Walking beside a man all men feared.

"I can't," she said, sitting up. "There's Denby."

"You don't love him." It was a flat statement.

She hesitated. "No, but I feel guilty about him. If he'd struck gold . . . but he didn't." Feeling suddenly sad, she looked away, felt his hand run delicately along her spine. She sighed and turned to see that his expression was puzzled. "How could you be raped by mistake?" he wondered, toying with her breasts. "How any man could mistake your body puzzles me. Surely there could not be another so lovely."

"I was wearing a mask and a wig and another girl's costume," said Roxanne gloomily. "And it was dark."

"Ah," he said, "that explains it, then. I did not think you could love a madman."

She tensed in fury. "I do *not* love him!" she cried. "I only thought I did—and it was only for a little while! I hate him and am glad of what you did to him."

Something flickered deep and dark behind the murky silver of his eyes—it might have been mirth. "Then stay with me," he said. "Sleep with me every night and punish him, Roxanne. I promise you he will writhe in misery."

She gave him a black look and would have risen, but for his restraining arm that rested lightly on her lap. His fingers idly played with the triangle of dark-blond hair. "Don't go yet," he said.

"Case, I must. It's nearly morning."

"I'll buy you from Denby. I'll send him away with as much gold as if he'd struck it rich on French Hill."

Her face softened, and tears glittered on her lashes as she suddenly flung herself forward and kissed him—kissed his eyebrows, his eyes, his mouth, pulled him to her for a last embrace. "I do love you a little," she murmured. "But I must go. I'd never forgive myself, otherwise."

He held onto her wrist. "But you'd rather stay?"

"Yes," she sighed. "I'd rather stay."

He let her go then and got up, strode to the other side of the room and, picking up her clothes, handed them to her. When she put on her stockings, she discovered he'd handed her a new pair, and that her garters were new too, beautiful ones of red satin.

"I want to keep these," he said to her quizzical look, indicating the pink satin garters she'd been wearing. "Souvenir of the prettiest girl in the Klondike."

She looked up from fitting the garters over her shapely legs and smiled at him. Regret passed over his face as she stood up, slim and elegant and naked except for her stockings, and slipped on her chemise. He stood watching as she pulled it down over her white breasts and tied the satin bow that held the drawstring. Quickly she donned her petticoat and dress. She gave him another smile as she put on her hat.

"Your hair's awry," he observed. "Want a comb?"

She sensed he was finding excuses to keep her there; the thought warmed her. "Thanks, it won't show under my veil. I'll comb it back in Marge's room. I must get back."

"I'll escort you."

She hesitated—but yes, of course he must escort her through that rowdy crowd in the saloon downstairs, and through the almost equally rowdy street. She'd have to take the chance Denby might see her.

She tossed the black veil over her head. Gravely, as if she were a great lady, Case offered her his arm. With a little smile, she took it. He had an elegant walk, she thought. A tall aristocratic sway, lithe and supple, as he moved down the stairs, making way for her through the drunken carousing crowd below.

Midway across the room a woman in a red dress lurched against him. "Damn you, Case, you two-timing so-and-so!" she muttered. Case frowned at her and she subsided, but Roxanne recognized the woman as Yvonne. *Case's woman*, she thought with a pang, and hurried on where he led.

In the street the crowd was thinning out, but Roxanne kept her head bent and stayed close beside Case, holding up her skirt against the mud. He lifted her over one deep rut, holding her for a moment before setting her down with obvious regret.

At her hotel, she turned to him suddenly. "Case, in Seattle you said I reminded you of someone. Who?"

"A girl who's dead," he said. Suddenly he swept aside her veil and kissed her, lingeringly. Then he threw open the hotel door and led her inside. "I'll see you to your room," he said.

"No." Her cool fingers rested on his arm. "No. We'd better say good-bye here."

She was aware that he stood and watched her as she ran lightly up the wooden stairs.

At the head of the stairs, she collided with a man, and his arms closed around her to keep her from tumbling backward. The impact caused her hat to fall off, taking the veil with it. She looked up and realized it was Leighton who had caught her. The look of complete consternation on the golden giant's face shook her.

"Where is Denby?" she asked fearfully.

"Gone to bed," he said. "Roxanne, where've you been?" His blue gaze took in her disheveled hair, her hastily buttoned dress that hadn't come out quite evenly at the neck.

"This had nothing to do with Denby," she whispered desperately. "It had to do with me and a person from my past. It was something I had to do, Leighton."

Looking up at him, she could see he wanted to believe her, but his world was struck down at the sight of her like this.

"Leighton," she pleaded. "Oh, Leighton, don't tell Denby. So much has gone wrong—it would destroy him."

"I won't tell him," he said stiffly. He had a wounded air. "After all, it's not my affair, is it?"

He reached down and picked up her hat and veil. As she put them back on her head, she knew she had hurt him too.

Quietly she slipped back to Marge's room, gave the ghost of a knock. Marge threw the door open. "Well, about time!" she muttered. "A little longer and you might have missed the boat!"

"Has Denby been by?"

"Nope."

Roxanne tossed her hat on the bed, stood before the wavery mirror and rebuttoned her bodice carefully. "Can I borrow your comb, Marge?"

Silently it was passed to her.

"I suppose I owe you an explanation, Marge."

Marge shrugged. "Not unless you want to give it.

You're a grown woman, Roxanne. I guess you know what you want to do with your life."

Roxanne, combing out her hair, hesitated and gave the older woman a sober look. "Yes," she said sadly, "I suppose I do. At least I know what I have to do with it."

Marge snorted. "If you're throwin' in with the Hard Case, you're makin' a big mistake. Any day some sharpshooter might take a potshot at him and remove him—permanently. He's got enemies who don't like the way he deals the cards."

"I'm not throwing in with Case," said Roxanne wistfully. "I'm going back to San Francisco with Denby."

"That's the spirit," approved Marge. "Although to be honest, I thought someone would get you before you left here. I just thought it would be Leighton."

Comb upraised, Roxanne stared at Marge.

"On account of he loves you so much," amplified Marge.

"Leighton is going exploring up the Koyukuk—not to San Francisco. If he loves me so much, why isn't he taking the boat?"

"He's tryin' to get over you," Marge told her soberly.

Roxanne remembered the hurt look in the golden giant's eyes. "I met him just now," she said. "On the stairs."

"Maybe that'll help him get over you," said Marge dryly. "Now shut up and let me go to sleep. I paid good money for this bed and I mean to get my money's worth. You can sit up in that chair or you can go down and tell your husband I'm better, whichever you want. He'll ask you where you got those red garters and those new stockings though."

Roxanne, who was adjusting her garters and smoothing her stockings, said, "I'll tell him they were a going-away present from you."

"And I'll back you up," sighed Marge. "I got no sense either."

But Denby noticed neither her red garters nor her

new stockings when she changed her clothes in their room before leaving for the steamer, even though she made a point of letting him see them. He was excited and preoccupied. She supposed he was thinking of San Francisco and the new problems he must face there. Certainly he was intent on hurrying her to the boat; it was obvious that he could not leave Dawson fast enough.

Hurrying along beside them down Front Street, Marge grumbled to herself; she looked sleepy—understandably. Leighton loped along in silence. Roxanne looked up to find him watching her, a hurt, perplexed look on his face. She gave him a tender smile and patted his hand. He had kept faith with her; he had not told Denby. Impulsively, just before they went up the gangplank, she pulled his big shaggy head down to hers and kissed him good-bye. He looked very shaken.

From the rail, she thought she saw Case in the crowd watching the steamer depart, but she could not be sure. Then the gangplank was up, and the ship was moving, and a roar from the crowd on the river's edge enveloped them. As they moved downstream, Dawson slipped away and out of sight.

It was all over for them, the Klondike experience. They hadn't found gold—only trouble. But at least they were getting out alive, which many had not. Roxanne leaned on the rail and thought dreamily of Case, of his silken lovemaking, of the yearning in his face when he'd offered to buy her from Denby. As if she were for sale for mere money! In Seattle she had given herself to him in sudden revulsion against everything in her life. In Dawson she had given herself to him for revenge.

But the taste of revenge was not sweet in her mouth. Somehow she did not like the thought of Rhodes lying beaten and drugged and broke in some whore's bedroom. He'd be waking up soon . . . he'd get her message. Her revenge, which she had wanted so much, would be complete.

She leaned on the rail and considered her feelings.

It seemed to her she should feel better than she did. Her old score with Rhodes was at last settled. Case's lovemaking had been wild, an outlet for her pent-up desires. Denby didn't know, would never know. She should be happy.

Why then did she feel so wounded? She decided she did not understand herself. On the other hand, she thought, people in general probably didn't understand themselves, and if all of us staggered blindly through life marking our shins, perhaps she was no more blind than the rest.

"Look at the boats." Denby interrupted her musings, his voice awed. "Looks like the whole population of Dawson is afloat and heading downriver. It's the rush to Nome, Roxanne."

Roxanne lifted her troubled eyes. It was true. The Yukon was alive with boats, rafts, Peterborough canoes, craft of every description. And as the day wore on their boat kept passing others that had started out the day before but were moored while their passengers camped on shore for the night. Later Roxanne would hear that seven thousand people had started out from Dawson, to be borne on the swift current for the seventeen hundred-mile journey to the Bering Sea.

Although Denby talked constantly and vivaciously of Nome, Roxanne hardly heard him as the days went by. Gloomy and sad, she stood by the rail and watched low blue hills glide past. The hot, short subarctic summer had painted the landscape with bright splashes of yellow daisies and arnicas, drifts of blue lupines, crimson-red fireweed. Past clumps of birches and through fragrant spruce forests the current swept them, their smokestacks a blotch against the brilliant blue of the sky. It was a world where birds sang and hawks hovered, blown by the wind.

Roxanne's glorious blue eyes reflected the blue of that sky and of the low pale clouds that scudded past to the accompaniment of Denby's enthusiastic running talk of Nome. Some Scandinavians, he said, had struck it rich on Anvil Creek in the Snake River Valley.

Roxanne pitied them. This brief and lovely subarctic summer would soon be gone, the mud would freeze to granite and ice cakes as big as houses would pile up in the rivers and blizzards would howl at seventy below zero. She couldn't see how Denby could envy anyone who must make his living here.

On a particularly lovely day when the birches seemed full of robins and even the Yukon's tawny face seemed to smile, Roxanne, in the tiny cabin she shared with Denby below decks, gave a last brush to her hair. Denby had already gone up on deck; he seemed nervous now that they were approaching the Yukon Flats and would soon enter the labyrinth of the delta. No doubt he was worried about finding a job when they reached San Francisco. She laid down her hairbrush and accidentally knocked her purse to the floor. As she picked it up she felt the sharp corner of Rhodes's wallet. She had forgotten it was in there.

It occurred to her that she should get rid of that wallet, throw it over the ship's rail. Case had said it contained lots of identification. Jealous Denby, who once again was an eager if incompetent lover, must not see a wallet with the name Coulter in her possession.

Soberly she took the wallet out, held it in her hands. It belonged to the man she hated, and over whom she had at last triumphed. But staring at it she felt no sense of triumph, only of loss. She turned it over in her hands and opened it slowly. Perhaps, she thought, wincing, he'd have a picture of a woman in it, one of his fancy women. He did! Three pictures, in fact. Her hands trembled slightly as she pulled them out. She froze and stared down at the pictures, transfixed. Her own face was smiling back at her. They were pictures that had been taken that first summer when Rhodes seemed to be courting her. Rhodes had taken them himself, telling her later they had not turned out, that the film had been bad. He had wanted them for himself, she now realized, and he had kept them with him all this time.

Her face turned chalk-white, and she moved over

to the bunk on legs that suddenly would not support her. Rhodes had come to the Klondike looking for *her*. Not to sight-see. And a man does not pursue a woman half around the world to some wild backwater unless he loves her. Incredibly, the fact beat into her consciousness:

Rhodes loved her!

All her world turned topsy-turvy at that moment. All her old hatreds and old loyalties crumbled into dust. Rhodes had come to Dawson because he loved her—and she had greeted him bitterly, lied to him, sold her very body so that he might be set upon and beaten and robbed and left stranded in a town whose heart was as cold as its climate. She caught her breath. Ashen-faced, she imagined him sitting up in bed holding an aching head, nursing a bruised body, while some insolent prostitute delivered her message:

Roxanne did this to you. She wanted to be sure you knew it.

Her hand flew to her mouth, pressed against it so hard her teeth hurt. *Oh, God, what had she done*? Rhodes had come seeking her, his love so great he did not care that she was married, did not care that she had gone to the very ends of the earth He had sought her and found her, and she had promptly destroyed him.

She sat there crouched in the bunk, staring at the pictures in her hand, but not seeing them. She felt as if she were dying.

The cabin door opened to admit Denby.

Automatically, she threw a fold of her skirt over the wallet and pictures. She glanced at Denby and turned away.

"Roxanne." His voice sounded loud and strangely contrite. "Roxanne, I changed our tickets."

"Did you?" she said absently.

"Roxanne, we aren't going to San Francisco. We're going to Nome."

Slowly that sank in. She turned and looked penetratingly at Denby. "What did you say?"

"I said I'd changed our tickets for Nome—before

we boarded. Oh, Roxanne." He seized her arm, his voice pleading. "It's our chance. Don't you see, we were too late for the Klondike—everything was already staked: Bonanza, Eldorado, French Hill. But in Nome, we'll be in the first wave! We'll be rich, Roxanne."

She pulled away from him. At that moment, she could not bear his touch. "It doesn't matter," she said in a soft, tense voice. "I don't care where I go, Denby. To Nome or to hell, it makes no difference!"

Denby's jaw dropped. Whatever response he had expected from his fiery wife, it was not this. "Then you—you don't mind?" He sounded amazed.

"No," said Roxanne woodenly. "I don't mind."

Denby took a deep breath and squared his shoulders. Still a bit stunned, he left the cabin.

A little while later Roxanne dragged herself from the bunk and went up to the deck. She found a deserted space at the rail and with a sob she tossed the wallet and the three pictures into the river. The wallet sank immediately, but the three pictures drifted for a while before they slipped below the surface. Roxanne watched them go, drowned like all her hopes. Then she put her head down on the railing and wept.

Now she knew she had loved Rhodes all the time—had indeed never ceased loving him. Fate had given her a second chance, and she had thrown it away. She had come to understand herself too late. Her folly had cost her everything.

The storm over, she lifted her head and stared through tear-blurred eyes at the river bank drifting by. They were winding through a low tortuous maze, the labyrinth of the Yukon Delta.

Nome. They were going to Nome. But what did it matter? Her life was finished, over. She had realized too late whom she loved—after she had gratuitously destroyed him. And Denby, poor Denby, she had destroyed him too. Had she not cuckolded him with the most notorious man in Dawson? Case had held her body and Rhodes her heart—what was there left for Denby? Only that sense of guilt that held her shackled to him. Perhaps Denby would discover gold in Nome after all, perhaps it would make him happy. She never could.

Yet she would not spend her life in tears, no matter what happened. With fierce determination she dried her eyes and set her hat more firmly on her head.

At that point Denby found her. He peered at her. "Roxanne, have you been crying?"

She shook her head. "Some soot got in my eyes from the funnel."

"Never mind," he said, not believing her. "Things will be better in Nome."

She gave him a bleak look. Things would never be better, anywhere.

Nome, Alaska 1899—1900

Chapter 27

Roxanne was still silent and pale when they transferred to another steamer to make the trip across Norton Sound toward what Denby insisted on calling "the golden gates of Nome."

Those gates did not open very wide, Roxanne observed cynically, for while one could journey to within sight of Nome, it was almost impossible to land there. Their ship, as did most others, anchored miles offshore, and they waited for days for the sea to be quiet enough so that a landing barge could take them close to the narrow strip of dark sand fronting the driftwood and tent community that was Nome. Leighton was not with them, so Roxanne lifted up her skirts and waded through the rough surf with the others.

Built on a spit along the mouth of a sluggish river, Nome was a man's town. A boom town. A gold town. Above all, it was a rough town. The only women Roxanne saw on her first day there were prostitutes and dance hall girls. From one saloon raucous laughter spilled into the street. From another two men erupted, shouting angrily; they were being thrown out. Past a driftwood shack, she saw a public latrine: tickets available here, twenty-five cents. All around she could hear the sound of hammering and once, of gunfire. The law was far away here and tempers were short.

In Dawson she had seen Indians. In Nome she saw Eskimos, and turned to call Denby's attention to them, fascinated by their round rather Oriental faces, their exotic dress of fur parkas and mukluks. Many Eskimos owned handsome teams of malamute sled dogs. Denby ignored the Eskimos and their dogs. His only thoughts were of heading for Anvil Creek, which he did at once. He found it staked, of course, and came home haggard to the hotel room Roxanne had managed to get for them by flirting with the proprietor.

She wondered what they would do now.

In the morning, sharing a three-egg breakfast—it cost a dollar and they were almost out of funds—they heard a hoarse cry from the street. "There's gold in the beach sand! Feller down there has a pan that shows color—musta been washed in from the ocean!"

The men in that jerry-built restaurant jumped up so fast they overturned their rude benches. Denby was among them. "Got to stake my claim, Roxanne!" he cried and was gone, leaving Roxanne to finish the overcooked eggs alone. When she finished breakfast, she sauntered past Wyatt Earp's place, with its sign proudly proclaiming it *The Only Second Class Saloon in Alaska.* Continuing on down to the beach, she found the scene there quite incredible.

The dark sands swarmed with people, digging with shovels, swirling sand in their pans, perspiring, calling to others. From the sea more landing barges spilled out eager new arrivals who promptly joined the fray. As Roxanne stood watching, a group of prostitutes with fancy hats and fancy hairdos rushed by with shovels, which they thrust energetically into the sand. One of these women, a big coarse redhead, saw Roxanne watching them and straightened up to call, "Business bad, kid? Try this!" To the accompaniment of general laughter among the redhead's overdressed friends, Roxanne turned away. Eventually, in the excited mob she found Denby, flushed with perspiration and digging madly. "I need a pan," he shouted, a desperate note in his voice. "Can you find me one, Roxanne?"

Back into town went Roxanne. As they had on her way to the beach, the men in the streets turned admiringly to watch her pass. Several tipped their hats, some of them spoke. Many of their faces she knew from the mines around Bonanza, and to those she gave a civil nod. The others she ignored. Recognizing one of the regular customers of Marge's laundry standing in a group, she asked him about acquiring a pan. He gallantly lent her his. She thanked him with a brilliant smile and hurried back to the beach.

Roxanne soon discovered that, although they both worked hard, neither she nor Denby was very good at panning gold. After hours of back-breaking work they had only a couple of dollars worth of fine dust—not enough to feed them for one day in Nome.

Finally, Roxanne straightened up stiffly and studied Denby.

"Come on, Roxanne," he cried in an encouraging voice. "It's light almost all night here. We can keep working."

"No," she said. "I'm tired. I'm going back to the hotel."

All the saloons she passed were bursting with customers. Men tried to pick her up, but she brushed by them, eluding one clutching drunk by dodging behind a group of miners. Several places she heard brawls erupting. From many doorways came the tinkle of tinny music and sometimes thin female voices or husky whiskey ones, singing. The bright white night of Nome was beginning.

Tiredly, Roxanne sank down on the narrow cot she was to share with Denby and looked around at her room, which was little larger than a closet. That Denby wasn't going to strike it rich mining the beach sand was all too apparent. Finding a way to survive was going to be up to her. She lay there, exhausted.

When she'd rested a little, she tipped the tin pitcher into the cracked washbowl and bathed as well as she could. Putting on her only party dress, a peach georgette much the worse for wear—it had been worn almost the whole of last summer at Bonanza—she unbuttoned the high neck and adjusted it so that it was almost off the shoulder. Carefully, she combed her hair into a tall pile of gold, from which she allowed a curl or two to escape coquettishly and bob along her white neck. Ready at last, she started out to find work.

Whistles and delighted catcalls followed her from the hotel. In the street it was worse. Miners whooped at the sight of her, but with the help of a friend from Bonanza, a young man named Toby Hart, she made it to her destination—the town's only "first class" dance hall.

If this was first class, Roxanne decided, she would have hated to see second class. The place barely had a roof. In the center of the hall stood a crude, raised wooden platform, sprinkled with sawdust, upon which three homely perspiring women were dancing doggedly with a trio of booted miners. At a raw wood bar, drinks were served and the proprietor, Big Mike, a man with heavy shoulders, beady eyes and a slick kind of smile, collected a dollar for each one-minute dance with his bevy of beauties.

"You sure you want to do this, Miss Roxanne?" Toby asked uncertainly. "Ain't much of a place, is it?"

"I'm sure," said Roxanne steadily, and stepped up to ask for a job.

The beady eyes took in her sumptuous figure, her low-cut dress that tantalizingly exposed the white tops of her round, young breasts, her silken dark-blond hair and reckless sapphire eyes. "Ma'am," was the prayerful response, "you've sure come to the right place. Hey, ain't I seen you someplace? Dawson, maybe?"

"You might have," sighed Roxanne. "I might have washed your shirts."

His eyes widened. "That's it!" he cried. "Step right up, boys," he bellowed. "This here's the Dawson blond! Right up on the platform there, Miss—"

"Roxanne."

"Miss Roxanne. We split fifty–fifty, Miss Roxanne," he muttered in an aside. Then his voice rose again to a roar. "Best-looking woman ever to hit the Klondike. You're in for a treat tonight, boys. Step right up and dance with Miss Roxanne—the Dawson blond!"

Roxanne climbed up on the platform so they could see her better. She took a deep breath and lifted her head and looked up at the roof, then down to the hot eyes of the men who crowded around the platform. Her beauty as she stood there, a delicate figure of peach and gold, caused a sudden silence—perhaps the men were remembering the girls they'd left behind them. The silence was broken by a stampede as the piano struck up a tune and men fought to pay their dollar to dance around for a minute with the celebrated Dawson blond.

With first one man swinging her about, then another, this way and that way, Roxanne went home that night exhausted but a hundred dollars richer. The streets were still bright as she entered the hotel, for the long summer days had come to Nome and it was still light at midnight. She was glad she had had the presence of mind to button up her high-necked peach dress before she got back to the hotel, because she found Denby sitting on the narrow cot glaring at her accusingly. He looked exhausted.

"Where the devil have you been?" he growled.

Roxanne, giving him a level look, showed him the hundred dollars. "I've been working." And at his aghast expression, added, "A dollar a dance—you must have seen the place. It's called Big Mike's."

Denby groaned. "Roxanne, you're a lady. How could you?"

Roxanne pulled off her shoes to ease her throbbing

feet. "Denby," she asked, "how much did you make today?"

"Three dollars," he growled.

"And do you think that can keep us? Here in Nome where it costs more than that a day to feed just one of us? It will be snowing soon. Even the sea will freeze over. Where will we sleep? The beach?"

He looked away, mumbling.

"Denby, if you strike it rich, I promise to quit. It isn't a job I love, you know."

Moving away from her on the cot, he turned his back to her. Roxanne looked at his rigid, angry back and sighed. She took off her peach dress and, edging onto the cot against him, was soon asleep.

The next morning she bought a flashy dress from one of the other girls who worked at Big Mike's. It cost her fifty dollars, but it was worth it. For Roxanne had had an idea. She didn't intend to stay in Nome for the winter. Passage to San Francisco could be had for three hundred dollars now. That meant she needed six hundred for her and Denby. They'd need money to get started when they got to San Francisco, but most of all, they needed money to live here even in miserable conditions—big money; she could see that.

Denby, home early from his back-breaking work on the beach, toiling just a shovel's length away from the next digger, lay on the cot and watched her dress for her evening. His expression was one of pure horror. "Roxanne, you aren't going to wear *that*?"

Peering into the little bit of foggy cracked mirror that hung on the wall, she finished combing her upswept hair and smoothed the red satin dress down critically over her hips. It had fit her bustline readily enough. But Flo—from whom she'd bought it—was on the plump side and the waist had had to be taken in with a needle and thread. Roxanne hoped she had done a neat job. Denby's horrified expression told her she had.

"What's wrong with it?" she asked.

"It's cut too low," he cried. "Your—everything shows!"

"Nothing shows," corrected Roxanne. "Except a little bosom."

"And it's too tight," he said, aggrieved. "You might as well be naked."

Fine. That was exactly the effect she had hoped to achieve. She turned to face him. "Will you walk me there, Denby?"

"No," he said, looking sulky.

Roxanne sighed. She tied a black satin ribbon around her neck and another around a narrow wrist; they accentuated the gleaming whiteness of her lovely skin. She was sorry she hadn't shortened the skirt so her trim ankles would show, but she decided that since the dress had a little train, she could always gracefully hold it up with one hand and give a glimpse of pretty leg as she danced. Yes, that would be very good. She started for the door.

On the cot, Denby suddenly sprang to a sitting position. "If you go out in that dress, Roxanne, I'm going to leave you!" he cried.

Roxanne gave him a look. Without answering, she turned and went out the door. As she closed the door, she could hear him cursing.

Once again she found an old friend from Bonanza to escort her through the streets. The men, all very admiring of her white shoulders and plunging neckline, couldn't take their eyes off her. On the way to Big Mike's, Roxanne collected quite a following.

When she arrived, Big Mike himself stepped forward to greet her. His eyes gleamed. "You're looking very fetching tonight, Miss Roxanne."

"And I've brought a lot of people with me." She indicated the small crowd milling behind her.

"That's good." He rubbed his hands together.

"As your stellar attraction," she said soberly, "I think I should get a better cut than fifty percent. I think it should be seventy-five–twenty-five."

Big Mike looked affronted. "Fifty–fifty is generous!" he protested.

Roxanne bluffed it out. "On the way here," she said, "a fellow I danced with last night stopped me and asked me if I would dance for him if he set up a dance hall. He said he'd give me seventy-five."

Her employer looked aggrieved. "I was the one started you out," he said reproachfully. But when Roxanne turned as if to go, "All right, all right, you got a deal, sister."

Briskly, Roxanne stepped up onto the platform, posed to show her white shoulders in the low-cut dress to best advantage. She took a deep breath and smiled brightly.

"Step right up," roared Mike. "Step right up—"

Afterwards Roxanne was sure she had danced with half the men in Nome that night. Her feet felt like it. Still, she was going back to the hotel with a hundred and fifty dollars.

She found Denby gone when she got there.

That surprised her. But she was so tired she fell onto the bed and went to sleep. She rose again only in time to eat and dance.

Two days later, when she was again dressing for work, Denby came back, tired and dragging. She guessed he hadn't been able to pay for a cot and feed himself too, even with shoveling and panning the heavy beach sand all day.

"Roxanne," he said, sitting down wearily. "Why don't you find decent work like you did at Bonanza?"

Roxanne, in the red satin dress, adjusted her garters and gave him a cold look. "Denby, at Bonanza I washed half the dirty clothes in the Klondike. I am not going to do that ever again."

Denby grumbled, but he stayed. She supposed it was because he had no place else to go.

Late one evening a man paid his dollar and stepped up to the platform. Roxanne, weary, hardly looked at him.

"I remember you, Missy," he whispered. That voice, so close to her ear, was strangely familiar. Roxanne took a good look at him. She knew that rat-face, that big gold watch with the huge fake ruby watchfob.

This was the man who had accosted her on the train from Kansas to Baltimore, the man who had threatened her and accused her of killing poor old Mary Willis.

Roxanne broke free of his arms and, to the amazement of the ogling watchers around the platform, she drew back one white arm and delivered a stinging slap to Ratface's surprised mouth.

"Mike," she called angrily, "this man insulted me."

Even though it was a frontier saloon, women were protected after a fashion. Surging through the crowd, Big Mike found the platform edge, grabbed Ratface by the legs and pulled him off. As he sprawled in the sawdust, several enraged miners—enamored of the lustrous Dawson blond—kicked him. Cursing, Ratface staggered away and stumbled into the arms of a reporter from a New York tabloid. "What happened up there, man?" cried the reporter, who was just off the boat and looking for a story.

"That goddamn wench nearly got me killed," howled Ratface. "Because I recognized her."

"Recognized her?"

Bruised and shaken, Ratface was glad to accompany the reporter to a nearby bar. There, he downed a whiskey and said in an ugly voice, "I was on a train when a woman died—an old woman with money, name of Mary Willis. I seen this girl steal from her purse and"—his eyes narrowed—"I seen her slip something into the old woman's drink."

"Did you report it?"

"No . . . she were young," mumbled Ratface. "I didn't want to believe it of her."

"But when you recognized her tonight, she struck you," mused the reporter. "Sounds like an admission of guilt, doesn't it?"

Ratface nodded and drank another whiskey.

After that the New York reporter began making discreet inquiries about the Dawson blond.

Roxanne was not aware of this unwelcome attention. She was making money fast, but of course, it cost a lot to live. And the northern summer days were flying by. She danced her feet off; her partners became a blur of faces. She bought another dress from Flo—this one of orange satin trimmed in black lace, cut very low. She decided to shorten the skirt. The glimpse of trim legs in black mesh stockings kept the miners' eyes focused on her.

But as she danced, she worried.

Denby was in trouble.

Along with many others, Denby had decided the strip of beach sand he was working was too crowded, and he had moved his diggings some distance from town. The new beach diggings were adjacent to a claim called "tundra rights"; the original claimant had sold out to a mining company, and the mining company, insisting it owned the shoreline, ordered the diggers to pay royalties or leave. The tired, bearded men shoveling up the beach sand had ignored the order. The mining company had called in the troops, and Denby, along with hundreds of others, had been arrested. Roxanne had tried to see him, but the soldiers had refused to let her.

Now as she danced, she considered the problem. She must go to see the commandant tomorrow. Army men were notoriously susceptible; she would use all her wiles to get Denby released. Smiling mechanically as she was whirled around the platform, she planned how she would do it.

To her surprise, Denby woke her from an exhausted sleep the next morning, grinning broadly. There was no jail in Nome, no civil judge—the commandant had decided to release them. Along with the rest, Denby went back to digging up the beach sand. And Roxanne with a sigh went back to sleep, ignoring the insistent hammering outside.

The sound of hammering was constant in Nome, a kind of background noise that went on around the clock. Shacks were made of imported lumber, for the driftwood had long since been exhausted and the little stunted willow along the streams was used mainly for fuel. The hovels were going up at an alarming rate, and, with space at a premium, they were being constructed right onto the beach where the first hard gale would wash them away. Despite the construction, much of Nome was still an insubstantial tent city with the air of a carnival.

Roxanne's life was a round of dancing and exhaustion, high prices, bad food, honky tonk music and tired feet. Most of the men who danced with her were discouraged men. They'd tried Dawson, they'd tried Nome; they hadn't made it. They wanted to hold a girl in their arms, if only for a minute. During those short dances, they could imagine themselves back in the States, in better times, with girls of their own. Roxanne understood that. Resplendent in her orange satin dress, she smiled at them and gave them dreams. In return, they were giving her the money to go home and start a new life.

Some of them fell in love with her. It was inevitable. They looked at her with big soulful eyes and stumbled over her feet and would have spent their last dollars dancing with her, but she gently refused to let them. Roxanne liked the miners. Sometimes she loaned them money, small amounts to keep them going. Her popularity increased. Any man in Nome who dared to speak out against the Dawson blond in those days would have found his mouth silenced by a large and purposeful fist—as the New York reporter found out to his sorrow. One night he made a disparaging remark about Roxanne and found himself spitting out teeth. And it made him vengeful. He watched her from then on with ferocious interest, hanging around Big Mike's almost nightly noting those who came to see her.

Serenely unaware of this, Roxanne whirled about the platform night after night. Eventually she managed to save nearly a thousand dollars, which was being held for her by the hotel owner, whom she trusted. Soon she'd be going home. She was dreaming about it when, looking down into the crowd of avid faces below the platform she saw Buck Wentworth, looking much as he had in Kansas, only older and wearing a red mackinaw. The big farm boy stared back at her, his mouth gaping open. Roxanne finished her dance and hurried down the steps. She signaled to Big Mike that she was taking a break and pushed her way through to Buck, hugging him impulsively—to the envy of the watching miners, who could hope for no more than a dance bought for a dollar. Quickly, she guided Buck to the little bar.

"Roxanne, I couldn't believe it when I saw you up there on that platform." He looked at her satin dress in amazement, averted his eyes quickly from her deep decolletage. "What are you doing in Nome?"

"I might ask you the same question," she smiled, nodding to the bartender to bring them drinks.

Buck's ruddy face saddened. "Well, after you left, Julie and I got married and she—she lived a year, Roxanne. I think she was happy."

Roxanne's face clouded. Poor Julie, poor wonderful generous Julie. At least she had had a year with the man she loved.

"And after she was gone, I"—he looked sheepish—"I married Nadine."

So flirtatious little Nadine had got him after all.

"What did Nadine think of your coming to the Klondike?" she asked curiously when he fell to silently studying his glass.

He looked up. "Oh, it was Nadine that wanted to come. She kept after me until I sold everything I had. We took the boat from San Francisco, came up the inland waterway. We got to Alaska too late in the year, awful weather, blizzards every day. Spent a couple of months just trying to get our stuff over the Chilkoot Pass."

The Chilkoot . . . how well Roxanne remembered that high white notch in the towering wall of mountains that shut off the mighty upper Yukon Valley from the outside.

Buck seemed to be laboring under great emotional stress. He downed his drink at a gulp. Roxanne signaled for another one.

"We'd been snowed in for so long," he said, "waiting there at Sheep Camp. Nadine was just rarin' to go. She'd never let nothing stop her, you know that. And people warned us about that six feet of new wet snow that had fallen on that big glacier that overhung the pass."

Roxanne's blue eyes widened. With a shudder she recalled how that glacier had looked suspended above her, glittering in the sunlight, beautiful and deadly and diamond bright.

"It was on Palm Sunday. The blizzard had stopped. About a hundred people started up the pass, and Nadine wanted to go. So we did. We were about halfway up when there was this awful noise. . . . It was—it was like the sound of a tornado, Roxanne. Just fearful!" Roxanne could still recall that sound; her ears rang with it.

"And the wind seemed to rush out of the east at us, and all this snow and ice came down. At first we were lifted up and tossed around and then it came down like a wall falling and buried us under about twelve feet of snow."

She was afraid of what he was going to say. "But you fought your way out?"

"No, it held you like cement. Like concrete. You couldn't move at all." Roxanne looked at Buck, so big with his sturdy farm-boy frame, and asked, "Then how did you get out, Buck?"

"They dug us out. They could hear us groaning and calling out from under the snow. And they dug some of us out, but it took a long time. There was so much snow. I was under there three hours. They thought I was dead when they got me out, but they were able to revive me."

"And Nadine?"

Buck's eyes were haunted. He gripped his glass. "It was awful, Roxanne. The people who were buried, we could hear each other. We could talk to each other under the snow, and we could hear the people up there shouting at each other and trying to find us. We could talk to them too. It was the carbon dioxide that got us. After a while you got sort of numb. You got drowsy and just went to sleep. I was talking to

Nadine, and she was begging me to get her out, and I—I couldn't move, Roxanne. I couldn't move a muscle, the weight was so great. The last thing I remember was calling out to them to save her, and then I don't remember anything until they brought me to. It was seven hours before they got Nadine out . . . she was dead by then."

Wordlessly, Roxanne patted his hand. Poor Buck, he'd been through so much.

"I didn't know what to do then." He sounded bewildered, beaten. "I thought I might as well go on. On the upper lakes I went snowblind from all that glitter on the ice. And when I got to Dawson, everything was staked. I spent all my time out on the Stewart River, but never found nothing."

It was strange, she thought. Buck might have met Denby there along the Stewart, might even have talked to him, and never have known Denby was her husband.

"After a while I got a job working for a fellow who had a claim on French Hill, and saved enough money to come up here to Nome. I been working the beach sands, but it doesn't pay much."

Roxanne squeezed Buck's hand. "Buck," she said, "why don't you go home to Kansas?"

He sighed, a big deep sigh that shook his chest. "I would, Roxanne, but I got no money."

At a dollar a dance—and sometimes with big chunky nuggets for tips—money was easy for Roxanne to come by. And ship passages didn't cost as much as they had at the height of the Klondike boom.

"Wait here," she told Buck. "I'll go talk to the boss."

While she waited to talk to Big Mike, who was busy arguing with two heavyset drunks at the bar, Roxanne studied Buck. The Klondike had aged him, wearied him. She supposed it had done that to them all.

Memory flowed over her like a wave. How she had wanted him once! And when he had taken her, wordlessly, there on the Kansas prairie as the great tornado raged above them, how thunderous it had seemed to her. She looked at those big defeated shoulders and remembered how strong he had been, remembered the feel of his arms about her, his muscular body straining, demanding, against her own—and her own sudden, impassioned response. At that moment, she knew that he too was thinking of those wild moments beneath the storm-tossed Kansas sky, knew he was waiting for some sign from her that she remembered. She had had her first wild fling with Buck, but she did not yearn to resume where she had left off.

It came to her suddenly, in a dispassionate sort of way, that Buck was not the man she cared to grow old beside, that his were not the features she desired to see in her children. Her desire for him had been a young desire, based on inexperience and rebellion. Now that she was older, her feeling for him was warm but maternal. She had had a young girl's crush on Buck, but she was over it now.

By the time she got back to the table, after she had persuaded Big Mike to give her a loan against her wages, she was sure of her feelings. Handing Buck the money, she said, "This will get you to Seattle, Buck. From there you can work your way home."

His face flushed. "Gee, I can't take money from you, Roxanne."

"Why not?" she said. "I took money from you once and—you'd do the same for me, Buck, right now if you had it."

"Yes," he said sheepishly. "I sure would." He looked wistful. "I've missed you, Roxanne."

She gave him an appreciative smile, and said, "I have to get back on that platform and dance. It's what I'm paid to do. Listen, don't even go to sleep tonight, Buck. Somebody might roll you. Just stay up and don't drink—walk around until morning. There's a boat leaving for Seattle in the morning. Be on it."

With a quick, affectionate kiss she told him goodbye. There was longing in his eyes as she left him. Longing . . . but hope too. He was going home.

Briskly, Roxanne stepped up to join the other girls on the platform. She put her hands saucily on her hips and stood so that her figure in the satin dress was displayed to its best advantage. Beside her Sal, a buxom brunette, said, "What's with you, Rox? You look like the cat that et the cream."

Roxanne gave Sal a big smile. She felt good, having paid off an old debt. Buck could go back to Kansas now. Back to where he belonged. There he'd find some other girl. A fellow with Buck's good looks and strong physique would always find another girl.

Chapter 28

Several days later, Roxanne decided that she had had enough of Nome. The brief northern summer was ending, and the swift transition to the dread arctic winter was imminent.

Fearfully, she watched the weather. It was chancy to delay. She had almost enough money saved up to pay off the loan from Big Mike and to buy their tickets home. Two or three more evenings would give her the rest. She had already decided to forget the plan of waiting until she had enough money to tide them over for a bit in the States. What she wanted was to get out while it was still possible.

She didn't make it. On what was almost her last evening, a violent storm roared in from the Bering Sea across Norton Sound. Their hotel was swept away and with it all their possessions save the clothes on their backs. Roxanne would never forget that first wild storm in Nome. The lashing sea spilled into the streets and turned the shanty town into a northern

Venice. People lashed their shacks with ropes to the bulkheads to keep them from being swept away. Sometimes, the ropes broke and the shacks were lifted up and carried into the sea, riding the surf until they broke up and their debris joined the broken sluice boxes and mining gear that littered the beach.

After the storm, Big Mike let Roxanne and Denby move into a tiny cubbyhole at the back of his dance hall. From there Roxanne watched bitterly as the sea became a solid ice sheet. They were frozen in, stuck for the winter. Despondent, Denby came down with typhoid. Nome's bad sanitation had gotten to him at last. As Roxanne nursed him through it, she tried to comfort herself with the thought that once her nursing stint was over, if she danced all winter at Big Mike's, she'd return to the States a rich woman. It didn't help much.

She was almost ill herself when, finally, she got Denby through the crisis and fell into an exhausted sleep to recover. She woke up to realize she'd missed a lot of dancing hours on the platform, but Big Mike hadn't said a word. Believing in fairness, she danced free for a week and then went back to fifty percent; Big Mike glowed. But people hadn't as much heart to dance in the bleak winter weather, so Mike expanded his bar in a makeshift way from wreckage left by the storm and salvaged from the beach, and during certain hours Roxanne became a barmaid. Mike's business boomed. Roxanne was not only beautiful to look upon; she had a strange rapport with these rough men, for had she not endured as they had, sticking it out with back-breaking work so near the riches of Bonanza and coming away, as they had, with nothing? It was a society of the lost, the overlooked, the unwanted—all those Lady Luck had passed by, this winter crew.

Lady Luck had bypassed a good many that year, and there was trouble abroad in Nome. United States law decreed that no foreigner could stake a claim on United States soil, and Nome was part of Alaska. Many claims had been made there by Scandinavians.

The Scandinavians were especially bitter, for three of their number had made the first discovery on Anvil Creek. Claim-jumping and murder were commonplace, and only the military managed to keep an uneasy peace among the turbulent miners of Nome—sometimes by the use of fixed bayonets. The Scandinavians, feeling dispossessed, smoldered. Lars Nelgren was one of these.

He was a big man, utterly devoid of humor. Night after night he came into Big Mike's and stared silently at Roxanne as he drank his whiskey. The way he watched her with those blank pale blue eyes made Roxanne uneasy. Lars wasn't like the others—those who pinched her when no one was looking, or gave her sheepish admiring glances, or told her drunkenly about the girls they'd left back home. His rigid countenance never melted into a smile, and for some reason that frightened her.

Oddly, Lars struck up a friendship with Denby, who was still recovering from his bout with typhoid. Roxanne wondered if Lars had bestowed his friendship on Denby because he was her husband, then decided it was unworthy of her to think that. Normally, Denby had a pleasant personality, but he seldom exhibited it anymore, sitting instead dark and dejected in a corner of the bar as he watched Roxanne work. In any event, Lars had no other friends, and Denby's friends had drifted away, finding him gloomy company.

Having given up the search for gold himself, Denby now loudly championed the cause of the Scandinavians. He harangued Roxanne about it. Afraid Denby would get into trouble with the law again, she questioned him closely about Lars.

Lars, it seemed, had arrived early in Nome. He had an Eskimo mistress he called Gin-Gin, who, Denby said, was young and pretty. Lars also had a team of precious malamutes—those magnificent sled dogs of the Eskimos whose feet and legs were different from those of ordinary dogs; their leg temperatures ran fifty degrees lower than their bodies, allowing them to sleep in the snow without freezing in the terrible arctic temperatures. Lars insisted that he'd been run off his claim because he was a foreigner, and Denby thought that was a crying shame.

Roxanne agreed with Denby, but she was afraid for him. He had never really regained his strength after his bout with typhoid. So she tried to soothe Denby, to cheer him and make him think of other things.

As the winter wore on, big Lars with his expressionless face, and Denby, gaunt now and with his eyes sunk deeply into their sockets, continued to mutter together in a corner of Big Mike's, while Roxanne in her orange satin dress—the only one she had been able to save from the storm—served whiskey to a bar crowded with standing, shuffling men. Above the bar hung the usual picture of a reclining nude. Sometimes, when a lock of Roxanne's blond hair came loose and fell temptingly down to a white shoulder, the men at the bar looked up at the picture and back at Roxanne's softly glowing white bosom and sighed. She realized they were stripping her with their eyes, seeing *her* in that sensuous picture, lying naked and inviting. But she did not care. She had to earn a living the only way she could, and tending bar and dancing with the big shaggy miners was less back-breaking than working at Marge's laundry had been. She remembered Marge's happy bellow of "It's clean work!" and smiled wistfully. Big Marge was one of her happier memories of this bleak north country; she hoped the winter was being kind to Marge.

And Leighton—she thought of him occasionally, and hoped he was faring well on the bleak northern reaches of the Koyukuk River. Kind Leighton, who had carried so many heavy washtubs for her, who had fashioned her a pair of snowshoes and gladdened her heart with his warm admiration, and who had saved their lives half a dozen times on the terrible journey over the Chilkoot Pass and down the Yukon to Dawson.

And Case, sinister and deadly and complex . . . she had never met a man who made love so well. She remembered the lean length of him lying beside her and shivered. Why couldn't she have loved him?

But no, she had had to love Rhodes. . . . She could keep her face steady now, but the knife still twisted painfully in her heart whenever she thought of him. Rhodes, the only man she had ever truly loved. If only he had said, *I came to see you, Roxanne. I came to Dawson because I love you.* But Rhodes had his share of stiff-necked pride, too, and so he had not said the words that were in his heart. Nor had she.

While Roxanne dredged up old memories, on the other side of the bar, the New York reporter who was busy trying to glean human-interest stories from Nome's frozen heart for his paper saw the sad look in her eyes and wondered what the Dawson blond was thinking about. He doubted any of these dance hall trollops had a heart—certainly not this one. He'd made careful note of what Ratface had told him about her killing a woman in the States. When he got enough material, he'd write a story about her, and it would be a humdinger!

Roxanne, with worries enough of her own, was unaware of his interest.

In midwinter Josie Mawkins, muffled to the eyes in furs, came over to Big Mike's to see her. Josie, like so many other Dawson madams, had transferred her establishment to Nome, setting up Nome's snootiest sporting house. Roxanne looked up from polishing glasses at the bar to see her stamping snow off her boots on the sawdust floor.

Josie threw open her fur coat to reveal a pink boa over an ample bosom, brushed snow off wisps of brightly hennaed hair, and came right to the point. "Rox," she said, "you could make more money in my place in twenty minutes than you can here in two hours." She looked around her disparagingly. "You know dancin' only whets their appetites for the real thing. These fellows come over here and get all stirred up dancing with you for maybe ten dollars—and then they rush over to my place and spend two hundred. I could use you. Two of my girls got in a fight and knifed each other something awful. You want to consider coming over?"

Roxanne grinned at earnest Josie, resplendent in her furs and pink boa. "I've still got that jealous husband, Josie."

Josie shrugged. "Just stopped by to tell you if you ever change your mind, the offer's still open. You'd like it over at my place," she declared. "High-class clientele, real overstuffed chairs, lace doilies, servants to fetch and carry, red hot stoves—not freezin' like this place." She shivered. "I don't see how you can wear a dress cut so low with that draft comin' through the door! 'Course my girls wear even less. Mostly they romp around in their underwear—or nothin' at all—so's they need it a little warmer. But then my girls are hothouse flowers—and you are too, if you'd only realize it."

Roxanne gave Josie a warm look. For all their obvious differences, there was something about Josie that reminded her of Marge. Something forthright and honest.

"It's a nice offer, Josie," she said. "I'm sorry I have to say no. It would be nice to be actually warm without dancing!"

They both laughed, and Josie refused a drink, saying she had better liquor back at the house. The New York reporter, craning his neck to see them through the crowd at the bar, scowled. Here was another thing to chalk up against the Dawson blond: she kept bad company. He rather hoped to see them leave together, but he was disappointed, for at that moment, Josie and her pink boa and her hennaed hair and her furs floated out into the snowy street. And Roxanne went back to earning her living as a barmaid.

As that winter of howling winds and blizzards and disasters wore on, Roxanne grew more and more worried about Denby. He and Lars seemed to have retreated into a kind of private world as they skulked about together. Nome itself was an eerie place that winter. Bored with huddling like captives indoors, eating monotonous food, doing nothing, the miners traded stories at the bar, and Roxanne listened. Frightening stories of things that had wafted out of the fog, stories of a subhuman monster that lay in wait on the glaciers, grinding its teeth, or came roaring out of the subarctic darkness to crush a man. Men listened and nodded their heads soberly. Many believed in the hairy monster of the glaciers.

As bitter winter slipped into frozen spring, Denby took up a new tune. Now he muttered about a great discovery Lars had made, a claim Lars was afraid to stake lest—as a foreigner—it be taken away from him. Lars called it the Gold of the North. Denby's eyes glittered as he told Roxanne about it. Somewhere beyond the low hills behind Nome it lay; Lars hadn't told him exactly where. That Lars was willing to share this vast mother lode with Denby made him proud. Roxanne listened with a sense of frustration. She was thoroughly tired of being waltzed about by strangers, having her feet tramped on, listening to tinny music and tired jokes, serving cheap whiskey for high prices. She was tired of Alaska. All she could think of now was summer, when the ice would break on the Bering Sea and the steamers would thread their way north—steamers that would take her home.

Preoccupied with thoughts of leaving, she didn't pay much attention to Denby, but she was glad his health had improved, even though his eyes were more sunken than ever and had a fanatical gleam in them that bothered her. Sometimes she heard him talking to himself as she went to sleep beside him on the hard bed. Roxanne covered her ears; her work was hard and demanding. She needed her sleep.

It all happened so quickly, she was never sure later in which sequence the events occurred. Vaguely, she remembered dressing for work while Denby babbled about Lars's need to stake his claim—*their* claim—to the Gold of the North before others found their way there. Roxanne, smoothing down the orange satin dress around her hips, ignored him. She looked up when he muttered that he'd have to go too—suppose Lars forgot to stake a claim for him? She sighed and began combing her hair. Later, she remembered how Denby had watched her, a curiously sly gleam in his eyes.

To her surprise, Denby, as if to make amends for past treatment, brought out two brimming glasses and insisted Roxanne have a drink with him—something he had never done before, for he disapproved of women drinking. As Roxanne sipped her drink, Denby raised his glass and said with a flourish, "Here's to the States. Drink up!" That was one toast Roxanne could drink to heartily; she swallowed the rest of the hot liquid at a gulp, smiled at Denby and went back to fixing her hair.

Shortly after that she passed out.

She awoke feeling smothered, with fur tickling her nose. She was being jolted too, and there was a loud yelping somewhere ahead of her. When she struggled to sit up, she found to her horror that her hands were tied. Something—she thought at first it was a fur rug—had been thrown over her face. Her body felt strange too; there was fur against her skin. She moved her legs in disbelief; her feet too were encased in fur, and beneath the soles of her feet she could feel something stiff and rasping.

She cried out. Abruptly the jolting ceased.

"She's awake," said a voice, Denby's voice.

The fur covering—it was called a parka—was thrown back from her face, and she was almost blinded by the white glare of an icy world. When her vision could focus, she saw that she was wrapped in furs and riding on a dogsled. Nearby she saw another sled, and behind it, his hands on the handlebars, stood Lars.

Denby's face loomed up beside her. "I had to tie you, Roxanne." His voice was apologetic. "I didn't want you to jump off and try to get back to Nome. You'd get lost and you might die."

"Denby," she wailed, "where are we?"

"Remember I told you we had to stake our claim?" he told her importantly. "Lars is leading us to the Gold of the North."

Bewildered, Roxanne looked around her. As far as the eye could see stretched a white wilderness: snow, ice, undulating hills. "Why did you bring me along?" she gasped. And then, in horror, "Denby, you drugged me! You put something in my drink!"

"I *had* to, Roxanne," he mumbled. "I couldn't leave you there in that place. Besides, I needed your money to buy these dogs and this outfit." His voice grew defensive. "And you wouldn't have given me the money. You know you wouldn't."

Grimly, she stared at Denby. Indeed she wouldn't have, not for this mad venture!

"Your clothes," he said cheerfully, "they belong to Lars's Eskimo girl friend, Gin-Gin. They'll keep you warm."

Gradually it all sank in.

"Denby," whispered Roxanne, "untie my hands. Isn't it enough you took the money for this wild-goose chase? Take me back to Nome. We could all die out here!"

"No," said Denby, sticking out his lower lip childishly.

"Denby." She was very near to tears. "What have I ever done to you that you would do this to me? How *could* you drag me out into these wastes of ice?"

"We're going to be rich, Roxanne." Denby turned his face away from her and said it as if it were a litany, repeated many times and memorized. "You aren't going to have to work anymore. We'll be as rich as those millionaires in Bonanza."

"Come along," called Lars impatiently. "Suppose they come looking for her from Nome?"

"He's right," said Denby. "They mustn't follow us. They might kill us for the gold."

"Gold!" wailed Roxanne. "Denby, there is no gold—there's only snow and ice. Oh, Denby, untie me!"

For answer, he tossed the fur over her head again. She heard his muffled voice, "So your face won't freeze in the wind, Roxanne."

Immobilized in darkness, she lay back, tears swimming in her eyes. Dear God, how could Denby *do* this to her?

That first night on the trail Denby untied her so

she could eat and drink. She sat on the sled, sheltered by an overhanging boulder of ice and looked around glumly.

Lars and Denby were dressed like Eskimos in fur parkas and tunics and mukluks. Roxanne studied the clothes that Lars had borrowed from Gin-Gin for her. Sewn with thread made of sinew, her undergarments consisted of a tunic and parka with the fur turned inward, fur pants made of caribou tucked into sock-like boots with the fur side inward. The boots fitted loosely and were packed with dry grass, which had to be changed frequently, Denby told her, to keep her feet from freezing. Over those fitted first another low boot, like a slipper, and then a pair of big fur boots. As an overgarment she wore a tunic, fur-side out. The tunic was loose-sleeved so she could pull her arms inside and get warm.

"That fur around both hoods is made of—well, one's wolf and one's wolverine," Denby told her importantly. "Lars told me that's because those furs won't collect ice from your breathing."

Roxanne looked down at her hands, stuck into fur mittens that extended to the sleeves. "I look as if I've gained a hundred pounds," she muttered, indicating her warm but ungainly costume, and Denby laughed as if she had said something hilarious.

She gave him a resentful look. "You aren't up to this trip, Denby," she said coldly. "We may be dressed as Eskimos, but we are not Eskimos. If there's a bad blizzard, we won't survive out here."

His lips thrust outward and his eyes glittered. She knew that look—it was his "gold look." "We've come a long way, Roxanne. We aren't going back to the States empty-handed."

Roxanne sighed. They wouldn't have gone back empty-handed. She had made enough, saved up in their mattress, to get them started. But Denby, with his misguided pride, wanted to be the one to make the money. She fell silent, sitting there by the tiny campfire and trying to eat the food Lars handed her silently. Still lashed to the sleds, the malamutes growled and barked and scrapped over their meal of frozen fish. Overhead, a brilliant green aurora borealis cascaded down like a giant waterfall against the inky sky. Over the campfire's thin yellow flame, Lars's pale, expressionless blue eyes watched her. Roxanne thought she read a kind of triumph in his look, and she shrank back. When they had finished eating and rested awhile, Denby said apologetically, "I've got to tie you up again, Roxanne. I know you'd take one of the teams and start out alone. Don't try to say you wouldn't—I know you."

Neither pleas nor common sense restrained Denby, and he tied her up again. She spent the night thinking bitterly about how Denby had thrown away their chance of going back to the States with enough money to make a good start, and wondering about big silent Lars, and why he had taken part in this—this kidnapping!

The next morning Denby untied her hands, saying they were now too far from Nome for her to have any chance of making it back alone. Lars called out to Roxanne that she should learn to handle the dogs, and should practice riding on the sled runners and running behind the sled as the men did. Roxanne gave him a black look, but flexed her fingers and moved on stiff legs up to make friends with Denby's lead dog. He was a big malamute sled dog of a type found along the Bering Sea. Stocky and short, he weighed a good seventy-five pounds. His shoulders were powerful, his arched tail was a bushy plume, and there was resolution in the way he stood, in the way he forged ahead, leading the other dogs. The other dogs were grays, but this handsome dog was snowy white. He was named Snowman and he had cost a packet, Denby told her cheerfully. Snowman was reputed to be smarter than a man at finding his way. Roxanne found the dog friendly and surprisingly tame. He snuffled her hand with his pointed nose and waved his bushy tail when she patted his head. She was warned not to feed the dogs, since it would make them fight and perhaps injure one another; one had to be careful about feeding them. On the trail they were given just a little bit of frozen fish at a time, because if they were allowed to eat all they wanted, they'd simply lie down and sleep. As she petted the big handsome dog, Roxanne wondered if she could seize the sled when Denby wasn't looking and make her escape. But the bleak white countryside with its absence of recognizable landmarks daunted her. How would she find her way to Nome? Would she not just wander deeper into this glacial wilderness?

Lars seemed to have read her thoughts, for he suddenly pulled out a long rifle and inspected it. She shuddered, wondering if he would really bring her down with that if she tried to leave. She turned to study Denby's pack. Sure enough, Denby had a Winchester. Her eyes traced their fresh sled tracks in the soft snow. Could she follow those tracks to Nome? Perhaps . . . if the wind did not come up and blow them away, or if new snow did not fall and cover them up.

They kept traveling and the weather held. Roxanne believed they were headed north and that frightened her too. North lay the Arctic Circle. Around them the white countryside was rougher now. Chunks of ice like crags jutted up out of the snow and caused them to make sudden detours. For two days they followed a frightening crevasse and, at one heart-stopping point, Denby's sled veered and nearly slid into it. The crevasse had sheer sides and was incredibly deep. Around them the ice made noises, like a great creature stirring, and Roxanne thought of the monster of the glaciers that the miners had muttered about in Nome.

Once when Lars's sled was too far away for him to hear, she confided to Denby, "I don't think that man knows where he's going. He keeps looking around him for landmarks and doesn't seem to find them. I think he's lost."

Denby gave her an uneasy look. "Lars can't be lost. He knows this country."

"I doubt that," said Roxanne sharply. "Why don't you ask him where we're headed?"

But when Denby questioned Lars, all he got was a laconic nod of the head that included half the landscape.

By now Roxanne had learned to manage the dogs fairly well and to hold onto the handlebars while running along behind the sled. It was exhausting, but her long hours of dancing had conditioned her for it. She was holding up somewhat better than Denby.

Lars seemed to be changing before her eyes. Every night now, when they camped, he looked at her more fixedly and his pale blue eyes were beginning to gleam; she felt violated by that look. It was frightening. She mentioned it to Denby.

"I've noticed," he growled. She had almost forgotten how jealous he was.

"Suppose you are hurt," she pointed out. "I'll be completely at his mercy."

Denby wavered. "The Winchester's loaded," he said thoughtfully. "Do you know how to use a gun, Roxanne?"

"Yes—though I'm not a good shot." She had learned while he was out prospecting along the Pelly.

"You don't have to be a good shot," said Denby. "If Lars comes at you, just aim it at him and cock it and pull the trigger. The gun'll take care of the rest."

The fourth day out, Roxanne had occasion to test the truth of that. They had spent a trying day with yet another arctic delight inflicted on them: a type of mirage called "looming," in which distant objects appeared near and close. Crawling like ants over Alaska's white face, they never seemed to come any nearer to a distant lip of ice that projected sullenly ahead of them.

When at last they stopped by a low wall of ice, Lars sent Denby around to the other side of the white wall to see if it contained a better campsite than the one he had chosen. As soon as Denby left, Lars strode over to Roxanne. His big fur-clad figure looming over her, he asked, "Tired?"

Bone weary, she looked away from him and did not reply.

"We're only a couple of days away from where we're goin'," he said. "Gin-Gin's people—she's my Eskimo gal I left back in Nome—have a camp somewheres up here. We can't be more than a couple of days from it."

A camp—people. Hope sprang up in Roxanne, but she kept her face averted.

His voice harshened. "Damn it, look at me when I'm talkin' to you, woman! Now you get on that sled and holler 'Mush!' and make tracks out of here after me. You hear?"

"Denby isn't back," she pointed out.

"We don't need Denby. We're leavin' him behind," Lars said heavily.

Roxanne whirled to stare at Lars, her worst fears realized. Lars was going to leave Denby behind to freeze!

"Unless you'd rather I shot him," said Lars sarcastically.

She must warn Denby. She made a dive for Denby's Winchester on the sled to fire a warning shot, but Lars was too quick for her. He grasped the gun just as she reached it. Still, Roxanne did not give it up easily; she struggled with him for it. Contemptuously, he wrested the barrel from her and sent her sprawling.

"Now you get up from there," he snarled. "I want to do this the easy way, you hear? We're leaving Denby here and heading for the igloos of Gin-Gin's people. We'll have an Eskimo marriage, you and me—I'll take you for my second wife. Come on, don't look so glum, you won't find it so bad—they play games in the igloos sometimes; turn off the lamp and everybody undresses and we all find each other in the dark—finders keepers. Life's real relaxed in the igloos. All you'll need to wear is that short fur top, no bottoms. Gin-Gin's brother's wife never wears the bottoms in the igloo."

Roxanne scrambled to her feet in the snow and turned to run. Lars's big body barred her way, standing between her and the dogs. With a sob Roxanne fell back before him, and Denby's voice, almost a shriek, pierced her consciousness. Turning toward the sound, she saw that Denby had just rounded the corner of the ice wall.

"Lars, you cheat! We're up here for gold!"

Lars lifted Denby's Winchester. "There was never no gold," he said heavily. "*She* was the gold. I been planning this all winter."

With a maddened roar that was half sob, Denby lunged at Lars. He didn't make it. The Winchester spoke—once. Struck in the chest, Denby fell, a look of disbelief spreading over his haggard young face. He lay wincing, clutching his chest where the red lifeblood was ebbing fast away.

"Denby! Oh, Denby!" Roxanne ran and knelt in the snow beside him, cradled his head in her arms with a sob, shielded him with her body from Lars's long gun.

"I'm—sorry, Roxanne," Denby gasped, and she could see that his eyes were glazing. "I . . . did it for you . . . make you rich . . ." His voice was drifting away, like his life. "Loved you so. . . ." he murmured, and his voice was gone, lost in the crunch of the ice beneath Lars's big mukluks.

"Oh, Denby." She didn't know if he could hear her, but she hoped so. "Denby, I loved you too!" Hot tears spilled from Roxanne's eyes, fell to his cheeks, froze there. And she *had* loved him. Those long-ago words of his, *I love you anyway*, rang in her ears. Denby had tried—in his way he had tried to make her happy, to give her what he thought she should want. If he had failed, the fault was as much hers as his. And now . . . the glover's son lay dead in the arctic snows.

Lars's mukluks had come to a stop beside her. With a snarl deep in her throat, Roxanne hurled herself upward against the long gun cradled in his arm, and felt her shoulder connect with it, knocking it from his grasp. Off balance, Lars staggered backward. She plunged madly forward, threw herself on the gun, grasped it, rolled over and pointed it at him.

But before she could fire it, he was on her and had wrested the gun away. His hot breath was on her face, melting the ice on her lashes.

"Goddamn wench," he muttered. "I'll make you pay for that!" Her head rocked as he slapped her face, first this way, then that. Though the fur parka protected her a little, her neck felt almost broken from the blows. She would have sagged back into the snow, but he dragged her to her feet with a curse. "Don't you pass out on me now! We got us a way to go yet!" He shook her as a great bear might shake some small animal. The loose snow flew from her parka as he shoved her toward the sled. "You take Denby's sled," he said, "and you go just where I tell you. Or"—his voice rose to a roar—"I'm going to shoot you, do you hear? Just like I did him. Now take hold of those sled handles and make tracks!"

Out of the pain of her ringing head, Roxanne found her voice. "You aren't going to leave him?" she cried. "Not here where the wolves—?"

Lars paused. She could see indecision on his angry face. A fierce light burned in those blank blue eyes. "Come here," he said. She came reluctantly. Swiftly he lashed her to the sled, took up Denby's slight body in his arms as easily as if it had been a child's, and stomped to the edge of the crevasse. Lifting the body high, he hurled it over. Roxanne closed her eyes. Her head reeled. Poor Denby, walled in forever by the ice. For when spring came, this whole mass would move, closing up the crevasse, holding Denby eternally in its dark crystal depths. She was only half conscious when Lars strode back and untied the thongs that bound her, stood her on her feet and pushed her toward the sled. To steady herself and keep from falling, she grasped the sled handles.

"Now *mush*!" shouted Lars, and she leaped on the sled runners and cried out to the dogs in a voice that had tears in it, "Mush! Snowman, mush!" Head bowed, she clung there until minutes later they hit a rough spot and she was tossed off. She caught up and in stunned misery, whipped by the wind, ran along behind the sled, gripping the handlebars. Sometimes to catch her breath, she stood on the runners and buried her face in the fur of her parka. Sobs wracked her slight body encased in its heavy furs. Denby had not been much of a husband, nor had her marriage brought her satisfaction. Between them they had brought each other only heartache and despair. But for him to die in that forbidding place and in that terrible unnecessary way! It was unbearable. Pain blurred her vision as she stood on the runners, her hands gripping the handlebars, and felt the yelping dogs sweep the sled farther into the frozen north.

Then slowly, rising even over the numbing pain of Denby's death, the horror of her own situation penetrated her misery. *She* had been the prize all along, and Lars had killed Denby to possess her. And now they were headed God knows where. . . .

Her tears dried and her courage returned to sustain her. She looked across the open space at Lars's watchful figure, tall and bulky and with a bearlike strength, running behind his sled. Dull hatred burned in her eyes. If only she had the Winchester, she would kill him now! Whatever happened, she swore silently, she would never be Lars's woman. But she had only until they made camp to make her move, and time was running out.

Before they had gone another two miles, she had figured out what she would do. She planned to wait until the trail narrowed and Lars had to go around a difficult blind turn to maneuver past some jagged chunk of ice that barred their way. The moment he could not see her, she would wheel the dogs about and run for it. She was lighter than Lars, and her team was every bit as good as his—Snowman, in fact, was better than his lead dog. She would run with all her strength and leap on the runners only when her strength failed her. No matter if they went in the wrong direction at first; they would take the easiest path, whichever way it lay. But she would escape from Lars, even if she died in that white frozen world out there.

Lars must have guessed her intention, because they had not gone another quarter mile when he reined up his sled and came to a halt. Roxanne halted behind him, blocked by his sled. At his approach she shrank back.

"I don't trust you," he muttered. "Tricky, that's what you are. Here." He pushed her onto Denby's sled, pulled the fur wraps around her and tied her down. "That'll keep you nice and warm for me tonight," he said grinning.

Haggard, Roxanne stared back at him, hatred burning in her sapphire eyes.

"You'll come round," he chuckled. "You'll find out you got no other choice."

As she watched, he untied his own sled and cut it adrift. "We've used enough of our supplies to get rid of it anyway," he grunted. "And Snowman's a better lead dog." Tying all the dogs so that they fanned out before the sled, he roared to Snowman, "Mush!" Roxanne thought she heard the sound of wolves in the distance.

A red aurora hung shimmering in the sky when at last Lars made camp. He built the fire, cooked their food, brought Roxanne's portion to her and untied her hands so she could eat. Though she had tried to writhe free, she was still tied securely to the sled. The events of the day had kept her so distraught that she could not force her food down.

"You better eat," Lars advised in a surly voice. "You'll need it." And when she shook her head and looked away, "Don't matter none. After I've got you broke in, you'll be plenty glad to eat—and cook, too. You'll do whatever I say and jump when I tell you."

Roxanne gave him a bitter look.

He sat hunched before the fire, talking to her, while the dogs growled and snarled, sniffing the food. From the distance there came a howl. Lars looked up alertly. "Probably wolves," he muttered.

Still tied, Roxanne shuddered. Wolves . . .

Lars leaned back and contemplated her. "You think I'm in a hurry to get my hands on your white skin," he said lazily. "But I ain't in no hurry. Me, I know how to wait. I seen you up there on that platform with your hips swingin' in that orange satin dress, and I swore I'd have you. I'd have took you back there in town, but half of Nome would have been gunnin' for me. So I figured out how to get rid of your fool of a husband and get you at the same time."

"What about your Eskimo girl friend?" asked Roxanne. "I'm even wearing her clothes. Do you mean *she* won't mind?"

Lars shrugged. "I got Gin-Gin broke in real good, same as I'll have you broke in soon. When Gin-Gin acts too uppity, I just give her a taste of the whip."

Roxanne paled. That long whip that he cracked over the dogs . . . she could almost feel it lashing her own bare skin. Well, he would have to use it on her, because she did not mean to give in to him without a struggle.

He sat a while, staring at her. Then he rose casually. "Now," he said, "you and me is going to share a sleeping bag. And inside that sleeping bag you're going to do anything I want you to do. And you're not going to give me no trouble. On account of," he added reflectively, "I killed the last one who give me trouble. Sort of forgot myself and found I'd broken her back. . . ."

Feeling like a trapped animal, Roxanne glared at him, her own back stiff. She'd rather lie dead in the snow, or buried in some crevasse like Denby, than share a sleeping bag with Lars!

He stepped forward and unbound her. Roxanne stumbled to her feet, feeling numb at first from lying there so long.

"Walk around a minute," he suggested. "Restores the circulation. I want you in the pink when you crawl into that sleeping bag."

Roxanne flexed her leg muscles. She wondered how far she could run before Lars caught up with her.

She was poised to run, seeing Lars's big shape as a shadow against the red aurora that lit the night sky, when a voice she had never expected to hear again said, "Drop to the ground, Roxanne, so I can get a shot at him."

Over the low, icy embankment that sheltered their little camp from the wind, a man vaulted toward them. He was wearing mukluks and a fur parka, and inside that parka—was Rhodes's grim face.

With a curse Lars whirled and grasped his gun. Since Roxanne was between them, Rhodes paused for an instant, while Roxanne, coming out of shock, flung herself to the snow. But that momentary delay had given Lars his chance. He turned the Winchester on Rhodes and both of their guns roared at once. In the explosion of sound, Roxanne saw Rhodes waver, heard Lars's gun roar again. Silently, blood dripping from a wound in his head, Rhodes fell to the ground, his gun exploding once more as he went down.

Roxanne scrambled up and ran for Rhodes's gun. As she grasped it, brought the barrel up and whirled, she saw there was no need to fire it. Rhodes's first bullet had got Lars full in the face. Lars could only have fired one shot—the other must have been the result of a reflex. Appalled, Roxanne turned away from that sight; Lars was unrecognizable. What had been a face was now a bloody mask.

But it was not Lars who concerned her. Through some miracle, Rhodes was here—and he was hurt, perhaps dying. She bent over him fearfully. His eyes were closed, and blood was oozing from a cut on his scalp. It did not appear deep, but she did not know what damage might have been done. Then she saw that the blood was also trickling down his sleeve and staining his wrist. So he had taken both bullets.

Quickly, she stanched the bleeding with a woolen shirt from Denby's pack. Her desperate gaze swung round. In all its fearsome beauty, the trackless arctic lay before her . . . unique, awe-inspiring, relentless, forbidding and remote. In the snow at her feet lay the only man she had ever loved—who might be dying because he had come to save her.

Roxanne's jaw hardened. She looked out at the grim white distance, stretching ever away, and then down again at Rhodes's prone figure.

By God, neither of them was going to die! Rhodes had come for her, and she was going to get him back to Nome! She would lash him to the sled, just as Lars had tied her. The same furs would cover him.

The hardest thing would be getting Rhodes onto the sled. And it had to be done at once or, she feared, he would freeze in the cold arctic night. Swiftly she founds Lars's knife, cut off Lars's outer clothing and wrapped Rhodes in the furs, being careful not to reopen his wounds. Then she enlisted Snowman's aid. After she had untied the dog—risking bitten fingers from the other irritable snapping dogs, who smelled blood and were excited—she lashed Rhodes's legs to Snowman's harness, and together they heaved him onto the sled. She wrapped Rhodes in furs more carefully than she had ever wrapped anything, warmed her hands at the fire, swallowed the food Lars had prepared, retied Snowman and, leaving Lars's body to the mercy of the wolves, started out by the light of the aurora. They would travel for short distances and make brief rest stops, she decided. Surely the dogs would last longer that way and could cover more distance. She feared the weather and the loss of the plain line of sled tracks that led back toward Nome.

With a start, she realized Rhodes must have dogs, a sled somewhere. His dogs must not be left to starve! She mushed her yelping pack back along Rhodes's tracks, which followed their own across the snow, and found his dogsled. Roxanne fastened his dogs' traces to her own sled and reassessed the situation. Since there were many dogs to pull a relatively light load, they would be able to travel fast. Even though they were lightly provisioned, she would not starve, having found some supplies on Rhodes's sled and transferred them to her own. She had also tossed Denby's Winchester and cartridges onto the sled, so if she met a wolf pack, she would be able to deal with them.

But wolves were not to be the enemy.

The arctic was.

Chapter 29

Two days later Rhodes still had not regained consciousness though Roxanne tended him anxiously. She tried to take care of herself too, forcing herself to eat, remembering to change the straw inside her mukluks to keep her feet from freezing, for the burden was hers now. Somehow she must bring them both home.

The way seemed endless and their food had almost run out when a light snow blew in from the north. Doggedly, Roxanne kept going as long as she could, then took a short exhausted nap on the lee side of a long ice shelf. She was awakened by the sounds of two of the hungry dogs fighting—they were on necessarily short rations now—and rousing herself, she struggled to her feet. Standing there, in the new-fallen snow, she was overcome by a feeling of hopelessness. Half blinded by the snow-glare, she climbed to a little hillock and surveyed the faceless landscape. No sign of the sled tracks she had so faithfully followed. The new snow lay like powdered sugar frosting, covering the ice with deceptive softness.

Walking heavily, she returned to where the dogs stood and checked Rhodes automatically, making sure he was warm and well-protected by his furs. The dogs had ceased quarreling and were resting in their harness. The animals were used to her way of travel by now, short runs and short rests—indeed, they seemed to like it. They were gallant dogs. She gave them and Rhodes a heartbroken look. She had no idea of which direction she should take. She might well be headed toward the Arctic Ocean or the Chukchi Sea instead of Nome. Nightmare stories she had heard of starving sled dogs eating their traces, of starving Eskimos eating their sled dogs, flashed through her mind.

Grimly, she headed in the direction she hoped was right and called to Snowman, "Mush!"

For the first time, Snowman balked. Roxanne looked at the powerful dog in amazement. Then suddenly she understood. Those intelligent eyes were looking at her anxiously; he was trying to tell her she was heading the wrong way. Impulsively, she went over and threw her arms around his beautiful shaggy neck. He licked her face sympathetically.

"Snowman," she whispered huskily, "get us home."

The dog made a soft growling sound in his throat. When Roxanne straightened up and resumed her position at the handlebars behind the sled, she snapped the whip high over the dogs' heads so they could hear its singing message and let Snowman have his head. Straight and true he led the yelping pack off to the right of Roxanne's original direction. Head aching from the white brilliance, Roxanne leaped on the runners and closed her eyes for a moment against the blinding glare. It would never do to get snow blindness; then they would surely all die. She closed her eyes whenever she stood on the runners, and sometimes briefly even as she ran behind the sled. But she feared falling, too—a broken bone could be just as fatal as snow blindness. Snowman seemed sure of himself as over that desolate wilderness he led his yelping pack.

And Roxanne, hanging on, tending Rhodes as well as she could, somehow keeping him alive, followed the big dog's lead and prayed.

The trip became a race against time, against the elements, for a hard east wind was blowing which could mean more snow. If they were slowed down by a blizzard Rhodes's fate was sealed, she was sure, and perhaps all of them would die.

Miraculously, the weather held.

Out of the trackless arctic, they made it into Nome. Exhausted, staggering, Roxanne brought them in, zig-zagging a ragged course behind the sled as Snowman, that redoubtable malamute, tirelessly led his flagging fellows. On the sled, slumped in his furs, Rhodes lay insensible. At that point, Roxanne did not know if he was alive or dead.

Down Nome's snow-packed streets, aglaze with ice, they sped. Past Wyatt Earp's Only Second Class Saloon in Alaska. Past the jerrybuilt stores and the gawking miners who watched these gaunt furry apparitions sweep down out of the north where no one ought to be at this time of year.

They came to a collapsed halt in front of Josie's place. Remembering Josie's boast that she had the hottest house in Nome—steamy warm, for the half-naked women roaming about—Roxanne was sure that delivering Rhodes there was his best clear chance of survival.

Josie, who had been looking out the window through her lace curtains, came out and stared at Roxanne. Bulky in her furs, Roxanne surged toward that over-dressed flashy figure in red taffeta and jet. She threw back her parka and cried in a panicky exhausted voice, "Oh, Josie, I need a doctor. Rhodes is hurt—I don't know how bad. Can we get him inside?"

Josie took one look at Roxanne's haggard face and let out a holler. Two of her minions came rushing out and unstrapped Rhodes's inert figure. Having lifted him from the sled, they carried him inside and up to one of the rooms. Within minutes, Josie ushered in a man she proudly introduced as "the best sawbones in Nome."

As the doctor took over, Roxanne staggered back downstairs, went out into the street where the dogs had collapsed panting in their harness, threw her arms around Snowman and wept uncontrollably. She was too exhausted to notice that a curious crowd had gathered to witness the Dawson blond's dramatic return to Nome. Now one of the miners approached her. Gently he disengaged Roxanne's arms from the gallant dog, lifted her from the icy street and stood her up. "I've got to get food for my dogs," she whispered, wavering on her feet. "We wouldn't have made it without them and they're starving."

"We'll feed your dogs," he said gruffly and made a grab for her arm as her knees buckled. After all she had been through, Roxanne lost consciousness for the first time. He carried her into Josie's.

When Roxanne awoke that afternoon, Josie told her that Rhodes could stay in the room where he'd been put. Tiger Lil, as Josie called the Chinese girl, whose room she had appropriated for Rhodes, could take her tricks behind a hastily constructed partition in Yukon Cassie's room. Roxanne was so grateful she wept again. Josie, her own brown eyes bright with tears, plied her with nourishing hot soup and scolded her. "Come on now, Rox. Nobody's goin' to die. With you nursin' him, your fellow will get well soon—you'll see."

"Do you think so?" asked Roxanne, her eyes big and luminous in her thin face. "Oh, Josie do you think so?"

Josie nodded and hustled Roxanne off to be with Rhodes. To Tiger Lil's complaints about being dispossessed Josie bellowed, "You ain't never loved a man like that! Rox can have the room for as long as she needs it!"

Upstairs in that tiny room, Roxanne, thin and pale from her bitter adventures in the snows, willed Rhodes to live. His eyes were still closed, his lashes dark on his wasted cheeks. He still had not spoken a word to her.

"Concussed," Josie's sawbones called it. The shoulder wound was infected, he'd lost a lot of blood, his pulse was weak. As for the head wound—well, you just couldn't tell about those, the doctor said, might come to for a minute and sink right back. Asked if Rhodes would make it, the doctor shook his head. No telling, he said cheerfully. These miners were a tough breed.

But Rhodes wasn't a miner, thought Roxanne wistfully. He was a salt-water sailor, and somewhere his ship, the lovely proud *Virginia Lass*, awaited his return.

But the important thing was the fact that Rhodes had come for her, come to save her. Out of the trackless wastes, how many weary miles he must have come across country that even Leighton, with his taste for wilderness exploration, called desperate. . . . He must love her very much to have done that. A glow warmed the ice that had built up around her heart since leaving Dawson, and it broke inside her with a thunder greater than the spring thaw along the Yukon. The passion she felt growing within her was like the brilliant subtropical verdure that rose as if by magic in June across the barren subarctic slopes of the Yukon Valley.

Rhodes loved her, loved her . . . nothing else mattered. He had to live. Her fists clenched. She would snatch him from death. She would make him live.

In her narrow room, Roxanne sat and waited while outside, once again, the Dawson blond was the talk of Nome. Some said she had been drugged and kidnapped, others that she'd run away with Lars, and that Denby had pursued her. Some were of the opinion that Roxanne had killed them both and fled back to Nome with the lover who'd come all the way from Dawson by dogsled to claim her.

In the downstairs front room of the posh sporting house where booted miners clomped in and out, Josie shrugged and said not to ask her about it—then they'd hear no lies. Fact was, Rox was holed up, nursing a fellow who was more dead than alive. And if he died, Josie added pessimistically, from the desperate look of her, Rox would hurl herself into the Bering Sea.

The miners listened gravely. They'd long ago put the Dawson blond on a pedestal, and in their sentimental hearts they respected love.

On a night when the swirling aurora outside the small window spilled a sparkling shower of light onto the bleak white landscape, Rhodes opened his eyes. For a moment he stared vacantly at Roxanne in the lamplight, and she thought his lips silently formed her name. Then his eyes closed again, and he went back into that night of the mind that concussion brings.

The next day, still unconscious, he developed a raging fever. Quickly, Roxanne summoned the doctor. Shaking his head, the doctor explained that every kind of disease was rife in Nome, and this feller, worn out with his long trek in a state of shock from his concussion, and weakened by loss of blood, had been ripe to pick up any bug that was goin' by. Could be malaria; he wasn't sure. If this man's constitution was tough enough, he'd come through it. If not . . . the doctor shrugged.

"He'll come through it," Roxanne said grimly, and the doctor, looking into her pale determined face, believed he would.

That little upstairs room had become Roxanne's prison—her heaven and her hell. She scarcely left it. Wild with yearning, she sat besides Rhodes, spooning broth and whiskey and life into his wasted body. Aching with tenderness, she wiped his broad forehead gently with damp cloths. And when, after one of the assaults of burning fever, he shook with chills, she warmed his lean, sinewy form with her own warm naked body. Her very heart trembled at the sound of that loved voice when delirium shook him and he raved. Any injury he might have done her in Baltimore was long forgotten. He had loved her in Baltimore and she had not known it . . . then as now, he had loved her. She blanked from her mind the savagery of his attack on her body after the ball. It all seemed so long ago.

Nothing mattered, except that Rhodes loved her.

From gossip and rumors overheard by Josie and the girls, Roxanne was able to piece together some of what had happened to Rhodes after she had had him rolled in Dawson. He had taken a job in one of the mines and had gambled his wages at the Last Nugget Saloon, where he had won heavily from a "black hatted gambler." Roxanne smiled. Case always wore a black hat. Perhaps he had let Rhodes win deliberately; Case had told her that rolling a man in an alley wasn't his style.

With his winnings, Rhodes had bought a team of malamutes, a sled, heavy fur clothing and provisions, and had set out overland toward Nome.

When he finally reached Nome he had found his way to Big Mike's saloon, where he met Gin-Gin, Lars's disgruntled Eskimo wife. She had been the one who told Rhodes about Lars and Denby, and how they had taken off in two sleds with a bundle that later proved to be Denby's wife. Gin-Gin was sure that they had headed for her people's camp far to the north. She was in a murderous rage at Lars, who had taken her clothes and her dogsled and left her to starve in Nome.

Rhodes had set out again almost immediately after his talk with the Eskimo girl.

The rest Roxanne had to imagine: how Rhodes had followed their tracks. His dogs must have been the wolves she and Lars had heard howling that night. Finally, Rhodes must have come upon Denby's abandoned sled, must have seen the blood and kept on going, cautiously. No doubt he had recognized the glow of their campfire from the distance and left his dogs and sneaked up to find Roxanne and Lars battling over the gun.

And he saved me, she thought, thrilling to the wonder of it.

Rhodes, tossing and turning, sometimes came to enough to talk wildly, eyes staring, unseeing, face burning hot. Roxanne stroked his hair lovingly, spoke soothing words and pressed a damp cloth to his forehead.

One night, he began talking again. And this time, with stunning force, she understood what he was saying.

". . . going to kill her," he panted, eyes bright and feverish. "Got to get there . . . going to throttle her with these hands. . . ." He lay back, exhausted, eyes shut.

All the joy left Roxanne's face. So did the color. White and drawn, she stared down at him, this man she loved more than all the world's gold.

Rhodes had made that terrible journey, had come to Nome *not to save her but to kill her*. Silently she stared at him, and then she covered her face with her hands and sobs rocked her body.

Oh, she had done her work well. She had made him hate her. There was no bright future for her with Rhodes. If she had thought him lost to her on the Yukon; now, in Nome, she knew it to be true.

After that she tended Rhodes as lovingly as ever, perhaps a bit more desperately, for she knew that when the fever broke he would try to revenge himself on her. At the very least, he would send her away. So, grieving, she looked out the tiny slit of window at the wheels of light that were a feature of this strange landscape. She stared at these wonders without seeing them, listening to Rhodes's feverish ravings. When the aurora was a high golden glow outside her window, she kissed him and tasted the salt of her tears on her mouth.

She knew that she was kissing him good-bye.

Soon after that, the doctor assured Roxanne that Rhodes was mending, even though he seemed barely aware of what was going on around him.

When she was not caring for Rhodes, Roxanne passed the time downstairs in the plush Victorian parlor with Josie and the girls.

"This here's Roxie," Josie had introduced her. "She's a lady. So mind your language when she's around."

"I just don't understand you, Rox," Josie puzzled one day as they all lounged around the front room in various stages of dress and undress. Yukon Cassie was playing solitaire on a pine table that struck a rude note in this luxury, but the rest were gathered around a marble topped table set on a handsome oriental rug, drinking tea or whiskey or gin according to their tastes.

Roxanne put down her teacup and looked at Josie a little sadly. "There's nothing to understand, Josie. I followed my husband up here, and now he's dead. That's all."

"You ain't the type to be here," insisted Josie. "You with those clear blue eyes that look right through a man and make him want to do right by you."

"I was never after gold," admitted Roxanne.

"Then why the hell *are* you here?" wondered Josie, giving her bronze taffeta skirts a shake and adjusting an ornate pin that held her orange boa in place. "I could understand your being lured to the Klondike, but why *this* godforsaken place? Why Nome?"

"Denby—my husband—changed our tickets without telling me," admitted Roxanne.

"So you was bamboozled into it by a man." Josie nodded with understanding.

"Like the way I got into this business in Duluth," drawled a whiskey-voice, and Roxanne turned to acknowledge the voluptuous strawberry blond in a transparent pink combination who lounged in an overstuffed chair. "A psalm-singing loud-mouthed praying—"

"Shut up, Flossie," Josie told the Titian beauty. "Can't you see I'm trying to understand how a lady's mind works? Who knows but what I might want to be one myself sometime."

"Works the same as ours," said a black-eyed Mexican girl, whose big gold earrings dangled against her creamy satin skin and gleaming long black hair, and whose silken negligee was open to display a lithe naked body underneath. "Only maybe," she added, laughing, "not so good, eh, *chiquita*?"

Her laughter was joined by that of a French girl wearing high heels, silk stockings held by black garters, and a lacy shawl through which her pink skin glowed.

Josie frowned to silence them both. "Rox, you bring in this fellow who lit out after you in a dogsled—you bring him in half dead and you're all broke up, and then the doctor tells you he's goin' to live and your eyes light up like stars, but now the fellow's gonna come to any day and you're all downhearted again."

"I'm a fool," said Roxanne sadly. "I just remembered it, and it's made me sad."

The girls looked at each other. If this was being a lady, give them a life of sin any day.

No one, not Roxanne, Josie or the girls had been given a clue that the young newspaper reporter for the New York paper had been busy "researching" again. After Roxanne's dramatic return to Nome, he had made swift inquiries and discovered that she had set out with her husband and another man, but had returned from the white wilds of the north with yet a third. To the reporter the situation was more than clear. Roxanne had undoubtedly plotted with her lover to dispose of Denby and Lars had been caught in the crossfire; then she had brought her wounded lover back to Nome. Roxanne, to the reporter's overheated imagination, was clearly a murderess.

At last, he sat down to write his article.

"Her name is currently Roxanne Barrington," he wrote. "No one knows what it was before that. She is blond, blue-eyed, beautiful beyond belief. She has a fake Southern accent, but all indications are that she hails from Seattle. A reputable source says she killed a woman in the States, a certain Mary Willis, but was never tried for the crime. Arriving in Dawson City in the spring of 1898, she promptly became notorious as 'the Dawson blond,' but I prefer to call her 'Klondike Roxie.' In Nome she fraternized with the lowest types, and her flashing skirts and pretty legs could be seen—yes, and danced with any night for a dollar—at Big Mike's. But deadly Klondike Roxie has now made another kill—her husband, Denby Barrington, a man of the shadows, and perhaps his friend Lars Nelgren, one of Nome's stalwart citizens. Although the three of them started out together by dogsled over the barren icy hills, only Klondike Roxie returned. She arrived weeping, in the company of a wounded man reputed to be her lover, one Rhodes Coulter, said to have pursued her from Dawson City. Since her return, Klondike Roxie has retired with her lover into the infamous establishment of a certain Madam J——, Nome's plushiest sporting house."

The article concluded, "Watch this paper for the next episode in the scandalous affairs of Klondike Roxie." It reached the telegraph by dogsled. It was yellow journalism at its worst, but so the legend of Klondike Roxie was born.

It made sensational reading in the States as well as the Klondike. It was picked up by the wire services and printed across the nation.

Among those who read the article was Leighton Clarke.

Chapter 30

The ice broke early on the Bering Sea that year of 1900. An old whaler was the first to penetrate the ice barrier that shut Nome off from the world. Not long after that, a ship reputed to be filled with people from Dawson arrived. Since almost everybody in Nome had friends in Dawson, most of Nome's population turned out to greet the ship. Roxanne, like the rest, came down to the dark beach sands, hoping to see someone she knew. Her expression was somber, as she watched the ship approach. How she wished she could leave on that vessel, so that she would not have to face Rhodes when he was fully recovered. Twice already his green eyes had opened and he had looked at her for a moment as if he knew her, then he had slipped back into a sleep-like state. He was mending nicely, the doctor said, not realizing that to Roxanne "mending" meant she must give him up.

So it was with a serious face that she stood on the dark beach alongside fancy women with their big leg-o'-mutton sleeves and gaudy dresses, and hip-booted miners staring out to sea. As Roxanne watched, surrounded by almost the entire population of Nome, she saw the ship cast anchor off the ice pack, saw a crewman jump onto an ice floe. They watched him approach, probing with a long pole through the ice to find a path for the smaller landing craft that followed.

When the first small craft, filled with exuberant passengers, landed, a general cheer went up from the beach. Roxanne, peering at the men who waded ashore in the icy water, shouted out her own cheer. For there, sloshing toward her, looking just as he had in Dawson, was a golden giant with smiling blue eyes—Leighton Clarke.

She fought her way through the crowded beach toward him. He was easy to find—he was taller than anybody else. Then Leighton saw her and moved purposefully through the throng.

"Roxanne," he yelled over the heads of people standing between them, "I heard about Denby's death in Dawson, and I came as soon as the ice broke."

"You . . . heard?" She looked at him blankly.

They had to shout over the din.

"It was in the papers. Dawson's got a telegraph office now, telephone, three newspapers, churches, banks. It's one of the biggest Canadian cities west of Winnepeg."

Roxanne looked up at him, her eyes brimming. She didn't care about Dawson's surging growth; returned to her was the lovely golden giant she'd missed so much. When Leighton managed to edge by the obstructing crowd, she threw herself into his arms.

"Oh, Leighton," she cried out of the hurt in her heart, "I'm so glad you've come."

His strong arms enfolded her. "There, there, Roxanne," he soothed her gently. "There's nothing to cry about. I'm here now. I'm going to take care of you."

Against his big chest she found release for all those pent-up tears she had not shed. She sobbed and sobbed as he held her, soothed her, amid the jostling crowd.

"You'll forget, Roxanne," he told her earnestly. "In time you'll forget him." He could not know that it was not for Denby but for Rhodes she wept. Leighton was so good. Her soft body sagged against him until her sobs were stilled, and then she dried her eyes and looked up at him trustingly. In that moment, as their eyes met, they melted together as one.

That look was an acknowledgment that since Denby no longer stood in the way, they could become lovers.

Another ship was due to leave later in the day. It would be carrying little but passengers—some of them lucky miners laden down with gold, bent on rollicking home to the States to spend their fortunes. When the ship left for Seattle, Roxanne and Leighton would be sailing with her.

With Leighton, Roxanne went back to Josie's to see Rhodes one last time. Having left Leighton downstairs in the front room talking to the girls, she passed the doctor leaving as she went up. Rhodes was better, the doctor said cheerfully. Soon he'd be talking to her good as new. Roxanne winced. Where Rhodes was concerned, she was a coward. She didn't want him talking to her. She didn't want to hear the things he'd say, didn't want to face the stormy accusation in his green eyes. She looked down at him lying asleep in the bed, planted a last wistful kiss on his forehead, and fled. She didn't want to be there when he woke up.

In the hall outside his door she ran into Josie, resplendent in black lace and magenta taffeta. "I meant to work and get money to pay you for keeping Rhodes and me here, Josie," she choked. "But now I'm leaving Nome. I've got a friend waiting downstairs. I could borrow money from him to pay you now, or I could send you—"

"Ain't no call to give me money, Rox," said Josie briskly. "I've enjoyed havin' you around. And anyway, I promised Case back in Dawson if I ever ran across you, I'd look out for you."

"You didn't tell me that you and Case were friends."

Josie nodded emphatically. "We'd have come to

Alaska on the same boat, but I found there wasn't room for my girls, so I had to take a later one."

Roxanne's eyes widened. "*You* were the madam he got out of jail?"

"Sure as hell was," said Josie with feeling. "I owe Case a lot."

"So do I," said Roxanne sadly.

"But what's this about you leavin' Nome, Rox?"

"Yes," Roxanne sighed. "With Leighton, the man who's waiting for me downstairs, Josie. On the ship that leaves today."

"Why are you runnin' away?" demanded Josie, bewildered. "The way you looked when you dragged this Rhodes fellow in, the wild way you acted when you thought he might die, I figgered you and he—" She broke off, studying Roxanne's set white face. "Someone's bound to tell Rhodes you left Nome with another man," she warned.

"He won't care," said Roxanne, her voice bleak. "It's what he expects of me. He'll tell you that."

Josie peered sharply at her. "Rox, you sure ain't what people say you are."

"Neither are you, Josie." Impulsively, Roxanne hugged that magenta taffeta figure. "Oh, Josie, take good care of him for me, won't you?"

"Well, I must admit he looks to be the kind of man I'd like to have around the house," grinned Josie. "Not that he'll stay long after he's up and about. He'll be hot-footin' it after you again!"

"No," sighed Roxanne. "Never again. Though he's fair-minded and this time he'll say we're even . . . I'll never see him again, Josie." Her eyes filled with tears and she could not speak. With a wave, she hurried downstairs to where Leighton was waiting. She found him seated on Josie's red plush sofa talking to doll-faced Tiger Lil in what sounded like Chinese. The girl's limpid oriental eyes were very animated, and she moved her shoulders expressively as she talked, so that her red silk negligee fell away from the golden skin of her firm round breasts. Josie, who had followed Roxanne down the stairs, frowned at

Tiger Lil and jerked her head toward the door. With an angry look, the Chinese girl jumped up, her red silk negligee swishing, and went out a door, banging it.

Leighton rose to greet Roxanne, but his smiling gaze followed the Chinese girl's retreat. "I must say you have interesting friends," he murmured to Josie.

Roxanne said in a teary voice, "Come on, we have a boat to catch, remember?" and took her broken heart into the street. Josie's "Good luck, Rox—but I think you're makin' a mistake" followed her as they trudged past the saloons, down to the shore and the waiting ship.

Book III

The Adventuress

Part One:

The Departure

Chapter 31

Roxanne stood by the rail beside Leighton and watched the dark sands and the lights of the tent-and-driftwood city that was Nome slip away behind them. Past chunks of ice in the dark northern sea they glided as the steamer struck out for Seattle, for the States, for home. In silence, Roxanne looked back and saw Alaska receding. She would always remember it as a land of crystal white, beautiful and dangerous, a land of snow and ice and gold and heartbreak.

There was a new hardness in her eyes. She had lost Rhodes, lost him as surely as if he were dead—lost him not once but twice. It made her see the world in a different light. But Denby was gone too. She no longer had to look out for him. She would make her own way.

She had come to Alaska a wife, hoping somehow to resurrect her battered marriage. She left it a widow in the prime of her beauty.

She had come to Alaska still hopeful that life had

something to offer her. She left it an adventuress, determined to take what she wanted.

Night had fallen, and as the steamer moved across Norton Sound into the cold waters of the Bering Sea, Roxanne brooded over those distant lights of Nome reflected in the dark, almost still water across the ice floes.

The Alaskan venture was over; Dawson and Nome lay behind her. With Leighton she would sail to warmer seas. Of the men who had loved her, one lay dead in an icy crevasse, one was headed back to the Kansas prairies, one was dealing out the cards in self-imposed exile in Dawson, and one, the most important one of all, was recovering—his broken head and body slowly mending—in the raw boom town of Nome. She had brought none of them luck, she thought, but she would be good for Leighton, that much she promised herself. She would do her golden giant no harm.

There in the cold sea air, they stood at the rail watching the northern lights. A great aurora spanned the heavens like giant, shimmering blue curtains. It was a breathtaking sight.

Roxanne lifted her chin and looked up at the aurora, suspended majestically above them. Those shimmering blue curtains were opening for her. The next act of the drama of her life was about to begin.

She turned to look at Leighton, standing possessively beside her. She was his now. His woman. Neither of them had spoken of marriage, both had understood the way it would be.

Her face softened as she remembered how tenderly the big blond giant had cared for her and Denby during the dangerous crossing of the Chilkoot Pass and the wild journey from the high lakes down the upper Yukon to Dawson City. And how he had kept their spirits up that first terrible winter frozen in at Fort Yukon, had fed them with the wild game he had shot.

And now Denby was gone and she was his. Leighton's. She remembered big Marge saying wisely that

Leighton had gone up the Koyukuk "trying to get over you." Marge had known Leighton loved her, even when she herself had not been sure. In his arms she would find solace and comfort for her battered heart.

Leighton suggested that it was growing late, and they started below deck. But Roxanne stopped, murmuring, "Wait for me in my cabin—there's something I must do first," and hurried back to the rail. Slipping off the narrow band of gold that had shackled her to Denby, she dropped it over the side of the ship. The ring sparkled for a moment as it fell, then sank into the dark sea. Roxanne sighed. She did not need a ring to remember Denby; she would forget the bad times and remember only that his was the young intense voice that had once said, *I don't care what your name is or what you've done—I love you anyway.* She smiled and her eyes frosted over with tears as she thought of the young Denby who had known her for what she was and loved her anyway.

The chill wind from the ice dried her tears. Steady now, she lifted her head and went on down to meet her new lover.

She found him waiting in her cabin. He was pacing about, golden head bent, arms behind his back, deep in thought. As she opened the door, he looked up and an anxious frown passed across his usually calm face.

"Roxanne," he said abruptly, "there is something I must tell you. First."

Roxanne sighed. She was not in any mood for confessions. She had need of a strong shoulder to lean against, soft murmurings to comfort her. But she crossed the room and stood before him, looking up into his face, listening.

"I must tell you that I can never marry you, Roxanne. I'm already married."

A wife! Leighton had a wife! Roxanne sank to a chair and stared at him. Somehow she had not expected that from innocent Leighton.

"Her name is Allison. We are separated. I met her

long ago, loved her long ago. She was a part of my youth, Roxanne. In Washington. Her family lived near mine in the Georgetown section near Dumbarton Oaks. After we married we lived in different parts of the world, wherever my father was stationed. But Allison was ambitious—God help me, I never was. She thought I was throwing away my life. She had dreams of my becoming Ambassador to the Court of St. James—impossible dreams. I disappointed her. When we returned home to Georgetown, she took to seeing other men. I knew about them, but I closed my eyes. Then one night she did not come home at all. She had run away with her lover. I drifted to the West Coast and then to the Klondike. Now you know all about me."

As if once he had started, he had to keep talking, Leighton continued. "She's still a little girl, Roxanne. Charming, spoiled—she never really grew up. She has soft brown hair and trusting gray eyes and the sweetest smile—I could never stand up before that smile; it always rocked me. Whatever she wanted I was willing to do. But becoming Ambassador to England was beyond my grasp—and that was what she really wanted."

Roxanne gave him a slightly crooked smile. In his heart Leighton was shackled to someone else—just as she in her heart was shackled to Rhodes. It was fair, she supposed, but it was a blow too.

"It doesn't matter," she said quietly. And then with a slight frown, "I suppose you've never considered divorce?"

His voice was muffled and he kept his head averted, but she could see a vein throb in his neck. "It would be like divorcing my right arm. Allison is part of me . . . even if I never see her again."

Ruefully, she understood. In silence she leaned over and unbuttoned her shoes, kicked them off and leaned over to remove her garters and stockings. Leighton could hear the silk rasp against her elegant legs, but he did not turn to watch her. Perhaps the talk of Allison had made him feel shy.

She stood up. "These hooks down the back of my dress, I can't manage them alone." It wasn't true, but it would bring him closer. She could no longer bear the subject of Allison.

Obediently he came to her and worked on the hooks, fumbling with them awkwardly. As the last one came free, Roxanne shrugged the dress off and tossed it on a chair. As she stood in her petticoat, her back to Leighton, she felt his big hands close over the bare skin of her shoulders, felt his touch tinglingly. Very gently he turned her around to face him, lifted her up with an easy gesture and sat down with her on his lap, burying his face in her blond hair.

"Thank you, Roxanne. For understanding." His voice was humble.

She ran her fingers through his hair, thick and golden. "I'm a realist, Leighton," she said with a sigh. It might not be true, but she hoped it was. "I think we'll be happier together than apart."

He lifted his head and smiled down at her. Once again he was the steady blue-eyed giant who had guided them down the wild rivers. "I know it's very soon after—but . . . I have wanted you for so long," he said and bent down and kissed her parted mouth. Roxanne snuggled against him. He thought he was comforting her for Denby's death, she knew. But it was the loss of Rhodes for which she needed to be comforted—Rhodes, who had walked across her heart in dusty boots and left an indelible mark. But she would not tell Leighton that. Her good golden giant must think her only a grieving widow who had endured scarring experiences in the Alaskan wilds.

Pensively, she let him ease her out of her petticoat and combination, so that she sat on his lap nude, her elegant legs dangling against his trouser legs. His expression was blissful, and his big gentle hands stroked her all over. She felt almost inclined to purr, so warm and enveloping were his strong arms, so resilient the big shoulder on which she leaned. In those arms it would be easy to relax, to seek love, to drowse off and dream.

But, as she rested against his deep chest, quiet and docile under his exploring touch, her breath came raggedly faster. Always tinder to the match, her body responded to him, gave him back for each caress its sweet promises of passion. Feeling her response, his arms gripped her more firmly and his lips moved with urgency, trailing down her neck and down the tingling column of her spine, until she turned her torso about and pulled his face against her own and murmured little broken phrases from the language of love. He might have taken her in that fiery instant, but there was a quietude to Leighton's lovemaking that night, the gentleness of touching loved things that made him unique in her brief experience. Only once did he reveal the triumph that must be roaring through his veins—and that was when he rose, scooping her up as he did so and, lifting her naked form lightly, tossed her exuberantly in the air. He caught her as gently as one might a baby and bore her to the softness of the big bunk.

He stood studying her loveliness with smiling eyes for a moment. Then, with a shyness Roxanne found appealing, he took off his clothes and joined her in the bunk. He had taken a long time about it. She wondered if Allison had ever felt impatient.

But once those steely arms had closed around her, all impatience was at end. Tenderly, possessively, with charm and grace, Leighton took her to him, melded her body to his own. Smoothly, lovingly he made her his, cradling her so that his weight rested upon his own encircling arms, and only the sensuous length of his big form moved against her, within her. Desires rising, she wound her arms about his neck to draw him closer, heard her own breath sob in her throat as his naked passions drove him fiercely onward, and she, too, was borne on wings of pleasure to heights that rivaled the aurora. Eyes closed, she seemed to float and drift and soar in ecstasy. Finally, gently, she came to earth in Leighton's arms.

Still lying in those arms—lazy arms now, with gentle hands that savored her body, lingering, urging—she felt that she had found the enfolding arms that would shut out the world. They were the arms that would heal the wounds life had given her. Those hands, which caressed her fiery body so gently, would take her own trembling hand and lead her into a happier golden land. Beside Leighton she would walk proudly.

"I wish I had known you long ago," she sighed and snuggled against his powerful naked chest.

"And what would have been so different?" he asked, stroking her long blond hair.

"If I had married you instead of Denby," she smiled, "you'd have appreciated me."

"You know," he said meditatively, "I was always afraid to make love to Allison. She was so little, so fragile, I was afraid I'd hurt her. With you it's different."

She moved restlessly beneath him. Allison . . . Of course, it was too much to hope that the ghost of Allison was exorcised.

"You're very good for me, Roxanne," he said humbly. "I'm very grateful."

She moved again beneath him, and he slid away from her, leaned on one shoulder as she turned over on her side, the curving line of her naked back presenting itself to him. Something akin to jealousy beat in her breast. She didn't want him to be grateful, she wanted him to love her. Consummately. Passionately. She wanted him to make her love him by sheer force of will . . . so she could forget. . . .

She realized that that was unfair. So, when he said, "You're so lovely," his voice muffled as he planted a kiss on the satiny shoulder that rose in a soft impish mound toward him, she turned to face him, eyes wide and luminous.

"I'm glad, Leighton," she said softly. "I want to be lovely for you—and to make you happy."

The glow on his face rewarded her simple gesture as he pulled her to him. Luxuriously, savoring each moment, they made love again. In wonder, Roxanne shared his joy. She realized that she represented a loved pet, to him, a joyous plaything, to be humored and cared for and cherished. For a woman who had struggled through four years of a hellish marriage, and who had endured all the travails of the Klondike and Nome, it was a bewildering and delightful experience.

At last, he eased away from her and she turned to look at him affectionately. His huge body was stretched out, his feet hanging over the edge of the too-short bunk. Her head pillowed on his muscular shoulder, she considered his mighty arms, the broad deep expanse of his chest with its light frosting of golden hair, the lean hard stomach and loins and sleek heavy-muscled limbs.

His eyes opened to regard her. "I haven't had a woman since Allison," he said. "For a long time I felt they weren't for me." He reached out a big hand and smoothed back her hair and smiled into her face, and she felt a warm glow steal over her body. "You've broken my run of bad luck, Roxanne. You've made me whole again."

Later, when he slept, Roxanne rose and went to the porthole. What had Allison wanted? she asked herself, puzzled. Ambition . . . Leighton said that was what drove Allison. But Allison had sought the arms of other men. And after tonight that seemed strange to Roxanne, for surely Leighton's lovemaking was like himself, whole-souled and ardent and warm—he was enough for any woman.

Determinedly, as the days went by, Roxanne forced herself not to think of Rhodes. She was Leighton's now. She would cleave to him.

Their steamer did not seek the path of the inland waterway down Canada's rugged coast. Instead they plowed through the drifting ice of Norton Sound and out into the cold Bering Sea. The first port they touched—in a driving rain—was Dutch Harbor on the Island of Unalaska, where the Aleutian chain began, and so into the broad Pacific on the long journey south to Seattle. On its way south their steamer also called at Vancouver Island, and it was there that Roxanne and Leighton left it.

Leighton told her, at last, about the inflammatory newspaper article in which she had been called a murderess. Law was coming fast to Nome, and he feared for her. She had been tried and convicted in the newspapers for the murder of her husband and one Lars Nelgren. Perhaps she could escape that, but there was also this business of the woman in the States, Mary Willis, that had been dredged up.

"I've killed no one," Roxanne told Leighton with a stricken look. "You know I'd never have hurt Denby. As for Mary Willis, I *did* impersonate her after her death when I needed a job so badly, but I never harmed her."

"I know you'd never harm anyone," said Leighton gently. "But we can't be too careful. Your name might be recognized in the States right now. There might be some unpleasantness."

He meant she might be jailed, tried, convicted—hanged. She drew a ragged breath and looked out at the serene blue ocean. It wasn't what you *did*, she perceived anew, it was what people *believed* you did that mattered. For that, they would bring you down.

Sadly, she realized that it also meant she must become an exile. She might never see her own country again.

Within a week, they were on their way again. They had transferred their baggage which included the glamorous new wardrobe Leighton had purchased for her in the shops of Vancouver to a ship bound across the wild reaches of the Pacific. They steamed toward the sunset and that lovely gateway to the mysterious Far East, lying midway between India and China—Singapore.

She would like Singapore, Leighton predicted. A jolly town; he was well known there. He had been there with his father before he had married Allison. People there might know he was married but they had never met Allison. Roxanne was relieved to hear it, and felt a stirring of pride when she discovered that, as he had on the way south from Nome, Leighton had taken separate staterooms for their journey across the Pacific. He was protecting her reputation, she realized. Dear Leighton, she would sometimes think, Leighton, who had hurried to Nome to save her from jail or worse. Bless him for it! She would reach out to him then and hold him close.

She told herself she didn't care that he could never marry her. She asked only that he love her and be true to her. To Roxanne the difference was absolute.

During their crossing, they mixed very little with the other passengers, holding themselves aloof—from each other as well as from the general public, eating even at separate tables. And although Leighton was dignified, even courtly, in his treatment of her in public, in the privacy of her stateroom at night he was a roguish lover. Slowly, through his lovemaking she began to understand him. He was a man hurt so deeply that it had left a hole in his heart—a hole in his affections which should have been filled by a wife, children. Her own relationship with Leighton, she felt, was a healing scar tissue that eased the pain of an old wound. Sometimes on cool nights when the sea air coursed through the stateroom, he wooed her as a woman, with tenderness. At other times he played with her delightedly, roguishly, as if she were a child —until, remembering she was his mistress and belonged to him wholly, he clasped her in firm arms and took her with urgency.

It was a beautiful Pacific crossing. Calm, healing, in every way. In the private world of their stateroom she felt they were both sixteen again when Leighton gamboled with her like a kitten, and they both abandoned themselves to joy and a love as innocent as any first love.

Though under the laws of God and man Leighton belonged to another woman, to Roxanne he was husband, father, lover. In her contentment she began to feel dreamily that she was in love with him, that they could build a new life together.

Part Two:

Singapore 1900—1903

Chapter 32

Singapore was, as Leighton had predicted it would be, a constant round of gaiety, garden parties and balls for the international contingent. At the magnificent Raffles Hotel—named for the redoubtable Sir Stamford Raffles of the British East India Company—Leighton took a room for himself and a suite for Mrs. Barrington, the independent young widow with whom he had struck up an acquaintance during their voyage to the Far East.

As a beautiful and soft-spoken expatriate, vouched for in the diplomatic set by the well-liked and socially impeccable Leighton Clarke, Roxanne found herself sought after in circles that would have closed ranks and excluded her back in Baltimore. She reveled in it, and Leighton enjoyed her childlike delight at being launched into the social set. In elegant, welcoming homes she waltzed with diplomats and dignified civil servants and handsome British naval officers stationed on warships anchored nearby—for Singapore was a giant British naval base. On manicured lawns resplendent with flowers, she chatted with diplomatic wives dressed in sweeping hats and daintily patterned chiffon dresses. On cool shaded verandahs she took tea with officialdom. Her progress a triumph, Roxanne made her way beside the ever-popular Leighton with aplomb.

For his elegantly gowned blond beauty, Leighton had concocted a romantic background that was difficult for the prying to check. Child of wealthy parents whose private yacht had sunk in the Mediterranean, Roxanne had been a lonely little girl brought up in cloistered surroundings by an elderly recluse in a Southern city. She had married, briefly, tragically, and her young husband had been killed. To solace herself, she had taken this trip to the Far East and, by great good fortune, Leighton had met her—and was showing her about Singapore, a city he knew so well. Everyone accepted the story. Or if they did not, they kept quiet. For the beautiful blond with the elegant figure and sparkling sapphire eyes was welcome everywhere—as was her handsome escort.

Roxanne was enchanted when Leighton, tired of surreptitious visits to her hotel room and nervous lest this pleasant habit attract unfavorable attention, found for her a small two-story house with a balcony overlooking the sea. The rooms were large and airy with thick plastered walls painted white. Leighton kept it abloom with huge bunches of the orchids and gladiolas that abounded on the island. Daily he called for her decorously in a carriage and squired her about the city whose architecture was almost as diverse as its population: big tropical-looking houses overrun with vines, Chinese bungalows set behind waving palms, and interesting Malay houses built on stilts, as well as the more staid government buildings and shops, the handsome Raffles Hotel, and the colorful tinkling Chinatown.

Along with its other ethnic groups, including Bugis and Malays, Singapore had a burgeoning Chinese population. Roxanne had a staff of four Chinese servants for her small house, and when Leighton dined with her—which was often—they ate Cantonese food prepared by a cook who knew no English, who bowed Mandarin style whenever he saw Roxanne, and who received his instructions via a bilingual housekeeper who moved about the house on tiny bound feet conveying Roxanne's orders.

Leighton was very discreet about his visits to her. All of Singapore knew he was in love with the charming American widow, but only the shrewd guessed he was sleeping with her. Leighton's manner was impeccable as he squired her through long receiving lines at Government House, stood about with her at garden parties, introduced her to cricket matches and polo—and played croquet with her on manicured lawns. They caused heads to turn enviously, the golden giant and his golden lady, when he whirled her across the dance floors at many a ball. Attired in the lovely gowns he had bought for her in Vancouver or in the even more elegant gowns she had had made in Singapore of exotic sheer silks that came by ship from India and China, Roxanne was stunningly beautiful.

Roxanne never tired of accompanying Leighton about the sultry exotic city. From a minaret in the Sultan Mohammed Mosque on North Bridge Road near Arab Street she heard for the first time a muezzin calling the faithful to prayer. By rickshaw they visited Chinese temples with exquisite names—the Lotus Mountain Temple, the Monkey God Temple, the Temple of Heavenly Happiness. And came home to excellent meals served by the efficient Chinese servants, and to spend languorous nights in a big bed rustling with silks. Making love there, as the soft wind from the South China Sea blew across the great port city.

She felt happy with Leighton—and safe.

Leighton, she had discovered, was very wealthy. He lived on a semi-annual stipend from a trust fund left by a maternal grandmother, which was paid regularly to his bank in Singapore. Because he had starved along with them in the Klondike whenever the hunting brought no game, Roxanne had thought him poor as herself, but she now knew it was only the difficulty of receiving money in the Klondike that had held up his flow of funds. In Singapore, he spent money lavishly, purchasing for her small house handsome dark carved Chinese furniture and interesting jades and Chinese silks and sumptuous Chinese rugs that were everywhere in the city, one of the world's busiest ports.

To Roxanne it was a kind of Cinderella dream come true. Although her true relationship with Leighton was clandestine and would have shocked her well-bred preening hostesses, she was enjoying the kind of social season that would have delighted a young debutante. Sometimes she thought of Clarissa in Baltimore, with her round of parties and balls, and laughed to herself. But memories of Baltimore brought her achingly back to Rhodes, and she would stop laughing, and the pain of an old, old knife would turn again in her heart. At those moments she would hurry off to ask Leighton with a fierce gaiety about his plans for their day.

They celebrated the Chinese New Year amid jostling crowds and papier-mache dragons and exploding firecrackers. And when Leighton went tiger hunting to Johore she remained faithful, awaiting him in the house by the sea—even though roguish eyes and contemplative glances were cast at her daily by the handsome British Army and Navy officers who were ever in Singapore. Roxanne paid them no heed because, although neither law nor church had blessed it, she felt her relationship with Leighton was a marriage, and she had vowed in her restless heart to be faithful to him.

Sometimes in the big bed on nights when the sultry air was stirred by the soft winds and the silken hangings rustled at the balcony windows, she would open her eyes and find Leighton leaning over on an elbow looking at her with a gentle smile in his eyes, and she would feel a warm glow, knowing that she had made him happy. At moments, the far-off shadow of his wife Allison still haunted them, but for the most part Roxanne was optimistic. Eventually, she told herself confidently, someday lovely spirited Allison would wish to marry her lover. In far-off America Allison would divorce Leighton, and then he would be able to marry again. They would leave this jangling foreign city and return to the States. They would have a house somewhere and a brace of blond, blue-eyed children. When in her dreams she got that far, Roxanne would laugh at herself, and tell herself ruefully that today was enough.

For she had found comfort for her bruised heart in Leighton's encompassing arms and a regal yet light-hearted life by his side. For Leighton treated her with respect; he treated her as a wife.

And if he never read her the letters that reached him occasionally from Washington, if when he received them he cancelled his social engagements and shut himself in his hotel room for the better part of a day and came back to her looking grimmer and older—well, we all have things in our past, she counseled herself. Leighton had loved his young wife too well, and the pain of her betrayal could still reach him half across the world.

Roxanne always knew when those letters came. She tried to be gentle with him then, and understanding—seeing to it that the Chinese cook prepared Leighton's favorite dinner, served his favorite wine. And after dinner, when the night wind blew cool across their balcony and rustled the light curtains, Roxanne would change into a favorite negligee of delicate blue silk from India, tissue thin. She would take him in her arms and try to make him forget, as he had helped her to forget, that other world that had hurt them both.

And always the next day he was the old Leighton, smiling, debonair, with a tenderness in his gaze that was its own reward.

They lived together in Singapore more than two wonderful years, years in which Roxanne could almost believe she had never been unhappy, never been poor. With Leighton beside her, she skimmed the surface of life. All was glitter with no looming tomorrow.

The blow, when it fell, caught her unaware.

Leighton, who had planned to take her to an afternoon cricket match, sent word that something had come up and he would be along later. Roxanne shrugged and waited. She waited all afternoon, through a dinner that congealed on the table. At last she heard a creak as the front door opened to admit him, and flew downstairs to meet him in the cool shadowy downstairs hall. She thought he looked tired and hastened to take his hat before the servant could.

"It's too hot for all this running about," she said, lovingly smoothing back the golden hair from his damp forehead. "Remember only the mad go out in the noonday sun—and from the look of you, you've been out all day!" She preened a little, displaying her lovely bustline through the shimmering jade silk. of her negligee. "I've had a bath and a lovely nap while I waited. . . ." She gazed provocatively up at him through her lashes and took his hand to lead him upstairs.

"Roxanne." His voice stayed her, and a spasm of pain crossed his face. "Send the servants away."

She clapped her hands, heard a door close, and looked at him wonderingly, for the first time feeling alarm. He reached into his pocket and pulled out a letter, changed his mind and put it back. His expression was irresolute. Her alarm grew. Something was very wrong . . . he was looking at her queerly.

Tension mounted inside her as she waited.

"I've got to go back, Roxanne." His voice rang loud and harsh in the shadowed hall.

"Back?" She was bewildered.

"To Washington. Allison has had an accident. There's been an auto smashup. *He* was driving." *He*, she guessed, was Allison's lover. "He was drunk and he hit a train. He's dead."

"And Allison?"

"She's expected to live, but she'll never walk again. Oh, God, Roxanne, she was always so bright, so active. And now—my sister writes that she won't eat, won't talk to people, keeps saying she wants to die. Nobody knows what to do. She needs me, Roxanne. She never needed me before, but she'll need me now."

Roxanne's thoughts were chaotic. Leighton's haggard face pleaded with her to understand. She looked down, past the shimmering green folds of her gown and studied the floor tiles. His desperation was a felt thing. She had no real hold on Leighton, she could not ask him to stay. Nor could she go with him. In Washington she would only be an embarrassment to him. Whatever they had had between them was over now. It was over the moment he heard his Allison needed him.

He seized her hand. His voice was anguished. "Allison—she's like a child, Roxanne, little and helpless. I *couldn't* desert her now. . . .

Relentlessly, her mind finished his sentence for him: *And you, Roxanne, are not helpless. You can stand anything. You have.* With a bleak expression, she turned away. "Of course you must go, Leighton," she heard herself say in a mechanical voice. "Of course you must." And then with a little break in her voice, "When—when are you leaving?"

"Tomorrow." He sounded drained. "I've already bought my ticket, Roxanne . . . I've deposited money to your account in the bank. It will be enough to live on, enough to take you back to the States if you want to go."

"Thank you," she murmured.

He seized her by the shoulders, turned her around to face him and stared down into her woebegone countenance. "Oh, Roxanne," he said huskily. "If I had known you first, loved you first . . ."

"I know," she said softly, bright tears glimmering on her long lashes. She had thought herself a wife, but . . . there was a real wife who had surfaced once again, a woman with a prior claim. And she, the make-believe wife, was to be cast off. Bitter tea indeed. . . . She straightened her shoulders. "Then since it's our last night," she tried to smile, "we must make the most of it. Have you eaten?"

He had not. Roxanne clapped her hands. Swiftly food was prepared—but neither of them was hungry. They sat on cushions in friendly fashion on either side of a low carved teakwood table and toyed with their food, and afterward lounged on the balcony and drank. They spent the entire evening together in misery, while Leighton—as if he owed it to her—told her the whole heartrending story of his long love affair with the reckless girl in Georgetown who had at last come to grief.

Leighton talked about Allison—but Roxanne did not hear him. She let the wind from the South China Sea blow her hair and looked out at the ocean that would take him away from her, and listened to the sound of his rich voice with its undertone of tragedy—Allison's tragedy that had seared him too. Through his tortured eyes, Roxanne could see Allison standing there, lovely and shallow and spoiled. Wanting her golden giant, but wanting other men too. Unwilling to give up a single iota of her sparkling life to make her marriage work.

Roxanne dropped her lashes to her cheeks, lest Leighton see this stark accusation in her eyes. He was blind to his Allison's faults—let it be so, now that she would never walk again. Perhaps Allison would change, perhaps she would love him now. Desperately, Roxanne hoped so. Leighton deserved love.

It was a long evening, awash with champagne. And at the end of it Leighton did not make love to her. She wished he had. Instead he kissed the top of her fair head and then, almost reverently, her lips.

"If it weren't for Allison . . ." he said.

Her sapphire eyes big and dark with suffering for them both, Roxanne nodded wordlessly. She understood. Suddenly she flung herself against him and clung to him. "I wish you all the luck," she whispered against his deep chest. "I hope Allison gets well and that everything works out for you."

The sky in the east had turned to gold and she realized they had talked all night.

Still feeling it could not be true, she dressed in the thin blue linen dress that was his favorite and set atop her fluffy pompadour a wide-brimmed straw hat topped with tulle and linen bows. In brilliant sunshine, she went with Leighton to the docks. He had already checked out of his hotel; his luggage was waiting for him at dockside. Seabirds wheeled overhead; the docks were crowded, full of strange sights and smells; and the sounds of a dozen languages swirled about them. Bending down from his great height, Leighton gravely kissed her good-bye, a lingering kiss full of sweetness . . . and gratitude for the time they had spent together. But even as he kissed her, she knew his heart and mind were elsewhere, with a woman who lay in a hospital bed and who had beckoned him back across the miles.

Roxanne drew back from him and stood quietly, back straight and head held high in the wide straw hat, and watched him ascend the gangplank. From the top he turned to wave. Roxanne swallowed and waved back. With the wind whipping her bell-like skirts and fashionable leg-o'-mutton sleeves, she stood and watched as the ship steamed away from her, watched until it was only a distant speck that disappeared across the horizon and the smudge of its smokestacks was lost in the blue cauldron of the sky.

Soberly she stared out at that empty ocean that had swallowed him up and then turned back to her rickshaw with a sigh. She had lost her golden giant. Whether Allison lived or died, she knew he would never come back to her. That part of her life was over, gone like precious jewels tucked away in a velvet box to be taken out and wept over in remembrance.

It was a sad woman who closed her dainty parasol and wended her way by rickshaw back to an empty house filled only with yesterday's flowers and impassive servants who spoke Chinese. She looked about her gloomily. She had felt herself married and now, without warning, she found herself divorced.

Chapter 33

Leighton's going did not pass unnoticed. Word was whispered around Singapore soon enough of an injured wife who had managed to call Leighton back to her bedside. Quietly Roxanne found herself dropped from the garden parties and the balls. No longer did she take tea in rose gardens with diplomatic wives. Her calls were not returned. Those on whom she called, ones whom she had thought friends, were unaccountably out. She was no longer received in polite society.

She was not without friends, of course. Men flocked around. And if Roxanne on many occasions felt the hurt of being cut dead by women with whom she had taken tea only a short time before, she refused to show it. Although she might have collapsed in her house in silent misery, this sudden ostracism stiffened her spine. Determinedly, she appeared in public, wearing her best, her brightest clothes, her most spectacular hats. Let them talk—*she* would not skulk in corners!

Soon she began to take spiteful amusement in luring

away the husbands of her former friends—even though she did not want them. She surrounded herself by men, admiring men attracted by her beauty, her sparkling wit. But her bruised heart found little solace in her newfound popularity. Many men pursued her. She had brief affairs with several of them.

The first was a British colonel who bragged about her in the officers' mess, who escorted her proudly about the city by rickshaw and squired her to such parties as Roxanne was now invited to—parties given by women who, like herself, had been dropped for various scandalous reasons, some of them mere unfortunates, some the genuine demimonde. Roxanne did not much like these parties, but they were noisy and crowded and they filled in the time before she had to go home to face an empty house—so empty without Leighton. She lost her colonel when his wife came out from Hampshire, bringing with her their two charming children.

Fiercely, Roxanne told herself she did not care. Her Chinese cook was stabbed in an altercation in the marketplace, and Roxanne got herself a new cook—an Indian one, and switched from Cantonese dishes to chutneys and curries. They were very hot, but no hotter than her burning pride. She would not give up!

During the winter, she began going out with a British civil servant, a quiet mustachioed widower who had bided his time in the hope of catching the beautiful American widow on the rebound. He squired restless Roxanne about Singapore's noisy Chinatown, with its *wayangs*, Chinese opera, puppet shows and nerve-wracking percussion musical instruments. Because he loved her too much and she was afraid she would hurt him, she brought the affair to an abrupt halt in early spring and took up with a rubber planter.

The British civil servant went back to Liverpool, and the rubber planter began to educate Roxanne by enlarging her view of the Malay Peninsula. Along with other friends, a raffish lot, he took her on excursions into the interior of Johore to see palaces and temples that seemed to her Western eyes older than time itself. Together they explored Singapore in depth. Joss Houses, even opium dens—they saw it all. But somewhere, he too had a wife, one who loved the isolation of a plantation and never came to town. To Roxanne that woman was a shadow wife, unreal. But she was made aware of her presence forcefully when the rubber planter returned to his trees and was never seen again.

A woman alone, she found herself once more at loose ends, and during the next months she played the field, refusing to ally herself with any of the interested and amorous gentlemen who found pleasure in her company. Most of them, she knew, regarded a liaison with her as something to be remembered later, reckless and romantic evenings to be recalled for the telling when they journeyed elsewhere. In officers' quarters, in men's clubs, in casinos, over cards and dice and after-dinner brandy. . . . *Ah, let me tell you about the blond I knew in Singapore*. . . . Thinking about that, her sapphire eyes hardened. At their jokes she smiled, their gifts she regarded lightly. The men who gave them were to her but ships that passed in the night and meant little to her.

Sometimes as she regarded herself in her teakwood mirror, silently gazing at her figure, clad in the light silks, the drifting organzas that suited this hot climate—a figure that was the envy of every woman in Singapore—she would ask herself why it had all turned out so badly. Why, she wondered, had her startling good looks not brought her happiness? Why on hot restless nights, did a man's face float accusingly before her so that she could find no peace.

Then, with a sigh, she would turn and give an order to her watchful servants in her worldly, throaty, sophisticated voice and get ready to go out. She was always going out. For the round of parties continued like a merry-go-round that never stopped and from which nobody ever got off—except to die. Like the others—those exiles who had begun the slow terrible slide down into the dark depths of the East—she needed parties and frivolity to raise her flagging spirits, to assure her that the final inevitable degradation was not going to happen.

At a party given by a down-at-the-heel Russian countess whose husband had long since cast her off, celebrating the Festival of the Chinese Moon, Roxanne met Jan van Vlynen, a Dutch planter from Sumatra on holiday in Singapore.

It was a breathless night, starless, with the promise of rain in the air. The French windows of the countess's living room were thrown open to the night, and from the garden outside the heavy scent of tropical flowers reached her guests. Wearing a daringly low-cut black lace dress, which exhibited the full lines of her white bosom, and the pearl necklace that had been a gift from Leighton the Christmas before, Roxanne sat on a teak and cushion sofa toying with a stemmed glass of champagne. Around her, conversation buzzed and laughter rippled as the decaying oddments of exotic Singapore—proud outpost of a British empire on which the sun never set—laughed and flirted and drank themselves into oblivion.

Beside her, his glittering eyes fixed lasciviously on her white shoulders and softly rising and falling bust, sat a cashiered Army officer who managed to swagger even when he was seated. Roxanne was only half listening to his bragging tale about having shot fifteen tigers during his recent stay in India, when she turned to see across the crowded room a deeply tanned man of medium height with dark brown hair and brown eyes. He was looking at her with the mute beseeching intensity of a drowning man grasping at a straw. As she met his gaze, that expression instantly left his face, to be replaced by a look both courteous and bland. But she had seen it for a flashing instant, that raw naked need, and she responded to it with a touch of pity.

She gave him a vivid smile of encouragement and

lifted her glass, meaning by that slight gesture to say: *Take heart. Life is not yet over for either of us.*

Taking her smile as an invitation, he came over to meet her.

Their hostess, the Russian countess, standing nearby, introduced them with an arch look. The cashiered Army officer stiffened with irritation as van Vlynen gave him only the barest of greetings and, bending, formally kissed Roxanne's hand. Immediately, the Dutchman seated himself on her other side and engaged her in conversation, to the fury of the officer. This amused Roxanne, who hated tiger-hunting and thought it too bad to see the beautiful beasts brought down to make a stuffed head or a fur rug for someone's feet. She turned an insolent white shoulder to him and concentrated on van Vlynen. After a few seething moments, the officer leaped to his feet and transferred his attentions to their hostess, a woman who was glad enough to receive them.

Roxanne hardly noticed his defection. Something about the Dutchman's weathered leather-like face held her attention. Perhaps it was the quality of his concentration; she had the odd feeling that they were alone in the room as he told her in his fluent but accented English that this hot evening was "cool compared with Sumatra" which lay directly under the equator.

Sumatra . . . Roxanne thought of steaming jungles. She asked him about it and listened attentively as he told her of his pepper plantation in the interior.

After the party, van Vlynen drove her home to her rented house in the carriage he had borrowed from his own host, a former Sumatran planter now residing in Singapore. The stars were out, brilliant against the blackness of the sky.

"I will see you again, yes?" he asked earnestly when the carriage stopped.

Roxanne, alighting with his help, smiled up at him, her eyes reflecting the brilliance of the myriad stars that floated above the city. "If you like, Mr. van Vlynen."

Before the week was out she was calling him Jan. Before the month was out—and he had overstayed his vacation in Singapore, he told her gravely—they were seen everywhere together. He brought her flowers and little gifts such as one might give a lady, not the expensive trifles that one might give a scarlet woman. She found that very sweet. As they rode through the busy port city, Jan filled her ears with stories of Sumatra—and of Amsterdam, the city of his youth. Roxanne's mind was full of tulips and windmills as they wended their way past pagodas and Chinese bungalows and huge "godowns," or warehouses filled with goods from all the countries of the world.

They attended dinner parties and balls in some of the handsome houses they passed in these drives. For although van Vlynen's credentials were not so overwhelming as Leighton's, and although aristocratic English did not receive him with open arms, he still had many friends among the wealthy planters. With a bright defiant smile, Roxanne faced the speculative gaze of the men and their wary wives, who were undoubtedly aware of her fast reputation. Beside her, a man of leather and steel, van Vlynen was impassive. His cool manner announced to all that Roxanne was a woman under his protection and therefore above reproach. Roxanne, who had suffered so many slights, found her heart softening toward the stern-eyed Dutchman.

She told herself she was tired of the tinsel merry-go-round of her existence, tired of being feted for her beauty alone by people who cared nothing for her. She was ready for the look she saw in the wiry Dutchman's eyes. But before he had time to present his proposal, Roxanne was on her way to a very different sort of liaison.

It happened on the balcony of her small house overlooking the sea. After a rather stuffy dinner party at the house of one of van Vlynen's friends, Roxanne, who had been bothered with a slight headache, had sent the Dutchman on his way when he escorted her home. Resting now, sipping a cool drink, she gazed up at the stars and tried not to think of the depressing alternatives her future promised. Half overcome by the oppressive heat and too lazy to get ready for bed, she put her glass on the floor and closed her eyes in the hot darkness.

How long she lay there she did not know, but she came awake to a large dark shape looming over her, a shape that obscured the moon. As she sprang up, opening her mouth to scream, a hand was clamped over it. Then a cloth—a sheet, perhaps—was thrown over her, and she was swept up, kicking and clawing, to be held against a hard body. She could hear padding footsteps, as her captor carried her downstairs . . . and out into the small scented garden at the rear, where she could feel the slap of the lush tropical vegetation as vines and leaves and branches brushed her; but her face, covered by the material, was pressed tightly against a thudding chest, and she could see nothing.

Stifled, fighting for air, and more frightened than she had ever been in her life, Roxanne felt consciousness slipping away. She was jolted to awareness again when she was set down in an uncomfortably cramped space. As she lay face down, whatever had been thrown over her head was loosened, and a piece of cloth was stuffed in her mouth to prevent her from screaming. Her streaming hair obscured her vision. She struck out, but a pair of arms promptly pinioned her and held her fast as some sort of wheeled vehicle took her and her captor away.

Part Three:

The Indian Ocean
1903—1904

Chapter 34

They were moving through the water; she could tell.

Pirates, she thought, half-fainting. *I've been abducted by the Chinese pirates everybody talks about!*

She felt herself being carried up the side of a ship and heaved over the rail. Then she was taken across the deck, a door opened, and she was tossed onto the softness of a bunk. And left there, face down, bound and gagged in the darkness as the door closed behind her. Weakly she struggled for air. Around her she could hear the creaking of a ship, feel its motions as its sails took the wind. They were bound for somewhere, God knew where, on a sailing vessel. In silent terror, Roxanne prayed.

A great deal of time passed and she had the feeling they must be far out at sea.

Although she was bound and turned so that she could not see the door, the shaft of moonlight that came into the cabin when it opened showed her a man's shadow on the wall. Then the door closed, and there was darkness again until a lamp flared up. Footsteps padded over to her. She was untied and ungagged, and she heard her kidnapper step back away from her.

Like some proud, fierce animal at bay, Roxanne sprang up and whirled to face her captor.

She stopped to stare in disbelief. Before her stood the man for whom she had daily yearned.

"Rhodes," she gasped.

Standing at ease, wearing crumpled white linen trousers and a white shirt that had seen better days, Rhodes still presented a daunting figure. Intent, amused, he studied her. "Who were you expecting?"

"Chinese pirates," she whispered. Suddenly weak, she leaned her trembling legs against the bunk.

The smile that spread across his lean dark face was not a pleasant one. "Perhaps you'd prefer them in the long run," he murmured.

She peered at him: at that well-loved, square-jawed face, so taciturn and deeply tanned and with a careless growth of dark beard; at his handsome frame, so strong and sinewy; at the gleaming dark hair that looked as if he didn't cut it, but rather hacked it off; at the eyes . . . especially at the eyes. Looking back at her, they were murky as a stormy green sea breaking across the deck. Windows of hell, she thought, staring into his haggard face.

She cast a quick look around her. She recognized the cabin. "We're aboard the *Virginia Lass*!"

His smile was thin. "The same," he said in a hard offhand tone. "Although I had thought to rename her *Delilah* in your honor."

Roxanne did not like the look in his eyes. Slowly she straightened. "What—what do you intend doing with me, Rhodes?"

He laughed. It was not the laugh she remembered. Looking into that handsome weathered face, with the grim lines overlaying the boyish lighthearted ones, she realized how thoroughly she must have destroyed his feelings for her.

"Do with you?" He drawled as he sat down on

the corner of a ship's table. "Why, I intend to enjoy you, Roxanne, as a man should enjoy you. And after that . . ." He shrugged.

She moistened her lips. "And after that?" she asked steadily.

"Why, then I may sell you to Yen Chiang or some of his friends. They'll give me a good price for you. Now or later."

Yen Chiang . . . . she shuddered. Yen Chiang was the most notorious of the Chinese pirates that infested the South China Sea and the Indian Ocean. With an effort she kept her face under control. Her eyes were as expressionless as his, but less hellish.

"Perhaps I would prefer Yen Chiang to you," she said coldly.

"Perhaps," he said indifferently. "But the choice is not yours to make."

Cold, so cold, she thought. So different from the old laughing Rhodes she had known. This was the bitter man who had come to Nome, hunting her. The man who had followed her out across the barren wastes of ice not to save her but to kill her. He had saved her there only because he wanted the pleasure of killing her himself. And now . . . he planned another kind of retribution. She had thought that by nursing him through his fever in Nome, she might have won some measure of forgiveness, but obviously, he had not forgiven her.

"How can you do this to me?" she demanded. "I saved your life when Lars shot you!"

"Oh, I heard about that," he drawled. "They told me about it at the same time they mentioned you'd run off with another man. I suppose he brought you to Singapore. He's said to have money. Bright lights, parties, men to entertain you—that's your style."

Her teeth closed with a snap. "They'll hang you," she said, her voice low and deadly. "You know that, don't you? Kidnapping a white woman just isn't done —even in this godforsaken part of the world."

He shrugged. "Life is not so dear to me I wouldn't

risk it for what I want," he declared coolly.

As the force of that hit her, Roxanne swayed on her feet for a moment. "I should have left you to die in Nome!" she cried.

He gave her a bleak bitter smile. "But you didn't. That was your mistake."

Facing his taunts, she felt her blood boil with what she thought was fury, but might also have been fear. Did he really think she would stand for this? To be used like this? Sold to Chinese pirates, bandied about from man to man?"

That indignity at least she would not endure! Life was no longer dear to him. Well, it was not dear to her either. Half-blinded by tears and rage, she darted past him and ran from the cabin up to the deck. She would have hurled herself over the rail into the shark-infested waters, if Rhodes had not come up behind and, grasping her roughly, swung her about and dragged her back down to the cabin.

He held her shoulders in a grip that hurt. She could almost feel the triumph in him. "Did you think I would let you escape so easily?" he demanded, and his hard face above her broke into a wolfish grin. "I'll lash you to the bunk if I must. But you'll stay with me, Roxanne, as long as I wish it."

Angrily, she struck at that wolfish smile, and he bent her backwards and kissed her wet face. His lips clamped over hers as he silenced her mouth with his own. Not letting go of her, he withdrew his mouth and smiled nastily down at her. "A willing woman is a delight to any man," he said.

In white fury, she sank her teeth into his wrist. He cuffed her lightly, but hard enough that her head snapped back. "You will learn manners," he said, "Or I will teach them to you. The choice is yours."

Roxanne stood staring at him until there was a discreet knock and the door opened. A Malay boy clad only in torn white trousers slid into the room. Giving them both a curious look, he pulled a large metal tub of water into the cabin, and left. When the boy was gone, Rhodes released Roxanne.

"What's this . . . this tub?" Roxanne faltered.

"Your bath," Rhodes explained. "In this damned heat, you should be grateful for it. Undress and climb in."

"Then leave first!" she cried. "I won't bathe with you here."

"You'll bathe when I say—and where I say." His voice had a cutting edge to it.

"It's your tub, your bath—*you* use it!"

"I've had my bath on deck, thanks. This is for you. I choose to sit here and watch you take it. If you don't undress immediately—" he rose threateningly to his feet. "I'll rip the clothes from your back."

She winced. These were her only clothes. Still . . . anger and pride bade her defy him.

"I will not," she said, her face white.

With an oath, he sprang across the room and seized her. As she fought him, his impatient hands began systematically stripping the clothing from her body. She struck at him wildly, but he pinioned her arms behind her. Ignoring her flailing legs that kicked at him, he tore off her dress and flung it aside.

"You were not always a savage!" she cried.

"I am what you and the Coulters have made me," he said.

"But *you* are a Coulter," she panted.

"Not in truth, and you know it." His voice was grim. "Gavin was right. My fair maid of a mother *did* cuckold Joab Coulter—and so she should have—and I'm the result of it." He jerked the fabric from her shoulders so that her soft breasts were bared to his view. Roxanne winced. A moment later, with another yank he swept her up and pulled the rest of her underthings down around her hips and off her kicking legs.

She stood naked and panting before him, her bright hair tumbled, clad only in a pair of silk stockings and garters and her high-heeled shoes. "Faith, I like you like this," he observed coolly. "As far as I'm concerned, you can take your bath in your shoes and stockings."

With an angry exclamation, Roxanne turned her back and tugged off her own garters and stockings. She was spine-tinglingly conscious of Rhodes's eyes boring into her naked back, but—these were her only stockings. The memory of his ungentle hands upon her was vivid. Her whole body flushing pink at his critical inspection of its trim profile, her outthrust breasts only partially concealed by her slender arms—she stepped into the water and sank gratefully into it, slumping down so that only her white knees and whiter shoulders could be seen above the water line.

Rhodes, coming to stand over her, dropped a sponge and a bar of soap into her hands. "Would you like me to wash your back?"

For an answer, she threw the soap at him, which he gravely retrieved and tossed back to her, then resumed his seat on the edge of the table.

It was a very long bath. The water had cooled before Roxanne, feeling almost shriveled, decided enough was enough. The imperturbable Rhodes was regarding her through half-shut eyes. Plainly he would outstay her.

"I would like a towel," she said irritably.

He rose and tossed her one. Clutching the small inadequate towel around her, she stood dripping in the tub, her long white legs gleaming and wet.

"Come here," he said, and something in his voice had softened.

"No," she said, glaring at him. And then defensively, "I'm all wet."

His voice hardened. "Wet or dry, you belong to me. Come here."

Something dangerous in the green eyes that considered her so sternly made her move sullenly toward him, barefoot and dripping. He reached out and took the towel from her. She suffered him to do it, half afraid and half mesmerized by the look he gave her. She could not fathom it.

Methodically, he began to towel her soft body. She gave him an affronted look, and he laughed, spinning her about so that he could dry her back. She felt the towel rasp along her spine, felt her muscles contract sharply as, slowly, he toweled dry her buttocks, her inner thighs and ran the towel down her legs. Then he spun her around again and gently toweled her breasts and stomach as she trembled at his touch.

Tossing the wet towel from him, he laughed down at her.

"Now we've washed the touch of other men from you at last," he said, "and you're ready for me."

She backed away.

"Odd you should be so lovely," he murmured. "It's enough to make me believe in Joab Coulter's devils, sent to earth to tempt men. But you've little cause to worry, Roxanne. I'm sure you'll land on your feet wherever there are men to be deceived."

His words, heavy with irony, lashed at her, but she stood up stiff and straight and returned his gaze scornfully. Whatever he did with her, he would not find her a coward.

"I never deceived you, Rhodes."

"Oh, no?" There was almost pleasure in his smile as he advanced upon her, towered over her slight arrogant figure, lovely in its nakedness. Suddenly he reached down and tilted up her chin so that her gasping parted lips were close to his own. "Lovely, lying lips," he murmured. "Hard to believe you arranged to have me rolled and half killed in a Dawson alley."

She started to object, but he said, "Doesn't your consciousness ever bother you when you ruin a man, Roxanne?"

"Have I ruined so many?" she asked bitterly.

"All the poor fools who loved you, I've no doubt," he said, and his lips followed his fingers, nuzzling, tumbling that delicate pink nipple this way and that way with his tongue.

Roxanne looked up at the ceiling and steeled herself. With savage determination, she tried to make her body stiff, unyielding. Felt fierce anger at her body's rippling betrayal as, in spite of herself, she quivered to his touch. This was the man she had yearned for so long, so long . . . and now he was going to take her—without love. The thought screamed through her brain.

"You can't!" Despair forced out the words as she made a last desperate effort to twist away from him.

"Can't?" His voice was lazy, amused.

"No," she cried raggedly. "It's wrong—because you don't love me!"

"Roxanne," he said softly, "what would you know of love?"

He tired of the game then, and his hands tightened around her slender waist. Suddenly, she was wrenched up in his strong arms, held so that she was looking directly into his eyes—and what she saw there chilled her. After a moment, he carried her over to the bunk, and flung her down upon it.

Silently, Roxanne studied the savage grace with which he moved until he stood naked before her. Shoulders and chest deeply bronzed, contrasting with the paler skin of his muscular hips and thighs, Rhodes stood smiling down at her. It was not a pretty smile. She turned away from that smile and closed her eyes as he lowered his body onto hers.

And then—something miraculous happened. The hands that were moving over her exploringly were a lover's hands. The lips that softly probed her own were lover's lips. Rhodes's face, his manner, his voice had told her that he hated her—that he had brought her here only to punish her, but now his body, with a gentle yearning tenderness, was telling her something else. Telling her that he loved her.

His love was there in every touch, every movement: in the delicacy with which his strong hands caressed her, in the elegance of his entrance as he brushed aside her leg with a gentle hand and claimed her. In the strength and, yes, the beauty of the way he moved within her, rhythmically, pulsingly. In the exquisite way in which he led her on to passion.

Perhaps Rhodes was not a better lover than she had known before, but to her he *seemed* so. Every light touch burned her, every pressure of his lips or tongue roused in her a silken madness more violent than any she had known. Her heart beat suffocatingly. And it was all because it was Rhodes. Rhodes holding her intimately, lovingly in his arms at last.

She knew now with certainty that he had not raped her, could not have raped her that night in Baltimore. The housekeeper had not lied after all. It had been some stranger who had followed her, slipping in from the dark street and quickly out again. This magnificent lover who moved with such grace, such authority, such all-consuming fire, could never have struck her down and raped her brutally.

In his arms, Roxanne forgot Baltimore, forgot Alaska. All the other arms that had ever held her dimmed to insignificance. Something wild, something elemental was unleashed in her. A new feeling, like nothing she had ever known before, washed over her, drowned her in its reckless sweetness.

It was not sex that held her so in thrall. This was true mating—this was love. Golden and wonderful, she tasted its pleasures fully.

Wildly, she clasped him to her. Her breath sobbed in her throat as with passion and yearning she answered his kisses. She felt for a moment his surprise at the sudden unexpected heat of her response, but she did not care—she *wanted* him to know, wanted her body to speak to him as his had spoken to her, telling him with wordless abandon that she was his and only his forever. She could feel the exultation in him as he drove onward. Her whole body clung to him feverishly, wanting him with a desire greater than any she had ever imagined, until at last she reached a shivering ecstasy of joy that left her spent and unable to face him, as he lay beside her on the bunk, his lean naked body touching her own.

After a while he moved, and she stole a look at him. He was leaning on one arm, watching her keenly, a thoughtful frown upon his deeply bronzed face. "You're a very good actress, Roxanne," he said, and with a lithe movement he rose, picked up his trousers and strode naked to the door.

In blind rage Roxanne grabbed the first thing her hand landed upon—one of his boots—and flung it after his departing back. As the boot struck the door beside him, he turned with a laugh, flung down the trousers he had picked up, and sprang back toward her.

"How lovely you are—like some wild thing no man can tame," he murmured, catching her arm easily as she tried to strike him, and looking down somberly into her mutinous face.

She tried to wrench away from him, but he held her easily. "This time it won't it won't be so easy, Roxanne. Once you held me in the palm of your hand. I was younger then, and fool enough to love you." His jaw hardened. "Now I'll take what's mine —and keep on taking."

She opened her mouth to scream at him, but he swooped down and closed his mouth over hers. Warmly, suffocatingly. At his leisure he explored her mouth with his tongue. And as her body stiffened and she tried to beat at him with impoteent fists, he held her tighter so that her breasts were crushed against his chest. She could feel his strong throbbing beat of his heart.

With a sob, she felt herself giving in to him, felt those wild emotions she could not control taking over once more as he eased his big body down on the bunk and took her again.

Afterward, he straightened abruptly, leaving her panting where she lay. "Nice to know you're warm-blooded," he said coolly. "There was a time when I wasn't so sure. When you decide to get up, put this on." He reached into a chest and tossed a length of material at her. His taunting laugh echoed in her head as he picked up his trousers and strode out naked, perhaps to lie on the deck and let the hot winds of the Indian Ocean cool his long hard body.

With turmoil in her heart, Roxanne watched him go. Could she, she asked herself savagely, have been wrong about the way he took her? Could his body have lied to her? Could what she thought was love have been merely lust?

She turned over and flung herself face down in the bunk, and dry sobs wracked her beautiful body.

After a while the heat grew so oppressive she felt she could not breathe. She got up, saw that her linen dress was badly torn, and reluctantly picked up the length of cloth that Rhodes had thrown carelessly on the bunk. It appeared to be a native sarong of a lovely silky material in blue and gold—she had seen them in Singapore. She wrapped it around her, noting that it was so long that she might also have been wearing a strapless gown.

Tossing back her tumbled dark-blond hair that had long since lost its pins, she climbed up to the moonlit deck, running her fingers through her hair to comb it. The hot wind fanned her hotter cheeks, and above her, silvery white, billowed the shrouds of the familiar *Virginia Lass*. Around her, she heard the creakings of a sailing ship making way through a dark and trackless ocean. Overhead were a scattered handful of big bright stars.

Catlike, Rhodes came up beside her. He was wearing only his wrinkled white trousers; his bared chest gleamed in the pale light. "The sarong becomes you," he approved. "I bought it for you in Singapore."

She whirled about, incredulous. "You *planned* all this?"

She couldn't read his smile. "I planned it before I left Nome," he said. "But you were hard to find, Roxanne. It was luck, my running across you in Singapore. You were riding by in a rickshaw with the Dutchman. I followed you home."

"You can't keep me here, Rhodes." Her courage almost failed her.

"Why not? I can go on doing what I've been doing —a little pearling here and there, hauling a bit of copra for some fellow who has the law after him and ready money to pay for the trip. My crew's loyal to me—I can lock you in when I'm in port and only take you ashore on islands, where to be left is to die."

Her face whitened. "You've changed," she muttered.

"You haven't," he said lightly. "You're just what Gavin said you were—a pretty cheat."

Blindly, she turned to strike at him, but he caught her wrist in a grip that paralyzed her arm. "You'll control yourself on deck," he said savagely. "In front of my crew you'll present a good face, or, by God, I'll lock you in that hot cabin below decks for the whole voyage."

She swallowed, rubbing her wrist as he let her go and her sapphire eyes smoldered after him.

Chapter 35

For days they sailed across the glassy surface of the Indian Ocean, bound she knew not where. The crew, at first reticent, soon became used to her and smiled at her as she walked about. "The captain's lady" they called her, and tipped their hats respectfully. They were a motley group, bearded cutthroats, the riffraff of the islands, but it was plain they adored Rhodes.

Then on the ocean's hot face the wind left them, and they sat becalmed in muggy heat and misery. By day, Roxanne panted on deck with the rest of them. By night Rhodes claimed her in the stifling heat of the cabin, and the heat they made together was hotter than anything the tropical winds could concoct. She hated herself for surrendering to him so completely, hated herself the more because he was so cynically aware of her body's hot response to him. But there was no helping it. When he touched her, she turned to flame. At night, with his long lean body pressed to hers, all the bright veneer of civilization was stripped away. It was not the Roxanne who had danced at Government House he held in his arms, but another woman aflame with elemental passions, as timeless as Eve's. Her breath would sob in her lungs as she fought to possess him more fully. Arms twined tightly around his muscular neck, her body would move in an aching savage effort to become one with him, welded together forever in a feverish lover's embrace.

It was madness. It was passion. It was wonderful.

And all because it was Rhodes, Rhodes in her arms at last. Always afterward, when sanity returned, Rhodes would give her a cool appraising look, a cynical look that said her body was desirable and his to command, but that she had lovely, lying lips. . . .

That look would cut her to the quick, and she would turn away, telling herself she hated him. But the next time he took her, her response would be just as wild. . . .

The weather worsened. With leaden heat, the sky pressed down upon them. The burning copper sun was so hot, it seemed the very decks would melt. Overhead the sails hung limp, and the panting crew, stripped down as naked as they could with a woman aboard, cursed and quarreled and lay inert.

As Roxanne made her way topside one afternoon, to her surprise, she had trouble keeping her footing. Around her the ocean rolled in deep oily swells.

"Dirty weather around somewheres," one of the crewmen remarked ominously, and another nodded. "Heard the cap'n say the glass is falling fast."

Listless, Roxanne leaned on the rail, watching the long monotonous roll of the waves. Then with a sigh, eager to take off the sarong that clung to her skin as if pasted there, she went back down to her bunk and, naked, fell into a heavy exhausted sleep. She woke soaked with perspiration and gasping for breath. Staggering at the violent roll of the ship, she struggled back into her damp sarong and hurried topside.

For all the heat, she found the deck a flurry of

activity. Above them the canvas flapped weakly in the heavy, sultry air as the *Virginia Lass* tried to run sharply west. With a frown, she turned to ask Rhodes the reason for all this effort and saw that he was using a glass to study the rakish sails of three distant junks looming over the horizon. As she came up beside him, he handed the glass to her.

"Looks like Yen Chiang," he said grimly. Roxanne took the glass and studied the strange-looking red and yellow craft. "They aren't making much headway in this calm—but then, neither are we."

Silently, she returned the glass. In her heart she had never really believed that Rhodes meant to hand her over to Yen Chiang. "Can we outrun them, do you think?" she asked.

"Don't know. But there are three of them, so we'll have to try." He frowned. "We have more than one devil to outrun today."

She turned and, looking in the direction of his glance, saw a murky yellow haze that covered the horizon to the south.

"You know this Yen Chiang?" she asked him.

Rhodes nodded. "I had a brush with him once. I was pearling in the Sulu Sea when Yen Chiang tried to take over our outfit. We fought him off. Oh, he'll remember me. He tried to cut my head off with his sword, and I shot him. Too bad I only got his arm."

All day, amid steadily worsening swells, they played tag with the three junks. All day the storm came closer. Copper twilight found them on an ocean that seemed composed of hills and valleys. The yellow haze to the south had widened and become dense olive, a low cloud bank that hung suspended over the rocking sea.

"Look your last on the stars for a while, miss," Bevin, the first mate, told her as he came by. "For all that we're tacking away from her, that storm will be on us by morning."

Roxanne give him an uneasy look. "It looks ugly."

Bevin, who was British, nodded. "Typhoon. They're always ugly."

"You've been in them before?"

"Once. On land—not on sea. I was on a little island in the Sulu—not on the charts. One of these storms came up and damn near washed the island clean. Bent the palms double, broke them like matchsticks. Except for a rocky cliff with a cave high up, I'd not be here to tell about it."

Rhodes came up behind him. "Stop scaring the lady, Bevin. We don't need to add hysteria to our other ills."

Roxanne gave him an affronted look. "I've been in storms before."

"Not like this one, I dare say," he said grimly. "Once it strikes, I want you to stay in your cabin. Understand?"

She turned on her heel, but staggered at the pitch of the ship and had to clutch the rail. She made a zigzag way back to Rhodes's cabin and lay there on the bunk in the sweltering heat.

After a while Rhodes came down. He did not touch her. Instead he climbed into the bunk beside her and immediately fell asleep. She gave him a disgruntled look in the light of the wildly swinging lamp, turned over and went to sleep herself.

Awaking to a grayish darkness that she took to be dawn, Roxanne gasped as a table came crashing against the bunk. While she watched, startled, the cabin floor reared up at an angle, and the table that had just crashed into the bunk slid wildly across the room, along with everything else that would move, and slammed up against the opposite wall. A few moments later the floor changed angles, and everything bore down upon her and smashed violently against the bunk. Shaken, Roxanne watched as the situation repeated itself, and she made a nervous lunge for her clothes. With a minimum of bruises she managed to dress and, finally, walking uphill it seemed, made the door. At first it resisted her, then suddenly it flew open, taking her out with it into a rush of rain that battered at her as violently as if it were hail. She fought her way topside. Around her was a wild tumult, with waves crashing green across the deck. Appalled, she clung to whatever she could and watched the sea.

Out of the roar and clamor came Rhodes, soaking wet. He grasped her with rough hands and escorted her back to his cabin, where she would have gone skittering to the floor had he not held her up. "Stay—there," he shouted above the wild shriek of the wind, slammed the door shut and left her.

To avoid the gamboling furniture, Roxanne made for her bunk and clung to it, pale and frightened. She was unfamiliar with typhoons, knew only that those who had been in them spoke of them with great respect. In the next few hours she would come to understand why. As the storm's fury increased, the crash of the waves seemed every moment to threaten to smash the ship. Instead of lessening, it grew worse until she was hard put to stay in the bunk at all. With the unremitting fury of an avalanche, the storm attacked them, bore down upon them as if to bury them. She heard ominous cracking sounds, sometimes of timber splintering. Sometimes the ship seemed to lunge from the water, to rear up and fall back again sickeningly—or to strike head on into something solid. Over her head, all around her, she could hear the great seas boom as they broke green and fierce and deadly across the deck. For hours it went on—the *Virginia Lass* locked in step with a gray gale that blew rain horizontally instead of vertically and caused the men to gasp for air as they howled directions to each other.

She who had once looked up into a tornado, had had no conception of the size and power of a typhoon. Over a thousand miles it ranged, and though she could not know it, they were being sucked savagely toward the center of those whirling winds that ever increased in their fury.

Slowly, as day wore into night, came the conviction

that they could not outlive the violence of this shrieking gale. Roxanne bit her lip and held onto the bunk, and for a despairing hour wished she had told Rhodes—told him in plain words while she had the chance—that she loved him.

The storm seemed to peak to a horrendous, deafening intensity, and then of a sudden the wind stopped. Roxanne felt breathless and weighted down, but she staggered up nonetheless. Happily, the battered furniture no longer flew about. Had they come through it?

She made her way topside, almost unable to do so in the heaviness of the oppressive air which weighted her limbs and seemed bound to press her to the deck. On deck, she saw how badly the ship had been battered. Most of the shrouds were gone; a few rags still flapped disconsolately above. One of the masts had snapped off and was nowhere to be seen, lost doubtless somewhere in the Indian Ocean. She sought out Rhodes at the wheel.

"Rhodes." Her voice sounded very loud to her ears. "Is—is it over?"

He turned a haggard face to her. "No. A typhoon is a circular storm, Roxanne. We're in the center of it now."

Sucked into the center of the storm! She looked about her fearfully and saw that it was so. The *Virginia Lass* seemed to be lurching uneasily at the bottom of some deep well. Far above them a few stars lit the black water, and their weak light illuminated tall clouds that swirled and moaned in a devilish circle about them.

Once before Roxanne had looked up into a circular storm—a tornado. But this was a tornado on so vast a scale as to dwarf the imagination. Appalled, she stared about her, at those whirling cloud-cliffs that swept upward to the stars.

"It will be on us again presently," Rhodes said in a tired voice. "You must be below when that happens. We'll have the full fury of it again, Roxanne."

"Will we . . . make it?"

He shrugged, looked about him with a touch of the humor that always lurked in him. "Well, at least we've lost the junks," he said.

She loved him for saying that, for finding some glimmer of hope in the raging hell that surrounded them.

Impulsively she hugged his sinewy arm and brushed his salt-crusted cheek with her lips. "I'll go below," she said.

"No—wait a moment." He gave her a smile and turned to his exhausted crew who were staring amazed at the whirling cloud-world that surrounded them. He began to give swift orders for lashing down this, shoring up that—while there was still time.

She watched Rhodes issue his quiet orders, giving the men heart, and she was fiercely proud of him.

A low deep-throated roar coming at them from those sinister cloud walls that loomed ahead grew into a tearing shriek that seemed to vibrate through them like a thousand drums. At the height of its brutal power, the holocaust rolled back toward them. It seemed to come from all sides, a thundering torrent of sound that blanked the mind and terrified even the brave.

"Get below," shouted Rhodes. "*Now!*" She could hardly hear his voice above that roar. Before she took her leave, Roxanne had time to see ahead through that whirling cloud wall a line of white foam inconceivably high, riding atop a tall black wave that would assuredly smash the *Virginia Lass* to kindling. Trembling, she stumbled below and got the door closed before that wall of water struck. She was hurled across the cabin with a force that stunned her, and then, before she could seize anything to hold onto, she was slammed back again, accompanied by all of the furniture in a bruising mass. The second time she had the presence of mind to clutch the bunk and hang on, though her arms were nearly wrenched from their sockets as the ship plunged and bucked and writhed like a mad thing. Suddenly, the ship seemed to have crashed into a brick wall. And then, as she clung to the bunk, another. And another. Tattered and tossed, the ship careened about in this pulsating holocaust until the whole world seemed to crash and rock and the unearthly noise was almost beyond human endurance.

Only once before had Roxanne heard a sound like that . . . and on that occasion she had looked up into a vision of hell itself laced by vivid blue lightning. Then she had lain in a ditch. Now she crouched on a bunk in what seemed a corner of a pitching dungeon, a dungeon that was wildly in motion, bent one moment on tearing loose from the waves and flying up into the sky, and the next crashing down as if to seek the ocean's bottom. Every moment she expected to see the door cave in and the green sea fill the room. Every moment she expected to be her last.

And then, after terrible hours had passed—she did not know how many—it came to her battered senses that the horrendous roar of the storm was not quite so fierce, that the giant waves, while still big enough to smash the ship, had subsided a trifle, that the hull was not taking such a pounding. More time passed and she listened fearfully, felt each blow the hull took. The poor weakened *Lass* could not stand much more. And then—yes, she was sure of it: Like the wail of some great dying animal, the moan of the storm was retreating.

A little later Rhodes came into the cabin. He looked a wreck, his hair and face and clothes encrusted with salt, but he gave her a wide grin. "We came through it," he said. "Not much left of us, but we're still afloat. Bevin can hold her now."

She stared at him wordlessly, her heart in her eyes. He seemed too tired to notice. Exhaustedly, he pitched forward into the bunk, still in his soaking wet clothes, and fell asleep.

She was content to have it so.

Morning came. Roxanne had lost count of time. How many hours the *Virginia Lass* had ridden the storm-tossed sea, she was not sure. But with the first light, she woke to find Rhodes gone. Wrapping her sarong about her, she climbed up on deck and saw him standing at the helm. The wind was blowing his dark hair. Like some hero of ancient tales he stood a mighty man and master of his ship, with the gray light gleaming off his spray-lashed back and shoulders, as he steered his ship through the afterwash of the storm.

Roxanne was shocked at the sight of the deck. She had seen the bones of better-looking ships deserted upon the beach. Gray with salt, the deck was a shambles of twisted wood and bits of torn sail. Two masts were gone—but one remained. And on that mast a gallant bit of canvas fluttered in the wind.

Roxanne clambered over the wreckage, past the crew making desperate repairs, to reach her captain. He turned to her a haggard face.

"We've made it," she declared proudly. "*You've* made it."

If Rhodes was surprised at the warmth of her tone, he did not show it. His green eyes held a fleeting sadness. "Not quite," he said gently, and nodded to the west.

There on the horizon bobbed a Chinese junk, its sail a shattered thing.

"Yen Chiang's flagship," said Rhodes tiredly. "We haven't lost him after all. The storm spit us both out together."

She studied the ship anxiously. "It looks to be in bad shape."

"Oh, you can count on that, all right. But she's heading for us nonetheless. Yen Chiang must have recognized the *Lass*. He bears me a grudge, as I told you."

"At least," she sighed, "there aren't three of them."

"Yes," he said with feeling, "we can thank God for that."

"I'll find some food below," she said. "I'll bring you something."

He turned and smiled at her. "You're a warrior's woman, Roxanne."

Still feeling the glow of his approval she found a tin of dry biscuits and an unsmashed bottle down in the galley. They would win through, she told herself stubbornly. They had survived the storm—they could survive anything!

She brought the biscuit and bottle up to him. He gave the wheel to someone else and took a deep swallow.

"Will we—get away?" she asked soberly.

Rhodes paused with the biscuit halfway to his mouth and considered that junk with the ragged sail, grimly inching after them. "Not likely. Yen Chiang has more sail. Perhaps we can get away from him in the night. If it's dark. If we're lucky."

She understood the need for flight. Chinese pirate junks carried many men, fighters all. The *Virginia Lass* with its small crew would be no match for her. Soberly, she watched the junk in the distance, pacing them as they rode the big swells that were the aftermath of the storm.

All day long Rhodes supervised the shoring up of the *Virginia Lass*. To make her seaworthy. To make her battleworthy.

Night came. The men cursed as the moon shone down across the great rolling waves that still swept the uneasy sea. It was late when Rhodes came below. For all his fatigue, she had never seen him look so dangerous.

"She's gaining on us," he said. "When dawn comes, we'll engage her!"

A thrill went through her. *He meant to fight*. It was there in every line of his square-jawed face, in the very stance of his powerful body.

"Roxanne." His voice was hesitant. "I want you to know, I'd never have turned you over to Yen Chiang. Or to any other man."

"I knew you wouldn't," she said softly.

"Yes, I guess you did," he said, his face grim. "I guess there are no secrets between us. We know what we are—and how we feel."

She was lying on the bunk, and now she lifted her face to him and threw out an arm in a lovely feminine gesture that outlined her soft figure in the lamplight. In the muggy heat, she was completely naked and had only pulled the sheet about her hastily as he came into the cabin. Now she swept that sheet away. "You'll win," she said confidently. "I know you will."

She lay there before him, a slender column of peach and gold in the swinging light of the ship's lamp. Her dark-blond hair floated gleaming around her bare shoulders. Her firm young breasts rose and fell softly with her breathing, and her whole lustrous body by its gentle mein invited him to embrace her. She put both her hands on his shoulders and, smiling, twined her arms around his neck. As her soft breasts brushed the light hairs of his chest, she felt his muscles ripple at the touch. Gently, she drew his tired, bearded face down to hers. "*I know you will,*" she whispered.

He took her then, wordlessly, and with a kind of desperation. His arms were warm around her and his lips satin smooth against her own soft parted mouth, her pulsing white throat, her tingling breasts. Her whole body seemed to vibrate softly as she drew to him. fitting her yielding flesh to his own.

His body was lit with feverish desire, consumed by a compelling overpowering need. She felt that, with his body, he was making a statement to the earth that bred him—in case he should be killed on the morrow—and a statement to her: *I am Rhodes. I am your lover. I am the man whose arms were made to hold you forever, who will fight for you and if necessary die for you.* It was all there in the wild wonder and tenderness of his embrace, and she knew as they clung together in desperate intimacy there in the muggy heat of the cabin, what it was to love a man feeling that she might be sending him off to die.

Passionately, she clung to him, and no embrace in her whole lifetime had ever had for her the meaning of this one. An exalted happiness consumed her, for he had forgiven her at last. It was all there unspoken in the fierce tenderness of that wild embrace. Their long and clashing battle as a man and woman that had spanned continents was over. Tonight they were one. Inseparable. Forever.

And so they went where passion led them. Driven upward to heights undreamed of, every sense alive, then swept gustily down into wild sweet valleys laden with the perfume of love. Up distant unexplored reaches to a peak of passion, a bliss that mounted into heaven and swept the world away.

From those heights they descended gradually as she held him in her arms. Rising a little on his elbows, Rhodes looked down at her and smiled a very tender smile that brought a tremulous response to her own lips and misted her blue eyes with tears of grief for the wasted years without him. Tears of wonder that she had found him again—and that he loved her.

"Don't cry," he said gently, and brushed her wet lashes with his warm lips. "I've spent my life getting out of tight places. I'll think of something."

Wordlessly, she nodded. He was thinking of tomorrow, while she had been thinking of all their reckless wasted lives. "I love you, Rhodes," she said, so softly it was only a whisper on the sighing wind.

"I'll take that with me," he said, "when I go to meet Yen Chiang," and for a moment buried his dark bearded face in the sweet valley between her breasts.

Then he rolled over on the bunk and slept as if there were no Yen Chiang with his crew of experienced cutthroats stalking them across the waves.

Listening to his even breathing, Roxanne lay on one arm and looked at him. Relaxed and naked by her side, one lean buttock gently pressed against her soft stomach, he was a noble figure, his back and shoulders and arms deeply bronzed, his hips and muscular thighs gleaming almost as pale as her own, his calves and feet bronzed where he had walked barefoot, with trousers rolled up, across the decks on southern seas.

What a man he was, she thought dreamily. She yearned to reach out and touch him again, to bring him back to her, but sternly she resisted the impulse. For he had not slept the whole time they fought the storm, and tomorrow he would meet in battle the most notorious pirate to harry these coasts.

She leaned back luxuriantly, stretched her body softly, and lived over again in joy the moments in which he had possessed her, every look, every touch, every vivid flame . . . ah, Rhodes, Rhodes. Her body glowed with memories.

And then to her surprise—because she had not expected to sleep the night before the battle—she slept deeply and well, lulled by the roll of the ship on the timeless ocean.

When she woke, Rhodes was standing dressed and looking very fit.

"We've had a bit of luck," he said, brushing back a lock of dark hair impatiently. "I was able to see through my glass that Yen Chiang has had to jettison the cannon he usually carries, so it will be a small-arms war."

Cannon. She had not thought of cannons.

"We've plenty of ammunition, but he outmans us. I've thought of a possible way to even the score. We've some dynamite on board, packed silky soft and lashed down tight—even the typhoon didn't rip it loose. It was a danger, and I'd have thrown it over but for the likely event of meeting someone like Yen Chiang again. I've fixed up some packets of it and fuses. When they get close enough to board I'll throw the packets over. Should account for a few."

She shuddered. "Be careful," she said.

"Well, it isn't a time for being careful," he said, and she knew from the reckless glint in his eyes why his men adored him. This man before her had subtly changed from the lover of the night before. This was the wild Rhodes who led his men through the storm and battles, this was the leader they admired.

She sat up. "I'll dress," she said quickly, meaning to accompany him to the deck.

"You'll stay below," he said sternly. "I don't want to expose you to a stray bullet or have any long knives slashing at you. And take this." He handed her a pistol. "Six shots in it. Remember, just in case, save the last one for yourself."

Soberly she took the gun. It felt heavy in her hand.

"Easy to fire," he said.

"I know," she said. "I learned in the Klondike."

"Good girl," said Rhodes. "Don't look so down. We'll make out, you'll see." He went out, whistling, a jaunty figure going perhaps to his doom. She watched his departure somberly.

It was not long before she heard firing. A spatter of shots, no more. And then more gunfire as the two ships began a desultory running battle. When she heard actual explosions, she knew that Rhodes must have thrown the lighted sticks of dynamite. There were shouts and screams and then a hard shudder that rocked the hull. The Chinese junk must have rammed them. Roxanne closed her eyes and prayed.

Up on the deck she could hear a terrible clamor. Her mind's eye saw it plainly. Wild-eyed, golden-skinned pirates, their black hair in tight queues, leaping across from the junk, slashing with wicked long knives and great curved scimitars. Rhodes . . . perhaps they were killing him now.

That single thought goaded her to action. She would not lie here below decks, hiding while above her the crew of the *Lass* were killed to the last man! There were six bullets in the gun Rhodes had given her, and she would make them count.

Furious with herself that she had waited this long, she flung the door open, dashed up to the deck—and stopped. Before her was a scene of horrible shouting confusion, a bloody madness beyond anything she had imagined. Up and down the *Lass*'s slanted deck, against a livid background of smoke and fire from the explosions on the junk, men fought—with guns, with knives, with spars, with anything they could lay hands to. Their feet slid and skittered on wet patches of blood and gore, and they cursed and roared and slashed in a frenzy. A bullet whistled by her head, and she winced back. But her questing eye had found Rhodes in the thick of it. At the moment her eyes spotted him, he was suddenly hurled backward. Losing his footing on a slippery spot he skidded on his back almost to her feet. Before he could regain his stance, a huge figure, swinging a scimitar with a golden hilt, leaped out of the pack and sprang toward him with a bellow. The figure was large and muscular and Chinese. His black hair was worn in a small neat queue. His black eyes glittered in a ferocious face. A jade amulet on a gold chain swung against his powerful sweating chest. That splendid physical specimen paused for a moment in surprise at sight of Roxanne, his black eyes widening at sight of this new and desirable prize. Then the big curved scimitar sang as he swept it upward. In a split second, it would flash down full force upon the fallen Rhodes.

And in that split second Roxanne raised the gun and shot Yen Chiang.

The scimitar that was upraised to strike down the fallen Rhodes was convulsively held by nerveless fingers. The stalwart towering figure with the amulet tottered forward on one foot, blood gushing from a wound in the temple, and crashed to the deck beside Rhodes. A terrible tortured cry went up from Yen Chiang's men to see their leader slain.

In wavering horror, Roxanne regarded her kill.

"Good girl," grinned Rhodes, scrambling up. "I think we've got them now." He took the smoking gun from her trembling fingers. "Get back below."

But she did not go. Weak and sick, she leaned against the hatch cover and watched the battle surge back and forth in the choking smoke. Sometimes she lost sight of Rhodes in the fray. Clinging to the hatch cover, she prayed in silent terror. Nearby the burning junk bobbed in the water, occasionally jarring against their hull, sending a shudder through the *Virginia Lass*.

Near the rail, Rhodes—his gun now empty and discarded—was grimly fighting two burly Chinese. As she watched, a third—a giant with a red sash tied around his waist, who seemed to have assumed command, surged forward. Bevin blocked his way, but the big pirate sent him sprawling. Catching Rhodes unaware, he brought his heavy fist up and crashed it full force into Rhodes's jaw. Roxanne screamed, as the force of the blow lifted Rhodes from the deck and hurled him over the rail, to slide along the junk's evilly lit and slanting deck.

With a roar this new leader plunged after Rhodes, and both men disappeared into a billow of black smoke. Roxanne ran forward, unmindful of the battle. But all the pirates were leaving now. In answer to their new leader's bawled commands, which reached them through the smoke, they disengaged and leaped wildly across to the deck of their own vessel. Pushing free with long poles, they widened the distance between the junk and the *Lass*.

In those wild moments Roxanne tried to hurl herself over onto the junk's deck in pursuit, but Bevin caught her and dragged her back. She twisted in his arms, clawing desperately at the hands that held her. "Can't you see they have him?" she screamed. "*They have Rhodes*!"

"Hold it, miss!" panted Bevin. "No point getting yourself killed! You'd never make it—it's too far to jump!"

And it was. Through a haze of horror Roxanne could see that murky strip of green sea, ever widening as the burning junk drifted away from them. On its deck all was activity as men rushed about fighting the fire.

"You can't leave him there!" she cried desperately.

Bevin stared at her, his face tortured. "Gates, you speak Chinese," he cried, turning to a bleeding crewman who was staring after the departing junk in fascination. "Yell at them heathen that we'll ransom our captain—but only if he's let go unharmed!"

Leaving a trail of blood from a gash in his leg, Gates staggered to the rail, yelling something in Chinese. His answer was given back to him by the junk's new leader, who appeared out of the smoke at the rail, roaring what could only be curses, and flung a piece of burning wood at him. Gates ducked as the burning wood flew across the slippery deck, leaving a trail of sparks. Bevin loosened Roxanne and leaped forward to stamp out the flames and kick the burning brand overboard.

Mutely Roxanne turned to Gates—his defeated look gave her her answer. "They ain't in no mood to bargain," muttered Gates, turning to stare at the junk through the smoke as the distance between them increased.

"Rhodes!" screamed Roxanne despairingly across the water. "Rhodes!"

But only the shouts and the roaring sound of the fire came back to her.

"We'll follow them, miss!" cried Bevin, pulling her back from the rail. "Come away! They could still have some ammunition—you could get yourself shot standing here!"

Limp and dazed, Roxanne let him lead her away.

All day they followed the junk as well as they could, two disabled vessels drifting. Her eyes dark with suffering, Roxanne clung to the rail. She refused food, refused to go below. Only to help cleanse and bandage the wounds of the men would she turn from her vigil. Bevin, himself unhurt, watched her with pity in his eyes.

Night closed down thick as smoke. The moon, which had shone so brightly the night before, now hid behind a bank of clouds. Bevin cursed as the junk's rakish outline disappeared into the murk.

Morning found them alone on an empty sea. Twisting nervous fingers. Roxanne turned to Bevin. "The junk didn't—didn't sink?" she asked anxiously.

"No, miss," he assured her. "They got the fire out. Most likely they're making for some cove where they know they can patch up their vessel." He studied her, chewing his lip as he thought. "It's a big ocean. We'd better take you back to Singapore—it's what the captain would want, miss. We got some patchin' to do ourselves on the *Lass*. And then we'll go lookin' for him."

Nor could she sway Bevin from his purpose. Even though she protested, pleaded and wept, he would not heed her.

Back to the exotic international port of Singapore the crippled *Lass* sailed; and Roxanne, still barefoot and clad in her blue and gold sarong, went ashore with Bevin and the rest of the crew. In the crowd of carriages waiting at the dock for a big white ocean liner to arrive, Roxanne passed the wife of a former French ambassador, with whom she had once been friendly. This woman, sitting dressed in the latest Parisian mode, stared at Roxanne in horror through her lorgnette from underneath a wide straw hat laden with tulle.

She believes I've gone native, thought Roxanne grimly, and gave the French woman a small ironic bow.

She was rewarded by a gasp as the lorgnette snapped shut and the carriage holding the lady abruptly departed. It was but a sample of what awaited her. She went directly to her house, walking barefoot for she had no money even for a rickshaw, and she was embarrassed to ask Bevin—whom she had left on the wharf—for help. She found her house now occupied by a Chinese family, who stared at her stolidly. Her things were gone, as were her servants. Even the furniture had been taken. Inquiries availed her nothing, only establishing that her young Chinese housekeeper had quickly sold off everything and disappeared. So, Roxanne thought, that pretty, doll-like face had concealed not the mysteries of the fabled East but simple treachery.

Tired and still barefoot, she went to the bank and made a withdrawal on the money Leighton had left for her. There was some trouble with her identification, of course. The clerk, horrified at her appearance, insisted on calling the bank manager, who blinked but identified Roxanne. Her balance was quite low, she realized. After all, the money had to run out *sometime*.

She rented a cheap room for herself in the native quarter and tried to get a job. After a while she realized the impossibility of that and gave up. This was a city bursting with cheap Chinese labor, and she—a scandalous woman by any standards—could hardly hope to be hired as governess or clerk.

Living frugally, she settled down to wait for word of Rhodes.

Two months she waited. Three. There was no word. She had tried to make inquiries, but they came to nothing. Rhodes seemed to have vanished into the wilds of the Indian Ocean or the South China Sea. The months dragged on to six, and Roxanne was near panic. She worked at menial jobs in restaurants for her food, and finally took in fine laundry from the houses of women where once she had taken tea. But her lovely marketable body she would not sell—that now belonged to Rhodes.

A whole year passed and finally, dully, the truth sank in on her: Rhodes was not coming. She did not believe him dead; Bevin would have returned to tell her that—if he knew. But the *Virginia Lass* had really been in no shape to voyage out; Bevin had docked long enough for only the most necessary repairs before setting forth again. Perhaps the *Lass* had been lost in one of the sharp squalls that rose up out of nowhere on the Indian Ocean. Perhaps Bevin and his crew were gone . . . as Rhodes was gone. Vanished into the blue wilderness of water.

At last, thin and disheartened, she faced the truth: Rhodes was not coming. She had lost him—this time for good. Sad and lonely, she took to walking on the docks, staring hungrily at the ships in the harbor, some of them bound for America. *Home* . . . so desperately she wanted to go home.

One day on the dock she paused to watch a steamer named the *Trade Winds*. And saw, coming down the gangplank, a miner for whom she had done laundry in Dawson City, and who had helped her in Nome.

"Toby Hart," she hailed him joyfully. "It's been a long time!"

"Well, if it ain't the Dawson blond!" he cried. "Beg yer pardon, Miss Roxanne, but that was startled out of me." He wrung her hand, saw her shabby mended clothes, the toes gone out of her cheap shoes. "Ain't things going well with you, Miss Roxanne?"

Sadly she shook her head. "Toby," she asked wistfully, "do you think you could get me signed on as stewardess aboard your ship? I don't care where she's bound—anywhere that's away from Singapore."

He meditated. "I could, Miss Roxanne, but—well, she's bound for San Francisco and I—I heard about your trouble in Nome . . . about your killing those men. Word was you had run away before they hung you."

She smiled at him through her tears. "The only man I ever killed, Toby, was a Chinese pirate. And I don't care if they hang me when I get there—I'm going home."

Toby was one of those who had loved her in secret, who had come to stare at her while she danced and served drinks at Big Mike's. He had a wife in Seattle and a baby on the way, but he cherished still a warmth for the lovely Dawson blond who had glimmered across his path as shimmering as the pale gold aurora that lit the northern sky.

"I'll stake you to some clothes, Miss Roxanne," he said. She started to protest, but he assured her, "You can pay me out of your earnings. We've need of a stewardess aboard, and when they see you dressed up in new duds, there'll be none to match you."

Roxanne gave him a blinding smile. She couldn't speak just then, her throat was closed tight.

When the *Trade Winds* sailed, Roxanne was on her. She would take her plundered heart back to the States and to whatever awaited.

Part Four:

San Francisco 1905—1906

Chapter 36

On a brisk winter day under cloudswept skies, as the *SS Trade Winds* steamed through the Golden Gate, Roxanne had her first sight of the United States since she had left Seattle bound for her strange adventures in the Klondike. She found the beautiful city on its seven hills fascinating—and uncaring. Although, boldly, she traveled under her own name, there were no policemen waiting for her on San Francisco's docks. Nobody showed any interest. She had been news for a day, a scandal for a day—and then forgotten. It gave her hope. Forgotten, she could make a new life, and perhaps a good one, here on her native soil.

Jobs for women were not plentiful in San Francisco that fall. Waiters rather than waitresses served in the best eating places. Desperate, without references—for she had had an altercation with one of the passengers on board the *Trade Winds* after he had surreptitiously pinched her—she took the first job she could find. It was washing dishes in a waterfront restaurant. The work was hard and grubby and ill-paid, but at least she got her meals there, and had money enough to rent a small room in one of the wooden shacks that clustered on down-at-the-heel Russian Hill. The room had one great advantage—the view. From it she could see, far below, the greenish-gray sea fog of the Pacific flowing through the Golden Gate toward California's hot inland valleys . . . and across the Bay, where beyond Belvedere and Sausalito, the wooden slopes of Mount Tamalpais rose. Roxanne was inclined to think the view was the only good thing about it, for her room was hardly bigger than a closet, and the house seemed tenanted by slatterns and bleary-eyed drunks whose raucous parties interefered with her sleep.

Overworked from long hours at the dish tubs, Roxanne concluded bitterly that life was no better at home than abroad. To cheer herself up a bit, she decided to do a little sightseeing one Sunday. She climbed Telegraph Hill, looked down its dizzy two hundred-foot cliff to the sea, then window-shopped here and there, and returned to Market Street. Waiting on the corner of Powell, about to step onto the cable car that led to the top of another hill she heard a familiar voice.

"Well, if it ain't Roxie!"

A handsome carriage with a liveried driver drew up, and an elegantly dressed woman in bronze taffeta, wearing a picture hat laden with five stuffed birds and innumerable ribbons and orange plumes, leaned out its window. A small pince nez perched over her brown eyes, and a broad dog collar of amber and pearls encircled her aging neck. But the hennaed hair that peeped out from under that sweeping hat and the whiskey voice and broad grin were unmistakable.

"Josie!" cried Roxanne and hurried over to the carriage. "I thought you'd still be in Alaska."

Josie shrugged. "I'm retired, Rox. Made such a pile up there I decided to stop fightin' blizzards and corrupt officials who were always tellin' me to pay off or they'd close me down. I sold out to my best girl—Angie.

You didn't know her; she was after you left. Anyway, I've bought me a place on Nob Hill, got it all gussied up, paintings by furriners, little gilt chairs and sofas won't hold you if you sit down! Come and see it!"

Roxanne climbed in beside perfumed, powdered Josie. The older woman considered her critically. "You look terrible, Rox. Whatsa matter, down on your luck?"

Roxanne thought of her job and grimaced. "Sort of."

"Money troubles or man troubles?"

"Both."

Josie sighed gustily. "They go together right enough. I always say, don't follow your heart. Look where it got me!"

Roxanne waited, fascinated; she had always wanted to hear the story of Josie's life.

"I fell in love with a no-good drummer when I was thirteen," said Josie. "Run away with him to Nashville, and he left me stranded. Took up with the hotelkeeper, and first thing I knew he was rentin' me out! That made me mad. I decided I'd go into business for myself. Made enough to set up as a madam in Chicago—ran a good house, if I do say so. Met Case there. Then I had to go and fall in love with a politician named Harps, and when he lost the election, his opposition got me run out of town. Harps didn't care; he just went back to his wife. I went on to Seattle, but found trouble there too. That's why I teamed up with Case to go to the Klondike, Rox. There was plenty of gold in the States—I didn't have to go any farther north for it, but I thought maybe all that ice and snow would cool me down." She guffawed. "It sure did! Damn near froze me solid! Well, here we are!"

Leaping out, the driver handed down the ladies with a flourish and Roxanne looked up at a handsome house set into the steep hillside.

"Not much to look at outside," remarked Josie. "But wait till you get inside!"

Inside, the mansion was indeed remarkable. Roxanne had never seen quite so many huge gilt mirrors, quite such extensive use of red velvet and velour. Josie's favorite color was red. "Always liked those red lights," she confided, chuckling. "I've got real white skin, and them red lights always made me look rosy. See them carpets, Roxanne?" She pointed the toe of her high-buttoned boot at the deep red Oriental rugs. "All made by furriners—Chinee, Injun. And them chairs, ain't they elegant?" Roxanne looked wistfully at the gilt chairs and loveseats, which were almost as delicate as Josie had described, all Louis XIV and upholstered in deep red velour. The drapes—of such heavy velvet that it took massive brass rods to hold them up—were red too, and completely shut out the daylight. Illumination was supplied by glowing globes with red painted roses. Even the satin brocade that covered the walls above the dark mahogany wainscoting was red.

"Josie, I can't believe it," said Roxanne inadequately.

"Ain't it pretty?" agreed Josie in a complacent voice. "Well, sit down, Rox, and tell me what happened to you after you left Nome."

Roxanne perched herself on one of the pretty gilt chairs. "Leighton and I went to Singapore, and then his wife got hurt back in Washington and he went back to her."

"They do that!" sighed Josie. "You sure can't trust men—always goin' back to their wives! Bring us some champagne, Princeton," Josie said to the liveried servant who hovered in the background. "So what you do then, Roxie?"

"I stayed there trying to find a place for myself. And then Rhodes found me and kidnapped me."

"Kidnapped you? That big fellow you brought in half-dead on a dogsled into Nome? Well! I always thought he was the man for you, Rox. What a man! You should have heard him when he learned you'd shipped out with some other fellow—like to tore the place up cussin'! He paid me for his keep by givin' me his dogs and his sled—said he had a ship somewhere."

"The *Virginia Lass*. We sailed away in it. But we were attacked by pirates and got separated." Roxanne's eyes were shadowed. Looking down into the sparkling wine, she could relive those golden moments with Rhodes spent on a tossing ship in sultry southern seas.

"I waited for him in Singapore, but he never came. I don't know where he is." She drained her glass.

Josie sighed. "Like I say, don't follow your heart, Rox. Follow your pocketbook. The road to the bank is the only road there is for women whose blood runs as hot as ours." She sounded sad, but roused herself suddenly. "Fill up the lady's glass, Princeton—I like that name, don't you, Rox? Sounds sort of genteel. His real name's John, but I renamed him. That's right, Princeton—splash it right up to the rim. The girl needs courage!"

Roxanne smiled. Warmed by the bubbling champagne, she was feeling better. When Josie asked, "What you doin' now, Rox?" she admitted she was washing dishes in a waterfront dive.

"Laundry in Dawson, dishes in Frisco—you must have a secret yen to be a housewife, Rox," observed Josie, looking swiftly at Roxanne's hands. Roxanne was glad she was wearing mended gloves so Josie couldn't see how red her hands were. Josie's keen gaze switched to her face. "This fellow you're in love with—he ain't worth all this," she said. "You've got to get on your feet, Rox."

"How?" asked Roxanne bitterly. "I've got no reference, I can't get a job and, no"—she lifted a warning hand—"I don't want a reference to some posh sporting house, Josie."

"I know you don't, Rox. That ain't your style. But . . ." She meditated. "Stand up, Rox. Turn around."

Feeling a little foolish, Roxanne rose and turned about for Josie's inspection.

"It's amazing," said Josie, studying her. "I think you're in even *better* shape than you were in Nome."

Roxanne sat back down. "What about the people we knew in the Klondike, Josie? What ever happened to Case?"

"Case never came to Nome, Rox. But I heard he broke up with that black-haired Yvonne he was livin' with. Heard he left Dawson. Nobody knows where he went. Australia, maybe. Most of the people we knew left Alaska long ago. Now shut up, Rox. I'm thinkin'." And as she thought, Josie mused aloud. "Never saw a face like it—sort of stuns you. Figure good as ever —better maybe. Hair likc sunshine through the clouds. Rox!" She banged her stemmed glass down on a little table inlaid with brass and tortoiseshell. "You're wastin' your time down on the waterfront. Why don't you come and live on Nob Hill?"

Roxanne sighed. "I can't accept your hospitality, Josie. I couldn't pay you back, and it wouldn't be right."

"Hell, I'm not asking you to accept *my* hospitality. I'm talkin' about settin' you up with good-lookin' clothes and your own place where you can wander about, an unattached woman—I've got a *few* connections, you know—so's you can snag yourself a financier! This is a man's town, Rox—all the money here is owned by men. And you could strike it rich!"

"You mean—marry?"

Josie shrugged. "Or some such like arrangement. You're not a woman wants to live alone—you need a man, Rox!"

It was true. She wasn't a woman who wanted to live alone. Roxanne looked at Josie and, for the first time since she'd taken that job on the waterfront, hope sprang up in her. Why not? She'd left her heart with Rhodes in equatorial waters, but she was stuck with a body that wanted good clothes, good food. What did she have to lose?

"Josie," she marveled, "you're a fairy godmother!"

"Come off it, Rox," shrugged Josie, growing as red as her drapes with pleasure. "I'm sittin' around here with a sliver spoon in my mouth and nothin' to do. I'm spoilin' to be doin' somethin' and it'll give me a rare old time to watch you shake golden apples off the trees here in San Francisco. You can pay me back when you get your man."

Smiling, Roxanne agreed, and together they toasted the future.

As she had promised, Josie costumed Roxanne. She paid for a honey-beige walking suit and a blue one that clung to Roxanne's figure and matched her eyes. And scented underthings, stockings, dainty boots. An afternoon dress of shimmering peach taffeta and a sweeping hat aswirl with exotic feathers and peach taffeta bows. Plus an evening gown of rustling black silk, low-cut and startling against Roxanne's fair white skin.

"Josie, you've done too much," murmured Roxanne, as Josie ushered her into a tiny but handsome town house she had rented for her.

"Nonsense. Jewels has got to have a setting, ain't they? Brush your hair a little fuller on the side there, Rox—and pile it higher atop your head. Sure, it looks like it needs a crown. Won't be long before someone will stick a diamond tiara on it, you'll see! And *then* you can pay me back and maybe—" her voice grew wistful—"maybe once in a while you'll have me to the house, maybe to some big ball you give?"

"Josie." Roxanne's voice grew husky at Josie's admission that she was lonely, that she wanted to be "in society." "Every ball I ever give, you're invited to right now!"

Josie grinned. "Shucks, Rox," she said. "You can't do that—people would drop you if they knew who I was. But maybe once in a while. . . ." She became businesslike again. "Now there's this sassiety woman, she meets her lover down at Belle's—you don't know Belle, but she's got a real plushy house here. Well, this sassiety woman is gonna invite you to her party next Friday night and introduce you around, because if she *don't*, a letter is gonna arrive at her husband's office in Montgomery Street suggestin' he stroll down to Belle's some afternoon and see what his wife is doin'." Roxanne stared. Her new career was to be launched on *blackmail*? "Don't look so shocked, Rox. How'd you think someone with a background like yours was gonna get herself launched? You've got a past these sassiety ladies would slam the door on, you know!"

Roxanne sighed. Of course she had. She had for the moment forgotten it.

Like a clucking hen, Josie made her plans. Roxanne

was to go here, appear there. A certain gentleman would introduce her, a certain lady. . . .

To Roxanne's surprise, it worked. The glamorous and somewhat mysterious young widow, Roxanne Barrington, found herself launched in a small way into San Francisco society. Parties, balls. Roxanne was reminded of Singapore and her years with Leighton.

Her beauty attracted men: rich men, important men. Josie told her who "had it" and who didn't. Josie had a housekeeper's mind. Afloat on a sea of invitations, Roxanne was wined and dined and feted. Even though she knew she had not yet stormed the citadels of the truly wealthy at which Josie aimed, Roxanne found herself wanting to drift, to postpone making up her mind. She knew it was because of Rhodes . . . she did not really want to marry any of these men.

The day she faced that truth, she came back to her tiny town house and found Josie waiting for her in the small second-floor salon. Josie was wearing an enormously gaudy ostrich feather hat adorned with amethysts, and her ample chest was ablaze with beaded lace overlaying magenta taffeta. She sat jauntily on one of Roxanne's little chairs, tossing down a whiskey that Roxanne's maid had brought her. She looked smug.

Attired in the peach confection, Roxanne swept into the room and tossed her hat to a chair. "I just don't seem to be interested in any man I meet, Josie," she sighed, stripping off her peach kid gloves.

"Well, that's good, Rox," said Josie surprisingly, "because I wouldn't want you to be." She chuckled. "We've netted our fish, sure enough, and he's the right one! I knew if I was to waltz you around the town you'd attract attention, and here's the proof I was right!" She waved a note gleefully. "I'd just arrived when all those flowers come—Emma's putting them in water now, but I had her give me the note." She patted her beaded purse.

At that moment Emma, Roxanne's maid, came into the room almost obscured by an enormous vase of long-stemmed red roses.

"Who sent them?" asked Roxanne.

"She don't know," chuckled Josie, "and I ain't tellin'. But it's a gentleman who's been in Europe. He just got back and he saw you riding by in a carriage and found out where you lived. He's from the East Coast, but he transferred his business out here. Says he knows you, Rox!" Her brown eyes sparkled.

Roxanne stared at her. Leighton! Allison must have died and he'd come to San Francisco to live. He'd probably been in Europe visiting his diplomatic connections there.

"Oh, Rox!" Josie went over and hugged her. "You got yourself a real tycoon at last! Hurry up, the gentleman's expecting you at his house."

Roxanne frowned. Why hadn't he come here? But then, she and Leighton had never stood on ceremony. Doubtless he had his reasons. Swiftly she combed out her hair, touched a little French perfume to her earlobes and throat and the white hollow between her breasts. Resisting Josie's urging to add a touch of rouge to her already flushed cheeks, Roxanne pulled on her kid gloves and studied her reflection critically in the tall pier glass that stood in one corner.

A peach and gold vision looked back at her. Her long dress, which rustled nicely as she walked, fitted her like her own skin and molded her firm young breasts and deliciously slender waist as if it had been painted on.

"Come on, you look good enough to eat," said Josie impatiently. "I'm droppin' you off at his house."

Roxanne found herself hurried out to Josie's carriage, which promptly clattered away to Nob Hill and stopped before a white marble mansion of awe-inspiring proportions. Plainly Leighton was even wealthier than she had thought. She tried to ask the butler who answered the door whose house this was, but Josie pushed her forward with a crisp, "The lady's expected," and went her way, chuckling.

The door closed and Roxanne looked about her nervously. She found herself in a large octagonal high-ceilinged entrance hall with floors of black and white marble squares. On both sides a heavy white marble stair curved upward to a balcony-like landing at the top. All the downstairs walls were of white marble and were hung with French paintings of nymphs in forest glades, of ladies in huge pastel hoop skirts and powdered wigs, dallying in dappled light and shade. About her she saw a sprinkling of small gilt furniture covered in satin brocade.

She was promptly escorted through tall white double doors to a huge room that was almost frighteningly magnificent. Its ceiling reached up two stories and was ornately carved and painted. The walls were of rococo plaster, gilded and painted with vast murals. Looming against one wall was a huge green marble fireplace that a horse could have stood up in, and on the black marble floor of this treasure house were several large Chinese rugs in soft, glowing shades of green. The furniture was heavy and ornate, with brass ornamentation and painted inlays—all of it looked as if it might have been stolen from a museum. Did Leighton really live this way? Roxanne marveled.

The doors closed behind her as the butler departed, and she took a turn about the room, studying it for clues. There were none. Impersonal as a museum in its grandeur, this haughty room resisted her curiosity.

She had a moment of trepidation when she heard a man's firm step sound across the marble floor outside. Then she lifted her head to present a picture of elegant composure as the double doors swung open, and a man, a tall aristocratic man, stood framed in the entrance.

Roxanne's heart missed a beat and her mind flew back across the years to Baltimore.

Once again she was standing face-to-face with Gavin Coulter.

He was older, but age became him. The silver wings in his graying dark hair only made him the more distinguished. His full sensual lips curved at the sight of Roxanne, and his cold dark eyes were bright with—lust? As he had in Baltimore, he both repelled and attracted her. She felt herself frozen into immobility before him, as if he were the hunter and she the prey.

For there was no doubting the authority in the way he stood, in the way he moved toward her. As the head of a mighty shipping empire, he had not only authority—he had vast wealth.

Now, as he stood facing her, there was a triumphant light in his dark eyes.

"Roxanne," he said with a little bow.

Still daunted, she managed to retain her outward composure. Gracefully, a woman of the world now, no longer a lady's maid, she extended a gloved hand. "Gavin." Her voice was light, disdainful. He would see how little interest she had in him now! She sank into the soft rose brocade chair he offered her. "How nice to see you again."

He smiled into her eyes; she returned his gaze coolly. "May I offer you something to drink? As I remember, you drank only tea or coffee."

"Many things have changed, Gavin," she said, still in that cool light voice, though her heart was thumping at this encounter. "I will have champagne."

He smiled again. "Shall I drink it out of your slipper?"

She shrugged a slender indifferent shoulder. "If you like . . . many have before you."

He chuckled. "So I'm to be punished, I see. Still . . . how wonderful to find you in San Francisco. I thought I had lost you, Roxanne."

Oh, you have lost me, Gavin, you have. . . . She remained silent, watching as a soft-footed servant brought champagne, poured it sparkling into delicate long-stemmed glasses, and departed. Gavin raised his glass, touched hers with a little tinkle. "To us—restored to one another."

Roxanne lifted her glass mockingly. "To us," she said. "Destined to remain apart."

He ignored her mockery. "I had agents looking for you, after you left Baltimore."

"And they found me quite easily in Augusta, I suppose. I was married then."

He nodded. "I received regular reports on your progress. I knew you had gone to the Klondike."

She was astonished and looked it. Gavin had searched for her that long?

"My man lost you after you left Nome. It was a long time before we learned you had gone to Singapore; when my man arrived there, you had disappeared."

No, only my heart had vanished. I left it somewhere on the storm-lashed Indian Ocean. . . .

"He reported he had lost your trail completely. Until he found your name on the steamship bookings enroute to San Francisco."

This had been no chance encounter, then. Gavin had stalked her and found her—just as Rhodes had stalked her and found her. Ah, the Coulters were good at that. Her lip curled.

"Where did you go, Roxanne? Or should I rephrase that and ask 'with whom?' "

She thought of Rhodes and her eyes grew moist. "Nowhere of consequence," she said shortly.

"Ah, I am glad to hear it," he said pleasantly. "So there are no echoes of old loves now that I have found you again."

No echoes! How wrong he was! She studied Gavin's face, remembering how calmly he had told her that he had married another woman.

"And now that you've found me?" The silkiness of her tone belied the deep anger in her heart.

"Ah, now that I've found you, Roxanne, I'll never let you go." He said it easily, but there was a hint of steel lurking below the light caressing tone. The eyes she looked into were cold too, accustomed to command. Obviously, here was a man used to having his own way. In Baltimore Gavin had been menacing; in San Francisco he was formidable. She realized that the man who stood before her would brook no opposition. He meant to have her.

And this was Josie's tycoon! Her laugh rang out, a brittle sound. Gavin's eyes took on a harder gleam. She decided to take the offensive. "And you, Gavin, are you still married?" she taunted. "I seem to recall you were a bridegroom on our last encounter."

He had the grace to wince. "Roxanne," he murmured, "must you remind me of how badly I behaved toward you? How many times have I cursed myself for it since. . . . No, I am a widower now. My wife died last June."

"I am sorry to hear it," she said politely. "But there is always Clarissa. Surely *she* would console you."

He frowned. "Clarissa married shortly after you left. She has three children now and resides on the Eastern Shore."

"Well, if Clarissa is no longer available, there are others. Most of the debutantes in San Francisco must be straining at the leash to land so eligible a bachelor as yourself." She set down her glass and rose.

Gavin rose too. "Stop needling me," he said in an irritable voice. "Now that I've found you again, I want to make it all up to you. I want to give you everything, Roxanne."

"Do you, Gavin?" On a sudden reckless impulse, she walked toward him, her smile infinitely sweet and enticing. To his startled look, she wrapped her slender arms around his neck, fitted her elegant body to his and kissed him.

When she pushed him away, he looked shaken. "God, how I've missed you, Roxanne," he choked.

"And you must go on missing me, Gavin," she said with a brief, bitter smile. She picked up her purse, turned on her heel. "For I am walking out of this door and right out of your life—as you walked out of mine when you married for money."

She was halfway across one of the green Chinese rugs, heading for the door, when he leaped forward to block her way. She would have gone around him, but he reached the doors first and blocked her passage. "Then why did you kiss me like that, Roxanne?" he demanded hoarsely. "Why?"

"Because I enjoy seeing you suffer." Roxanne chose her words carefully. "I am a worldly woman now, Gavin, and I have some idea of what a man goes through when the woman he wants does not want him."

"No," he said angrily. "There was a commitment in that kiss. You can't deny you felt something?"

"I felt nothing. Let me pass."

"Ah, Roxanne!" He seized her by her peach taffeta shoulders, moving her back a step by his sudden onslaught. "I have waited so long. I had men combing the capitals of the world—Paris, London, Rome."

"No one can call up the past, Gavin—you no more than I. Anything that might have existed between us is dead."

"No!" he roared. "Nothing is dead. I have dreamed about you, Roxanne. Dreamed I held you in my arms! Now that I have found you, I will find a way to keep you."

"Will you, Gavin?" Indifferently, she freed herself from his grasp. "Then you will have to have a long reach, for next week I am taking a train to New York, and from there I will sail for Paris. Who knows, I may never return again."

She rustled past him and had reached the door when his voice stayed her. "You knew that Rhodes was dead?"

A stillness came over her. She remained where she was, suspended in time, motionless. "What did you say, Gavin?"

He sighed. "Lost at sea. I have erected a stone in the family burial plot. In death—if not in life—Rhodes belongs among us."

A wave of dizziness took her. She felt as if she would faint.

Gavin sprang forward to steady her. "I felt I must tell you." His voice was rough, accusing. "In case his shadow stood between us. I can see you did not know."

"No," she said faintly. "I did not know." Blindly she pushed past him and made her way into the street, where she took in great gulps of air to compose herself. After a while, the world came back into focus and she found a cab to take her home.

Shutting herself in her bedroom, she wept. She lay in her bed and remembered him—wonderful, strong, Rhodes. No man like him would ever come her way again. And she had wronged him—he had not cast her aside. Had he not been dead, he would have come to her in Singapore; perhaps he had even been on his way to Singapore when his ship went down. So, she sorrowed through many dark hours, but at least she lifted her head. Rhodes would want her to go on, to make something of her life, to try to be happy. She must try—oh, God, she must try!

The roses arrived the next day—and the next, and the next. All week long they arrived, banks of them, in long florist's boxes—long-stemmed, blood red, beautiful. Grimly amused, Roxanne arranged them in tall crystal bowls, moved about the house through a forest of flowers. Each box bore the same curt inscription: "Yours, Gavin Coulter."

Emma, her maid, was most impressed. "You mean it's *him*? Mr. Moneybags himself?" she had gasped.

"The same," Roxanne had assured her. Emma's wide-eyed admiring gaze told her that she had risen vastly in the girl's estimation.

With Josie she had one abrasive brush over her recalcitrance, and then Josie swished off home and left her strictly alone. Roxanne felt it was just as well. Miserable as she was, it would be worse to be pressured by Josie.

The news of Rhodes's death, followed instantly by this unceasing barrage of flowers, hardened her heart toward Gavin still further. What she had said about the train and Paris had not been true, but now she decided to leave San Francisco, to choose one of the lovers Josie had paraded before her, and depart. She hoped sincerely it would break Gavin's heart. But it was hard making a decision when all she could think of was that Rhodes was dead, that she was never going to see him again. She shrank from people, cancelled all her engagements, and skulked about the house breathing the heavy perfumed scent of roses.

One day there were no flowers, but instead a dark velvet jeweler's box arrived. Roxanne's eyes widened as she opened it and a narrow necklace of diamonds spilled out, clear and glittering as tears. She clasped the necklace around her neck, and considered it critically. She would keep it, of course. Gavin deserved no better. She would wear the necklace in Paris . . . beside a new lover.

That same afternoon a note arrived on vellum edged in gold, requesting the pleasure of her company at the theater. It was signed "Gavin Coulter." A servant waited for her answer. On scented pink notepaper Roxanne penned her answer: she was otherwise engaged for the evening.

The next day Gavin came himself. He arrived in his big motor car, a chauffeur-driven Pierce-Arrow. Roxanne saw him alight at the curb, elegantly tailored and arrogant. She had told Emma she would not receive him, but he must have pushed past the girl, for a moment later the door to her small upstairs salon was thrown open and Gavin came in. He looked angry.

Roxanne came forward to meet him, keeping her face expressionless. "You are difficult to discourage, Gavin," she said dryly. "Must I find a lover and parade him before you to make you understand?"

His cold eyes flashed with anger. "You have found your lover," he said, "and I stand here before you."

She laughed, but warily kept her distance from him. There was a tension in him that she did not like. She might not find him as easy to fight off as she had in Baltimore.

"Will you not ask me to sit down?" he demanded in a stern voice.

"By all means," she said. "Find a chair."

Gavin pulled up a small straight chair, leaned forward intently. "Since I found you again, I have not been idle. I have *insured* that you remain by my side for as long as I desire."

Astonishment colored her voice. "You have what?"

"Perhaps you will remember an old newspaper article," he said silkily. "It mentioned two murders in Nome and a third—of one Mary Willis—on a train. It may surprise you to learn that I have found an eyewitness from that train who swears he saw you put a powder in the woman's drink before she died."

Ratface! It could be no one else. Somehow Gavin's investigators had found Ratface, who would do anything for money. Who else could have accused her?

"I see you are startled," said Gavin in a low, deadly voice. "This witness swears he was beguiled by your beauty and by your youth, and so, when you confessed this murder to him, he kept silent. But now he wishes to cleanse his conscience. And he has made out an affidavit swearing to these things. I have the document locked in my safe. The man himself waits here in San Francisco to testify at your trial—should there be one."

"I did not kill Mary Willis!"

"Oh, I never thought you did," Gavin said. "But will a jury faced with circumstantial evidence and an eyewitness take so charitable a view?"

Roxanne's heart shuddered within her. A trial! How her past could be brought against her! Would all those enemies she had made along the way turn up, urged on by Gavin, to send her to the gallows?

Flight was the only answer. She would pretend to acquiesce to whatever Gavin desired. This was a port city—she would take a ship, stow away if necessary.

As if he had read her thoughts, Gavin straightened. "I had not meant to do it this way, Roxanne." His voice reproved her. "But you leave me no alternative."

She lifted a defiant chin and looked at him steadily from accusing blue eyes. "Gavin," she said, "have you not harmed me enough? Must you add this?"

"I have men watching you, Roxanne. Trusted men. If you try to leave San Francisco, they will bring you to me. If you do manage to leave anyway, they have instructions to find you and turn you over to the law. Then your only hope will be to appeal to me to pay for the expensive defense you will need. Unless, of course, you choose to hang. But you are young, beautiful, desirable—all your life lies ahead of you. I do not think you will choose the gallows."

He had pushed her too far. Something cold flickered in her lovely eyes. Pretending to be distraught, she took a turn around the room, stooped to open the drawer of a small table and quickly took out the pistol

Josie had given her for protection. Calmly she pointed it at Gavin. "Why should I run? Why should I not shoot you here and now?"

Gavin's eyes widened. She saw that he had not foreseen this type of opposition. Had he expected her to crumble and grovel before him? she wondered scornfully.

"Come to your senses," he said harshly. "I have men outside watching the house."

A bitter half smile played around her mouth. "And why should that matter to me? You tell me that I am already to be tried for murder. Why not another?"

He was breathing harder now; his arrogant face had a hunted look. "I say that you shall be tried for none," he insisted, "*if* you will become my mistress."

"And if I do not choose to?"

"You will," he said grimly. "You love life. It is in the way you walk, in the way you look at men."

Ah, that had once been true. But she loved her life not so much now as she once had—when she had thought to live it with Rhodes. . . . She lifted her head. "As you say, I want to live. But I will not be your mistress."

He breathed a ragged sigh. "If you kill me, Roxanne, the authorities will give you short shrift. No charges have been filed against you as yet for the—the other. But I have the sworn statements, and I will not—"

"*If* I become your mistress," she supplied, and cocked the gun.

His face paled. "You need not decide now," he said smoothly. "I will give you time to make your choice."

Roxanne gave him a mocking smile and toyed with the pistol. "How much time?"

Gavin looked back at the beautiful woman who menaced him. Straight and lovely she stood, and the eyes that returned his gaze were very steady. But the muzzle of the gun had dropped; it was no longer pointed directly at his chest.

"Enough. Enough time to consider." His dignity had returned now that the imminent peril was removed. At the door he turned. "I could have you seized in the street, you know that. Drugged. Delivered to my bed in some out-of-the-way place. I could plunder your body at will."

Her eyes narrowed. It was true enough, a man in his position. "Then why don't you do that?" she wondered. And as he returned her gaze, she answered for him. "Perhaps it is because you do not wish to make love to a woman inert and senseless, or to a woman cold and stiff, with hatred burning in her eyes. No, you desire passion from a woman, Gavin. I have always known it. I knew it back in Baltimore. Like a reptile that seeks warmth, you seek to warm your cold heart at the fires of others'. You will not kidnap me or drug me, Gavin. What you want is to bend me to your will."

He gave her an angry look and went out, slamming the door behind him. She knew she had struck home.

After he had gone she rushed to the window. Below in the street stood two quietly dressed men in dark hats. One of them was gazing at the house, but when Gavin waved his hand, the man stepped forward briskly. They spoke for a minute. After Gavin's car pulled away, the man stepped back and said something to the other. Then, like sentinels, they resumed their positions, standing—facing her front door.

She hurried to the back of the town house, which had the blank walls of the adjoining buildings on either side. Just beyond the back court two more men paced up and down, as if deep in conversation, but quietly keeping the back door under surveillance. She was not to escape, then.

Roxanne retraced her steps and leaned against the door of her living room, feeling suddenly weak.

She had stayed in San Francisco too long. Gavin had trapped her, and this time there would be no escape. She sat down heavily and contemplated the pistol. She had almost killed him. A little goading from Gavin and she would have fired at him point-blank, no matter what the cost. For a long time she sat in that chair and reviewed her life. She sat there until the sun went down, and after, telling Emma to go home—she did not want any dinner.

Night came. The four men outside had been replaced by four others. A changing of the guard.

Thoughtfully, Roxanne undressed and went to bed. She had no fear that Gavin would have her secretly whisked away to his waiting car. That was not his style. He meant to break down her resistance, to bring her, begging and frightened, to his arms.

It would not happen! Her heart was harder now, more steely. She meant to survive.

The next day the roses began arriving again.

All that day Roxanne pondered. The next, she dressed in her honey-beige walking suit and went to see Josie. Two men followed her.

Roxanne was uncertain how Josie would receive her. After her visit to Gavin's house she had told Josie all about Mary Bridey and how Gavin had lied to her in Baltimore and turned up married. But Josie had felt Roxanne should forgive him.

"A lot of water's gone over the dam," she had counseled Roxanne. "And here's a shipping tycoon wants to give you everything. Why, I had no idea you knew the richest man in San Francisco, Rox!"

When she had told Josie stonily that she would never let Gavin Coulter touch her, Josie had flung out in a temper, and Roxanne had half expected to be evicted from her small town house.

Forgiving Josie, wearing a brilliant red taffeta gown appliqued all over with black lace and jet, received her warmly and seated her by the fireplace in her garish living room. "I guess you know your own mind, Rox," she sighed. "Me, I'd let bygones be bygones and have Gavin Coulter shower me with diamonds, but since you hate him so . . ."

"He's blackmailing me now, Josie," said Roxanne quietly. "He says he'll have me or see me hang—I can take my choice."

Josie drew a deep breath, and her ample bodice in its lace and jet quivered. "Them killings back in Nome," she said in a thoughtful voice.

Roxanne sighed. "You know I never killed anyone in Nome, Josie."

"Oh, sure," said Josie indifferently. "I believe you, Rox. Anyway, that Lars fellow deserved to die."

Roxanne studied her friend. Josie wasn't fooling her. Josie believed she'd killed Lars—but was justified. And that was what the world would think—except they'd doubt the justification. Ah, Gavin was shrewder than she; he knew which way a jury would bend.

"But I guess you'd better run for it, Rox. While you still can."

"It's a bit late for that." Roxanne's voice was bitter. "Gavin's men are guarding me to see that I don't escape. Two of them followed me over here. Look out the window and you'll see them."

"I only see one," reported Josie, going to the window and carefully peeping through the red drapes. "Maybe you can get out the back way, and get to the station. I'll give you some money to catch a train out of town."

Roxanne hurried after Josie to the back. "And there's the other one," she said, gesturing at the back courtyard.

"Ah . . ." said Josie on a long-drawn sigh, "So that's the way of it. Well . . . I guess he's bound to have you, then." Suddenly her brown eyes narrowed and she laughed. "Hold out for marriage, Rox. That's the way to bring him down. Spend him bankrupt, accuse him of goin' out with other women. Marry him, Rox, and make his life a living hell!"

Roxanne looked at Josie in surprise. Was that indeed the way out? Marry Gavin and slam the bedroom door in his face? Marry him and taunt him with her lovers? He had men guarding her now, but as his wife . . . she pondered. Cleverly done, it would work. Although her wild heart revolted at such a travesty of a marriage, she began to see it as a way out. Once she had married him, she could desert him—Gavin would never allow a woman who bore his name to be hauled through the courts; it would be too damaging to his reputation. And Gavin valued his reputation, that much was obvious. She could marry him with a bright smile on her face—and simply disappear. Where she would go would not matter. She would slip away, take a new name.

"I see you're thinkin' up mischief, Rox," chuckled Josie. "I can see it sparklin' in those big blue eyes."

Roxanne stood up with decision. Her voice was hard. "I've decided to take your advice, Josie. I'm going to marry him."

"That's the spirit." Josie came over and gave her a rollicking slap on the back. "And from the look of you, I wouldn't want to be in Gavin Coulter's shoes come your wedding night!"

"No," murmured Roxanne. "Nobody would."

Josie's laughter followed her out to the street where she amazed her guard by saying crisply, "Take me to Mr. Coulter's office. At once, please."

Gavin received her warily in his dark-paneled Montgomery Street offices in the Coulter Building, which was situated north of Market in the city's financial district. On the way there, an even more deadly idea had formed in Roxanne's brain. She would marry Gavin—but not for flight. Not for Josie's more heavy-handed methods either. Gavin was so proud, proud of his shipping empire, his grand house on Nob Hill, his showy car, his possessions, even the livery of his servants; it had shown in his arrogant eyes. And how necessary it would be for him to be proud of his wife. . . .

"I have come to offer you my terms," she said, resting her gloved fingers on the top of his shining mahogany desk.

"Terms?" He seemed thunderstruck. "It is *I* who offer the terms," he said dryly.

"No. Revenging yourself on me will not gain you what you desire. What you want is to roll back the clock so that we meet again as we did once before—in Baltimore."

"I'll not deny it," he said softly, and she saw his eyes kindle as they strayed over her figure.

"I have come to tell you that I will not be your

mistress, Gavin," she announced proudly. "I told you that in Baltimore. But—I will marry you."

He looked a bit startled, and hope gleamed in his eyes. He would have looked somewhat more startled if he had known the plans for a terrible revenge that were forming behind the blue depths of those sapphire eyes.

I will marry you, the devil behind those blue eyes was vowing. *First I will make you flaunt me before all of San Francisco, make society accept me by the power of your money and your iron will. And then I will choose some night when you entertain a president or a king, and I will become Klondike Roxie again—a Klondike Roxie worse than ever I was. I will show your friends that you have married a harlot lost to shame. You will not dare to prosecute me for my crimes because it will be the woman who bears your name who would be hanged. You will be forced to suppress rumors of my scarlet ways, to buy off newspapermen, cameramen, servants—oh, I will bring you down, Gavin Coulter, I will bring you down!*

Across the desk he looked at her carefully, and then his eyes caught fire. "Wife . . ." he murmured. "Yes, what a wife you would make. With your proud bearing and your beauty, I could present you to kings."

She stood straight and beautiful before him—and inflexible as he. "I will marry you only on one condition, Gavin."

"Name it," he said warily.

"That you woo me as you would a lady."

"You are playing for time," he said.

She shook her head. "Not so. I ask that you move me to a larger house than the one in which I live, furnish me with my own carriage and a staff of servants, clothes, jewels—that you tell the world, indeed *show* the world that I am independently wealthy. You must make society respect me. I must be received. And after a suitable interval—a month perhaps—you will give a great ball, and we'll announce our betrothal."

"And do you plan a long engagement?" His dark eyes were alight, though his voice was scathing.

Again she shook her head. "I will marry you immediately after the engagement is announced."

He was puzzled. She could see he was tossing her offer around in his brain, studying it. "It is some trick," he muttered. "You are planning to fool me, to run away."

She laughed. "I will have no need to run away." And to his quizzical look, "I have no wish to die, Gavin. And I know that you would surely hunt me down. But I will not live my life under a cloud of blackmail either. I will have the protection of your name—you would never allow the woman who bore your name to be arrested."

A smile lit his craggy features. "Checkmate!" he murmured. "At last I understand you. It is a plan worthy of you, Roxanne."

"It is indeed," she said with a hard smile. "But until I marry you—not till then will I lie in your arms. Until then you must be content with the stable of fancy women I'm told you keep."

He frowned, chewing his lip. She guessed he was surprised that she knew about them, but of course Josie was informed about such things.

"And you will keep your bargain, Roxanne?"

"I swear it. On those terms I will become your wife, I will sleep beside you—as long as you wish. But first you must blazen my name across San Francisco, Gavin. You must make the women of the haughty set you frequent accept me—I will accept nothing less."

He admired her—not just as he always had for her beauty, but for her indomitable spirit. "God, how you match me!" he murmured. "I agree to your terms, Roxanne. But"— his eyes narrowed—"lest it be still a trap, my men will continue to watch you."

Roxanne shrugged indifferently. "That pleases me. They will serve as bodyguards."

With enthusiasm, Gavin poured out drinks from the crystal decanter on a side table. Roxanne took one in gloved fingers. Gavin lifted his glass. "To our marriage, Roxanne!"

Brilliant-eyed, she touched her glass to his. It made a little ringing sound, like a tiny cry of pain. "To our marriage, Gavin." *And the hell I will make it.* "And you must pay Josie Mawkins for all she has spent in launching me."

Laughing, he nodded his agreement and drank his wine.

Roxanne was escorted back to her town house in Gavin's Pierce-Arrow. The chauffeur let her out courteously, and she hurried to her front door. A thick fog had settled over the city. Roxanne looked about her grimly as she set her key into the lock. That fog was no murkier than her plans.

The very next morning, her world was a bustle of activity. She found herself moving into a handsome Victorian mansion, fashionably high on Nob Hill and pleasantly above the fog that drifted in daily from the bay. Modistes called, and milliners. Boots were procured, and hats and gloves and fine French perfumes, and silk stockings with elaborate jeweled clocks, and lingerie marvelously sheer and dainty to the touch. Within the week she had a finely furnished house, a staff, a wardrobe of fine clothes, a Russian sable coat and a handsome carriage with a matched team of bays.

Silk-hatted, debonair, Gavin came to call, bringing gifts of flowers, jewels. In perfumed silks, Roxanne received him, serving him the finest wines and food—which his money had paid for. Over wine he bragged to her of his art acquisitions and of his business dealings. So vast was his empire now that his shipping enterprise had become almost a sideline. His market manipulations were frightening to her. He loved to fleece people. She knew more about him now, knew that she was not his only victim. One man he had ruined had taken a shot at him on the floor of the stock exchange—and had been shot by Gavin's bodyguard, Gavotti, a big man who was always in evidence whenever Gavin made a public appearance. Another unfortunate victim of Gavin's manipulations had committed suicide, leaving a widow and six orphans to fend for themselves. Gavin shrugged off these tragedies as a winnowing out of the weak. Roxanne sat and smiled and drank her wine and hated him. Those people would have their revenge—through her!

In the afternoons Gavin took her out, calling at the houses of his friends. Their wives returned her calls—whether coerced or on their own, Roxanne did not know. It did not matter to her. These were the women whom she would shock and horrify on some chosen night in the future, some night when Gavin's pride in her was at its peak.

Spring found her sought-after—and most of all by Gavin. Hard-pressed, for the thought of his touch repelled her, she let him set a date for their engagement party.

"You will be an April bride," he promisd her. "The ball will be on a Tuesday and we will be married on a Wednesday, and afterwards I will take you to Europe, Roxanne."

No, Europe did not suit her purposes. San Francisco—that was Gavin's world. "I would prefer to stay here," she surprised him by saying.

"Well, then, we will take a short honeymoon down the coast and return here."

A honeymoon . . . she had forgotten about the honeymoon. Well, she would find a way to cut it even shorter. "I want to meet all your friends, Gavin. I want to entertain them in our home."

Eager to humor her, he nodded. "I have brought the guest list for our engagement party. Does the ballroom of the Golden Palace Hotel please you?"

She nodded indifferently, studied the guest list. "There is one name you have omitted—Josie Mawkins."

He frowned. "Surely you know that to invite her would stamp you as—as—" He hesitated.

"A scarlet woman?" She flashed a look up at him through her dark lashes. "Yes, I suppose it would. Very well." *But only because we are not married yet, Gavin. After I am your wife, Josie Mawkins will attend every party I ever give!*

He looked relieved that she was not going to make an issue of it. "The ballroom will be decked with white gardenias," he said hastily. "I have ordered enough champagne to float away the guests. And here, I have brought you something."

She touched her throat, where a wide diamond dog collar glittered, her ears where pendant diamond earrings sparkled like icicles. They felt cold to her touch—almost as cold as her voice. "You have already been generous enough, Gavin."

"But this—" He slipped over her index finger a forty-carat marquise diamond, "is your engagement ring."

She looked at it, startled. Even for a man of Gavin's wealth, this seemed extravagant. On her hand the ring looked enormous. It was heavy and brilliant, but it seemed to have an evil glitter—perhaps because she hated the giver so much. "It is so large," she murmured.

"It will show people that you are mine," he said quietly. "I would not have it said in whispers but in a loud shout."

She gave him a grim look. The shout would come sooner than he expected. She turned her head away from his kiss.

"But you will be my bride soon," he protested sharply.

"Not until then."

"Until tomorrow then," he said moodily and stalked out. Coldly, she watched him go, her husband-to-be.

On the Monday night before the engagement ball, they attended the Metropolitan Opera Company's first performance of the season in the Grand Opera House. The opera was the *Queen of Sheba.* Although the next morning's papers panned the performance, the society columns were quick to note the beauty of the handsome Mrs. Barrington, who had attended clad in ice-blue satin and diamonds that surely must have cost a king's ransom. They might have mentioned that the beautiful Mrs. Barrington's expression was a little somber, but they did not see past her flashing diamonds.

Chapter 37

The Grand Ballroom of the Golden Palace Hotel was a blaze of lights that Tuesday night. Prominent guests were there in abundance—for even though some regretted that Gavin Coulter had chosen the night of Enrico Caruso's performance in *Carmen* to give his ball, few had stayed away. To do so might be to invite the ire of a man known to be both overwhelmingly powerful and vengeful.

Roxanne knew that Gavin had arranged it that way. Deliberately. His guests must make this sacrifice, an offering to his ego. Should any guest be so unwise as to default in favor of hearing the Italian tenor sing, Gavin would take note and revenge himself upon them at his leisure. Like an enormous spider, Gavin had chosen this great port city for his web. They were all caught in his toils, because his interests were far-reaching enough to touch almost everyone. That San Francisco feared him was apparent—for glittering and smiling and urbane, the elite turned out to welcome Roxanne into their midst.

Tales of the men Gavin had ruined haunted Roxanne. She thought she read fear in some of the bland faces that passed her in the receiving line. Smiling, newsworthy, people flowed past them. That woman whose gloved hand fluttered toward her—that was the mayor's wife, wasn't it? And the fat one with the enormous diamond dog collar set into her wobbly chins was a railroad tycoon's widow and San Francisco's most noted hostess. That tall thin woman in rustling green taffetas, the one with the envious dark eyes, surely Roxanne had seen her before . . . yes, of course, her picture had been in the papers: San Francisco socialite returns home after European tour. They were all here, the money, the names, all smiles . . . but their hearts were filled with dread of the arrogant man who stood beside Roxanne taking their measure.

Roxanne had never looked so lovely. Her dark-blond hair was pulled back in a gleaming golden mass of curls. Diamond earrings glittered like falling tears against her slender neck. The gown in which she stood was the loveliest she had ever owned and by far the most expensive. It had been ordered especially by Gavin from Paris and had arrived barely in time for earnest little seamstresses to fit it to her lissome body. A magnificent ball gown with a sweeping train, it was composed entirely of tiny white glittering beads sewn onto chiffon so that they swayed and rippled like tiny white icicles when she walked. The whole dress was supple and glittering and clung to her elegant torso, outlining her curving bust. From her diamond dog collar to the deep decolletage was an alarming distance, an expanse of sheer white skin that set Gavin's eyes aglitter. She wore a set smile upon her face that never faltered, and if her blue eyes beneath their sweeping dark lashes seemed shadowed and sad, no one noticed. She was a vision of beauty to stop the heart. The effect was stunning.

To this woman on whom all eyes were focused, the evening had a strange dreamy quality. She had come so far from those days as lady's maid in Baltimore. Tomorrow she would be the wife of the richest man in San Francisco—a woman to reckon with. Tomorrow night at this time Gavin would take her to his bed. Willing or unwilling, she would lie in his arms. . . . In spite of her cool elegance, her heart wavered within her. But she stood her ground beside him as together they greeted the important people of San Francisco, holding court in the magnificent Grand Ballroom of the Golden Palace Hotel, a mammoth room with a huge and celebrated beamed ceiling. From those gigantic beams hung the largest chandeliers in San Francisco—a fitting setting, Roxanne felt, for the ring she sported on her hand. Around the ballroom, in every conceivable place, there were sprays, garlands, banks of gardenias and flowing white satin ribbons. Truly a bridal display, for Gavin planned no church wedding. He and Roxanne would be married quietly on the morrow and afterwards would set forth on their honeymoon—he had not yet disclosed their destination to her and she had not asked.

When at last they moved among their guests and he led her out upon the gleaming parquet dance floor, she looked about her, surprised that she felt no great surge of triumph. Gavin thought her his prey, but instead he was hers. As a hunter she should have savored this moment. Oddly she did not; instead she felt sad, as if she were losing something—perhaps that pride that had always kept her from going willingly into the arms of anyone she did not love. But, she reminded herself, Gavin *was* forcing her; she did not go to his arms a willing bride.

Around the ballroom floor, through the glittering guests, they waltzed in stately fashion, and she knew this scene was a foreshadowing of the life Gavin envisioned for them: a dignified world of financiers and potentates, presidents and kings. Graciously, they would receive these notables in their palatial home atop Nob Hill. By day, Gavin would spin his financial webs on Montgomery Street. By night—no, she preferred not to think about the nights. Concentrate rather on the days, when she would always be there to be flashed about as if she were some great jewel he owned.

They were standing alone for the moment by a bank of white gardenias, and she was frowning at the sight of the ever-watchful Gavotti hovering near, even in this festive scene guarding Gavin's life—when she felt Gavin stiffen beside her.

"What is it?" she asked.

"A late guest," he muttered. "An uninvited one."

Lifting her arched brows slightly, Roxanne turned and followed the direction of his gaze.

And froze to stillness.

There, across the glamorous ballroom, wearing formal attire that did not suit his big body, was Rhodes.

His thick brown hair shone glossily beneath the light of the chandeliers. The light struck the planes of his deeply bronzed face as his vivid green eyes swept the room. Something in the swing of those mighty shoulders, so at contrast with his narrow waist and hips, something in the regal set of him, brought back to her the memory of him on the deck of the *Lass*, half naked, encrusted with salt, hands hard on the wheel as he warred with the Indian Ocean. He had seemed godlike then, and now across the gleaming parquet floor he was even more strikingly handsome than she remembered. This was Rhodes as she remembered him in Baltimore . . . Rhodes, come to find her.

A glorious look must have crossed her face, for Gavin suddenly grasped her arm in a grip that hurt. "I knew you were lovers," he whispered hoarsely. "But if you think to begin anew with him—"

Rhodes had spotted them, and he hurried toward them with long strides.

Roxanne's eyes never left him. But she heard her voice, floating softly away from her. "What makes you think we were lovers, Gavin?"

"I have always known it," he said bitterly. "And if I had not, I could see it now on your face. You are trembling."

Yes, she supposed she was. Gavin's voice rang out

harshly, "Have you come to congratulate me on my impending marriage, Rhodes?"

She never knew what Rhodes answered. She looked up at him, her heart in her eyes. She thought he asked her to dance. It didn't matter. His words, if there were any, flowed over her like bright jewels, like cascading water. She swayed into his arms. His touch was magic; she melted under it. He smiled down into her eyes—the old Rhodes, the wonderful Rhodes—smiled because they had found each other, they were together again. He did not ask her why he had found her with Gavin, or why she had consented to marry Gavin. Implicit in his look, his every gesture, was an affirmation of the deep bond forged between them. She was *his* woman and he had come to claim her. Nothing else mattered.

Out upon the floor he swept her in a dance of triumph. Her elegant gown swirled about her silken legs. Her head found his shoulder, rested there. Eyes closed, she sighed as the music enveloped her, as the rhythmic thud of his heart lulled her. In defiance of convention, she lay against his chest, blissful, content, and let the music and the dance sweep her away.

"Your dress is lovely, but I liked you in your sarong," he said, smiling down at her.

Stirred by the sound of his voice above the music, she looked up at him. "We chased the Chinese junk, you know, but lost her in the dark," she said. "You'll never know what I went through, thinking what they must be doing to you on board her."

He laughed wryly. "Putting out the fire wore them out, and they forgot me till next day. They were about to start on me with hot irons when they hit a submerged reef. Tore the whole bottom out of the junk and she sank like a rock. A mail ship happened by and saw us hit, rescued the survivors and slapped everybody in irons. They wouldn't listen to me—thought I was one of the pirates. We ended up in Borneo, and it was months before I got out of jail and was able to go looking for Bevin. By then he'd about given me up. We went back to Singapore, but you were long gone.

Luckily a sailor in the waterfront dive told us a friend of yours had got you a job on a ship bound for San Francisco. We started right out."

"And sailed the *Virginia Lass* across the Pacific?" she marveled, remembering how shattered the *Lass* had been from her bout with the typhoon.

"All the way to San Francisco," he smiled. "A couple of times it was touch and go, but she's anchored in the Bay. I read in the papers about your engagement party and decided that I'd better come and claim my bride."

Come and claim his bride! Her heart leaped at the words.

"And it's a good thing that I got here today," he added lightly, "or I'd have found myself kidnapping Gavin's wife."

Gavin! In the white heat of Rhodes's return she had forgotten Gavin! Now her gaze swung to the wall where, beside some ornate pillars, Gavin was talking to a group of guests. An unhealthy pallor had spread over his face, but at this distance she could not read his expression.

Roxanne knew that she would have to tell Gavin. But she pushed the thought aside—for she knew very well that he would prefer to see her hanged rather than see her in Rhodes's arms.

When she tried to draw away, the arms that enfolded her tightened around her like a steel band.

"Having found you again, I'm in no mood to lose you," Rhodes said. "I've a mind to dance you right out that door and on to the deck of the *Lass*. We'll up anchor and be away before they miss us."

Gavotti, she noticed, had left Gavin's side and hovered as near to the dancing couple as he could. "Oh, Rhodes, let's not leave yet. The music is so wonderful. Let's dance the night away!"

He considered her gravely. "Haven't you tortured Gavin enough, Roxanne? It must hurt him to see me hold you in my arms."

Tortured him enough? Silent laughter rang through

her and was instantly quenched by a flood of inner tears. Still, she kept that bright smile on her face.

"Forget Gavin," she whispered, and melted into his arms.

Curious looks were directed at them as they continued to whirl among the dancers. Strange behavior for a bride-to-be, people muttered. But Roxanne did not care. She was looking up into Rhodes's face with a terrible intensity, as if to photograph his features to hold forever in her heart.

"I'm willing to dance with you till dawn," smiled Rhodes. "But at dawn we sail on the *Lass*."

All the love she felt for him was reflected in her blue gaze and the yearning in her breast was almost unbearable. "I was faithful to you, Rhodes—all that time in Singapore. I nearly starved, waiting."

"I never doubted you," he said softly. Tears glimmered on her lashes. "No doubt they told you I was dead, or you assumed I was after so long. I can't blame you for wanting to get back to the States.

"I didn't want to believe you were dead, but the alternative was that you didn't want me, that you'd proved your point and were willing to let me go."

"You know me better than that," he said comfortably.

Wild sweet magic engulfed her, lulled her senses. She drifted across the shining floor with him in sweet content, knowing her heart had found its home. Around the room, with whispers, comments, and sidelong looks, the guests wondered who the stranger was that kept the bride-to-be dancing the evening away in his arms. But to Roxanne, these were treasured moments. These last few dances under the brilliant chandeliers were all she would ever have of the man in her arms. This last evening she could spend with him—the rest of her life would be spent in prison. For she was sure that when she told Gavin that she would not marry him, he would carry out his threat to have her arrested. And as for dancing out of the room in Rhodes's arms . . . there were too many of Gavin's henchmen about for that to be possible.

Rhodes had sailed half around the world to reach her—but he had come too late. These golden moments must last her the rest of her life, for with the dawn she would have to send him away.

Someday, she told herself, he would be hers. Though she must die to win him, some kindly heaven would give him back to her.

His chest in its dark broadcloth coat brushed her breast, and a silken passion rippled through her. A sweet, overpowering tenderness. *Oh, Rhodes*, her heart yearned, *I love you so. . . .*

And she could not bear to tell him that these short hours with him would be her last.

The mayor and his besatined wife were leaving now . . . but Roxanne danced on. Other socialites and financiers and their ladies said their good-byes to a tight-lipped Gavin, casting curious glances at Rhodes and Roxanne, clasped together endlessly in a lovers' waltz. Roxanne, her eyes half closed, her lashes lying dark upon her flushed cheeks, gave them not so much as a nod.

In her wild heart, she found herself wishing for some great holocaust, so that she might die in Rhodes's arms, might never leave him as her body returned to dust.

The night wore on, and still they danced, the woman in the gorgeous white gown and the green-eyed stranger who had everyone buzzing. The ballroom was almost deserted, but with the reckless smile of the damned, Roxanne kept on. From a corner Gavin brooded, his sunken eyes on the waltzing pair. Finally, when all the guests were gone except for a straggler or two, Rhodes said restively, "It's nearly five. I think Gavin is sending the musicians home."

Roxanne, who had been dancing with her eyes closed, looked up, startled to see Gavin speaking to the musicians. Like Cinderella, her ball was over—and now the piper must be paid.

She drew a deep ragged breath. Then, with her head held high, she led Rhodes toward the table where Gavin sat. At their approach, Gavin rose mockingly.

Rhodes would have stayed her, but Roxanne sank down on the chair Gavin held out; and Rhodes, puzzled, eased his big form down across from her.

Both these men hungered for her. It was on their faces: Gavin's watchful and cold, Rhodes's with a little quizzical smile, as if wondering why they had not spun from the ballroom floor directly into the early morning air.

"It seems you must choose between us, Roxanne," announced Gavin. She had heard horseshoes ring on stone more softly than that voice.

"She has already chosen between us," said Rhodes easily.

Gavin gave Rhodes a black look. "Roxanne has by now considered her future." His voice was stern, ominous. "Roxanne . . . did you hear me, Roxanne?"

"I . . . heard you." Her voice was suddenly soft and slurred.

"Then you can give me your answer," said Gavin. He leaned forward, *willing* her obedience. "Besides, how could you choose Rhodes? Have you forgotten how he raped you?" Gavin's sneering voice was raised against the last blare of music. "Of course, Rhodes was drunk, and it wasn't as if you were a virgin . . ." Gavin stopped, realizing that his blinding anger had made him taunt her once too often.

It wasn't as if you were a virgin. . . it wasn't as if—! Who but her rapist could have known that? Roxanne paled and sat thunderstruck. Then, she sprang to her feet with a single violent motion that sent her gilt chair skittering.

"You!" she choked. "*You* raped me that night in Baltimore!"

Her last words were lost in a sudden grinding roar. For even before they were spoken, a giant earth-rip had burst out of the sea at Point Arena, ninety miles to the north. Racing down the San Andreas Fault at seven thousand miles an hour, scattering redwoods and bluffs and lighthouses as it came, the earthquake struck a sleeping San Francisco like the vengeance of God, and buckled the city with a single hammer blow.

To the accompaniment of a deep, terrible rumble that welled up from the moving grinding earth mass below, buildings danced upon their foundations, water mains and gas lines burst and thrust up jaggedly through broken pavement toward the sky. Streets undulated like ocean waves, and trolley tracks flashed blue as they twisted like snakes across a nightmare landscape. Chimneys tumbled, towers toppled, walls collapsed, roofs caved in—and everywhere, as the ground beneath the churches rocked, church bells tolled discordantly of doom . . . doom to the West Coast's proudest city.

And in the Grand Ballroom of the Golden Palace Hotel, there was first the terrible jarring rumble of the earth that tilted the floor and swung the great chandeliers wildly. A rumble that merged into a new din as the lights went out, the chains snapped, and the chandeliers crashed ot the polished parquet floor, sending shards of broken glass everywhere. Following their deadly sparkle, the ceiling fell in, bringing with it the network of heavy beams that arched over the dance floor. As those great polished beams—now instruments of death—came crashing down about them, both Gavin and Rhodes, galvanized, leaped forward to save Roxanne. Gavin, who was nearer, flung himself at Roxanne just as a falling beam struck him. Her body was knocked away from him as the beam drove him to the floor with killing force.

Roxanne, stunned by the weight of falling plaster, her mind shocked by the screams and the earth-rending noise as the building buckled, was hardly aware that Rhodes had plunged forward and that, as he had grasped her, his foot had slipped on the polished parquetry. It was a lucky slip, for it had carried them both headlong beneath a crazy tepee-like structure comprised of broken beams that had crashed to the ballroom floor, and off which other falling timbers and chunks of plaster ricocheted.

For a moment, lying there stunned, Roxanne thought she was dead.

Then she grew dimly aware that a voice—Rhodes's,

she thought—was shouting in her ear, "Are you all right? Roxanne?"

Choking on plaster dust, she tried to satisfy that voice that she was among the living. "Yes," she gasped, a strangled sound.

Rhodes set her on her feet, where she swayed unsteadily, coughing in the suffocating cloud of dust that rose about them. The front of the building, she saw in disbelief, had fallen outward; and now, through the rising dust and further avalanches of plaster and timber, weak daylight illuminated a scene from hell itself. The Grand Ballroom was a forest of broken beams and mounds of rubble. And from that rubble, where before there had been screams, there was only an occasional deep-buried groan. Overhead, the sight was even more frightening, for the multi-storied building, suspended on a framework that was slowly buckling, hung insubstantially above their heads, ready to crash down.

Nearby, almost buried under a heap of plaster, his body not quite cut in half by a heavy beam, lay Gavin. Whatever he'd been, whatever he'd done, his last act on earth had been to try to save *her*. With a little cry, Roxanne shook off Rhodes's arm and knelt beside Gavin. His lips were moving.

"To me it wasn't rape, Roxanne—you were mine . . . meant to be mine." He was sinking but he rallied. "You didn't love me, but . . . you'd . . . have learned to, Roxanne," he murmured—and was gone.

Rhodes grasped her roughly. "Come on!" His fingers dug into her arm. "With the next shock the whole building will go!"

She straightened up. Dead at her feet lay the man who, more than any other, had wrecked her life, whose evil reach had pursued her across a continent. The man for whom she had planned a terrible retribution. And yet . . . . in his way he had loved her. Sorrow filled her and spilled over into hot tears that ran down her dusty face as they clambered over the rubble.

Through the ruins of that silent ballroom in which nothing living could now be seen, she let Rhodes hurry her to the street. There stunned-looking people ran about, and she could see that San Francisco's skyline had changed—hideously. No sooner had they reached the street, stumbling, picking their way amid the crumpled girders and fallen bricks and stones, than the second great tremor struck. Staggered by the shock wave, Roxanne looked up to see the great broken edifice that had once been the hotel shudder like a living thing and collapse in upon itself with a great roar of crumbling masonry and splintering timbers, while all around them buildings slithered and slanted and cracked and disintegrated.

They stood among the ruins.

The little group of stunned people who had made it out of the hotel and nearby buildings to stand motionless for the moment, shaken by the immensity of the collapse of the great hotel, did not yet know the vast extent of the catastrophe that had overtaken California that day. In San Francisco Bay the water had dropped—pushed back from the shore, it had formed tidal waves in the Pacific that surged back, battering the shore. Up and down the coast, cliffs had crumbled, beaches had sunk, and spouting mud geysers had appeared, spewing up hot blue shale. In the aftershocks, giant redwoods that had withstood the first hammer blows now succumbed and fell to earth. Up and down the coast raged the terror.

And in San Francisco itself, everywhere around them, they heard the hiss of escaping gas, the screams and groans of the dying, the further rumbles and crashes as damaged timbers and cracked walls broke at last. But in that first awful stillness as the dust settled and new collapses threatened, in those stunned moments as she swayed against Rhodes and his strong arm held her up, Roxanne realized that besides death and destruction, the earthquake had brought them something else. In the shock of the catastrophe, she had almost forgotten: Only minutes before she had been about to lose either her life or her love. But now Gavin was gone and nothing stood between them—she could stay with Rhodes again.

And then suddenly they were both aware that the stillness around them was disintegrating. Groans began to be heard from the dusty heap of rubble and broken walls that had once been a great hotel.

At the sound, Rhodes leaped forward and began tossing away timbers and heaving aside blocks of stone. "Go find help," he cried over his shoulder to Roxanne. "A cart. Shovels. Crowbars. There are people buried under all this—we've got to dig them out."

Silently, swift-footed, Roxanne obeyed. She found a place where the sewers were being repaired before the earthquake struck. There were plenty of shovels. Help was harder to find. Everyone was distracted, everyone had their own problems. People were buried under hundreds of structures. The city was a scene of incredible carnage.

She brought the shovels back to Rhodes.

With grim determination, all day long she worked beside him. They did manage to rescue a number of people from the rubble before a new collapse brought the last wall of the building down and the groans ceased forever. Panting, they leaned upon their shovels for a moment, each realizing the other had made a gallant effort. Just as all across San Francisco, other survivors had scrambled up and made valiant efforts to save themselves and their city.

And they might have done it—except for the fire.

Chapter 38

The fire began in fifty places at once, even as the earth shuddered and rocked, and raged through some five square miles. Before it had burned itself out four days later, most of four hundred ninety city blocks—including the entire business district and most of the residential areas of San Francisco, lay in smoke-blackened ruins. The conflagration had burned like a mighty torch, reaching some two thousand degrees Fahrenheit, a fierce chattering fire-storm of flames that melted glass and exploded stone, an ocean of fire that terrified beholders and charred the very earth in its path. All through it sweating men dug people out of the rubble. All through it the horse-drawn fire engines clanged wildly, and people shouted and lugged their possessions—what they could save—through broken streets, heaved up by the earthquake. As fires raged uncontrolled, a torrent of refugees fled down Market Street toward the Ferry Building. The city came under martial law, and the roar of the fire and the clanging engines were augmented by great booms as buildings were dynamited in an effort to halt the spreading flames.

Some of the loveliest buildings in San Francisco

were blown up in an attempt to halt the fire, some of the grandest homes. One of the worst moments came for Roxanne when she found Josie Mawkins lying with a broken leg on a white cot in one of the makeshift hospitals that had been thrown up. Under Josie's anxious questioning, Roxanne had to admit that Josie's house had been reduced to rubble. To her surprise, Josie thought about that a while and then shrugged. "You know, Rox," she said, "I was tired of retirement anyway. Think I'll go back into business when this is over—that is, if the bank's still standing." Roxanne assured her it was and left, marveling at Josie's resilience.

All through those terrible days, Roxanne and Rhodes worked tirelessly, digging out those who had been buried alive, assisting them onto carts that would take them to doctors, sometimes even driving those carts themselves. They ate what scraps of food they could snatch, and ignored their own needs. What a sight they were: the powerful man in torn evening clothes with the grimy face; the supple woman with her wild, dirty blond hair working beside him in what remained of her glittering white ball gown. Doggedly they worked until either the long terrible tongues of the rapidly spreading flames or the grim-faced bayonet-carrying troops drove them back. Through the town rushed wild-eyed people, clad in whatever they had been wearing, or whatever was most valuable or closest at hand: women in nightgowns, weighted down by furcoats, wearing picture hats and pushing baby carriages; men in long johns and shawls dragging carts; even an occasional night-shirted old man in a stocking cap wandering about lost and barefoot.

But somehow, through incredible efforts, a kind of order was at last restored, and Rhodes and Roxanne, leaning on their shovels to rest, gazed into each other's dirty faces.

Although they had hardly spoken to each other except small necessary phrases like, "Help me with this plank," or, "I think I hear someone under that pile of bricks," or, "If we could raise this beam—" now, at least, they knew their long ordeal was ended. They smiled at each other; together they had won through.

But the smile on Roxanne's face faded as she saw Rhodes grow serious.

"One thing I must know, Roxanne: Why did you promise to marry Gavin in the first place?"

"He told me that you were dead," she answered wearily. "Lost at sea—and what was I to believe when you had not come for me in Singapore?" She straightened up, and her face flushed under the dirt as she added," He was also blackmailing me with trumped-up charges—it was marry him or hang. So, I promised to marry him. Though I fully intended to marry him and wreck his life, God forgive me." She paused for a moment to consider all that had happened these past few days. "But then, at the ball, when you appeared, I knew that I would rather die than give you up."

"Why didn't we make a run for it then, Roxanne? Instead of waltzing away the night?" Rhodes asked.

"Because Gavin had his bodyguards all around; they would have not let us out of the hall," she explained. "And he promised to hunt me down wherever I went if I left him again."

Lifting her smoke-blackened chin with his finger, Rhodes looked into her sad blue eyes. "Roxanne, Roxanne, I could always handle Gavin."

She shook her head. "No one could handle Gavin. He had become too powerful." Her voice was sharp. "Well, now you know what kind of a woman I am, Rhodes. I meant to stand up and vow to love honor and obey a man—but all the time, I was plotting to ruin him."

"Well, I never thought that either of us was good," Rhodes said cheerfully. "I just knew that we were made for each other. It was worth crossing the world to claim you!"

Hope and life and a surging happiness returned to make her sapphire eyes glow. Crying, laughing, Roxanne hurled herself against Rhodes. "Then you forgive me!"

His strong arms were holding her close. "There's nothing to forgive, Roxanne."

She pushed him away, gazed up at him intensely. "Oh, Rhodes, let them think we died in the fire! Then we can start again, salvage something of ourselves."

"I'm 'way ahead of you," he said, his voice deep and caressing. "When I was driving a cart yesterday up to the tent camp on Nob Hill, I picked up a man who'd tripped over some broken pavement and sprained his ankle. As we rode we talked, and he turned out to be one of Gavin's lawyers. Would you believe that with the city in ruins about them, they're already trying to straighten out his estate? Seems I'm his nearest living relative."

She stared at him. "But you're not even related—not really."

Rhodes shrugged, shifting the rags on his big shoulders. "Who's to know that? I figure the Coulters robbed me of a lot of years—years I could have spent with you. So I'll take that inheritance. I told the lawyer that I was sailing tomorrow with the tide and that I'll be back in six months to the day. And he doesn't know it yet, but I'll return with a wife. Her name will be Anne. Eventually, we'll take up residence in New York and sell the shipping line and go into railroads or some such—I've no love for steamers. And who's to connect the wife of a railroad tycoon with an adventuress who died in the Great San Francisco Fire?"

Grimy and happy, Roxanne threw her arms around his neck, feeling the strong muscles under her touch. Six months they would have, six wonderful months together before they had to come back and face respectability. Six wonderful carefree months just to be lovers. Six months to be venturesome with Rhodes before he became an industrial giant, hemmed in by lawyers and accountants. Six months to be wild free Roxanne before she became that conservative matron Anne Coulter, who wintered in her Fifth Avenue town house or in the south of France, who summered in her marble villa at Newport and hired an English nanny for her slew of adorable children.

With all their recklessness, Roxanne's eyes gleamed up at Rhodes. A sun that set red in the smoky west touched kindly their dirt and rags, and gilded their handsome silhouettes against a burned-out ruined city that would soon rise Phoenix-like from the ashes. Just as they would rise anew from the ashes of their shattered, misspent lives.

They left their shovels behind them in the rubble and, with half a crew, they sailed the battered *Virginia Lass* out through the Golden Gate—a leaky old ship on which to brave the wild Pacific, but it would sail them to heaven. As she boarded the familiar creaking vessel, Roxanne looked up at the billowing white shrouds above her and took a deep breath. She could almost smell the perfumed scent of islands waiting in the sun, see coral beaches and hear the rustle of the waving coconut palms that fringed blue lagoons and black volcanic sands and great seas breaking green—seas no greener than the eyes that smiled into her own, breezes no warmer than the arms that would hold her fast.

That first night out, a sliver of moon scattered diamonds over the waters, and the old ship rode the waves like a fair young clipper. When the grime of their efforts in the scarred and lovely city had been washed away, Roxanne turned to Rhodes languorously. On deck, Bevin had the wheel, and they could hear him singing in his soft baritone, a sailor's chantey. He was happy to be at sea again and so were they.

Roxanne lay on her back in the bunk, the moonlight silvering her lovely body. Fondly, she watched Rhodes undress, toss his clothes to a chair. In matching silver perfection, he stood above her for a moment, smiling down.

And then Rhodes, for whom a loving fate had fashioned her, was in her arms again. He nuzzled her throat, his rich soft laugh rang in her ears. She sighed deeply and her pliant body melted against his own as she surrendered herself to the night, to the magic, to the man she would always love.